'ravis came around to Melissa's 'ide of the Jeep.

'he lowered the window. Their faces were only ıches apart. It was madness, but she ached for .im to kiss her. If he ever got the urge, would ıe pretend she was his wife? She couldn't bear the thought.

His eyes played over her features. "You made this evening more memorable for us than you know," he said. She felt his warm breath on her mouth. Only a little closer… "How do I thank you?"

The blood pounded in her ears. "You're already loing that by agreeing to track down the people naking our family's life miserable. It's a miracle /ou've already unearthed so much. Who else but a Texas Ranger could do what you've done?"

He let out a sigh. Maybe he didn't like remembering he had a job to do. "Speaking of your case, I was wondering if tomorrow you'd go hiking in the 'orest beyond the ridge with me. Since we're going o a new area, I thought we'd take my truck. Bring ı backpack with the things you'll want."

What Melissa wanted was

lidn't want to have to wait

e ready."

Dear Reader,

Have you ever been told you looked like someone else, or that someone else looked like you?

Did you like being compared?

Several times in life I've been told I looked like someone else, or acted like someone else, and I didn't like it. I wanted to be ME. It gets into all the questions of comparisons, whether good or bad. Though we simply brush off these comments and go on, I think we all care to varying degrees.

In *The Texas Ranger's Reward,* I thought about this problem and decided to magnify it to the point that it becomes one of the linchpins of the plot concerning the hero and heroine. Strongly resembling someone else can lead to all kinds of consequences. In my story it raises doubts, picks away at self-confidence, arouses anger, destroys trust. The more I wrote, the more fascinated I became to see the way it produced so many issues on so many levels. I hope as you read, you'll find this element in my story fascinating, too. Most of all, I hope you'll find the resolution satisfying.

Enjoy!

Rebecca Winters

THE TEXAS RANGER'S REWARD

BY

REBECCA WINTERS

First published in Great Britain 2013
by Mills & Boon, an imprint of Harlequin (UK) Limited,
Eton House, 18-24 Paradise Road, Richmond, Surrey TW9 1SR

ISBN: 978 0 263 90085 9
ebook ISBN: 978 1 472 00443 7

23-0213

Harlequin (UK) policy is to use papers that are natural, renewable and recyclable products and made from wood grown in sustainable forests. The logging and manufacturing processes conform to the legal environmental regulations of the country of origin.

Printed and bound in Spain
by Blackprint CPI, Barcelona

Rebecca Winters, whose family of four children has now swelled to include five beautiful grandchildren, lives in Salt Lake City, Utah, in the land of the Rocky Mountains. With canyons and high alpine meadows full of wildflowers, she never runs out of places to explore. They, plus her favorite vacation spots in Europe, often end up as backgrounds for her romance novels, because writing is her passion, along with her family and church. Rebecca loves to hear from readers. If you wish to email her, please visit her website, www.cleanromances.com.

To my dear sister Kathie, who is kind enough to read my novels and always gets the essence of what I'm trying to say. Even better, we have long discussions that thrill my heart.

Chapter One

Melissa Dalton pulled her red-and-black Jeep Wrangler into the parking lot outside the entrance to the Lone Peak Children's Physical Therapy Clinic with no time to spare before her first appointment at eight-thirty. She lived on Salt Lake City's southeast bench, in the Sandy area, close to the Wasatch Mountains, and the new facility was only five minutes from her town-house condo.

How typical of her that even though she lived so close, she was still going to be late!

Waving to her friend Rosie, another therapist who'd just arrived, she hurried into the building and then her office, ready to go. As was her custom, she'd caught her shoulder-length hair at her nape so it wouldn't get in the way while she worked with one of her patients.

Today she'd worn a floppy French clip bow in navy to match her short-sleeved navy-and-white print top, and designer jeans. She'd put pearl studs in her ears. Melissa believed in dressing up as much as possible so she wouldn't look clinical. No lab coat for her. It made the kids nervous. Children who had to see her on a regular basis liked it when she came wearing something fashionable.

What she wore on her feet had to be comfortable for work, of course, but little girls often commented on her cute candy-apple-red flats. And her bangle bracelets, which came in gold, silver and jeweled tones. It was also important that she smelled good and kept her nails manicured. Children noticed everything. When she was looking her best, the sessions seemed brighter for the kids. Which made Melissa feel better about herself.

After the trauma leading up to her divorce six years ago, she'd gone through a period where she hadn't paid attention to her clothes or hair. But once she'd gone into pediatric orthopedic physical therapy, the children asked so many personal questions that she'd begun to look at herself again and care about her appearance. It was her young patients who helped pull her out of her depression. She loved them and enjoyed working with them.

Susan, the receptionist, had put a new file on her desk. It was a pertinent history sent by a doctor. Melissa sat down in her swivel chair to read it.

> Casey Stillman, Salt Lake, seven, broken left femur after fall from a horse July 27. Plated and screwed while in surgery. See X-rays. Successful. Anticipate complete recovery. Given crutches. Was home-schooled during recuperation period. As of Friday, September 7, father indicates son still clings to crutches and is anxious about bearing weight. Patient should be done with them. No physical reason for them now. Is afraid to go

to school. Recommend therapy. Pain and muscle soreness expressed, but wonder if there's a psychological issue.

Melissa glanced at the calendar. It was September 10. At more than five weeks following an accident, most children were pretty well back to normal, but others…

"TAKE AS LONG AS YOU NEED, bud. It's okay." Concerned by his lack of progress, Travis Stillman eyed his son, who was still dependant on his crutches. According to the doctor, Casey shouldn't need them anymore, thus the referral to visit someone who could work with him.

Halfway from Travis's blue Altima to the door of the clinic, Casey stopped. "My leg hurts." He was close to tears.

"I know, but pretty soon it will go away." Travis prayed that was true. Today was Monday, Casey's twentieth day of missing school. Though he'd kept up with his lessons at home, who knew how long it would take before he was ready to rejoin his second-grade class?

Travis held the door as his son hobbled into the clinic. "I don't want to go in there," Casey wailed as they approached the front desk.

The receptionist smiled. "It won't take long." She indicated the therapist's office—the first door down the hall on the right.

Travis didn't dare offer to pick up his son and carry him. His boy was proud as blazes. Lately, Travis's sister, Pat, had been reminding him that Casey was a chip off the old block. But since his fall, too much pride had turned Casey into a hermit.

He wouldn't give up the crutches, and he didn't want to play with his cousins, let alone the neighbors' children. Forget going to school. Travis's friend Mitch Garrett, one of the P.I.s who worked with him at the Lufka Private Investigator firm in Salt Lake, had brought over his newly adopted son, Zack, several times to play. But Casey was having none of it—he'd been too down since the accident.

They were almost to the office in question when someone called out, "Hi, Casey! Wow! Look at you handle those crutches!"

The cheerful-sounding female voice caused Travis to look up. He did a triple take when he saw a knockout woman with ash-brown hair standing outside the office door. She looked like a model.

She walked toward them and stopped in front of Casey, making Travis aware of her flowery fragrance. "My name's Melissa. *You* look fine, but I want to hear what happened to your horse. Did it live?"

The question was so unexpected, Casey laughed. "Yes."

"What's his name?"

"Sugar."

"Isn't that kind of a wuss name?"

"Yes."

"Who's this with you?" Her dancing eyes lifted to Travis. For some reason the mix of blue and gray was disturbing to him, but he couldn't figure out why.

"My dad."

"How do you do, Dad," she teased. "Come with me, Casey, and let's talk about how boring it's been for you this past month."

A bemused Travis followed them and received another surprise when instead of into her office, she took them to the next door down the hall. The room turned out to be a sunny space containing physical therapy equipment. *What? No discussion first?*

While Travis looked on, the therapist said to Casey, "I'll take your crutches."

"What if I fall down?"

"I'll catch you."

Travis watched as his son thought about it, then gave them up. The therapist promptly put them on the floor. "Okay. Let's see you walk."

"I—I can't. My leg hurts."

"Don't you know that's a good thing?"

He blinked. "It is?"

"Absolutely. The muscles want to move and it means you're getting well. But if you'll walk without the crutches, it will help you get better even faster. Don't worry if it hurts. A little pain doesn't matter. My first dog lost his hind leg when a car hit him. He had to learn to walk on three legs, without any crutches."

"He did?"

"Yes, and it hurt to have to do that. But he was a trooper, and pretty soon all the pain went away. Have you ever had a dog?"

"Yes. We've got one now. He's a Scottish terrier."

"What's his name?"

"Dexter."

"Well, then…you need to take Dexter on lots of walks, but you can't do that with those crutches. Let's walk around the room together. If you think you're going to fall, put out your hand."

"Okay."

Travis was astonished that his son would actually do as she asked. When he began taking one tentative step, then another, Travis was elated, but also experienced a feeling of resentment that this Melissa could get his son to perform so easily. The feeling grew when Casey reached for her only once in the journey around the big room. Casey was still favoring his left leg, but this was the most he'd walked without help since the operation!

Melissa picked up the crutches and fitted them back under his arms. "You walked perfectly. And even though it hurt, you're still alive, right?"

Casey nodded with a smile, a reaction that shocked Travis.

"Come to my office and I'll give you a prize for doing a brilliant job this morning."

"What kind of prize?"

The way Casey was chatting with the woman, you'd have thought they were old friends. The change in Casey's behavior was nothing short of amazing. Too amazing, Travis thought, before realizing he was being uncharitable. She'd been working wonders with his boy.

When they walked through the door, he thought they'd entered a children's art museum. On one of the walls a large corkboard was covered in childlike drawings pinned up with colored tacks. Two other walls contained framed, stylized superheroes and animals painted in bright colors. He didn't recognize any of them, which meant they were original—and totally riveting. Casey looked around in delight.

Along the wall by the door sat a big pirate treasure chest. When the therapist opened the lid, Travis saw it was chock-full of store-bought toys in their packaging. This was much better than getting a look inside Santa's pack. Despite his conflicted feelings about Melissa, Travis couldn't seem to take his eyes off her sensational figure as she started rummaging through the toys.

"Hmm, let me see..." Travis could tell Casey's interest was piqued. In fact, he was getting impatient waiting for her to decide. "Ah. Here's the one I was looking for." She pulled out a package. "Hand me your crutches and I'll let you open it."

This time Casey hardly hesitated before he did her bidding. Travis could see that his son stood just fine without any support. She exchanged the crutches for the package. It took a minute for him to get it unwrapped.

"Look, Dad—a new leash for Dexter!" That was the biggest burst of happiness he'd heard from his son since before his fall. For the moment Casey had forgotten the pain in his leg.

"How about that, bud." Travis had tried bribery on him, but without the same result. Those were some pricey items he could see in that pirate chest. The therapist seemed to be doing everything right. His perturbance made no sense at all.

"When you get home, you'll have to take Dexter for a walk with it." She picked up the empty carton and tossed it in the wastebasket. "Want to give it to your dad to hold?"

Travis took it from him. The retractable leash would handle their twenty-two-pound Scottie without a problem.

After she'd helped him with his crutches, she said, "You can go home now."

Casey's eyes rounded. "You mean I don't have to get up on a table or anything?"

Her mouth curved into a big smile. "Nope. That's because you're all better. When you come back tomorrow morning, I'll let you look through the chest and pick out your own prize—*if* you walk all the way in from the car without your crutches. I'll be watching from the front door."

"I…think I'll be able to do it." His son was pretty transparent.

"Great! In that case I can't wait until tomorrow."

Casey grinned. "Thanks for the leash. Blue's my favorite color."

"Mine, too." She flicked her floppy bow to show him. Travis noted her bracelets, and saw she wore no rings on either hand. "I like blueberry popsicles, as well."

"So do I!" Casey actually laughed. "Are you really a doctor?"

"No, but don't I look like one?"

"No," Casey said. "You're too pretty."

Travis eyed his son in surprise.

"Well, thank you. I used to be a nurse. Then I trained

to become an orthopedic therapist. That means I work with patients after their doctor has seen them."

She finally glanced at Travis, just as he thought she'd forgotten him altogether. "We'll see you and your son in the morning. I'll put you down on my calendar for the same time, unless that's a problem."

"No. We'll be here at eight-thirty. Thank you."

"You're welcome. Bye, Casey."

"See ya," he called back.

Travis followed him out the door. Maybe it was his imagination, but he thought Casey walked most of the way, and used his crutches only for show. When they reached the car, Travis helped him in the back and fastened the seat belt.

In another minute they were on their way home. Instead of complaining, Casey played with the leash. "That was fun! I can't wait to get my prize tomorrow."

"Remember what Melissa said?"

"Yeah. I gotta walk all the way from the car into the building and not use my crutches. I can do that."

Travis smiled tightly and didn't ask any more questions. For the rest of the drive he remained immersed in thought. There'd been no preliminary discussion, and she'd given Travis no follow-up instructions. Nothing! It had irritated the hell out of him.

Not until he pulled in the driveway did he discover what was wrong with him.

There was an old saying about every person on earth having a double. This morning that saying had particular meaning for him.

He'd just come face-to-face with a woman who resembled, in looks and personality, his murdered wife, Valerie.

Travis was convinced that was the reason Casey had undergone a miraculous change at the therapist's hands. Although she was a younger version, Melissa Dalton had Valerie's sunny disposition and a way of making challenging things sound like fun. Her appealing energy had captured his son's attention, and he'd wanted her approval. But the very qualities about her that had caused the first therapy session to go so well haunted Travis.

He dreaded the thought of having to see her again in the morning. It had been fifteen months since he'd buried his wife in Texas. Melissa had unwittingly brought certain memories back to life. Casey's willingness to do what she wanted might have been unconscious, but his son had definitely responded because of deeply embedded memories, too.

It was going to be a long day and an even longer night, because Travis knew there'd be little sleep for him.

MELISSA LEFT FOR WORK on Tuesday morning curious to see if the skinny, brown-haired Stillman boy would let go of his crutches for good. She knew there was nothing wrong with him physically.

Probably never in her life had she seen such a handsome face or such sky-blue eyes. People would marvel over his remarkable features as he grew into manhood. Especially women. You needed to look no further than the boy's father.

But on the adult version—the man appeared to be

mid-thirties—there were differences. She'd seen the lines left by life and grief around his eyes and mouth, the shadow of a dark beard on his square jaw. The artist in her had caught the fierce gaze of arctic-blue eyes, distant and speculative. Almost forbidding. She shivered at the memory.

In the midst of her thoughts, she heard her cell ring. She reached for it and checked the caller ID. "Hi, Tom."

"Hey, how was your Labor Day weekend?"

"Semiproductive."

Unfortunately, she'd found herself looking over her shoulder quite a bit while doing her artwork. She'd been at the family cabin on her own, not for the first time this summer. Neither her parents, nor either of her two married siblings had used the place in August, yet increasingly she'd had a vague sense that someone other than herself had been there. Though she'd seen no signs of forced entry, there were little indications, such as books and lamps in places she didn't remember them being, the bedding not made up the normal way, and signs of dirty footprints on the floor by the back door. It made her nervous at night, so she'd turned on the generator, hoping the resulting sound and lights would ward off intruders.

If she'd still had her bulldog, Spike, Melissa wouldn't have felt so nervous. But soon after her divorce, her beloved pet had died of old age. She hadn't been able to bring herself to get a new one. She couldn't give an animal the time it deserved.

"Same here," Tom said, jolting her back to the present. "I'm afraid my children didn't leave me any time to write." That meant he'd had visitation through the long weekend. "I'm glad you're back. Let's meet for dinner at Rinaldo's in Bell Canyon Plaza after work."

"I'm afraid I can't. I promised the folks I'd spend the evening with them." Melissa needed to talk to her parents about the problem at the cabin. After their whole family had gotten together there for a Fourth of July celebration, her parents had gone to Laguna Beach, California, for two weeks on their own. "How about lunch there on Thursday?" She would have finished her renderings by then. "I'll bring everything you've been waiting for."

"Not till Thursday? I guess I can wait. What time?"

"One o'clock?" It would be right after the Denton baby's appointment. She had torticollis, a condition that curtailed her range of neck motion. Mrs. Denton fell apart emotionally every time she brought the baby for therapy. Melissa would need a break following the session.

"Okay, see you then. I'm looking forward to it."

Melissa hung up, unable to say the same thing back to him. Tom Hunt was a prominent patent attorney specializing in intellectual properties. He was also a talented writer of children's fiction. They'd met in March when he'd brought his son in for therapy because of knee pain. The eleven-year-old had Osgood-Schlatter disease, fortunately not too serious a case.

During the treatments, Tom had admired the paintings hanging in her office. When he'd learned she was the artist, he'd asked her if she'd be willing to do some sketches for a story he'd been working on. It was set during World War II, between two childhood friends whose countries were fighting on opposing sides. The subject appealed to her and she'd said yes. She'd started working closely with Tom, but despite his obvious interest, she had no desire for any sort of romantic relationship with him.

She knew he wanted to get married again, but in truth, the thought of marrying again herself filled her with dread.

Melissa had been young and in love when she'd married exciting, handsome Russell Dalton. But her dreams of living happily ever after were shattered when she realized she'd married an abuser.

Their seven-month marriage had come to an abrupt end the day he got home from his last college class. She was studying for finals at the kitchen table when he walked in, wanting to make love. Melissa had told him she needed to keep on studying, but he wouldn't take no for an answer. He'd jerked her out of the chair like a rag doll.

Shocked, she'd tried to push him away, and he'd responded by slapping her in the face so hard she fell to the floor. That blow had changed her life.

Though he was remorseful and swore it would never happen again, she'd grabbed her keys and run from the apartment and their life together. Divorce had followed.

Intellectually, she knew there were good men out in the universe who would make fine husbands. Over the past six years she'd dated quite a few of them. But the thought of taking the critical step into another marriage left her apprehensive.

To make her feelings clear to Tom, she never went out with him in the evening, or worked with him when his two children were on visitation. She shied away from any attachments. It wasn't fair to his kids, when there could be no future. He should have gotten the point long before now.

Since her divorce, Melissa had reached a restful place where she was in control. She wanted to stay there. When Tom's book was finished to his specifications, she'd decided, it would be the only project she'd do with him. After that, there wouldn't be a reason to get together again, and they could part with no hard feelings.

After parking in her usual spot, she headed for the clinic doors. She was almost there when she heard her name being called. Melissa turned to see Casey Stillman walking carefully away from a blue car toward her. He was dressed in shorts and a white T-shirt. His father followed, carrying the crutches.

She felt a burst of pleasure at the boy's taking up the challenge. When Casey was about halfway to her, he hesitated. "Keep coming, Casey!" she called. "You're doing great!"

The boy got a determined look on his face and picked up his speed. Once he reached her, she gave him a quick hug. "I'm very proud of you."

He looked up at her and smiled. Children smiled at her every day, but for some reason she didn't understand, Casey's expression tugged at her emotions. "It doesn't hurt that much."

"That's because you're so tough!" She let go of his

shoulders. "Come into my office. You've earned a gift of your choice. Do you need your crutches to get inside?"

Casey stared at her. "Will you hold my hand?"

"Of course." She took his hand and they walked through the main doors to her suite. She made sure they didn't go too fast. He was still favoring his leg, but not nearly as much as the day before.

Melissa walked him over to the treasure chest and opened it. "Take all the time you want picking out your prize. If you get tired, here's a little stool to sit on while you look."

He propped himself on the edge of the chest and started going through the presents. While he was occupied, she moved to her desk across the room and sat behind it. Casey's hard-muscled father, in jeans and a dark green sport shirt, took a chair opposite her and placed the crutches on the floor next to him.

"Mr. Stillman," she began quietly, "the doctor suggested your son's problem was psychological, so that's why I threw him in at the deep end of the pool yesterday. It's clear his leg has healed and he's able to walk just fine. Do you know any reason why his problem may have been so easily resolved? I don't. I know I'm close to being the perfect therapist, but an overnight recovery is astonishing."

The man's lips quirked at her joke, but she got the impression there was something about her he didn't like. She saw it in his wintry eyes. An odd chill went through her.

"I've discovered there's a very good reason," he answered, in a low voice so deep it resonated through her body. "But I would prefer to tell you out of his hearing." Casey's dad looked at her with such solemnity she took a quick breath.

"Understood. Since I'd like one more session with him, tomorrow morning, could you call me this afternoon? Say, around one? That's when I take my lunch break, and we can talk."

"I'll see that Casey is otherwise occupied, then phone you."

"Melissa?" his son called. "Can I have this Captain America toy?"

"Sure. It's one of my favorites. The gizmo shoots little disks."

"Awesome!"

"Did you know there's something else I'd like you to do for me?"

"What?"

"Just use one crutch on your way out to your father's car. Think you can do that?"

"Yes," he said. But he was so absorbed with his new toy she doubted he'd really listened. In a few long strides, his dad, carrying both crutches, reached Casey. He fitted one under his son's arm, then took the gift from him.

Melissa stood up. "I have one more favor to ask you, Casey." He finally lifted his head. "Will you come to my office tomorrow without your crutches? Just leave them at home. If you do that, I've got another surprise for you."

"Is it in the pirate chest?"

"I had something else in mind, but if there's another toy you'd like in there, that's fine."

She could almost hear his brain working. "Will I like it a lot?"

Kids. She loved them.

"I can guarantee it."

His eyes lit up. "Okay."

"Then I'll see you tomorrow. Bye, Casey."

"Can you thank her for being so generous?" his father prodded.

"Thanks, Melissa."

"You're welcome." She closed the door behind them to get ready for her next patient.

The morning seemed to pass much slower than usual. Melissa knew why. She was waiting for lunch, when Casey's father was supposed to phone. Not once in three years had she been given a case where it was over almost before it had begun. Mr. Stillman had indicated he knew the reason for his son's capitulation. She was eager for him to share it with her.

After her last appointment, she took a bottle of juice from her mini fridge and drank it while she typed the last patient's follow-up notes into the computer. At five after one, the receptionist told her she was wanted on line three. She picked up the receiver.

"Melissa Dalton speaking."

"This is Travis Stillman."

"Thanks for calling me, Mr. Stillman. Where is Casey right now?"

"In the kitchen eating lunch with the housekeeper. He's using her and Dexter to retrieve those disks."

She laughed softly. "From what I saw this morning, he should be picking them up himself. In my professional opinion he has healed beautifully. So why did he cling to the crutches until you brought him to the clinic?"

"Let me give you a bit of background first. Until fifteen months ago, I was a Texas Ranger living with my wife and son in Fort Davis, Texas."

A Texas Ranger. In Melissa's mind, Texas Rangers were legendary, and he fitted her image of one exactly.

"On my last case," he went on, "I went after a gang in a brutal racial slaying. I caught up with two of them, but a third one eluded me. They were known as the McClusky brothers. Soon after their capture, the third brother, Danny McClusky, murdered my wife in cold blood while she was driving home from the grocery store. It was a revenge killing. Thankfully, Casey was still at school."

His revelation stopped her cold. "I—I can't imagine anything so horrifying," she stammered. "Is that killer still free?"

"Yes. He's on the FBI's most wanted list. They'll get him in time."

"How do you live with that?"

"Not so well. Two other times during my career, my wife and son were threatened. After I buried her, I decided enough was enough, and resigned from the Texas Rangers. Casey needs me too much."

"He's so lucky you're still alive!" she said, before she realized how emotional she sounded. She knew what it felt like to be threatened. She'd gotten out of her marriage because of it. For both his and Casey's sakes, she was glad Mr. Stillman had moved to Utah, away from danger.

"I have a sister," he said, "who lives in Lone Peak Estates here in Sandy, with her husband and their two kids. Since the area's zoned for horses, she encouraged us to move across the street from her so we could ride their horses when we wanted. After the loss of his mother, I wanted Casey to have family close by."

"Of course," Melissa murmured, still shocked by the tragic story. For a child to lose his mother like that was utterly heartbreaking.

"He's had a hard time," Mr. Stillman continued, "but we were doing better until he fell off his horse and broke his leg. It happened soon after Pioneer Day, on the twenty-fourth of July. Having the surgery frightened him and set him back emotionally. He's been crying for his mother at night."

"That's only natural. Who wouldn't? In hellish times the child in everyone cries for his or her mother."

Melissa had wanted to cry in her mom's arms in the months before she'd run from Russ, wanting her to make everything all right. But she'd felt too ashamed to tell her parents anything. They'd advised her to wait another year before she got married, just to be sure. But oh, no. She knew what she was doing. What a fool.

She hadn't confided in her parents until after she'd left Russ.

Poor Casey hadn't had his mother when he'd fallen.

"When you greeted him outside your office yesterday morning, it was like something magical happened—he responded to you without even thinking about it. I was bewildered by his reaction until we got home. That's when I realized there's something about you that reminds him of his mother—the way you talk, your enthusiasm, even your physical appearance. You have a vitality like hers. Put all that together and you could be her double."

"Really?"

"Yes. At this point I believe he'd do anything for you. He proved that today."

Mr. Stillman had just given her a plausible answer for Casey's quick turnaround, but his own reaction was far more complicated. Melissa jumped up from her chair, suddenly putting two and two together. Whether he'd had a good, mediocre or bad marriage, seeing someone who reminded him so strongly of his wife must have come as a shock to him.

She'd known something was wrong. For some reason it made her feel strange. She didn't want to look like anyone else, especially his murdered wife. Apparently he didn't like it, either.

"Thank you for telling me all this," she said. "Considering his progress, tomorrow should be the last time he needs to come in." Working with children had made her careful not to allow attachments to form. "I'll send you home with a sheet showing a few exercises he can do. If you make a game of it and do them with him, he won't know you're trying to help strengthen those muscles. Keep in mind he doesn't have to do the exercises. Natural play will eventually work out any kinks, but it's something you can do together as father and son to speed things up. Do you have any questions for me?"

"None."

He seemed anxious to get off the phone. "Then I'll see you in the morning. We'll deal with the issue of his not wanting to go to school then."

Melissa hung up. She had no desire to prolong their conversation either. It would have been agony for Travis Stillman to have to discuss the tragedy with her. Heaven knows it was hard enough to hear about it. Any trauma that directly affected a child pained her. But murder… The poor boy. The poor father. He'd been forced to give up his life's work and move to a new state. None of that could have been easy.

She was glad she had a busy schedule that afternoon. It would get her mind off what she'd learned.

At four o'clock she left the clinic for her parents' home in Federal Heights, an area in the northeast region of the city near the University of Utah. Five generations of Robertses, all of whom had run the Wasatch Front Steel Corporation, had lived there. Melissa had grown up surrounded by tall, gorgeous old trees and a lush yard. Her town house, where the trees had been newly planted and there was no heavy foliage, was a big change.

While she ate dinner with her parents, she told them about the cabin. Her father rubbed his chin. "That's the trouble with such remote places, honey. After every winter, our neighbors up there complain of the same thing. Somebody's broken in and things are stolen."

She shook her head "Winter is one thing, Dad, but

for intruders to be that brazen in summer is really upsetting. I didn't see anything missing, but I know someone has been in there since July 24."

"Let's just be thankful you didn't surprise them when you walked in," her mother said. "I've never liked you going up there alone. This settles it. Please don't use the cabin again unless you have a friend or family member with you."

"Mom—"

"I don't care if you're a grown woman, Melissa. It's not safe."

"Your mother's right, honey. What about Tom?"

"He's a man I've done some artwork for, but that's all. I've never been interested in him. When the book's done, I won't be doing any more projects with him. Real-life paintings aren't the kind of thing I like to do."

Her dad glanced at her with affection. "I know. You love your world of fantasy."

"I always have." She put down her fork. "Fall is when I like to be up at the cabin every weekend. The atmosphere inspires me. My week's vacation starts next Tuesday. I planned to live up there the whole time, so I can hike and paint nonstop."

"If you're determined to go alone," her father said, "then you need to buy a gun and learn how to shoot it."

Her mother gasped. "William!"

"Well, it's either that or take a boyfriend along." Her parents despaired of her ever settling down again, and brought up the subject at every opportunity.

"I don't have one. What if we hired a retired policeman to be at the cabin when I go up? I'd help pay him."

Her father eyed her in frustration. "I guess anything's possible, but tell you what, honey. Some time tomorrow I'll call the police in the Kamas area and ask them to send someone over to the cabin and take a look."

"I don't see any signs of a break-in, so I don't think that will do any good."

"You have a point. Let me think about it. I don't like this any more than you do."

Her mother leaned forward. "I'll go up with you for a couple of nights, and I'm sure John and Linda will, too. In the meantime, why don't you ask Rosie from your work?"

"She's involved with a guy, Mom."

Besides, the problem with taking girl friends up there was that they needed to be entertained. At night they wanted to drive down to Kamas for a little fun, and to meet the local male talent. Melissa had done that years ago. It was how she'd met her husband. She had no desire for lightning to strike her twice in the same place.

Chapter Two

Travis was awake Wednesday morning long before it was time to take Casey to the clinic. His boss, Roman Lufka, owner of the Lufka Private Investigator firm, had intended to assign him a new case on Monday, but because Travis's son refused to go to school, the timing was wrong.

Roman was the greatest, and told him to take as long as he needed to work with Casey, but Travis was getting anxious. It was one thing for his son to convince the therapist that he could manage without his crutches in order to receive a prize, and quite another to agree to go back to school without them.

Travis heard his cell phone ringing when he came out of the shower. Hitching a towel around his hips, he hurried into the bedroom and reached for it. Maybe the therapist was calling because a scheduling problem had come up.

Last night, without knowing what he knew, his housekeeper, Deana White, had whispered to him that Casey seemed to have developed a crush on the therapist and couldn't wait until morning. Travis didn't want to think about the damage a cancelation could do at such a pivotal point in Casey's recovery.

Relief swept through him when he looked at the caller ID before picking up. "Hey, Chaz, it's good to hear your voice." Chaz Roylance was another great friend he'd made at the firm.

"Do you and Casey want to meet up for breakfast? I'll bring Abby." All the guys were trying to help Travis get through this rough period with his son.

"There's nothing I'd like better, but we're due at his therapist's in twenty minutes."

"How's it going?"

Travis sucked in his breath. "She challenged him to come without his crutches. Wants him to leave them at home. If he takes her up on it, I think we're halfway there."

"Only halfway?"

"The other half is getting him to go back to school."

"I hear you. As you know, our Abby is still having meltdowns over bees."

"The poor little tyke."

"When she sees one, it's the end of the world. Frankly, I'm glad cooler weather is on the way. Unless I can promise that bees won't be around, she refuses to do certain things, even for her mother."

For her mother.

In that arena, Travis had the edge on Chaz, because the therapist seemed to have the power to get his son to do anything. Travis ought to be grateful to her. Hell, he *was* grateful, but nothing seemed to alleviate his tortured thoughts since he'd met her.

"Thanks for the invite," he said to Chaz. "I'll call you tomorrow." He hung up and went back to the bathroom to shave. After putting on a crew-neck and dark trousers, he walked through the house to find his son in the kitchen eating breakfast. He'd dressed in jeans and a T-shirt. Travis didn't know if Deana had helped him or not.

And so far Casey hadn't gotten bored with Captain America.

"Good morning." The housekeeper, who'd raised three children of her own, put a plate of sausages and pancakes in front of him.

"Thanks, Deana."

Travis didn't have much appetite, but he ate what she'd served him, to be polite. His sister, Pat, had helped him find Deana. She'd been coming once a week to clean, and the rest of the time she picked up Casey from school and got dinner ready. Since he'd broken his leg, however, Deana had been putting in long hours, and Casey liked her.

Lately he hadn't been interested in food, and today he'd left half his breakfast on his plate, Travis noted in concern. "Hey, bud, it's time to go to the clinic. Put the toy down, okay?"

"Okay. What do you think she's going to give me this morning?"

He studied his son. "Are you going to leave your crutches here?"

Casey had laid them on the floor by his chair. "Yup."

"Then let's get going and find out. Do you need me to hold your hand?"

"I don't think so."

Deana sent Travis a private smile. What she didn't know was that although this was progress, the difficult part—school—was still to come. But he'd wait until they were in the therapist's office to bring the subject up.

Dexter followed them to the garage, and Casey gave him a hug. If people didn't look too closely, they might never know Casey had gone through his ordeal, Travis decided. Though his son took a little more time, he walked with a steady gait. Like any child, he loved getting neat things, but Travis feared that another gift wasn't all that was motivating him.

"There she is!" Casey spotted Melissa as they drove into the clinic parking lot five minutes later. There weren't many cars this early. When Casey climbed out she started waving. This time Travis didn't see any hesitancy on his son's part as he closed the distance between them.

Travis brought up the rear, surreptitiously studying Melissa Dalton. This morning she was turned out in a pair of latte-colored trousers with a dark brown waistband. With the fitted melon-colored blouse, it was hard to look anywhere else.

Her eyes appraised Casey. "Well, look at you. Good as new!" The boy beamed up at her. "I like a guy who makes a promise and keeps it. Where are those old crutches?"

"At home. I turned them into weapons." Travis blinked when Casey unexpectedly pulled a folded paper from his pocket and handed it to her. "See?"

"Hmm. What have we got here?" He giggled while she opened the paper with great ceremony. "Whoa, I certainly *do* see. How clever of you to make them into laser guns! Is that an interplanetary rocket they fit on?"

"Yeah."

She pressed it to her heart. "Can I have this and put it up on the corkboard for the other children to see?"

He nodded.

"When we get inside, you have to autograph it."

"Auto—?"

"*Autograph's* a fancy word for your name."

"Okay. I can print it."

"I didn't doubt it for a second. Come with me."

Once the three of them reached her office, Melissa walked around the desk and opened the top drawer. "Here's a good pen, Casey. Take the drawing over to the table by the books. After you print your name, you can put up your picture using those tacks on the board."

"Where shall I print it?"

"Anyplace you like. Make sure it's big so everyone can see it."

Casey got down on his knees to get to work. That's when Travis knew his son was no longer thinking about his leg. He chuckled as Casey's tongue rubbed against his lower lip while he carried out her suggestion.

"Here," she said when he was done, "I'll make a little more room for it." While she helped Casey mount the drawing, Travis returned the felt-tipped pen to her desk, then wandered over to see the finished product. But he found himself looking at the skein of lustrous hair caught at the nape of her neck with a coral flower clip. This morning she wore gold studs in her earlobes. Her fashion sense held strong appeal for him. Almost as much as her gorgeous body did.

"I love it!" she declared, drawing Travis's attention back to the drawing. His son had put his name coming out of the tip of the rocket, with each letter getting a little bigger. "I especially like the way you make your *y* with the curlicue on the tail."

Casey smiled again. Every time she opened her mouth, she built his son's confidence, Travis realized.

"This calls for a celebration." She walked back to her desk and reached in the drawer for a small envelope. Handing it to Casey, she said, "Inside this are three passes for your dad to take you and a close friend to a fun movie. And I have one more thing for you. It's in the clinic kitchen. I'll be right back."

Travis felt the gift giving had gone on long enough, and would have told her so, but she left the office too fast. He sat down with Casey. "That was certainly nice of her. Be sure to thank her for those passes when she comes back in."

"I will," he answered, sounding preoccupied. Travis didn't know how Casey felt about his latest present, but was glad he didn't say he'd have preferred a toy. "Hey, Dad, look at the picture of the huge bulldog! I wish I could take that one home."

Travis automatically complied, glancing toward the fabulous collection as he shook his head.

"Sorry, bud. That one stays on the wall." If he had a dollar for every time his son wished for something…

Pretty soon Melissa came back with a bakery carton

of iced cupcakes decorated in autumn colors, and put it on the table with some napkins.

"I noticed on your medical chart that you had a birthday a couple of weeks ago," she said, "but since you weren't in school, you didn't have a chance to celebrate. Every kid celebrates birthdays at school. Today would be the perfect day to take these to class. The other kids will love a treat. There's enough in the box for the three of us to have one before your dad drives you to school. Your teacher's waiting for you."

Casey looked as dumbfounded as Travis felt. "She is?"

"Of course. Doesn't everyone go to school on Wednesdays?" Casey nodded. "She's looking for one Mr. Casey Stillman to show up. Did you meet her at a parent-teacher conference before school started?"

"No. I couldn't walk."

"Well, you can now! Here—try one." She opened the lid. "You pick the color you want."

At first Casey couldn't decide. Travis reached for a yellow one and ate it in two bites, his eyes meeting Melissa's in amusement before she bit into hers. Finally Casey made his choice and devoured it quickly. She handed him a napkin, so he could wipe the frosting off his face. "If you're thirsty, there's a drinking fountain across the hall," she said.

"Okay." He slid off the chair and left her office.

Travis got to his feet, hardly knowing where to start thanking her for all she'd done. But before he could get a word out she said, "Quick—find your son and go. I'll follow you to the front doors." She picked up the cupcake carton and they left her office, gathering Casey along the way.

"I wish you could have stayed longer," she explained to him, "but I've got another patient waiting for me. Have fun at school." She handed the cupcakes to Travis. "Bye, Casey."

"Bye."

Her brilliant strategy had left his son confused. She'd been right; now was the time to act. Travis walked beside him to the car and they took off for his school, not giving him the luxury of thinking about what had just happened.

"Dad? I want Melissa to go to the movie with us."

Oh, no. He should've known! "She meant you should take one of your friends, Casey. I was thinking Blaine." He was a boy Casey often played with, who lived down the street from them.

"I don't want to go with him. She's more fun!"

She was definitely that. And maybe too clever? Travis wanted to believe the therapist had no ulterior motive when she'd handed him those passes, but he couldn't be sure. If she was interested in him, then this wasn't the first time a woman had tried to get his attention through his child.

Since moving to Utah, he'd met attractive women who'd come on to him, but he'd felt no answering spark and couldn't pretend otherwise. After one date, he couldn't bring himself to repeat the experience.

"We don't have to worry about it now. The passes are good for six months."

"But I want to see *Spider-Man* with her this week before the movie's gone!"

"We'll have to talk about it later." Relieved that the school was in sight, he pulled into the parking lot.

Because Travis had talked with Casey's teacher several times already, she handled the interruption to her morning class like the pro she was. The kids were delighted to get treats, and enough fuss was made of Casey that Travis could slip out before his son could decide he didn't want to stay.

Travis would never have thought of using his son's birthday as a way to get him back to class. But Melissa's tactic was the kind of thing Valerie might have done, and it had worked. He drove straight to the P.I. firm on Wasatch Boulevard, feeling as if he'd just survived a blizzard before reaching the top of Everest.

En route, he rang Deana and told her Casey was back in class, hopefully for the whole day. Travis planned to pick him up, but he would appreciate her staying until they got home, in case something went wrong before the school day was over.

Because of the therapist's clever handling of his son, life looked as if it might be getting back to normal. He was indebted to Melissa and her unorthodox methods. At the same time, he felt conflicted. He knew it wasn't her fault she reminded him of Valerie. And therein lay the problem. She *wasn't* his deceased wife. That woman was gone. More than ever he didn't want to be around her stand-in.

With a groan of frustration, he pressed on the accelerator, anxious to get to his office. What he needed was to dig into a new case, something that kept him physically active so he wouldn't have time to think. Roman had told him that a half-dozen cases he'd probably like were waiting for him. He could choose the one that appealed to him most.

As for Casey, he would have to go to the movie with his father and his eleven-year-old cousin, Jack. Or maybe just the two of them would go. He'd given in to his son's wishes long enough.

ON THURSDAY Melissa rushed inside Rinaldo's at the lunch hour. The place was crowded, but Tom had grabbed a booth and was waiting for her. She walked over and sat down opposite him.

"Sorry I'm late, but my last appointment lasted longer than I'd planned."

"Don't worry about it. I took the liberty of ordering our lunch, since I know you have to get back to work soon."

"I do. Thanks for going ahead. You'll be glad to know I've finished my part of our project." Melissa handed Tom the portfolio containing the artwork she'd done in watercolor for his book.

After the waitress brought their food, she ate while he looked through it. "These are perfect, Melissa."

"I'm glad you're pleased. Go ahead and take it to your office to scan everything before you send it off to your publisher."

"I want to do more than that," he said, with a look of longing in his eyes. "I've got ideas for a whole series of books based on World War II. Take a peek." He opened his briefcase and handed her a proposal he'd put together. "We make a great team."

No. Not in the way he meant. It was code for he wanted to marry her. This had to end now.

"Tom, I'm flattered that you want me to collaborate on your terrific stories, but I'm not interested in doing more of this kind of work."

He stared at her in disbelief. "I can't believe you're serious. You're a wonderful artist."

She'd been afraid of this, but it had to be said. "Thank you so much for giving me the opportunity, but I have my reasons."

"What are they?"

"Well, I've discovered that my work as a therapist keeps me so busy, I don't like the outside stress of deadlines. I've always painted for pleasure and don't want that to change now."

"Surely you realize a lot of money could be involved here—" The mention of money couldn't mask the hurt in his voice.

"I'm not after money," she stated quickly.

"Then it's me you don't like."

"Of course I do, or I wouldn't have worked with you on this."

He seemed to hesitate before he said, "Don't you realize how I feel about you?"

"Oh, Tom. Since my divorce I've been focused on my work. You're in a different place than I am. I love my freedom and don't want that to change." She hated it that he'd gotten emotionally attached without any encouragement from her. For him to have built a romantic fantasy about them was ludicrous. In Melissa's opinion he ought to go back to his wife, but she would never say that. All she could do was be firm.

When he didn't respond she added, "You're the writer and can attract other artists much more talented than I am. I don't doubt that in time you'll meet that special someone."

"Wait," he said, as she put a twenty-dollar bill on the table and got to her feet.

"I can't. I have to get back to the clinic. Let this lunch be on me. Naturally, I'll be available for anything else I have to do before the book goes to publication."

On that note she turned and worked her way through the lunch crowd, doubly thankful she'd never been anything but professional with Tom. He certainly couldn't accuse her of leading him on.

In truth, she'd been distracted by something else since she'd awakened that morning. For some reason she'd expected a phone call from Mr. Stillman, telling her Casey was back to not wanting to go to school. But then she did a rethink. If the little boy pulled another stunt, his dad would most likely go through another avenue to get help, and she would never know how things worked out for him.

For the rest of the afternoon she stayed busy, then left for the gym. A good workout was what she needed; it always helped relieve tension. But when she got home, she still felt at loose ends. She wanted to blame it on the unhappy moments at the restaurant earlier with Tom.

She should have been able to see his real intentions when he'd asked her to collaborate with him. But she didn't blame him. He was only doing what a divorced man would do to move on, and she must have seemed like a perfect start.

Casey's widowed father, on the other hand, wasn't looking. Any woman who hoped to draw the former Texas Ranger's attention was delusional.

In the end, Melissa climbed into bed with a portfolio of some of her old paintings. For years she'd been working on characters that one day might be the inspiration for children's cartoons for the screen. She worked with acrylics, and little by little she felt she was improving. But she hadn't yet achieved something she considered good enough to send to an agent who would approach a film studio for her.

After studying some of her paintings, she set the portfolio aside and began a new sketch.

The next thing she knew, it was morning. When she rolled out of bed, her right foot landed on the sketch pad, which had fallen to the floor at some point in the night. She picked it up and was shocked to discover a familiar face looking back at her.

Casey Stillman. Somehow he had worked his way onto the paper. An older Casey—maybe thirteen—astride an animal with three horns coming through a prehistoric-looking forest. Over his strong body he wore skins, and a thong around his forehead. One hand clutched a spear. His leg carried a jagged scar from thigh to ankle. A teen superhero…

Pleased with the drawing, she sat on the mattress and added a few more touches. Finally satisfied, she removed the sketch from the pad and slid it under the bed.

Later she'd take it to an art store and have it framed. After taking her pad and portfolio to the other bedroom, which she'd set up as a studio, she showered and dressed for work.

Since she would never see Casey again, she was glad she had a memento of him. That little boy must have really gotten to her, showing up in her art as he had.

But as she drove to the clinic a half hour later, she realized she needed to get her mind on other things. Tomorrow being Saturday, she would get up early and drive to the cabin.

Remembering the talk with her parents, she made a mental note to phone her brother, John, and ask him to bring Nedra and the kids for an overnighter. If they couldn't come, she'd call her sister, Linda. Maybe she and Brent would bring their children. Surely one of her siblings would be able to join her. But if no one could make it, Melissa decided, she'd stay till dark before leaving for home, and return on Sunday morning.

It angered her that strangers trespassed with no conscience and made themselves comfortable in a cabin that didn't belong to them. She'd felt violated. And then there was the fact that she'd seen no sign of a break-in. That disturbed her a lot. Someone had a key, or a way to get in, and could walk in on her at any time. She supposed the first thing she could do when she got up there was hunt for John's old baseball bat and keep it with her so she wouldn't feel completely helpless.

Kamas was only thirty miles east of Sandy. They had to drive another two miles on dirt roads to reach their property. The log cabin, built in 1935, was at a higher elevation and somewhat isolated from other cabins in the forest. She could see it made a perfect target for lowlifes—her father's term for people who made themselves at home on someone else's land.

If she found more signs of trespassers using their cabin, she'd tell her parents she was calling the police, and she'd meet them there herself. Something had to be done. The cabin had always been her retreat. It was important.

As soon as she reached the clinic, she made phone calls to her siblings. No one was free this weekend, though John told her he'd get back to her if anything changed. She thanked him, but didn't count on it. So she wouldn't be able to go up to the cabin. Melissa was deflated by that prospect, but knew there was nothing else to do but accept it and immerse herself in work.

Fridays usually turned out to be the busiest day of the week. That was a good thing. She'd barely said goodbye to her first patient when the receptionist told her she had a call on line four. Maybe it was John. She picked up and almost said his name, but caught herself in time. "Melissa Dalton."

"Ms. Dalton?" Her pulse picked up speed when she recognized that baritone voice. "This is Travis Stillman."

"Good morning. How's Casey doing?"

"He's the reason I'm calling." *Uh-oh.* "Would you happen to be free after work today?"

What?

"Casey wants you to go to the movie with us."

"I take it he's weaned himself from the crutches."

"He has, all because of you. He wants to thank you for the birthday treats. I told him you were a very busy lady, but he asked me to try and arrange it. Hopefully it won't interfere with your plans for the evening."

"No, it's a perfect time for me."

"You're through at four-thirty?"

"Yes. I'll meet you at the theater if you'll tell me which one."

"In the Bell Canyon Plaza. It's the latest *Spider-Man*. There's a showing at four forty-five."

"I'll be there."

"We'll meet you outside the box office to give you your ticket."

"Sounds good. Tell Casey thanks for sharing his gift. I'll see you both later."

"Until then."

She hung up, but when she thought about the invitation, her excitement quickly subsided. This had been Casey's doing, not his father's. And just as Melissa had avoided meeting Tom in the evenings, Travis Stillman had arranged this outing during the day.

No mention of picking her up beforehand or eating dinner afterward. He'd even gone so far as to say he didn't want to interfere with her evening plans. That didn't surprise her. The last thing he'd be looking for—if he were looking—would be a woman who reminded him of his wife.

Where Casey was concerned, she had to remember that children could be manipulative. He liked getting presents and it wasn't beyond the realm of possibility that he was hoping to wangle one more out of her. That was why she would show up empty-handed.

Melissa worked through until four-twenty, then left for the movie theater. The minute she climbed out of her Jeep, she heard her name being called. And there was Casey, running up to her. No one would know he'd ever had a broken leg.

His father, striking in a black polo and khakis, stood back with his hands on his hips. She noticed he'd drawn the attention of several women, not just her.

Casey broke into a smile. "That's an awesome Jeep."

"Thanks. I love it."

"I wish I could ride in it sometime."

"Maybe you can. It's up to your father. How's school?" She started walking toward his dad. Casey kept up with her.

"Pretty good. Thanks for the cupcakes."

"You're welcome. Thanks for asking me to come to the movie. After being at work all day, this is a treat." She lifted her gaze to find a pair of midnight-blue eyes staring down at her. They weren't quite as frosty this afternoon, thank goodness. "It's nice to see you again, Mr. Stillman."

"Casey and I are pleased you could come. We'd better go in. The previews have probably started."

He held the main door open for them, and they passed through the lobby to the theater itself. She was careful not to brush against him, but even without touching, she was aware of him. The place wasn't crowded yet, though the previews were on. Casey took the lead and walked down the aisle to an empty row. "Can we sit here?"

"I was just going to pick it," his father said.

Melissa moved ahead so Casey would be sitting between them.

"I'll get us some popcorn and be right back," Travis murmured.

"Thanks, Dad." When he'd gone, Casey turned his head to look at her. "Do you like Spider-Man?"

"I think he's amazing the way he swings around on his web, looking for bad guys."

"Except he's not real. But my dad is."

"What do you mean?"

"He looks for bad guys."

Melissa didn't know what to say to that, for fear she'd bring up something painful. His father might have moved to Utah, but he'd never give up the search for the criminal who'd killed his wife. "You mean a long time ago."

"No, now. He's a P.I. You know—he looks for people doing bad things."

She blinked. Travis Stillman was a private investigator? "Here in Salt Lake?"

"Yup. At Lufka's."

Lufka's? She'd seen that name written somewhere, but not in Casey's patient file. "I didn't know that."

Just as the main feature started, his father returned with a tub of popcorn and passed it down. Throughout the film she munched on it, but her mind wasn't on the film. While Casey sat there totally absorbed, she was thinking about what he'd told her. Until people got up to leave, she didn't even realize the movie was over.

"I wish we could watch it again," Casey said to his dad.

"I know, but we can't. We're due at your aunt Pat's for dinner. Let's go."

Melissa filed out of the row after them. They made their way through the lobby and outside. Without looking at his father, she patted Casey on the shoulder. "Thanks for inviting me. I loved the movie and the popcorn. Now I have to go or I'll be late for my dinner date." In this case she hoped she could be forgiven for a small white lie.

"I wish you could come with us."

"But she can't." His father's voice had an edge. "Have you thanked her for coming?"

Casey's blue eyes revealed a poignant longing that caught her off guard. "Thanks, Melissa."

She smiled. "I bet I had a better time than you did. Have fun at your aunt's. Are you taking Dexter with you?"

He nodded.

"Lucky dog," she said, and hurried off to her Jeep to prevent his father from having to say another word.

Once inside, she reached into her purse for her iPhone and searched for Lufka's in Salt Lake. A list with that spelling came up. She clicked on the first entry, and up popped the website for the Lufka Private Investigator firm on Wasatch Boulevard. Now she remembered where she'd seen it before. She'd passed their place of business hundreds of times.

Her eyes took in the information. The firm covered everything from surveillance and insurance fraud to missing persons, stalking cases, theft of property and protection to individuals. In Melissa's mind, Mr. Stillman had traded one dangerous job for another, and would make an adversary without equal.

Not wasting another second, she headed for her parents' home. She knew they had a business dinner tonight, but maybe they hadn't left yet. Melissa needed to talk to them. She had an idea.

Chapter Three

After dropping Casey off at school Monday morning, Travis drove to work. Despite the promise of another hot, beautiful September day, he was in a foul mood.

As he was getting out of his car, Chaz walked over to him. "Things must be better with Casey or you wouldn't be here." But when he got closer and scrutinized him, he added, "So how come you look like you haven't slept in a week? What's wrong?"

"Let's just say I've been haunted by a ghost."

Chaz frowned. The guys knew about Valerie and had always been sensitive to his moods. "That doesn't sound good. Want to talk about it?"

Travis let out a deep sigh. "Maybe I should." He looked around. Roman wasn't here yet. When his boss arrived, they were going to go over the new missing person's case he'd been assigned. Travis had barely started the groundwork, and had some questions only Roman could answer through his connections with the police department. "Sure you have the time?"

"I'll make it. Come on."

He followed Chaz inside. Somebody had brought SweetSpuds for the staff, probably Mitch. Since marrying Heidi Norris, whose family owned the SweetSpuds doughnut company, Mitch kept them in good supply. Before long they would all have to go on a strict diet, but not this morning.

Travis poured them coffee and took it to Chaz's office, while his friend carried the doughnuts. "You know the therapist Casey saw last week, and then he suddenly had a miraculous recovery?" He sat down heavily in a visitor's chair.

Chaz's eyes narrowed as he settled behind his desk. "Yeah?"

Travis rubbed his face with his hands before letting out a groan. "Weird as this may sound, she looks and acts like…Valerie."

A shadow crept over Chaz's face. "You mean…"

"I mean Melissa Dalton could be her double, in a superficial way, of course. I almost had a heart attack when I met her." His voice grated as he continued, "It hit me so hard, I couldn't respond naturally around her." He drank some coffee, but forgot it was hot, and the liquid scalded his tongue.

"And Casey?"

"I don't even know where to begin."

Chaz leaned forward. "Has he said she reminds him of his mother?"

"No. I think he's afraid to admit it to me, but I'm convinced he's already bonded with her. Since she went to that movie with us on Friday, he's worked himself up into seeing her again. I shouldn't have given in to him. I feared there'd be a price to pay, but the thought of him refusing to go to school drove me to it. I purposely made it for the afternoon and—"

"Travis," Chaz broke in. "I'm confused."

"You're not the only one."

"Try telling me this from the beginning."

He nodded. "Okay. Last Monday, when I took Casey to his first appointment with her, she challenged him to walk without his crutches. Just like that, he put them down and started walking around the therapy room with her. It was amazing. If I hadn't been there to witness it, I wouldn't have believed it."

For the next five minutes Travis unloaded to Chaz. When he'd finished, his friend stared hard at him. "My next question for you is might there be a part of you that wants to see her again?"

"Hell, no!" Travis shot out of the chair and began pacing. If he did want to see her again, he'd need his head examined. "But Casey does."

"How come you're so upset? If you don't want anything more to do with her, then Casey will have to accept it. Even if he goes into another funk for a week or two, that will be the end of it."

Travis sighed. "You're right. I just need to get over the shock. Thanks for talking to me. I'd better get to work. Roman should be here by now."

"Bring Casey over tonight. We've invited Mitch and Heidi. They'll bring Zack. It's still beautiful weather. We're going to grill some hamburgers out on the deck. Lacey and Abby will be thrilled if you two come."

"Thanks, Chaz. I think I'll take you up on that. It'll be fun for Casey. I'll bring the dessert."

His friend smiled. "Not necessary. Just make sure Dexter comes, too. Abby loves him."

"Will do."

Travis headed to Roman's office, feeling better after having aired his fears to Chaz. But he hadn't told him everything. On Friday he'd discovered Melissa Dalton was the only woman of his acquaintance who showed no personal interest in him. He knew it when he couldn't feel any vibes coming from her.

Travis wasn't a vain man, but the few times she'd glanced at him, she'd seemed to look right through him. Their conversation on the phone when he'd told her about Valerie had been brief and to the point. She didn't draw things out or show undue curiosity. Didn't voice the usual platitudes.

Generous as she'd been to Casey, Travis sensed she wouldn't like it if he brought his son around her again. She'd been professional and accommodating to her patient, but there was a limit, and Casey had reached it. *Travis* needed therapy if he allowed this situation to get to him. There was no reason they would ever see each other again. Ships passing in the night.

Roman had arrived, and motioned to him from his office. "Come on in and sit down. I've got something to discuss with you."

"I was just going to ask you a few questions concerning the new case myself."

His boss shook his head. "I've turned it over to Rand." Rand was one of the older P.I.s who'd worked there for several years.

Travis squinted at his boss. "Maybe you didn't realize that Casey is fine now and back in school."

"I heard and it's great news. But something else has come up and your name was mentioned as the person to get the job done. Ever heard of William Roberts?"

"No."

"He's the CEO of the Wasatch Front Steel company."

"*That* name I've heard of."

"Everyone has. Their family is one of the most prominent in our fair city. They've owned property in the Kamas area for close to eighty years, up in the Wasatch-Cache National Forest. The first Roberts settlers erected a cabin in 1935, and it has been used and maintained by the family ever since.

"After the twenty-fourth of July, his daughter went up several times alone and discovered that someone, maybe several people, have been using the cabin on weekdays. She's nervous to go up there at all now, and had a talk with her parents. Mr. Roberts told her he'd look into it the next chance he got.

"Apparently owners of other cabins farther down the mountain have had occasional break-ins too, but the police have told them they can do nothing unless they see a crime in action. To Mr. Roberts's knowledge, nothing in their cabin is missing, but there are definite signs of occupation. He phoned our company to look into the problem and catch the intruders. I talked with him yesterday. He requested you."

Travis was mystified. "Because of another case I've worked on?"

"No. Because you're a former Texas Ranger. It seems

his daughter has met you and learned you're now a P.I. She recommended you to her father and he called me."

The hairs stood up on the back of Travis's neck. "What's her name?"

"Melissa Dalton. Does it ring a bell?"

The news brought him to his feet. With a different last name, it meant she was either divorced or widowed. It would explain the absence of a ring on her finger, and her dinner date for Friday night. At the time he'd wondered if she didn't wear rings because she did a lot of physical therapy with children.

After concluding that she had *no* interest in him, Travis found, his thoughts going through a 180-degree reversal. He'd never told her that he worked as a P.I. now. The subject hadn't come up. Which meant she must have learned it through Casey.

Travis thought back to last week. The only time the two of them were alone was at the movie, when he'd gone out to buy popcorn. Had she asked Casey questions out of curiosity? Or had his boy just been chatty and told her the story of his life in those five minutes?

What kind of work Travis did since they'd moved from Texas wasn't a secret. But with Valerie's killer still on the loose, everyone kept quiet about his former occupation. For her of all people to find out, and then go to her father, came as a big surprise. Knowing how she felt—or didn't feel—about him made it an even bigger one.

"What's going on, Travis? This woman obviously means something to you."

Roman's question jerked him out of his thoughts. He

glanced at him. "She's the therapist who worked with Casey last week."

His boss smiled. Travis didn't miss the twinkle in his eyes. "Whatever went on, nice job."

"Nothing went on." Roman could be a terrible tease.

"Whatever you say." His boss stood up and handed him the new file. "Her cell phone number is in there, along with the notes I took. Mr. Roberts wants you to work with his daughter. She's the one who uses the cabin the most, and can tell you everything you need to know.

"He's made phone calls to his neighbors and indicated that a lot of well-heeled cabin owners up there will be indebted to you. The list is included. They're willing to pay any amount to get rid of the trespassers, and want you to start today."

"After that buildup, I guess I don't have a choice."

"There's always a choice. You know that." Roman had more integrity than anyone he knew. "Say the word and I'll give it to Rand."

Travis broke out in a cold sweat. This was a dilemma he could never have anticipated. But as long as Casey didn't know about it, and Travis kept any contact with Melissa Dalton to a minimum, he supposed it could work. "Today, you say?"

Roman nodded. "Gather your crew. Anything you need, just let me know. Jose and Lon are available for backup. Adam's on another case, but should be finished shortly."

Jose was ex-FBI with the Bureau of Alcohol, Tobacco and Firearms, and had worked for years on assignments in Latin America. Lon was a retired police chief who'd once headed the Salt Lake City SWAT team. Both were great resources among the many operatives Roman employed. Travis liked working with them when they were available. "That's good to know. Okay, I'm out of here."

"Keep me posted, comrade."

Travis chuckled. Because of his Russian heritage, Roman often put in an exaggerated accent when he spoke to the guys. He was a bit of a joker.

The first thing Travis needed to do was let Deana know not to fix dinner, because he and Casey were going to Chaz and Lacey's.

Next, he dipped into the file Roman had given him. After finding Melissa's cell number, he programmed it and the clinic number into his iPhone, then went out to the firm's shop to gather batteries, surveillance cameras and a listening device.

Everything for the staff's use was stored in there. Roman's brother, Yuri, manufactured electronic gadgets and sent them out from the East Coast for the firm to try out. The place was a gold mine for the latest state-of-the-art equipment. Sometimes Yuri flew out with his family. He was an even bigger tease than Roman. The two brothers were so entertaining, everyone flocked around.

Travis wore a smile out to the car, but once inside, he felt the reality of the situation hit home. *Just call her and get it over with, Stillman.*

Gripping his cell, he phoned the clinic and left a message with the receptionist for Melissa Dalton to call him ASAP. He needed a key to her family's cabin, and directions. If he didn't hear from her within the hour, he'd try her cell. With that accomplished, he headed for home to change clothes and load his truck.

MELISSA HAD JUST TAKEN a shower and was eating toast in the kitchen when her cell phone rang. Her heart kicked, which surprised her. It hadn't done that in years.

She checked the caller ID, wondering if it might be Travis Stillman. On Sunday her father had talked to the owner of the Lufka firm and had hired them, specifically Mr. Stillman, to check in to the problem at the cabin. But Casey's dad might be in the middle of another case and one of the other P.I.s would have to be assigned.

Even if Casey's father had been available, he might have declined taking the case when he found out Melissa had been the one to suggest him for the job. Then she would know in a hurry he preferred to have no more contact with her. Whether it was because she reminded him of his wife or some other reason, she would have to let it go. It surprised her that she even cared.

When she saw the clinic's number on her caller ID, she felt a double spasm of disappointment before picking up. Why were they phoning when she'd taken the day off?

"This is Melissa."

"Hi. It's Susan. Sorry to bother you at home, but Mr. Stillman just called the clinic and asked if you would phone him right back. It sounded important. Here's his number."

Melissa ran over to the counter where she kept a pad

and pencil and wrote it down. To her frustration, she saw her hand was unsteady. "Thanks, Susan."

After she clicked off, she phoned Casey's father, taking several calming breaths while she waited for him to pick up.

"Ms. Dalton?"

"Yes."

"I appreciate your calling me back so fast, but I didn't expect your receptionist to interrupt one of your therapy sessions."

"She didn't. I'm at home."

He was quiet for a second. "You're not ill, I hope."

"No. Nothing like that. I took the day off when my father told me he'd hired your firm. He wants me to be available for you."

"I see. Casey must have told you about my work."

"When he explained that Spider-Man caught bad guys, he also mentioned that you look for bad guys 'for real.' I asked him what he meant and he told me you were a P.I. who worked for Lufka's. I looked it up on the internet and found the website. When I saw the word *surveillance,* I thought it an amazing coincidence." She was talking too fast, but couldn't seem to stop herself.

"In what way?"

"Ever since the July 24 holiday, I've been entertaining the idea of hiring somebody to find out who's invading our cabin when we're not there. I told Dad I'd be willing to help pay for a retired police officer to stay at the cabin until winter. He said he'd try talking to the police again, but I feared we'd get nowhere there."

"I heard about that from my boss this morning," Travis replied. "Roman Lufka talked to your father, who told him you've got a problem up there. I've agreed to look into it, and understand you're the one who can help me get started."

She leaned against the counter, trying to recover from her adrenaline rush. "I didn't know if you'd be involved in another case, but I thought we should ask for you just the same."

"Actually, I'd been assigned to a missing person's case, but my boss took me off it after talking to your father. It's the least I can do after you helped my son realize he didn't need those crutches. You have a way with children, Ms. Dalton."

"Thank you. But would you please call me Melissa?"

"Okay, and you call me Travis."

"I will. We're very grateful to you. I, most of all, since I'm the one who spends a lot of time up there. Fall is one of the most beautiful seasons in the woods. I'm really angry about what's happened. We've been invaded."

"You have every right to be upset. Since you're free, I'll come by for you now and we'll drive up there."

"We can take my Jeep."

"Except that it will be familiar to the culprits if they've been watching your comings and goings."

Melissa shivered at the idea. "You're right."

"My truck won't raise suspicions. If you have any maps of the area, bring them."

"We have a drawer full of U.S. Geological Survey maps at the cabin. My brother pores over them at every opportunity."

"That's even better. I want to see everything inside and out. We'll come home in time for me to drop you off and pick up Casey after school. By then I'll have a much better idea of how I want to handle your case."

"I'll be ready in five minutes."

"Good. I've loaded some food and drinks in my backpack. When we reach Kamas, I'd like to go on foot from there. I understand your cabin is only a couple of miles up the mountain."

"That's right." Hiking was one of her favorite things to do in this world. Waves of delight swept through her. A picnic with a Texas Ranger among the wildflowers would be like something out of a fantasy. With him around, no way could she get hurt.

The biggest problem for her would be remembering it was only a dream. When he'd solved the case, the dream would be over.

"Give me your address." When she'd done his bidding, he told her he'd be there in ten minutes. Then he rang off.

She hurried upstairs to the bedroom and removed her robe, choosing to wear jeans and a peach-colored T-shirt. After putting on her hiking boots, she went into the bathroom to do her hair. If they were going to be doing a lot of hiking, she preferred it off her neck, and opted for a French twist, using a couple of inlaid-wood hair sticks.

After applying a liberal coating of sunscreen, she put the tube in one of her back pockets with apricot-frost lipstick. In the other one she stashed her keys and a twenty-dollar bill. That was all she needed. She kept a lot of art supplies at the cabin. In fact, her bedroom there looked like a painting studio. If time permitted, she'd do some drawings.

When she was ready, she went downstairs and grabbed two cold apples from the fridge. He might like one. Making sure the lights were off, she locked the door behind her and walked out to the drive to wait for him. She hadn't taken a day off in a long time. It was almost like being a kid again playing hooky.

Melissa was feeling so good she feared her latent divorcée hormones had finally decided to kick in. Until now she'd thought the whole idea was a myth.

A few neighbors waved on their way to the carport. No doubt they were surprised to see her out in front eating an apple as if she didn't have a care in the world. In another minute a steel-green metallic Silverado four-door truck pulled into the driveway with Travis at the wheel. She ran around to the passenger side and climbed in so he wouldn't have to get out and help her.

On a scale of one to ten, one being the most like the frozen Arctic, she decided the blue eyes that met hers were probably closer to a thawed-out four. The vast improvement lifted her spirits. If he'd really been turned off by her, he wouldn't have considered taking this case, no matter what his boss wanted.

"I brought you an apple, but if you don't want it, that's fine."

"Thanks." He took it from her and bit into it, studying her at the same time from head to toe until she was almost suffocated from inner heat. The way she'd done her hair seemed to fascinate him. If his wife had worn it this way, Melissa didn't want to know about it.

"You don't have a purse," he said. "Do you want to go back for it?"

She shook her head. "I have everything I need in my pockets."

"Incredible," he muttered. In the next instant he looked around and backed out to the street. Then they took off. Like her, he'd dressed in jeans and a T-shirt, but every inch of him was hard lines and sinew. Out of the corner of her eye she saw his backpack lying on the seat behind him.

"Have you been to Kamas before, Travis?"

"No, but I drove up Parley's Canyon to Park City to ski with some coworkers several times last winter."

"Those places aren't far apart. Our cabin is two miles beyond the town, farther up in the forest, at 8,500 feet."

He finished the apple and tossed the core with hers into the plastic bag he used for waste. "I thought the Davis Mountains of West Texas were amazing until I came here and saw the Uintas."

"All mountains have their own beauty. Unfortunately, there are lawless people who ruin it for everyone else." When he didn't say anything, she glanced at him and saw that his jaw with its dark shadow had hardened. "I—I'm sorry if what I said brought back your pain," she stammered.

"Don't worry about it. I've been living with pain for a long time. Because of Casey, I'm able to deal with my wife's death."

"I know what you mean. The children I work with

brought me out of my depression after my divorce. When they're around, you have to meet their needs. In the process, you forget yourself."

"Yup. The day my wife was buried, I wanted to crawl into the ground with her. Then Casey whispered that he didn't feel good and needed to go the bathroom."

In spite of her sorrow for Travis, Melissa laughed gently. "The day I received my divorce decree, one of my young patients caught me crying. She asked me what was wrong. Not thinking, I told her my marriage was over. She said, 'You're lucky. Now you get to sleep with your mommy.'"

Unexpected laughter burst out of Travis. It gave her a glimpse into that hidden part of him. She was pretty sure he was a man who'd once laughed a lot. How would it be to get to know *that* man…?

"Have you been divorced for a while?"

"Six years."

"You must have been a child bride."

"Being married at twenty-one does sound young these days. To make it worse, I was married to a child groom." One who was Dr. Jekyll to everyone else, but when they were alone, he became a version of Mr. Hyde, who watched and knew every move she made until she couldn't breathe.

"How long did it last?"

"Seven months."

"I'm sorry."

"I'm not. It wasn't meant to be. You know those boxes you have to check as the primary reason for the divorce?"

He nodded.

"Well," she continued, "instead of 'incompatibility,' the first one ought to read 'total and complete immaturity.'"

Her comment produced another laugh from him.

"I can laugh about it now, too," she said.

She actually could laugh about that part of it, but the other part… Russ's dark side… She'd since learned that he'd married again and moved to California. The news had made her euphoric, but if she ever allowed herself to think about it, she trembled for his unsuspecting wife.

"You know, I wish I could find that little girl again and tell her I didn't end up sleeping with my mommy, but I'm a lot happier now."

Melissa looked out the side window, knowing Travis couldn't say the same thing. Even if his wife's killer were caught and given the death penalty, it wouldn't undo the pain of losing her. The horrific murder had robbed Casey of his mother. Melissa heaved a sigh. It was all too sad, but to wallow in it wouldn't do either of them any good.

"I have several theories about the people breaking into the cabin," she said without preamble. "The first one is that they're probably deer hunters without permits, checking out their favorite spots ahead of time and using the cabin as their motel."

His lips twitched. "That's a possibility."

"The second one is that a couple of unemployed high school dropouts wanted by the police are hanging out where no one can find them."

"I like that one."

Apparently she was amusing him, but this was better than dwelling on his tragic past. "The third one is kind of outside-the-box thinking."

"Go on. I'm intrigued."

"A Sasquatch family has decided our cabin is the perfect retreat."

Again, laughter rumbled out of him. When it subsided he said, "Don't tell me. You're a regular listener of the *Stargazer Paranormal* radio show."

"I used to be, but the host was replaced so I don't listen anymore."

"You liked Lacey Pomeroy?"

Her eyes widened. "Did you used to listen to her show, too?"

"A couple of times."

"Ooh, I wish she hadn't gone off the air. Sometimes I work late and I loved to hear her talk about other worlds."

"Rumor has it she got married and retired into a life of obscurity."

"I figured it had to be something like that, but it's my loss."

Travis flashed her a glance. "Does this mean you do a night clinic?"

"No. I paint."

His gaze roved over her with new interest. "Am I in the presence of a famous artist?"

It was her turn to laugh. "I just play at it for my own pleasure." She could get lost in it, the best kind of therapy to rid herself of past demons.

He slowed down to make a turn. They'd be in Kamas soon. "The art hanging in your office—it's yours?"

"Yes."

"Why didn't you sign them?" He sounded surprised. "You're very good."

He sounded as if he meant it. "Thank you. Lest you think I'm crazy for putting up my own stuff and letting my art remain anonymous, I have my reasons."

"You mean besides making your office a place children love to visit? Casey said he wished he could take home that picture of the superhero sleeping against the huge bulldog."

"He did?" That pleased her. "I painted that soon after my bulldog died." She'd mourned the loss of him extra hard.

"But he had four legs."

The man sitting next to her didn't miss anything. When law enforcement failed, you called in a Texas Ranger to get the job done. She'd heard that all her life and couldn't believe she was actually sitting next to one.

"My bulldog, Spike, was my *second* dog."

"Spike?"

"Like the dog in the Tom and Jerry comics."

"I liked those old cartoons. Still do."

With those words, her feelings warmed toward him. "So do I. Anyway, it was my first dog, Cleo, who was missing a leg. She was a white Bichon. A real cutie. She was a happy little thing, quite unaware she had only three legs."

"Do you have a dog now?"

"No. With the hours I keep, it would be alone too much."

"I know what you mean. We have a part-time housekeeper who watches out for Dexter."

"A housekeeper who cleans and cooks is what *I* need, so I can have more time to spend on my hobby."

She felt him glance at her. "Lest I think you're crazy for exhibiting your talent in public, tell me your real reason for putting it up in your office."

His brain was a steel trap.

"Okay. One day I'd like to submit my art to a film company that makes animated cartoons. In the meantime I've brought my art to the office and mounted it, watching to see which samples appeal the most to my patients. But so far I've received such a wide range of responses, I can't decide which pieces would be the best to send to an agent who'll represent me."

She thought of her picture of Casey. If she dared put it up, she'd be fascinated to see if her patients found it more interesting than the others. But now wasn't the time to think about that. Melissa turned her head toward Travis, needing to change the subject. "What are some of your ideas about the cabin break-in?" Then she corrected herself. "I suppose I shouldn't say *break-in*—there's no sign of a forced entry."

His expression sobered. "Doesn't matter how they got in. After tracking criminals since my early twenties, I had quite a few scenarios springing to mind. But until I pick up some kind of evidence, I'm keeping the many possibilities open to investigation."

"That was a good nonanswer." She said it with a smile.

He shot her an amused glance. "We're coming into Kamas. Let's grab a bite at that fast-food place up ahead."

"You mean Grampy's. They used to make awesome hamburgers, but they're under new management. I hope the food's still good."

"We'll find out. After that I'll drive to a church parking lot to leave the truck and we'll head out on foot."

"Why a church parking lot?"

"They're usually safe places. Anyone looking to hot-wire it, *if* they can open the door, will think twice about stealing it. There's usually a custodian around who could walk out at any time and catch them."

"That makes sense."

He pulled off the road next to some other cars parked in front of Grampy's, where they had to get out to be served. She opened the cab door and jumped down to get in line behind half a dozen other people. Travis followed. In a minute it was their turn.

Melissa knew just about everyone who ran the businesses in town. But she didn't recognize the dark blond employee manning the window. Probably mid-forties, he had a buzz cut and a deeply burnished complexion, with that leathery kind of skin normally seen on a sailor or a beachcomber.

She likely wouldn't have noticed details about him if he hadn't given her that blatant kind of once-over some guys did. Closer now, she saw a glazed look in his eyes.

For a second it reminded her of Russ's crazed expression before he'd struck her.

This man didn't stop staring until Travis moved behind her. Then his gaze turned away to Travis, who didn't need a Texas Ranger uniform to be formidable. Melissa was thankful he was with her.

"What can I get for you and the wife?" The question didn't fool her. Neither she nor Travis wore wedding rings.

She leaned inside the window. "Is that your *wife* cooking back there?"

He glanced at the older woman at the grill, giving Melissa a glimpse of a tattoo on the back of his neck. "I don't have a wife." Melissa could tell that her question had angered him.

"I see," she said. "Well, as it happens, I don't have a husband. Now, I'll have a burger and fries to go. Heavy on the onions."

She pulled out her twenty-dollar bill and plunked it down in front of him. People in the line behind them must have heard her, for they started chuckling. She wasn't sorry. The man had disgusted her. He stood there with spots of anger on his cheeks. The spots went even darker by the time he'd waited on Travis and handed him his order.

By tacit agreement they took their food to a picnic table around the side of the building.

Chapter Four

Travis hadn't liked the way the other man had looked at Melissa. And when his shifty eyes had seen Travis, the way he'd tried to cover up. A woman as pretty as Melissa would always be a target, but there was more to it than that. After chasing down criminals for years, Travis had a gut instinct about them, and this man's behavior put up a red flag.

Obviously, Melissa had seen that look, too—she'd paled in reaction—but she'd camouflaged it by turning the tables on the man. But something had gone on inside her, and Travis planned to get to the bottom of it. He'd wait until she was ready to talk.

Melissa had been a constant surprise from the first moment she'd connected with Casey. Travis might have a problem getting past the similarities to Valerie, yet on the drive up the canyon, he'd enjoyed talking to Melissa, and recognized she was her own person.

Now she sat across from him and tucked into her burger and fries. He wondered how long it would be before they resumed conversation. Before long he'd finished his food, noticing she had, too. "If you're through, shall we drive to the church we passed?"

Her head lifted. "I don't usually behave that rudely to people, even if they deserve it."

He got up and threw their sacks in the receptacle. "The man *did* make a false assumption."

"You mean after he'd—"

"That, too." Travis broke in, reading her mind. "You were certainly within your rights."

"Well, things like that happen often enough." Travis didn't doubt it. "He just happened to pick on the wrong man and woman today."

Curious, Travis cocked his head. "Wrong man?"

"Because of my resemblance to your deceased wife. You must have hated the reminder."

Ah. Now he understood part of her reaction, but not all. She jumped up from the bench and started toward the truck. After they were both in the cab, he angled his head toward her. "Actually, it was probably the first time since her death Valerie wasn't on my mind, but I appreciate your sensitivity. Don't give it another thought."

The more he was getting to know Melissa, the more he realized how different she was from his wife. Since they'd be working together for a while, he needed to get over it. He started the truck and they drove down the street to the church. "How long ago did new management take over there?"

"Around the first of July. Why?"

"Have you noticed any other changes? New people in town?"

"You mean like teens who work here for the summer?"

"That and anything else you find unusual."

"Not really. Normally, I drive straight through to the cabin. But I have to admit that man gave me the creeps."

"You actually went pale."

She jerked her head toward him. "I did?" she asked in an anxious tone. That made him even more suspicious.

He nodded. "What would make you do that?"

"I have no idea."

He knew she was lying.

"Have you ever seen him before?"

"Never. He certainly has no social skills."

Travis agreed. "Do me a favor. Until I've had a chance to take a look around Kamas, don't go to Grampy's for a while." He was afraid Melissa could have made an enemy without realizing it.

"I wouldn't dream of it. Something wasn't right about him."

Amen. Travis would get the whole story out of her later.

He parked in the church lot, where the truck could be seen from the main street. He grabbed his backpack, and once the vehicle was locked they headed out of town and began the ascent to her cabin.

She flashed him a smile free of her earlier tension. "We'll keep heading up this road. It's not that far."

"I'm not complaining." She was entertaining, as well as incredibly beautiful. He took some invigorating breaths of fresh air.

Everywhere he looked, the quaking aspen showed some yellow. Signs of fall were creeping into the landscape. He saw a smattering of orange in various areas, but it would be another month before the heavy mountain foliage would turn into full autumn splendor. With the air still warm and a hot sun shining overhead, Travis felt a sudden infusion of well-being.

Maybe it was being out in nature again, but as they gained in elevation and he used leg muscles that had needed a workout, he found himself thinking he was glad to be alive. He couldn't remember feeling like this in a long time.

He glanced at Melissa. She was keeping right up with him.

"How do you stay in such great shape, Melissa?"

"I usually go to the gym after work."

"It shows. I'm probably holding you back."

She responded with a laugh that said his comment was absurd. He liked it that she didn't take herself too seriously. "You can see a few cabins here and there, but the higher we get, the more isolated things are."

"And more magnificent."

She spread her arms and whirled in a circle. "It is!"

Amused by her behavior, he said, "You sound happy."

"I am, and you're the reason. Since midsummer I've been nervous being up here alone, but today I've got you with me. Casey told me you go after bad people. I'm counting on you to find out what's going on up here."

"I'll do my best."

"That's good enough for me. The cabin is around the next curve in the road." She picked up speed, forcing him to move faster. In a few more minutes he saw the medium-size two-story log cabin half hidden by trees. Tons of pine needles and cones covered the ground. A lot of family life had been lived up here. He spotted an old swing and furniture on the front porch. There was a rope swing hanging from a nearby tree.

The branches of one enormous pine brushed against the eaves. Any agile person could climb the tree and get in an upstairs window using the right device. No glass would have to be broken. Two squirrels chattered noisily, then darted across the sun-dappled roof.

"Aren't they cute?" Melissa said in a quiet voice.

Travis smiled. "I recognize them from several of your paintings." They drew closer. "Before we go inside, I want to walk around and check all the windows and doors from the outside." He looked at the ground. "When you or your family come up, do you always park here in front?"

"Yes. There's no other place for cars."

With further inspection he could see what she meant. Foliage grew too close to the cabin for a vehicle to drive around it. "I see track marks."

"Those are mine."

"All of them? You always come in the Jeep?"

"Yes."

He walked over by some trees. "There's another set of tracks here that have dried since the last rainstorm. They don't match your Jeep tracks."

For a few minutes he took pictures and measurements. He felt her interest as he got out some material to powder the most prominent of the tracks, then lifted it with tape. "I'll drop this off at the lab. In time it might tell us something useful."

Melissa stuck with him as he moved around, trying to open the ground-floor windows. They didn't give way. At the back of the house he noticed cigarette butts leading from the back door into the forest. They were embedded in the dirt and pine needles. In some cases they were ground in.

"Does anyone in your family smoke?"

"No."

He pulled out a pair of disposable gloves and a plastic bag from his pack. After hunkering down, he retrieved what he could. There were enough butts to convince him more than one person had been here.

"I've never noticed those before!" Melissa exclaimed. "I have no idea how fresh they are."

"The forensics lab will run a test and let us know the approximate age and make." He zipped the bag and stowed it in his pack before walking to the back door. When he tried the handle, the lock seemed solid, but again, someone with special tools could open it. "Have you been in and out of this door recently?"

"Not since I realized it could be dangerous. But the last time I was here, I did notice dirt on the floor right inside and left it to show the police."

"Good thinking. I'll check for that in a few minutes." He made the full round of the cabin's exterior before asking her to unlock the front door. "Don't touch anything. When we go inside, what I'd like you to do is point out the items you've noticed that have been moved or disturbed over the last month. I might be able to get some fingerprints."

"Oh…okay."

He put on a fresh pair of gloves. For the next hour he followed her around, finding objects and surfaces to dust. The cabin had a straightforward floor plan. Two bedrooms and a bathroom upstairs, and on the ground floor two more bedrooms, a bathroom, a family room with a fireplace and comfortable furnishings, and a kitchen with a pine picnic table and benches. All very cozy.

With painstaking care Travis lifted the prints he'd found and put the tapes into bags. "So far, so good."

They'd finished in the kitchen where he'd gone through shelves and drawers. His gaze swerved to her smoky-blue eyes, watching his every move. "You have a very inviting cabin and it's…fairly secure."

"In other words, a child could get in with the right tools."

He chuckled. "Afraid so. Anyone wanting in here is a professional, and probably had a key made to the back door. Since I didn't find any cigarette butts in front of the cabin, it stands to reason they've chosen the rear entry, so they won't be seen from the road."

"You think there's more than one person?"

"Maybe three or four." She stood close enough to him that Travis felt the shudder that passed through her body. "My hunch is they've come on foot through the forest. Maybe they're the hunters, teenagers or the Sasquatch family you mentioned."

She smiled. "So what do *you* think?"

Now that he'd given himself permission to look at her, he wondered if he was more attracted to her than to other women because of the resemblance to Valerie. If so, did it matter?

Hell, yes. While they'd been moving around the

cabin, his mind should have been on the task, yet he'd imagined sliding his arms around her supple waist from behind and kissing the side of her neck the way he used to do with Valerie. And that was just for starters.

He was as bad as the letch at Grampy's. Worse even, because her father had hired him to find out who was trespassing on their property, and Melissa trusted him.

In frustration he reached for his pack and pulled out the mini cameras. "It's too early to tell. You say you come up on weekends, but so far you've never seen anyone hiding inside. I have to assume they only come after dark, on week nights. While I was gathering the dirt samples, I found some residue I didn't recognize mixed in, and I want to have it analyzed.

"In the meantime I'll install these cameras around and we'll get pictures on tape. One in the kitchen and one at the back door. Another I'll put at the top of the stairs. I'm also going to plant this listening device in the geranium pot on the kitchen table. The recorder will catch any conversation. "

"What if they notice?" She stayed with him and handed him things he needed.

"I doubt they will. You told me they've been coming around since Pioneer Day. Now that it's September and they haven't been caught or scared off, they feel safe and aren't looking for a trap."

He'd come up tomorrow morning and see if anything incriminating had shown up on the surveillance tapes. Maybe he'd get lucky and find some new cigarette butts and traces of anything else the intruders might have left outside. The garbage can out back hadn't revealed anything.

Except for the cigarette butts, Travis had to admit they'd been careful. No incriminating papers or wrappers in the wastebaskets or closets. Nothing had been hidden in the cushions or under the mattresses. Someone had been careful. Too careful for amateurs.

She cast him a questioning glance. "Does that mean you're through for now?"

It sounded as if she didn't want to leave. "I saw all your art supplies in the upstairs bedroom. You probably wanted to do some painting. But I'd prefer we go now, in case someone's scouting around to make sure it's all clear for tonight. I'm sorry."

"Please don't be. I'm grateful to you for agreeing to solve this nightmare. Our whole family is," she added.

Her pleasant disposition was one of the many remarkable things about her. "That's nice to hear. You can do some painting the next time you're able to come with me."

"I'm free anytime."

That news came as a revelation. "What about your work at the clinic? I don't understand."

"Today is the official beginning of my week's vacation. I take a week off every fall around this time of year, and another one in late spring when the wildflowers are in bloom."

Travis grabbed an extra breath. A whole week with her… "I can see why. The scenery up here is breathtaking." Including her.

He started across the family room. "We'll leave

through the front door and head down to town, looking like two hikers out enjoying the sunshine."

On the way back they drank from the water bottles he'd brought. She shared a granola bar with him and he experienced a period of contentment with her that had been foreign to him for too long.

Closer to town, a car drove past them. Melissa knew the couple, but they weren't neighbors who'd noticed anything disturbed or missing at their place. She provided an invaluable service to Travis by pointing out other cabins and the names of the owners. It all helped him put a picture together.

"How many cabins are above yours?"

"None. Ours is the highest one on this ridge. There's nothing else but forest."

Travis planned to go exploring tomorrow when he came back up, but now he realized he wouldn't be alone. "We've accomplished what I wanted, in time to get you home before I pick up Casey."

She darted Travis a glance. "Is he liking school?"

"I think so. He hasn't pulled a 'sore leg' on me yet." But his son had been plaguing him to go to another movie with Melissa. Before school that morning he'd asked if she could come over to see him walk Dexter with his new leash. Travis had muttered something unintelligible and told him they needed to get going or they'd both be late.

"That's a good sign."

"I live in hope for the peace to continue." At least in that department. But Travis feared his son wasn't about to give up on seeing Melissa again.

She laughed as they made their way back to the church. “Lo and behold, your truck is still here.”

“So it is.”

After he’d helped her inside, she pulled out her key ring. “I better give this to you now before I forget. It’s an extra key to the cabin so you can come and go as you please.” She handed it to him, and their fingers brushed. As if he’d just come in contact with a strong electric current, heat snaked up his arm.

It had happened earlier, too, when she’d held the tools he’d needed while he’d installed the cameras. Each time she’d handed him something, the friction of skin against skin had caused him to grow more aware of her.

MELISSA PUT THE KEY RING back in her pocket, but the tingling sensation from his touch was more intense than it had been inside the cabin while she’d been helping him. Something was wrong with her if she could still feel him in every cell of her body.

How embarrassing if he knew it.

Of course he knew it!

Travis Stillman was an extraordinary man who saw and sensed everything. *And she was a nitwit!*

On the way down the canyon, her cell rang. She checked the caller ID. It was Tom. If this had to do with her artwork, Melissa figured she’d better take the call. “Tom?” In the periphery she felt Travis’s eyes on her, disturbing her concentration.

“Hi. I’m sorry to bother you. The receptionist at the clinic said you were off today, so I thought I’d take my chances on reaching you at home.”

"Actually, I'm out of town. Are you calling because you heard from your editor?"

"Yes. I'm pretty excited. He's accepted everything and wants to be absolutely certain you won't be doing any more artwork. I sent him my ideas for my new series and he likes them. If you were going to be the artist on them as well, he would add some information about it in your bio in the first book."

The man didn't give up. "I'm positive, Tom, but I appreciate you telling me."

"Just checking in case you'd changed your mind."

"I'm afraid not, but congratulations. I'm very happy for you."

"You deserve the same congratulations. Your artwork helped sell it."

"Thanks, Tom. I'm sure we'll be talking again soon. Now I have to run."

No sooner had she hung up than Travis's phone rang. After he checked to see who was calling, his dark brows furrowed and he clicked on. A few seconds later he said, "I'll be there in five minutes," and clicked off.

"Problems at work?" she asked.

"No." She heard him draw in a swift breath, saw his face drain of color. "It was the school calling. Casey fell from the monkey bars at afternoon recess and is complaining of pain. They've got him in the office."

Her stomach clenched in reaction, but she didn't want to show her alarm in front of him. "Then I'm sure he's fine or they would have called an ambulance," she said. "Kids get hurt at school all the time."

His hands gripped the steering wheel so tightly his

knuckles were white. “Not one who’s barely mended from a broken leg.”

Travis had always appeared in control in her presence, but this was his precious son who was hurt again, and he’d already lost his wife. “I’ll come with you and check him out. If need be, we’ll drive him to the clinic and take an X-ray. The radiologist will tell you if you need to talk to his surgeon.”

“You don’t mind?” he asked.

“This is what I do all day long at work. It’s nice that Casey already knows me, so he won’t be as frightened.” Not as frightened as his father.

Before long they rolled into the school parking lot. Melissa jumped down the second he’d pulled to a stop, and they hurried inside to reach the main office. Casey saw both of them come into the reception room. His blue eyes widened before he slid off the chair. “Dad… Melissa…”

“Hi, Casey,” she said. “I heard you got hurt so I came with your dad to see how you’re doing.”

His face broke out in a smile. “I fell off the monkey bars and got hurt, but it’s feeling a little better now.”

Travis hunkered down in front of his son and gave him a hug. “I thought you hurt your leg.”

“No, my arm. See?”

Melissa leaned over to inspect the sand burn below his elbow. He moved his arm just fine. No fractures there.

“Ooh,” she said. “I bet that stung. But better your arm than your leg.”

He nodded. “It really hurt.”

"Like I told you before, you're tough, and now you've got a mark of bravery to show for it. I think this calls for ice cream. Don't you, Dad?"

If she didn't know better, she would say Travis was in a state of shock. If he'd stayed on the phone long enough, he might have heard a whole explanation from the receptionist and saved himself all this angst. But it showed his love for his son, and she found that trait in this tough man completely endearing.

Travis got to his feet, his color slowly returning. "Let's go, shall we?"

"Yeah." Casey turned to the receptionist. "Thanks for calling my dad."

"Anytime. Glad to see you're fine now." She winked at Travis and gave Melissa a smile before the three of them walked out to the truck.

"Can we go to Farr's?" He'd climbed in the back and fastened his seat belt. "They'll put M&M's in my ice cream."

"I like candy in my ice cream, too," Melissa said. "Peppermint is my favorite."

"Dad doesn't like pieces in his."

"Is that so." She flicked her gaze to Travis. "Are you a chocolate man?"

"Yup," Casey answered for his father. "How did you know?"

"A wild guess."

Travis shifted gears. "Melissa's pretty smart."

"I know."

She wore a smile on her face the whole time they visited the ice cream shop. Casey showed his sore arm to the salesgirl, who put extra candies on his ice cream. They all thanked her warmly.

On the way home Casey said, "She sure was nice." He glanced at Melissa. "Can you come to our house and see Dexter?"

Melissa knew what his father wanted her to say. "Do you know, I'd like that, but I have other plans I can't break. Thank you so much, though." Deep down she wanted to go to his house more than anything, but she didn't dare take advantage of the situation.

"Can you come tomorrow?"

By now Travis had pulled the truck in front of her town house. "Melissa will be busy."

"Oh."

"We'll make arrangements for that another time."

"Okay." But he sounded downhearted.

She opened the door. "When you get home, be sure and put some disinfectant on your arm."

His head whipped around to his father. "Do we have any?"

"I'm not sure. If we don't, I'll buy some."

"But it will hurt."

Melissa had an idea. "If you'll wait just a moment, I'll get some for you that doesn't sting." Leaving the truck door open, she darted into her condo. Once inside, she grabbed the can off her bathroom shelf and in seconds was back. Casey had opened his door and undone his seat belt, and now he waited for her on the end of the seat.

"Can you stick out your arm? This is a spray. It'll feel

cool." He nervously extended it. She pressed the nozzle and covered the long scrape with the mist.

"Hey! That didn't even hurt!"

"Nope, and now you're going to be good as new. I'm very proud of you."

Without warning, he reached out and gave her a hug. Luckily, she'd been standing right next to the seat. She hugged him back, then stepped away and shut the door. Her gaze flicked to his father. "See ya," she said, not daring to prolong this. She'd taken her cue from Travis.

"I'll be in touch about tomorrow," he assured her.

"See ya soon!" Casey exclaimed.

She chuckled as she walked back inside. Kids. They never gave up when they wanted something. She was crazy about them, but her feelings for Casey were growing deeper. Naturally, the loss of his mother had a lot to with her desire to comfort him, but that wasn't the only reason.

He was an endearing child in his own right. Fun to talk to. Bright, adorable. A son his father loved with a fierceness she'd noticed from the start. Casey was the reason Travis got up in the morning. She could see why, and she envied him.

After checking her mailbox, she let herself inside the condo without looking back. Because of their hike in the heat, she decided a shower was in order.

Later, when she'd dressed, she felt restless. For once she didn't turn to her painting. Vaguely disturbed without knowing why, she phoned her brother and asked if he'd come over to her place. He told her it would have to be later that night, because he was up at the cabin right then having a look around.

She was surprised and relieved. John was the one person she felt she could talk to about Travis. Her brother might be able to give her insight into how to handle the fact that Travis resented her looking like his deceased wife.

Without a good talk, she feared that when she eventually went to bed, she would lie awake half the night waiting for tomorrow to come. It had been years since she'd found herself wanting to be with a man again. But he wasn't just any man. Since the movie with Casey, she'd thought of his father as her own personal Texas Ranger.

Chapter Five

Travis drove away from the town house and headed downtown. He needed to run by the forensics lab to drop off the soil samples, fingerprint tapes and cast he'd taken.

En route he remembered what he'd wanted to ask Melissa before he'd received that phone call from the school, and everything else had gone out of his mind. He needed a list of any people who'd been in their cabin this year besides family.

Without wasting any time, he phoned her. When she didn't answer, he realized she could be anywhere, doing anything. He left a message for her to call him back.

"Dad? Where are we going?"

"To Lacey and Chaz's condo. They've invited us for dinner."

"Is Zack going to be there?"

"I think so."

"I wish I'd brought Captain America. Can we go home first and get it?"

"Afraid not. We're late as it is."

"But what about Dexter?"

"He'll live till we get back."

When they arrived a few minutes later, everyone noticed that Casey had come without his crutches, and high-fived him.

"Yup," he responded. "Melissa told me my leg was all better and I didn't need them anymore."

"Who's Melissa?" Mitch asked.

"She's my or—" He looked at Travis for help. Everyone in the room cracked up.

"Orthopedic specialist," Travis managed to say without laughing.

"She's awesome and drives a red-and-black Jeep. She used to have a bulldog named Spike, but he's dead now. She made my sore arm all better, too." He extended his scraped elbow for everyone to have a good look.

"Ew!" Zack blurted.

"Does it hurt?" Abby was very worried. Since her bee sting, she was overly solicitous.

"Nope. She put this spray on it."

"She *does* sound awesome," Mitch murmured.

"She is! She gave me a leash for Dexter, and tickets for *Spider-Man*. Dad and I went to the movie with her. Oh, and she bought cupcakes for my whole room. It wasn't really my birthday, but she said it was okay because everyone has a birthday party at school."

Heidi smiled. "That's pretty fantastic."

"Was it a good movie?" Lacey asked him, but her eyes were on Travis.

"Dad thought it was boring, but Melissa and I loved it!"

In the midst of everything Travis's phone rang. He saw the caller ID and said, "Excuse me for a minute."

He left the living room and walked down the hall where he could have some privacy.

"Melissa? Thanks for calling me back."

"Sorry it took me so long. I went to my folks' place for dinner. When I left, I couldn't find my phone. After searching my car, I went back to their house and found it on the couch. It must have slipped right out of my purse."

Her breathless explanation pleased him even more than the knowledge that she hadn't been out with some guy. Travis wasn't blind. She attracted every man in sight. Everywhere they'd been together, he'd seen men's eyes light up the minute they caught sight of her. The traffic in Kamas had slowed several times because some guy was staring at her from his car as they'd walked along the main street.

"No problem. Earlier today I meant to ask you if you would compile a list of people who've been in your cabin this year. I'm talking friends, neighbors, work-men—anyone. Your siblings might be able to help with names, and your parents, too, of course. I'm trying to explore every possibility."

"I'll do it before I go to bed. One more thing, Travis. You'll probably think I'm crazy, but maybe someone is looking for gold and using our cabin to hide at night."

"Gold?"

"I've been thinking about something my grandfa-ther told me when I was young. We were out hiking and he pointed out an old mine that wasn't active any-more. He said that most people thought the gold rush started in California. But he said gold was mined in the western mountains in Utah well before the first white settlers arrived.

"Apparently, Indians first worked the mines here, ones enslaved by the Spanish explorers, who came in the 1600s. In fact, what many originally thought were Indian hieroglyphics and pictographs are actually markers along the Spanish Trail. It led from Mexico to the Uinta Mountains and beyond."

Travis blinked. "I had no idea."

"If he hadn't told me, I wouldn't have known it, either. He said the trail was the main link between Mexico and Spanish outposts here. In the 1800s, pack trains of Mexicans were seen heading out of the Uintas laden with gold.

"Grandpa said all kinds of Spanish cannons and swords were found in our 'killer mountains,' as they called them. One cannon was found in Kamas. They had gold mines that few of the later European arrivals knew about. The ruins of rock homes, forts, tree carvings and various artifacts were clues that pointed the way to the gold ore. Silver, too.

"The Indians knew where the mines were because they'd been forced to work in them by the Spanish. After years of oppression they revolted, killing most of their captors, and returned the gold to the earth, leaving it in the mines. Grandpa told me that from time to time, men have come to Kamas in search of gold, and have checked out that mine right behind our cabin. I know it's a stretch, but since this has been going on most of the summer, it has caused me to wonder."

It *was* a stretch, but he wouldn't dismiss it out of

hand. "Thanks for the Utah history lesson, Melissa. Anything's possible. I'll keep it in mind while I look around."

"Uh-oh. I've got another call coming in, and better hang up. Good night, Travis."

There was a click. He'd wanted to keep on talking. Since that wasn't possible, he turned off his cell phone and returned to the living room. The guys eyed him speculatively, but it was Chaz who asked, "Talking to your latest client?" His friend knew about Melissa's resemblance to Valerie and the shock Travis had received because of it.

Travis nodded. And shouldn't have been surprised when Casey picked up on it immediately. Running over to him, he blurted, "Was it Melissa?" With that question, the guys' wives were looking at him, too.

"As a matter of fact, it was," he admitted.

"I love her! Didn't she want to talk to me?"

Out of the mouths of babes, honest and unabridged. "She had only a minute to answer a question for me," Travis replied.

"Oh."

He didn't know how much of Casey's exclamation had to do with his memory of Valerie, but one thing was certain. His son was hooked on Melissa, and everyone in the room knew it.

"It's time to get you home, bud. Tell Lacey and Chaz thank-you, and thank Heidi and Mitch for the doughnuts."

Casey did so, adding, "It was really yummy. Bye, Zack. Bye, Abby."

Mitch walked over to Travis with a gleam in his eye. "I've yet to hear about all this. Expect a call from me if we don't see each other in the office tomorrow morning."

Travis's friend would be relentless in wanting to find out the details.

Once they arrived home, Casey played with Dexter for a few minutes and took him for a walk on his leash. Finally, it was time for bed. "Come on, bud. Under the covers," Travis said.

As soon as Casey crawled in, the dog jumped up and lay at his feet. Travis kissed his son on the forehead. "Sleep tight. I'll see you in the morning."

"Are you going to take me to the clinic tomorrow to visit Melissa?"

"No. You're fine now."

"But you brought her to school to see me."

"That was different."

"How come?"

He had hoped to avoid the subject, but Casey wouldn't let it go. Since Travis didn't know how long this case for Melissa's family might go on, he realized he needed to tell his son a few facts.

With a resigned sigh, he sank onto the side of his bed. "The reason she was with me today was because I've been hired by her father to do some investigative work. I understand you told Melissa I'm a P.I."

"Yup. At the movie."

"Well, she told her dad. He asked me to look around their mountain cabin up in Kamas and find out who's been living in it without their permission."

Casey gasped. "You mean someone has been sneaking inside?"

"It looks like it. I took Melissa with me today so she could show me where it is and let me in."

"Is it far away?" His son's voice had a mournful note.

"No. Only forty-five minutes. It's up by Park City. Do you remember we went up there skiing?"

"Yes." But Casey looked unhappy.

"Melissa and I were on the way down the canyon when someone from your school called me."

"Is her cabin big?"

"Sort of. It has an upstairs and is made of logs because it's old."

"Cool. Can I see it sometime with you and Melissa?"

"I think it's a possibility." After fighting his conflicted feelings for Melissa from day one, Travis was surprised he'd conceded that much to Casey. Something was happening to him. Today, with Melissa, he'd had moments he wished could have gone on.

"Are you going to go up with her tomorrow?"

"Probably." She wanted to paint. Travis couldn't very well tell her she couldn't come, but the scenario was starting to get complicated in ways he didn't feel like examining.

"Why can't I go with you?"

"You know why. You have school."

"No, I don't. Tomorrow is teachers' work day."

Travis blinked. He'd forgotten about that.

"I don't want to go to Aunt Pat's. I want to be with you. What if you don't come back?"

Travis knew that deep-seated fear was always lurking beneath the surface. He pulled his son into his arms. "Tell you what. I'll phone her. Maybe we can all go up for part of the day. How does that sound?"

"Hooray!" In an instant, his boy became a happy child again. They high-fived. "I can't wait till tomorrow. Night, Daddy."

Travis discovered he couldn't wait, either, and reached for his phone to call Melissa for a second time. Hopefully, whatever she was doing, she'd pick up.

She answered on the third ring.

He liked her well-modulated voice. "Hi. I know it's getting late, but there's one more thing I wanted to talk to you about before you're in bed. Are you free to talk?"

There was a pause, then she said, "Is there a new development in the case?"

He frowned when she answered his question with a question. Something was definitely off. She wasn't the same warm woman from earlier, and she didn't mention Casey in the conversation, which wasn't like her. "I can tell you're not alone."

"My brother's here, helping me with that list. He just got down from the cabin."

Travis's blood turned cold. "Did he go alone?"

"Yes." She paused for a second. "Are you saying it wasn't a good idea? I thought it would be okay for him. He wanted to look around."

"After today I'm concerned, because I suspect that more than one person has been using your place to sleep. I don't like the implications, and feel it won't be safe for you or anyone in your family to go up there unless I'm with you."

He heard her quiet gasp. "You're not telling me everything you know, are you?"

"I'm operating on instinct right now, Melissa." He grimaced. "It's too soon to give you facts. What's important is that you and your family will come to no harm if you stay strictly away. If it's necessary for one of you to go up, and I can't be there, then I'll send some of my backup crew to protect you. Be sure you tell your brother how serious this is. I'm sorry it has to be this way."

"So am I. But if you say it's dangerous, I believe you. John's totally impressed with all your surveillance gadgets. He's fascinated by the work you do and can't wait to meet you."

"I look forward to meeting him. In the meantime, all is not lost. Casey's school is taking a teacher work day tomorrow, so he'll be free. We'll pick you up around ten and drive to the cabin. While I'm busy checking around the area, you can paint to your heart's content, as long as you and Casey stay within fifty feet of the cabin. Two of my crew will already be around to keep everyone safe."

"You mean it?" The excitement was back in her voice—the sound that had been missing. The one he'd wanted to hear. "You don't know how I long to take advantage of this weather. I love the mountains this time of year."

"I'm aware you took a week off from work to paint, Melissa. Even though your father hired me, and I need to be up there to do the job he's paying me to do, there's nothing to prevent you from being with me. Under the circumstances it will be best if we take your Jeep, so anyone keeping a lookout will know you're in residence and won't come around while we're there."

"No problem. Casey told me he wanted to ride in it."

"Now he's going to get his chance. On the way up the canyon we'll pick up pizza to take with us. There's a place in the Bell Canyon Plaza."

"I know the one."

"Since Casey learned you have a cabin, he's dying to see it. Is it all right if we bring Dexter?"

"Oh, yes!" Clearly, she adored animals. "He'll love it up there. I want to draw him. Terriers are so darling."

Melissa had Travis smiling. "Then it's settled. See you tomorrow." He hung up, excited to know he'd be with her soon. He was also pleased at the idea of taking their Scottie along. Besides being fun for Casey, Dexter made an excellent watchdog.

Too wired to go to bed yet, Travis went to his study. He needed to write up notes on the case and email them to Roman, to keep him abreast of his progress. Travis had no idea what he'd find up there tomorrow, but he planned to hike around and look for signs of people camping in an undesignated area.

Melissa's suggestion that people might be up there trying to find a lost gold mine might not be so far-fetched. She was a regular treasure trove of information. It was one more facet of her personality that drew him.

Next, he phoned Jose and asked him to drive up to Grampy's in the morning. Travis wanted photos of the employees who showed up for work. He gave Jose a description of the man who'd leered at Melissa.

"If he drives a car to work, I want you to get his license plate number. But whether in a car or on foot, follow him after he gets off work. I'd like to know what he does in his spare time. Find out if he has friends in the area. See if he lives alone or with someone."

The man might not have anything to do with the case, but Travis was curious about him and intended to check him out. Oftentimes evidence turned up that was helpful for an entirely different case the police were investigating.

"I'd also like you to find out who's the new owner of Grampy's. Melissa said the place changed hands in July."

"Okay. Anything else?"

"Will you check the water and electricity bills for their cabin? Let's monitor the usage and compare this last month's activity to the bills for last year. I'm looking for any disparities or an unexpected spike."

"I'll get on it first thing tomorrow."

After they got off the phone he contacted Adam and asked him to set up surveillance while he was up there with his son and Melissa tomorrow.

Finally, Travis had done everything he could for the moment, and left the study. A shower sounded good. He headed for the bathroom, full of anticipation for tomorrow.

He could see why Melissa loved the cabin so much. Salt Lake was unique. Within a half hour you could be in a remote mountain wilderness, thousands of feet above the valley floor. He'd hated leaving the Davis Mountains in Texas, which he loved, but today's outing with Melissa, in a more primitive setting, where the peaks knifed the rarified air, called to the deepest part of him.

And when they'd been up in the rustic bedroom she'd turned into a studio, their eyes had met across the room. For a moment he'd imagined the cabin being theirs. Everything appealed to him, from the artwork on the walls to the colorful quilt her grandmother had made years earlier. Mellow with age and life having been lived, the cabin's interior had a warmth he could feel. Casey would love it. Especially the rope swing.

He saw black when he thought of the intruders who'd ruined Melissa's pleasure. Travis now had another enemy he was tracking besides Valerie's killer. This new project had become personal.

THE MINUTE MELISSA EMERGED from her town house on Tuesday morning, Casey came running, with an adorable black Scottish terrier at his heels.

"Hi, Casey!" she called out, and was rewarded with a hearty hug around the waist. "This must be Dexter. Hiya, fella." She hunkered down to rub his head and ears.

After lots of licks from his pink tongue, she got up and unlocked the Jeep. Travis picked up the dog and put him in the backseat with Casey.

"Quite a change from the first time we showed up at the clinic," he whispered as he came around to shut her door.

Their eyes met. "But he *did* look so cute using his crutches," she whispered back.

"Are you talking about me?"

She turned to peer at the dark-haired boy, strapped in with the dog lying next to him.

"Yes. We're glad your leg is all better. Let me see your arm." He showed it to her. "You're going to have a scab, but it's healing just fine."

"Since you sprayed me, it doesn't hurt anymore."

His father grinned at Melissa, turning her limbs to water.

She'd confided in John about Travis's deceased wife and her own resemblance to her. John didn't have specific answers to that problem, but had warned Melissa to go slowly. In time, things would change with Travis one way or the other. Her brother advised her to just play it cool while the investigation was going on.

Hah. So much for trying to distance herself from Travis. This talk with John had come too late. She was already in up to her hairline where the Texas Ranger was concerned. Any more looks like he'd just given her and she'd drown.

Melissa started the engine and they took off. "I'm glad you're so much better," she said to Casey. "I was thinking maybe you'd like to do some painting with me. Around the side of the cabin is a big rock where a family of woodchucks play. They have five burrows I've counted. Sometimes they stand still on their hind legs, listening for intruders, and then they whistle to warn the others."

Casey laughed. "They whistle?"

"Yes. Some people call them pig-whistlers. My brother calls them pot guts, because they have such big tummies." Both father and son laughed this time. "I think they're fun to draw," Melissa added.

"I wanna see them."

"You will, but we'll have to sit quietly for a while until they come out."

"I can be quiet, huh, Dad?"

"When you're asleep," his father teased. "But I can't vouch for Dexter."

"I'll keep him in the cabin. Will that be okay, Melissa?"

"Of course." She pulled up to the pizza place in the plaza. "I've got some old doggie toys of Spike's I couldn't bring myself to throw away." Travis sent her a compassionate glance. "Dexter can play with those while we're out watching for the woodchucks. Then we'll let him come outside so he can have fun."

Casey beamed while Travis went inside to pick up their lunch. After he came back, the smell of pizza filled the car while she drove them up the canyon. By the time they reached the cabin, everyone was starving, so they decided to eat before doing anything else.

When Travis announced he was off to do some hiking, Casey seemed fine with it. So was Melissa, because she knew some of Travis's men were outside, guarding them. But though she pretended nothing affected her, underneath, she worried about him. He'd said it was too dangerous for her to be up here without him and his crew, but who would protect Travis?

After asking herself that question, she realized how important he'd become to her. So important he was all she thought about. She'd had a life before he came into it, but she couldn't remember what it was like.

Melissa knew he enjoyed her company, but he'd done nothing overt to act on any feelings he might have for her. As she'd told John, if Travis still saw his wife when he was with her, you wouldn't know it. Her brother had suggested it was possible Travis was holding back because he was doing a job for her family, and didn't mix his private life with his professional one.

Melissa didn't have answers yet, but something needed to change soon. She couldn't bear to be with him like this, not knowing what was going on inside him. Maybe *nothing* was going on, and she was fantasizing at her own peril. That thought just about killed her.

Travis didn't return until it was getting dark and time to go home. She'd fixed peanut butter sandwiches. Luckily, it was food Casey liked. When his dad walked in, Casey asked if they could sleep over, but his father nixed that idea so fast it surprised even Melissa. Since his return she'd sensed his preoccupation.

In the car on the way down, Casey made up for his father's silence by telling him about the squirrels that had come out to play instead of the pig-whistlers. While he regaled Travis with their activities, Dexter chewed on one of the toys he'd commandeered.

They looked like a happy family coming home from a trip to the mountains, but the picture was false. Melissa's stomach was in knots by the time she drove them back to her town house.

They all got out of the Jeep, and Casey said, "I wish I didn't have school tomorrow."

"But you do," Travis said, without his usual warmth.

Melissa bit her lip. "Good night, Casey. Thanks for bringing Dexter."

"He loved it. We had fun!"

"So did I."

"See ya!"

"Good night, Melissa." Travis's low voice worked its way beneath her skin, igniting every nerve ending. She felt as if he'd brought her out of a deep sleep. Now she didn't know where to go with all these awakened feelings.

Travis bundled his son and dog into his truck before she could say good-night back. When she reached the door of her condo, he waved to her before she let herself inside.

Too uptight to relax, she got busy doing laundry, then talked with her mom for a few minutes before taking a shower. When Melissa was finally ready for bed, she still couldn't settle down.

After wrapping a robe around herself, she went into the living room to watch the ten o'clock news, hoping it would help her get sleepy. She'd just pressed the remote when her cell phone rang. Her heart thudded as she reached for it. When she saw who was calling, she could hardly breathe.

"Travis."

"Sorry for calling you this late."

"It's all right." *More than all right.* "I'm still up."

"I got a call from work while I was out hiking earlier. Something's come up that requires me to be in the office tomorrow. But the guys are keeping you under constant surveillance, so you can go up whenever you want."

"That's great. Thank you." Except the idea of being at the cabin without him suddenly didn't seem as appealing. Their two sojourns up there had spoiled her. It wasn't just a matter of him making her feel safe. She'd come to enjoy his company. Really enjoy it. "Do you think you'll be able to get away from the office at some point?" *You're pushing it, Melissa.*

"I'm counting on it. After school I'll pick up Casey and bring him to the cabin with Dexter." The news gave her heart a workout. "I'm afraid my son worries about me leaving him when I have business away from Salt Lake. He's still afraid that I might never come back."

"That doesn't surprise me at all." Her voice caught. Losing Travis was too tragic to contemplate. Casey needed him terribly. "Tell you what. If you're going to do that, I'll fix dinner up there," she said without hesitation. "I promise I can do better than peanut butter sandwiches." She'd been afraid she might not be seeing him tomorrow, and now was ecstatic. "What else does Casey like besides pizza?"

"Candy and doughnuts."

MELISSA'S LAUGHTER WAS like sunshine.

"Hot dogs are a safe bet," Travis told her. "He's not a big eater."

"And what about his dad? Would he like steak fajitas?"

Travis lounged against the wall, enjoying their conversation more than a little. "I've heard he's rather partial to them."

"Then I'll inform the cook. If I know her, she'll make a surprise dessert guaranteed to satisfy your boy's sweet tooth."

"Tell the cook he gets that particular tooth from me."

She chuckled quietly. "Thanks for the tip. Give me a ring when you reach the church parking lot in Kamas and I'll drive down to get you."

"We'll be watching for you. Good night, Melissa."

"Good night."

No sooner had Travis turned off his bedroom light to go to sleep than his cell phone rang. It was quarter to eleven. His excitement that it might be Melissa with something else she wanted to tell him subsided when he reached for it and saw the caller ID. Jose. He must have something important or he would have waited till morning to phone.

"Jose? What's up?"

"I'm still in Kamas. The guy got off work at eight. I followed him to a cabin in the forest about a mile west of town. It was shuttered and looked locked up for the season. There was a garage next to it, and he went inside there."

"Give me the coordinates and I'll check to find out the name of the owner." It was possible Melissa would know. After jotting down the information, Travis said, "Then what happened?"

"After a while he and another guy came out. It was too dark for details, but the second guy was smaller. More wiry. They locked the garage door and took off into the forest with a flashlight. I figured I had time to look around, and undid the lock. Inside was a 2005 Fleetwood Tioga 25' Class C RV camper, but it was locked."

"Something's definitely going on."

"Agreed. It had a Utah plate and up-to-date registration. I walked back to my truck before phoning it in. They'll call me when they know anything. What do you want me to do next?"

"Ask Lon to coordinate with you and Adam. I want to know where that camper goes when it leaves the garage."

"Will do."

"Thanks, Jose."

Travis hung up, gratified that his suspicions hadn't proved wrong, even if the situation might not have anything to do with the Roberts case. He stretched out in bed, reliving the day with Melissa. So far he'd seen her only with her hair done in different styles away from her face. He wondered what that light ash-brown hair would look like loose and flowing. How it would feel to bury his face in it…

When Casey woke him up the next morning, the last thing Travis remembered thinking was that Melissa had been on his mind, not Valerie. That was a first.

Now that he thought about it, he recalled that Chaz had experienced something similar. His friend had lost his first wife to cancer before he'd done his stint with the Navy SEALs. Not until last spring had he become emotionally involved with another woman. One night he'd confided to Travis that he knew Lacey was the one when he'd found himself dreaming about her, instead of his deceased wife. It had happened the first night he'd met Lacey, during his investigation of her stalking case.

Travis wasn't thinking Melissa was "the one," far from it. He wasn't in the market for another wife. But he had to admit no other woman since Valerie had interested him to this extent. The problem was, he didn't trust this attraction. Was it because, deep down, he wanted a woman who reminded him of Valerie? Maybe. How sick was that?

Casey followed him out of the bathroom, where Travis had just finished shaving. "Can Melissa come to dinner at our house tonight?"

Travis wasn't surprised that that was the first question to pop out of his son's mouth. He could hardly avoid this situation while he was working her case. Once he'd pulled on jeans and another T-shirt, he turned to his son. "Guess what? I'm going to pick you up after school and we're driving to the cabin again. Melissa's fixing dinner for us."

"Hooray!" Casey ran to the kitchen, whooping the whole way. Travis followed, to fix them fruit and cereal. Once they'd fed Dexter, they left for school in the truck.

After dropping off Casey with a hug, Travis stopped for gas, then headed to the office. Jose and Roman were waiting for him with coffee and doughnuts. The boss had a big smile on his face. "Come on in."

Bemused, Travis reached for his coffee and sat down, eyeing both of them. "What's going on?"

"Congratulations are in order."

Chapter Six

"What are you talking about?"

Roman smiled. "I'll let Jose tell you."

Travis eyed the other man. "Is this about that camper?"

His colleague nodded. "An hour after I phoned in the license plate number, I got a call. That Utah plate was stolen off a new blue Jetta on June 5 of this year. So they checked to see if the camper was stolen."

"Wait till you hear this next part," Roman interjected.

Travis was all ears.

"The police in Cochise County, Arizona, have been looking for the killer of an elderly couple, a crime that happened on June 3 of this year. They were found in their home in Douglas, with their camper stolen. I checked the VIN number, and it's their camper, all right. As you know, Douglas is in that border territory between the U.S. and Mexico."

Travis's heart dropped any time he heard that another innocent person had been murdered. It hit too close to home. But a part of him was elated that his hunch had been on target.

"What about the man you followed?"

"Adam said the guy came back to the garage about an hour later and got in the camper. He was in there all night, and still is. He thinks the guy's living there. The other man disappeared into the woods and never came back."

Travis's mind was reeling with possibilities. "This could be connected to what's going on at the Roberts cabin. Considering the close proximity between the camper and their place, that other man could be making himself at home there. But it's still early days."

"I agree," Roman said.

Travis looked at his boss. "Let's sit on what we know for now, and just keep them under surveillance. I'll be talking to forensics in a few minutes, to see what they've come up with so far. Later on I'll be going up to the cabin again, to check the tapes and the listening device.

"Before we make official inquiries, I'll ask Melissa if she knows who owns that vacant cabin and garage. I meant to ask her earlier, but got distracted. If the intruders were there last night, then we'll know a lot more than we do now, and can decide how to proceed. Jose? Have we found out who bought Grampy's yet?"

"Lon's still working on it. Hopefully he'll get back to us sometime today."

Roman leaned forward. "You're on to something big, Travis. I feel it in my bones." His solemn expression changed to a gleeful one. "I barely put you on the case and already you've turned up a couple of possible killers."

Travis eyed Jose. "Thanks to a great backup team."

"Agreed," Roman said. "How did you know about the hidden camper?"

"On Monday the guy with the buzz cut waited on Melissa and me at Grampy's, this burger shop in Kamas. He leered at her in a way that alarmed her. I sensed something about him wasn't right, so I asked Jose to check him out."

Their boss grinned. "And just like that you've helped solve cases that have stumped lawmen in two states. I'll get the police chief on the phone. He'll contact the cops in Douglas, but I'll make it clear you're in the middle of a sting and don't want anything to leak until you find out what's going on at the cabin."

"Appreciate that, Roman."

"You were born with an instinct for this business, comrade. Talk to you later."

Travis nodded and stood up. "Come to my office, Jose. Let's listen to what Forensics has to say."

A few minutes later Travis had Rudy, in Forensics, on the line. He was the best in the business. "What have you got for us?" Travis turned on the speakerphone so Jose could hear.

"That tire print was pretty good. I saw two cuts that could have been made by rocks or glass. They're year-old Goodyear tires.

"As for the fingerprints, you got some decent ones off that pine table you noted on the tape. I've sent them on to headquarters, and they'll run them through the database. The other items had some interesting elements."

"Like what?" Travis hadn't realized he was holding his breath.

"For example, the soil sample contained traces of mashed foliage typical of that area of forest. It also contained marijuana."

"Marijuana?" Travis's eyebrows lifted as he stared at Jose in amazement.

"No doubt it was clinging to the soles of someone's shoes. The particular type is called Early Misty. It's a short, bushy plant that flowers in eight weeks. The sample was pretty fresh. So were the cigarette butts you brought in last evening. They matched the others that were days old, and in some instances, a couple of months old."

"Were you able to identify the brand?"

"Yes. That's interesting, too. The tobacco is a type grown in Japan and shipped to Europe, where it's made into cigarettes with the brand name Monte Carlo. These are the long, slim kind you find in cellophane bundles."

"I've heard of them. Thanks, Rudy. Couldn't do this without you." Travis clicked off. "Jose? What do you know about Monte Carlo cigarettes?"

"They're the strong-flavored variety and the cheapest on the world market. You can buy them online in the U.S., but they're distributed and sold in Switzerland, Germany, Monaco, the Emirates and Colombia."

"We're narrowing it down. These boys have to be illegals sent by some Colombian drug cartel to work here."

Jose nodded. "The traffickers come primarily from the Valle del Cauca region or from the Caribbean north coast. The latter operate more independently than the Cali mafia, but are very powerful. By working with counterparts in Mexico and the U.S., they're responsible for most of the world's cocaine production and wholesale distribution."

Travis leaned back in his chair. "I wasn't in Utah three years ago, but I remember hearing Roman talk about a crop of marijuana plants with a street value of $60 million found growing on a mountain farther south in this state."

"You're talking Boulder Mountain in Wayne County. It was headed by a Mexican cartel."

"Could be the Colombians have done the same thing around here in the back country. The man you saw come out of the garage could be one of that group. Then again, maybe there's no connection."

"Maybe not," Jose murmured, "but I'm planning to get a look at the left front tire on that camper, in case it made a trip to the cabin. That will give us the link you're trying to find."

"Good. While you do that, I'll be busy hiking in the mountains, looking for marijuana plants."

As Jose got up to leave, Travis called him back. "I have another question for you. While Melissa and I were getting our hamburgers, I noticed the guy with the buzz had a tattoo on the back of his neck." Travis's eyes narrowed. "Does a solid silver star with eight points mean anything to you?"

Jose looked astonished, then shook his head in disbelief.

Travis half laughed. "What?"

"You just solved another piece of the puzzle. That star is in the middle of the Barranquilla flag, the northern port city of Colombia. It was carried by Simon Bolivar, signifying the eight provinces of the confederacy."

Again Travis's mind was off and running. "The bunch of them could have come up through the Caribbean to Mexico. When they got across the Arizona border, they killed that couple for the camper and drove straight here."

"It's more than a possibility."

"We don't know how many illegals are involved in this operation, but it's been well orchestrated up to now," Travis theorized. "Otherwise, they wouldn't have found a garage to keep the stolen vehicle hidden two days after that couple was killed. Roman needs to hear about this new development."

"While you talk to him, I'll drive back up to Kamas and try to get a look at those camper tires. When I find something out, I'll phone you. Oh, one more thing. I checked the bills with the water and electric company for this year and last. There was no abnormal usage of either utility."

"These men are being careful. It's more evidence that this operation has been in the planning for a long time."

"Watch your back, Travis."

"Ditto."

After Jose left, Travis went back to their boss's office and gave him the latest update. The news about the marijuana blew Roman away. They talked strategy before Travis went back to his office and called his resource at the database down at police headquarters. He wanted to know if any of those fingerprints were a match for wanted felons operating illegally in the country. The Feds would have a field day.

Later, Mitch dropped into his office, and they decided to go to lunch. Travis told him about Melissa, and they talked shop. Before long it was time to pick up Casey. His son worried when Travis didn't get to school right on time, but his anxiety level hadn't been as high since he'd met Melissa.

Casey was crazy about her. There were moments when he seemed to be as happy around her as he'd been when his mom was alive. And he wasn't the only one….

Time had something to do with the healing process, but Travis had to admit Melissa was playing a big part. Otherwise he wouldn't find himself this eager to be with her again. For several days he'd been wondering what she would taste like. Before much more time went on, he would have to find out—or go mad with wanting.

MELISSA REVELED IN BEING able to paint for a whole day without fear. At three o'clock she put her things away and started dinner. Around four she drove down to the church parking lot to wait for Travis and Casey. Her heart thudded when she heard the phone ring. She clicked on and said hello.

"Melissa?"

"Casey, hi! Where are you?"

"Dad says we're just coming into Kamas."

"Well, I'm right here watching for you."

"Okay. Don't go away."

She laughed. "I promise I won't."

A few minutes later they pulled in alongside her, and

everyone, including Dexter, got into her Jeep. The hug Casey gave her was so natural, she was thrilled to the core. It was sheer delight to hear about his school day. She caught Travis's warm glance. No ice, no shadows today. Her spirits soared.

Once they reached the cabin, Travis disappeared outside, while Casey ran around examining everything. After he'd teased Dexter with more of Spike's toys, he became Melissa's shadow.

She set up an easel for him and they painted out on the front porch. He chatted about some of the kids in his class at school. Robbie had asthma and had to carry around a spray. Cindy's daddy had to move to California because her parents got a divorce. Melissa loved listening to it all, but when she heard Casey's tummy growl, so loudly they both laughed and Dexter barked, she knew it was time for dinner.

Travis came in as she was putting supper on the table. To Melissa it felt like they were a real family. She found it harder and harder not to fantasize about what was going on. While he washed his hands at the kitchen sink, her gaze took in his rock-hard physique. The play of muscle across his back and shoulders kept her attention riveted.

When he suddenly turned toward the table, he caught her staring at him, and she felt herself blush to her eyebrows. Casey saved the moment. "Come on, Dad. We're hungry."

"So am I."

After they'd tucked into their food, Travis glanced at her. "I did some hiking and made the rounds of the cabins in the area you identified for me. There was one with a detached garage near the main road, about a mile from town, but it was boarded up. Do you have any idea who it belongs to?"

"You must mean the Gledhills. They're a retired couple from Reno, Nevada. They were willed that cabin by her father, but only come up here every other year. On the off year they like to boat on Lake Tahoe."

"That explains it," Travis murmured. "This afternoon I was able to talk to most of the people in the other cabins. When I showed them my ID, they were very receptive and anxious to talk to me. However, their complaints had more to do with thefts of fishing gear and items of furniture taken mostly over the winter months.

"I found it interesting that so far none of them have complained of intruders living there when the owners aren't about. Yet that seems to be the particular problem of *your* cabin. My hunch is because it's the highest one on this side of the ridge, out of sight."

"I'm sure that's true. The very thing I love about this location is what makes it a natural target for evi—for bad people," she corrected. Casey picked up on everything.

His father's eyes went an intense dark blue. "They won't be doing it much longer. That's a promise." The almost primitive note in his voice convinced her he knew more than he'd told her. The Texas Ranger was on the hunt. Melissa's hand trembled as she reached for her water glass.

"If you two will excuse me," Travis said next, "I have some work to do upstairs."

"Go ahead, Dad. We'll make dessert."

Travis exchanged an amused glance with Melissa, then left the table.

"Okay, Casey, let's get busy." She brought a dish from the counter. "These chocolate chips are melted. I'll let you ice the brownies."

She scooped the chocolate onto the cold peppermint butter cream frosting, then handed him the spoon. "While the chocolate is hot, you spread it around lightly and quickly till the brownies are all covered. Try not to mix the two together too much, so it will stay layered."

"Like this?" He made big fast swirls.

"That's perfect."

He worked with concentration, biting his lower lip. "I've finished! Now can I lick the spoon and the pot?"

Melissa chuckled before setting the brownies aside. While he went to town on the leftover chocolate, she cut a big brownie for Travis and put it on a plate. With a napkin in hand, she walked upstairs and found him in the hall, putting more film in the video camera. Melissa couldn't help watching him.

His jeans molded to his long, powerful legs. Her gaze traveled to a well-defined chest covered in a coffee-colored polo. In the dim light coming from downstairs, half of his chiseled features and rich chestnut hair were hidden in shadow. No superlative would do him justice. She only knew that when she looked at him, her senses came alive.

"Do you need my help?" she asked.

"I'm all through here, thanks." He put the camera back in place at the top of the stairs.

She moved closer. "Here's a treat for your efforts."

When Travis turned to her, his eyes swept over her before he took the brownie and bit into it. After swallowing, he said, "You have to be kidding."

"What do you mean?"

"I thought you told me you needed a cook. This brownie is too good to be true." He ate the rest in one swallow. "You could make your living selling these. Move over, Bauer Doughnuts. Dalton Brownies is the new company in town."

"Travis..." Warmth spread through her like the chocolate Casey was licking in the kitchen.

"It's true. The fajitas were wonderful, too. I don't think there's anything you can't do. I thought the same that first morning in your office. Like magic, you got Casey to give up his crutches long enough to walk around the room with you. You're like the Pied Piper of Hamelin."

Outwardly, Melissa smiled, but inside she was sad because there was one thing she couldn't do. She couldn't change her appearance. The reminder of his wife would always be there whenever he looked at her. "Thanks for the compliment, but I'll let you in on a secret. You don't realize it yet, but you've seen my whole repertoire."

"I don't think so." He smiled. "Every time we're together you do something that surprises me and delights my son."

"*He* delights *me*. I believe he'd make a great Texas Ranger. He notices everything. I know about every kid in his class—whose parents are getting divorced, whose grandma has cancer, whose daddy bashed in his mother's car when he drove into the garage, who keeps snakes in their basement."

Travis's shoulders shook with laughter.

"He reminds me of someone else I've recently met," she teased. "And you're right. He does have your sweet tooth."

"You just said the magic word," Travis murmured. "Let's go downstairs. It's so quiet down there, I need to check on him. But the real reason is because I have to have more of these brownies." What would it be like if he ever kissed her and told her he had to have more kisses?

When they entered the kitchen, Casey looked up. "Hi, Dad!" The smile on his handsome little face was wreathed in chocolate.

Travis crossed to him. "It looks like you licked the platter clean."

"Huh? This is a *pot*."

Travis shot Melissa an amused glance. The old Mother Goose rhyme was wasted on his son, but she got the message and smiled. When he smiled back, she felt like she was floating.

To hide her reaction, she wet a paper towel for Casey to use to wipe off his mouth. Travis stood at the table and downed two more brownies in quick succession.

"Can I have a brownie now, Dad?"

"A little one. You've got enough chocolate in you to keep you awake for a week."

"Huh?"

"Your dad doesn't want you to get a stomachache,"

Melissa interjected. "I'll wrap up the rest of the brownies so you can take them home."

"Thanks! Can we play Go Fish now?" She'd found a deck of cards in the game closet.

"One round," his father decreed. "After that we've got to get you home to bed."

Melissa cleaned up the rest of the dishes, then joined them. Casey made the most matches, and was proclaimed the winner in no time, before they turned out the lights and locked up. This evening had filled her with such contentment, it was scary.

She put Casey in charge of the brownies as they walked out to the Jeep. While she drove, he sat in the back and chattered all the way down to the truck parked in town. When she pulled up next to it, Travis got out and put his son in the backseat. She hated it that their marvelous evening was over.

After buckling him in, Travis came around to her side of the Jeep. She lowered the window. Their faces were only inches apart. It was madness, but she ached for him to kiss her. If he ever got the urge, would he pretend she was his wife? She couldn't bear it if that were true.

His eyes played over her features. "You made this evening more memorable for us than you know." She felt his warm breath on her face. Only a little closer… "How do I thank you?"

The blood pounded in her ears. "You're already doing that by agreeing to track down the trespassers."

He let out a sigh. She thought maybe he didn't like remembering he had a job to do. At least for a little while.

"Speaking of your case, I was wondering if tomorrow you'd come hiking in the forest beyond the ridge with me. This evening didn't give me nearly enough time to do all the necessary exploring. I'm aware you want to paint, but you grew up here and know the area better than most people."

Melissa needed to remember the man wasn't asking her out. He needed her help. Since she'd been the one to tell her father about Lufka's, and spearhead this investigation in the first place, she wanted to do whatever she could for it to be solved.

"Finding the culprits is more important than my painting. Besides, I got in a full day today. I told you I'd help all I can, and I meant it. What time do you want to leave in the morning?"

"I'll be by at eight-thirty, after I've dropped Casey off at school. In case you didn't notice, he's had a wonderful time with you today. Thank you for taking the time to paint with him and play games." Travis's eyes held a faraway look just then. "He's been missing that."

Travis had been missing it, too, Melissa knew. She had a hard time swallowing. "The feeling's mutual. Your son is precious. Do you want me to drive my Jeep tomorrow? If so, I'll need to fill it with gas when I get down the canyon tonight."

"Since we're going to a new area, I thought we'd take my truck. It shouldn't be too much longer before I get a lead. Bring a backpack with the things you'll want."

What Melissa wanted was right here, and she didn't want to have to wait until tomorrow. "I'll be ready."

It was all she could do to start down the canyon

without breaking into tears for the no-win situation in which she found herself.

Yes, she knew Travis was grateful for her help. The three of them got along well and they had a lot of fun, but she'd been playing house the whole time. When he caught the people invading the cabin, it would all be over, and she'd be headed for heartache.

He followed her all the way to her town house, but that came as no surprise. Travis had had sound instincts to guard and protect. After Russ, she was lucky to meet a man like Travis and get to know him. He was living proof that some men were a breed apart. Valerie had been blessed to know his love.

Melissa took a deep breath as she parked her car and got out. She noticed Travis was still out in front. He hadn't pulled away yet. "You don't need to watch while I go inside," she called to him.

"I beg to differ. If I'd gone to the store with Valerie, she might still be alive."

With that revealing response, joy went out of Melissa's world. But it was the wake-up call she'd needed to get out of her dream state.

Tonight's activities had brought back happier memories for him from the past, but it couldn't be clearer that he would always miss his wife. Up until now Melissa had assumed her resemblance to Valerie had worked against her. But after what he'd just said, she decided he wasn't interested in any woman. He had a son to raise. That was enough for him.

Heartsick, she resolved to keep the situation between

them strictly business. It might be the end of her, but that was the way it had to be.

"See ya!" Casey shouted.

She waved to him from her front door. It was a good thing neither of them could see the tears in her eyes. "See ya," she said softly.

Chapter Seven

"Bye, Dexter," Casey said. "You've got plenty of food and water. I left you a doggie treat."

Travis glanced over his shoulder. They'd just finished breakfast and were ready to leave the house. He put some bottled water in his backpack for the hike. "Casey? What are you doing now?"

"I'm cutting some brownies to take for my school snack." He got out the foil and wrapped them up before putting them in his backpack.

Travis couldn't help laughing because he'd had the same idea. He went over to the counter and cut two brownies for himself, which he proceeded to eat on their way out to the truck.

"I think Melissa's food is as good as Mom's."

Whoa. Travis hadn't been prepared for that, but it was clear his son had moved on. "Yeah, these brownies are the best I've ever tasted."

"Yup. She makes good hot dogs, too. Can she come over tonight?"

"We'll see."

"You always say that."

Travis glanced at him. "What would you like me to say?"

Casey looked at him with innocent eyes. "Just say yes."

Travis chuckled at his son's remark. It was so…adult. He was still chuckling when he dropped Casey off at school and then pulled up in front of Melissa's town house five minutes later. She came hurrying out to the truck before he'd even opened his door. He got out and put her backpack in the rear seat with his.

"What's so funny?" she asked.

When he told her, she chuckled, too. "He's an original if ever there was one."

"So," Travis said, "after our hike, do you want to make his day and come to our house for dinner? I'll order Chinese."

She didn't hesitate. "Only if I can bring something to contribute."

"I think Casey's hoping you'll make more brownies. Me, too."

She rolled her eyes. "More?"

"There was only one left when we walked out the door this morning. It'll be a race to see who gets it when Casey and I return to the house later."

"If that's what you really want."

"It is. Believe me."

Her fragrance, whether from the shower or her shampoo, met his nostrils. He was becoming addicted to it. "I do believe you're the most punctual woman I ever met."

As she climbed into the cab, the action revealed the lush curves of her body. She'd come dressed in denims and a long-sleeved crew-neck in an oatmeal color. He helped her in and shut the door before going around.

After they were on the road she flashed him a guileless smile. "My brother says that a girl being on time makes a guy nervous. He says it's one of my most irritating qualities."

Travis chuckled. "If he's rarely on time, then you make him feel guilty. In my business punctuality is an absolute necessity."

"Oh, good," she said drily. "Now I feel much better."

"I was paying you a compliment."

Melissa laughed. "I know. Thank you. What's the plan for today?"

"I'm going to let you decide where we go. We'll hike beyond the ridge and look in the high back country for people who might be up to no good. It'll be better if we don't talk while we're moving. When we stop, we'll whisper."

"Okay."

He pulled a Geological Survey map out of the glove compartment and handed it to her. "This is one I took from the cabin drawer. Let me know how much of the terrain you're familiar with. I'll drive us up to one of the firebreak roads. When we find a good spot, we'll pull off and walk from there."

She opened the map. He glanced at her as she studied it. Her lovely profile was beguiling, and with her hair caught back in a tortoiseshell clip, sheerly elegant. For once he wished he was on vacation and they could enjoy the day doing whatever they wanted. From the first she'd gotten to him, thrilling him at odd moments.

Now those moments were merging. When he was away from her, he thought about her more and more....

Yet part of him still felt an illogical resentment for those thoughts. He and Casey had been surviving in a numb state until that first day at the clinic. When she'd greeted them at the door, it was as if Travis had walked out of a black-and-white movie into a world of blinding Technicolor. Besides conjuring up remembered pain from the past, new feelings burgeoned. Longings and yearnings had taken hold, surprising the hell out of him.

He understood the initial attraction because of her similarities to Valerie. But to go on seeing Melissa as anyone but a client, desiring her to the point that he ached to act on his feelings, thrust him into an unexpected realm of guilt. Valerie hadn't been gone that long. It seemed a desecration of her memory that he wanted this woman sitting next to him. But he couldn't stop what his body was telling him.

Outside Kamas, Travis took a right and drove up an emergency access road into the forest. When he found a natural turnout, he pulled into it and parked. "What do you think?" He leaned over to look at the map. Her warm cheek was too close to his, distracting him from the business at hand. He'd become acutely aware of her.

If she was disturbed by his closeness, she hid it well. "I've hiked all through the forest this side of the ridge. But I hiked on the other side only once, with my grandpa. That's the area with the mine. The slope is steeper there, and the forest is thick, making it difficult to walk."

"Okay then," he said, "we'll hike in the area you're

most familiar with and see what we can find." From what he could gather, much of the western end of the Uinta Mountains was unroaded and relatively pristine country, accessible only to those willing to hike or go in on horseback. He'd seen no sign of anyone else in this area so far. "I've brought my thermal-image goggles to help us. Let's go."

They got out of the truck and she put on her backpack without waiting for his assistance. The more he got to know her, the more he noticed how independent she was, always protecting her body space. But there'd been a slight change in her from last week. Last evening he'd caught her staring at him a few times. That had to count for something. He planned to find out what during their hike.

Today there were clouds overhead, but they weren't threatening rain. When they blocked the sun, the forest air just grew cooler. The endless varieties of trees and undergrowth created a world of enchantment. Somewhere in this greenery a plantation of Early Misty marijuana was growing. He needed to stay focused to spot it, though Melissa's presence was a constant distraction.

The only sounds were of small animals and birds, and their own movements. For Travis it was as if they were the only two people on earth, encased in an almost spiritual solitude. He pitied anyone who'd never walked through a forest like this.

They'd been hiking for about two hours when he spotted movement in the distance. He stopped and waited until an elk with the biggest rack he'd ever seen walked into view. Signaling for Melissa to stop, he took off the goggles and helped her put them on. He stood behind her and pulled her against his chest while she took a good, long look.

"Oh, Travis," she whispered in awe, "he's magnificent. I think he must weigh a thousand pounds. Casey wouldn't believe it. I'd love to bring him hiking up here so he could see the elk, too."

"You'll have to draw him a picture," Travis suggested, speaking into her hair.

He felt a tremor run through her body, but she didn't move away. "I hope no hunter ever finds him."

"A rack that size proves he's eluded them for years."

Slowly, she peered around her, through the goggles. "I can see everything!" she exclaimed softly. She kept turning until she faced him. "There's nothing more beautiful than nature's creations."

"You're right." Without conscious thought he removed the goggles and set them down. "I'm looking at one of them right now. You have no idea how beautiful you are to me, Melissa." He'd loved watching her move quietly through the forest, a gorgeous human creature if there ever was one. His hands closed around her upper arms. "I want to kiss you, but you already know that."

"Because I look like your wife?" she asked with a daunting frankness.

He drew in a fortifying breath. "I don't know how to answer that. Maybe. Partly."

"That's honest, anyway. I can see in your eyes you'd give anything if I were her. But I'm me. I don't think you have any idea who *I* am."

His hands cupped her face. "Then there's only one

way to find out, isn't there?" He lowered his head and found her mouth with his own. It was sweet to the taste. So sweet. She'd been eating rcd grapes from her pack. He proceeded with slow deliberation, teasing her, pressing kisses against her throat and around her lips, invading her mouth a little deeper each time until she opened to him, like a rose opening to the sun.

He groaned before pulling her body to his. After Valerie, he'd thought he would never experience this kind of passion again. But holding Melissa in his arms, exploring her warm, pliant mouth, showed him he knew nothing about the mysterious alchemy stirring up his fire.

The world faded away as she wrapped her arms around his neck, allowing him to embrace her fully. He'd been craving this since she'd helped him put up cameras inside the cabin. While he'd been working, he'd had to fight the urge to reach out and touch her. Now he didn't have to hold back.

It wasn't his imagination that she wanted to get closer to him. Their bodies gravitated together in mutual need. One kiss didn't begin to satisfy and could never be enough for him. After such a long time in a state of limbo, the rapture he felt with this woman was almost beyond bearing. But it came to an abrupt end when she cried, "No, Travis!" and slid out of his arms.

He was so far gone, it took him a minute to realize what had just happened. Bereft after such ecstasy, he stood there breathing hard while he attempted to pull himself together. "What did I do that you didn't want me to?"

WITH THE CLOUDS SHUTTING out the sunlight, his eyes looked black. Melissa shook her head. "Nothing."

"But you wanted me. You were with me all the way."

"I don't deny it." Being in his arms, undergoing that explosion of joy when he'd kissed her breathless, had been a transcending experience Melissa had wanted to go on and on.

"Then what caused you to pull away? Did I frighten you?"

She rubbed her arms with her hands. "No…. Yes…. I don't know…."

He put his hands on his hips. "I *did* frighten you."

"No. It wasn't you. It's me. I frightened myself."

"Because you responded to me? Help me out here. I want to understand."

Melissa shook her head. "You had the power to make me respond when I had no intention of doing so."

"*Make* you? That's an odd choice of word. It takes two willing participants to feel what we were feeling."

"I don't want to talk about it. I—I can't," she stammered. "If you don't mind, I'd like to go back to the truck."

The safe world she'd created for herself since the divorce had just blown up in her face. For the first time in six years, she felt confused and out of control.

It was cruel to blame him for wanting his wife to still be alive. He could no more help it than he could fly. And Melissa knew it was sheer insanity to accuse him of trying to dominate her, when he'd done nothing of the kind. For days now she'd been wanting him to kiss her. Now that he had, she was a writhing mass of contradictions. She'd ruined it with him and could have bitten her tongue off for speaking to him like that.

Without saying anything, he put the goggles on again and started back the way they'd come, pacing his strides so she could keep up with him. When they got back to the truck, she checked her watch. It was one-thirty. They'd been out longer than she'd thought and they hadn't seen a soul.

He left her to remove her own pack and put it in the backseat. When she climbed into the cab, she still felt devastated by what she'd done. "Travis…I owe you an explanation, but I don't know where to start."

"You owe me nothing," he said in a remote tone of voice. "I felt like kissing you and I did, until you stopped me. We both know it happens to males and females all the time. It's just as well I got it out of my system so I can concentrate on finding the people invading your domain."

After starting the engine, he turned the truck around and they headed down the mountain. "I have to go to the cabin," he said, "so I can gather the memory cards from the cameras and put a new listening device in the flowers. I'll drive into Kamas and you can do some shopping there, or wait in the truck at the church, while I go up on foot. It won't take me long."

"I want to stay with you."

"I don't think so. Not after what happened back there."

"Please forget what I said." She was starting to panic.

"That would be impossible."

Melissa stirred restlessly. "I've made you angry, when it was the last thing I meant to do."

"If I'm angry, it's at myself. There's an unwritten law. No fraternizing with the clients. I've never crossed the line before and now I know why. Believe me, I won't do it again." The ice was back in his eyes.

She realized this wasn't the time to explain herself. He wasn't in a mood to listen. Perhaps by the time they reached the cabin, he'd be more approachable. For the rest of the drive to town she sat back and stared out the window, not seeing anything.

At one point his phone rang. He checked the caller ID before answering it. The call was a short one, but she sensed it was important. He didn't bother to explain, however.

When they reached Kamas, he parked at the church and said nothing as she headed up the road with him. But with every step, she grew more and more uncomfortable. Travis had surrounded himself with an invisible shield that no plea for leniency could penetrate.

Once at their destination, she followed him around the back. Melissa saw fresh cigarette butts outside the door the second he did.

He spoke at last. "There were more visitors here last night, but they didn't come from the area where we were hiking today. That leaves the section of forest I haven't explored yet."

He opened his pack to collect the samples and bag them. Returning to the front, he unlocked the door and they moved inside. "The lanterns have been transferred from the end table to the floor," she blurted.

"So I noticed. Your squatters have grown careless."

While Melissa drank water from the kitchen tap, he got busy removing the memory cards and replacing the batteries in the cameras. His last action was to hide a new listening device in the geraniums and pocket the other one.

"Shall we go?" he asked, his tone frigid.

She couldn't let things continue this way. The thought of trekking back to the truck and then driving down the canyon with him without saying a word was too painful to contemplate. In desperation she reached the front door ahead of him and flattened herself against it, so he'd have to remove her physically to go outside.

"We're not leaving until you let me explain."

His face was a study of lines and shadows. "It's not necessary."

"When I told you the reason for my divorce, I didn't tell you everything."

With that remark, he lifted his head. She had his attention. "Go on."

"Russ and I met in Kamas at the beginning of the summer. He was at his parents' summer home in Park City, and drove to Kamas with friends. We met at a local dance. He was good-looking, fun, funny, smart. He had lots of friends I really liked, and he liked my friends. I fell for him. In the fall, we got married."

Travis looked at her through veiled eyes. "What happened?"

"My parents had paid for my college education, and suggested that we wait and get another year of schooling behind us first, but we both wanted to marry. My siblings were married. All my friends were getting married. Love was in the air. I wanted what every girl wants, and didn't want to waste any more time. Mom and Dad got behind me, like they always do, and provided the beach honeymoon. It was great."

"You were still in love at the end of your honeymoon?"

"Yes. He was terrific to me and I assumed our wonderful lives would go on forever. Russ's father is a prominent, well-to-do Realtor, and he gave us a luxury house in an elegant neighborhood near the University of Utah for a wedding present. We had everything the upwardly mobile couple could ask for. Except for one thing I didn't see coming."

"What was that?"

"You've heard of Jekyll and Hyde."

Travis's features tautened. "How soon did he turn into Mr. Hyde?"

She averted her eyes, remembering the moment as if it was yesterday. "The day after our return from Laguna Beach. He wanted to control me." Her voice shook. "I'm not talking once in a while. I'm talking about every aspect of our lives. It was like a sickness."

"Why don't we sit down while you tell me the rest."

"I can't sit. Let me just tell you everything so you'll understand me better."

He folded his arms and stayed silent.

"Russ dictated when I went to bed, when I got up, what I cooked, what I ate," she stated numbly. "What I wore, what I did, where I went, what I read, who I did things with, how I spent his money. He curtailed the amount of time we spent with my family. He hated the cabin. He hated it when I painted. He chose what we watched on TV. When I was home from school, he checked on me all the time."

A pained expression crossed Travis's face, but he didn't interrupt.

"At first I thought I was living a nightmare. I prayed I would wake up, but it went on and on, and I knew I had to get out. But being beholden to both sets of parents, and knowing what our getting a divorce would do to them, I was afraid to tell them what was going on, afraid his parents would never believe me."

"You were trapped," Travis said with conviction. "I've seen it with other victims."

She nodded. "The only thing he couldn't control was my schoolwork and nursing classes. I immersed myself in my studies to stay mentally and emotionally away from him. I couldn't bear for him to touch me. One afternoon he came home while I was studying for midterms. He wanted to make love. The thought was so abhorrent to me, I did the only thing I could do, and told him I didn't have time.

"He got this crazed look in his eye and yanked me out of the chair. I tried to push him away, but he wouldn't take no for an answer and slapped me in the face, with such force, I fell to the floor."

"Melissa—"

"Luckily, when I got up, he saw that my cheek was all red and swelling, and he asked me to forgive him. He promised he'd never do it again." She swallowed hard. "I didn't give him the chance, and fled the house with my car keys."

"Thank heaven."

"The next day I filed for divorce. He didn't contest it. To my relief it went through without a hitch, and I never saw him again. But I heard he remarried, and it makes me ill for his new wife, just thinking about it."

Travis studied her for a tension-filled minute. "When I kissed you, it was the first time a man kissed you since your divorce, wasn't it?" His voice was low.

She drew in a deep breath. "I've dated a bit, but yes, you're the first."

His dark brows met in a frown. "And it brought that horrific moment back."

"No, that's not it. From the first time we met, I found myself attracted to you. When you told me I reminded you of your wife, I was utterly dismayed. Last night, when you watched me go in the town house, you said it was necessary because if you'd been on guard for your wife, she'd still be alive. To think that after six years I finally meet a man who appeals to me, and then I learn you only see Valerie when you look at me…

"On the drive up the canyon today, I told myself I was going to be strong and fight the attraction I felt. But when you told me you wanted to kiss me, that's what I wanted, too—more than anything. You know I did, and you know how much I enjoyed it. That's what I meant earlier when I said you had the power to make me respond when I had no intention of doing so. I lost control with you, but that was my problem, not yours."

Her explanation appeared to satisfy him. "So after giving in, why did you stop?"

"Because I remembered you were kissing *her,* not me. You were remembering your wife, and how you felt when she was in your arms. I could have gone on kissing you back, but I would have been lying to myself that it was me you really wanted."

He rubbed his jaw. "I can see that you and I both need more time together to dispel our ghosts from the past."

Melissa wished he hadn't said that. "I'm glad you feel that way," she whispered.

His gaze was centered on her mouth, causing hers to tingle in response. "We'd better get going. I have to drop off the latest samples at the lab before I pick up Casey."

"I'm ready."

Together they left the cabin. Unburdening herself turned out to be cathartic. By the time they reached the truck in town, Melissa felt a lightening of her spirit.

Once they were sitting in the cab, he gave her a searching glance. "Tell me something," he said. "Were you reminded of your ex-husband when the employee at Grampy's leered at you?"

She nodded.

"When you went pale like you did, I knew you'd been deeply disturbed."

"No wonder you Texas Rangers are so legendary. Nothing gets by you."

His disarming smile chased away her earlier fear that she might never see it again. "Let's hope that holds true during my investigation." He pulled the listening device from his pocket. "We know from those fresh cigarette butts that someone was in your cabin last night. I'm curious to hear what this picked up." He turned it on so they could both listen.

She heard a number of male voices. That alone made her shudder—to think a bunch of men were in the cabin's kitchen as if they owned the place. Melissa listened more intently. "They're all speaking Spanish. Do you understand what they're saying?"

"I can pick out a little, but they're not conversing in the kind of Spanish I used to hear in Texas. This is a fast-paced dialect with certain phonetic changes I'm unfamiliar with. I'll need Jose for this. He's our expert."

Melissa watched Travis turn off the device and put it in his pocket. "What are you thinking?"

"This and that."

"Travis—" she half moaned in frustration "—that was one of your nonanswers again."

His jaw hardened. "After I get back to the office, I'll look through the camera memory cards and will know a lot more. Once I've pieced everything together, I'll tell you my suspicions."

He didn't have to say it; a bunch of men up to no good had to be armed and dangerous.

He switched on the ignition. On the way out of town he stopped in front of the Quickie Mart. "I have to go inside, but I'll only be a minute. Do you want anything?"

"No, thank you."

Maybe he needed to use the restroom, Melissa decided. But with him you never could tell, because he operated on his own private agenda. Whatever was going on, the tension was building.

Travis entered the mart, where he'd arranged to meet Jose back by the cold drinks section. His friend had driven up in the R & T Painting Company truck from the P.I. shop. It had been parked alongside a dozen other vehicles. There were still a lot of tourists on vacation.

When Travis found him, he was dressed in a painter's overalls and cap. They both reached for a Coke. Travis took a second one in case Melissa wanted one. "What did you find out so far?"

"The same man and a woman I tailed Tuesday showed up at Grampy's for work at five to ten. They drove the same cars as before. I checked with the DMV and found out there's no police record or warrants out on them. Both driving records are clean.

"Our man with the tattoo left the camper on foot and arrived at Grampy's at eleven. I'll watch till he goes off shift and follow him again. When I find out anything else, I'll let you know."

Travis nodded. "I'll check to see if those fingerprints taken at the cabin produce results. Who knows? We might get lucky and some names will turn up, his among them. You've got enough backup?"

"Plenty."

"Good. When you've got a minute, listen to this and give me your expert opinion." He handed him the listening device. "I pulled it from the flowers in the kitchen."

"I'll do it as soon as I get back in the truck."

"Thanks."

Travis went to the checkout stand first to pay for his drinks, then joined Melissa in the truck. "I bought you a Coke."

"Thank you."

On the way down the canyon he decided to share some information with her. He was aware he'd been secretive, yet she never asked about the case. That was a quality he respected in her more than she could possibly realize.

"I went in the mart to meet up with Jose and give him the listening device. He'll translate for me when he gets a chance."

She nodded. "You don't do anything without a reason."

They had just emerged from the canyon when Jose phoned. Travis picked up. "What's new?"

Jose whistled, and that alone told him plenty. "Give me five minutes and I'll call you back," Travis suggested.

"It's probably a good idea you're alone when I tell you."

He didn't like the sound of that. "Understood."

He drove straight to Melissa's town house and pulled up in front. She climbed out in a hurry and retrieved her pack from the backseat.

"Casey and I will be over at six to get you," he said.

"You still want me to come?" She looked anxious.

"At the cabin I thought we agreed we needed to get to know each other better. Or have you changed your mind?"

"No," she said quickly. "No. But let me come to you. Give me directions to your house and I'll be there at six, okay?"

He agreed. And her positive response relieved him.

They had things to work out. After she'd unburdened herself today, he feared she'd retreat emotionally before they got to know each other better. Travis didn't think he could handle that. Much to his surprise, he recognized she was becoming important to his existence.

And he realized that he was seeing Melissa in her own right and not as a clone of Valerie. In time he hoped to prove it to her.

"Okay, see you later."

She nodded. After she'd gone inside the condo, he pulled out his phone and rang Jose. "Go ahead and tell me what you heard. I'm alone now."

"It's all coming together, Travis. Those men in the cabin are from Colombia. I counted four distinct voices. They're speaking the Choquano dialect from the northern coastal region. They talked about the hard work and the isolation. One of them said the pay was going to be great, so stop complaining. Another talked about finding women when this was over. They were getting tired of the job.

"One complained of a bad toothache. Another guy said he was going to jump the woman whose bedroom was upstairs before they cleared out. He described in detail what he wanted to do to her. His friend suggested they wait to get paid, then kidnap her. She would be of interest to the boss, who'd want her for himself.

"It could be worth a lot of extra *dinero* for them if they took her back with them, he said. Her family wouldn't know what had happened to her, and would never be able to find her. There was laughter and then silence."

Rage curled Travis's hands into fists. The mention of their plans for Melissa twisted his gut. If Casey hadn't told her about Travis's job while they were at the movie, she might not have sought help soon enough to avoid the fate awaiting her. At least he could be thankful that Valerie hadn't been molested before she was killed.

"Travis?" Jose said in concern. "Are you all right?"

Travis struggled for breath. "No. And I won't be until these vermin are caught and put away in prison to rot. If this is a big operation like the one on Boulder Mountain, then there's a lot more at stake and we're dealing with men who'll kill to protect their crop."

"Which means there's a lot of money behind them."

"I've got my work cut out finding those plants, so we'll know exactly what we're up against. Let's hope the next recording gives us some kind of time line for their activities. With it being mid-September, they have to be coming to the end of the harvest."

"Agreed. I'm here on surveillance when you want to talk."

The call ended. Travis dropped off the new samples at the lab, then swung by the school to pick up Casey. In a couple of hours they'd be seeing Melissa again. He could hardly wait.

Chapter Eight

Melissa followed Travis's directions to his house in the Lone Peak Estates and pulled up in front. She loved the country-cottage-style home on sight. White trim enhanced the stone exterior and matched the white fencing.

Casey answered her knock. Apparently Travis was tied up on the phone, so Casey and Dexter took her on the grand tour. Dark honey flooring ran from the foyer throughout the downstairs. The mix of traditional and contemporary furnishings reflecting the wood tones against soft yellow walls gave the interior a warm, livable feel.

She accompanied Casey into the formal dining room with its decorative columns. It led to the two-story great room with a stone fireplace, and beyond it, the kitchen and breakfast room done in sage accents.

He then led her to their bedrooms at the rear of the house. At the first one he announced, "This is my room."

She could tell. It had everything a boy could want. "I love it, especially your posters of Spider-Man and Optimus Prime."

But there was something else she loved more: the framed photograph of his father in his Texas Ranger uniform hanging over the bed. Travis looked younger in the picture and handsome as sin.

Her gaze darted to more family photographs propped on his dresser. Casey took one and showed it to Melissa. It was a head shot of his mother, wearing a crew-neck top like the one Melissa had worn today.

She gasped, seeing the smiling woman. They *did* have definite similarities. In this picture, her light brown hair was pulled back the way Melissa's was. It revealed the tiny blue sparkling jewels in her ears that matched her blue-gray eyes. Eyes like Melissa's.

To see this photo of his wife, after hearing of their likeness, explained so much about Travis's initial reaction to Melissa at the clinic. She put it back on the dresser before looking at Casey.

"You must miss her very much."

His sigh spoke volumes. "Yup, but she's gone to heaven. You're nice and pretty, just like her. I wish you lived with us all the time."

Melissa moaned inwardly, while her throat swelled. "Thank you, Casey," she whispered, knowing she didn't dare tell him the same thing back. "That's the greatest compliment I ever received." She couldn't deal with the pain any longer. "Shall we finish the tour?"

"Okay. Come on, Dexter."

They went to Travis's bedroom, which had a coffered ceiling and luxurious bath. Melissa didn't stay to look around for other pictures of his wife.

There were two more bedrooms at the top of a

white staircase. The house was utterly charming, but she found the real character of their home came from the prints and two oil paintings hanging on the walls. Casey said they'd brought them from Texas. The big one in the dining room showed a field of gorgeous Texas bluebonnets.

The other oil, a very large one in the great room, showed a black stallion racing ahead of some other horses. It was obviously a favorite, and had been signed. The artist had caught the beauty and swiftness of horses in motion. From experience Melissa knew it was a hard thing to capture.

"This is fabulous," she told Travis as he walked into the room.

He studied it for minute. "Before Casey and I left Texas, the Rangers in my district took up a collection to buy this for me. The artist is becoming famous. Nothing could have surprised or pleased me more." His voice was thick with emotion.

Tears stung her eyelids, but she refused to cry. "They must have thought the world of you. Did you ride a lot?"

"All my life. Mostly for pleasure, sometimes on the job."

"Are your parents still living, Travis?"

"No," Casey answered for him. "They were killed by a train when he and Aunt Pat were babies. Their truck stalled on the track and they couldn't get out in time."

Melissa gulped. "That's awful."

"I know. My grandpa was a Texas Ranger, too!"

"I didn't know that."

"Yup. Daddy and Aunt Pat had to go live with their aunt and uncle."

"And we were very fortunate," Travis confided. "They became our parents and they were horse people. After my aunt May passed away from a lung clot, it was just the three of us. When Uncle Frank died of a heart attack, Pat and I inherited their house and lived in it."

Casey nodded. "And then Aunt Pat got married and moved to Salt Lake, and then Daddy met Mommy and they got married."

Melissa smiled at Travis's adorable boy. "And then *you* came along. That was a really lucky day for your parents."

Sadness tinged his smile. "I didn't want to move to Salt Lake, but now I'm glad we did. Do you ride horses?"

After their little talk in the bedroom, she realized where this was leading. "I have done. There's a stable in Kamas where you can go for rides, but I'm not very good. Are you thinking of getting horses again?"

"Maybe," Travis said. "We're taking this one step at a time."

No doubt he'd ridden with his wife. After her death he'd probably lost his love for it. Certainly Casey's recent fall wouldn't put him in any hurry to do something about it.

"Who's ready for dinner?" Travis asked. "Our Chinese food arrived while you two were touring the house."

"I don't like that stuff," Casey said in dismay.

"I made you mac and cheese, bud."

Melissa grinned. "And I brought you more homemade brownies."

"Yippee!"

TRAVIS CAME IN the breakfast room after putting Casey to bed. While they were gone, she'd cleaned up the kitchen. He brought his laptop with him and sat down at the table. From his pocket he pulled out the three tiny micro SD cards taken from the mini cameras.

Melissa looked at him. "Is Casey asleep?"

"Not yet, but I think he's on the way."

Suddenly, they said each other's name, at the exact same time. "You go first," Travis told her.

"Casey showed me a picture of his mother. I—I can see why you were taken back when we first met." Melissa's voice faltered.

"I didn't know you then."

"Still—"

"Still, nothing." He cut her off. "Even identical twins have differences when you get to know them."

"All I'm trying to say is that I'm not so sure Casey has made that distinction."

"Does it matter?" Travis watched her fidget.

"It might. That's why I made up the excuse about doing the dishes instead of going in his room to read him a bedtime story. I don't think it's wise that I get any closer to him."

"Are you sure you're not talking about me instead of my son?"

"Travis, please listen to me. After talking about his

mother, he told me he wished I lived with you all the time."

"That shouldn't surprise you." It had become Casey's mantra.

"No, but it troubles me. When you told me about his immediate turnaround after coming to the clinic, I only halfway believed your explanation. Not because I thought you were lying, but because it sounded so unlikley."

"But now you know it's true. So what if it is? Why are you so worried about it?"

She eyed him in confusion. "Because he has unrealistic expectations. One day, when I don't meet them, he's going to be let down."

"I haven't seen any sign of it."

"You're not hearing what I'm saying."

"I am hearing you. We both know he's transferred his feelings for his mom to you."

"Yes, but I'm not his mom, and when he eventually realizes it, his disappointment could present problems."

Travis had known the day would come when Melissa saw Valerie's picture. Now that she had, she'd started doubting him, fearing he couldn't separate his feelings about the two of them any more than Casey could. In fact, she was making sounds about wanting to distance herself from him as well.

Travis refused to allow that to happen before they could explore what was going on between them. Those kisses in the forest had been earthshaking for him.

"Then we'll deal with them if and when that time comes, okay?"

He stared her down. At last she gave him a small smile. "Okay," she said.

"Good. Right now we have a case to solve. Let's take a look at these tapes and see what's on them. This one is from the back door outside the cabin." He inserted the first memory card into the adaptor so they could view it on the laptop, full screen. "The time indicated says ten fifty-five."

"What on earth are they doing out in the forest so late at night?"

"I'm working on the answer." Travis knew exactly what they were doing. Tomorrow he'd hike with Melissa over the ridge in the other direction. In all likelihood he'd find what he was looking for, otherwise these drug traffickers wouldn't be using her family's cabin rather than some cheap motel miles from there.

Out of the darkness came the beam of a flashlight, moving around like a firefly. Melissa gasped as she counted one, two, three, four silhouettes coming toward the camera before they disappeared into the cabin.

"How dare they!" she said, appalled.

Travis picked up another memory card and put it in. "This one will be from the upstairs camera. It says ten after eleven." Again there was movement of a flashlight beam, followed by two silhouettes climbing the staircase.

Melissa shook her head. "How convenient! A bedroom for each of them."

"They probably had another one on watch outside the cabin, in case they had to get out in a hurry, but the camera didn't catch him. That might explain the number of cigarette butts."

He removed the card and put in the next. "Ten fifty-six." The tape caught the backs of four men in long-sleeved jackets entering the kitchen, one still wielding a flashlight. The man holding it put it on the picnic table, while they all crowded around the sink for a drink from the tap. They didn't use glasses from the cupboard. In another minute they assembled on the benches in the kitchen.

Melissa glanced at Travis. "Judging by the look of them, they're all Hispanic. That certainly explains why we heard Spanish on the listening device."

He nodded. "When Jose translated the audio, he picked up four voices, all of them native speakers." That was as much as he was willing to tell her.

"What were they talking about?"

"How hungry and thirsty they were. One had a toothache."

"But nothing about what they were doing in the mountains?"

"Not yet. But when we go up to the cabin tomorrow, I'll put in yet another listening device, and hope we pick up more chatter."

"Tomorrow's Friday. They might not come, since it'll be the weekend."

"We'll just have to wait and see. I plan to come by for you at eight-thirty in the morning. We'll spend the day up there. I'll ask Deana to pick Casey up from school, so it will give us a little more time to hike."

All of a sudden there was movement on the tape. The

kitchen became shrouded in darkness as one of the men took the flashlight and got up from the table. Another left with him, presumably to go upstairs. Which meant the other two were left in the dark. When there was nothing more to see, Travis pulled out the memory card.

Melissa shot up from the table. "I can't wait till they're caught. They sicken me. About a month ago I was watching an old Hollywood war movie where the enemy shot everyone inside this gorgeous French château before they took it over. It was winter. They chopped up the furniture and parquet floors for firewood.

"Some of the soldiers used the fabulous Sèvres china urns for chamber pots. They showed no mercy or regard for anything. I know it was just a movie, but it was based on a thousand true stories. I remembered thinking, what if that were my family? Our château? Now I have an inkling what it feels like for an enemy to invade your home as if it's their divine right."

Travis reached for her and wrapped his arms around her. She didn't resist. "I'm so close to catching them, I can taste it." He kissed her cheek and hair. "Bear with me a little longer and I promise you'll soon be rid of them for good."

"You think I don't know that?" she cried into his neck. "What if Casey hadn't told me you were a P.I.? It's a miracle you've already unearthed so much. Who else but a Texas Ranger could do what you've done?"

The warmth of her body proved to be an aphrodisiac that drove everything else from Travis's mind. He kissed his way to her mouth and began devouring her.

His hunger for her had been building. Whatever reservations she had about him seemed to have dissolved, because she was soon kissing him back with a fervency that matched his own.

He had no idea how long they stood there, locked in a feverish embrace. But when Dexter's bark registered, Travis realized they were no longer alone. Melissa had heard it, too, and eased out of his arms. He noticed her flushed face and swollen lips before he turned to discover Casey standing nearby. His son's blue eyes stared at them with a soberness that was puzzling, and he didn't say anything.

"What are you still doing up, bud?"

"I couldn't sleep."

Travis sighed. "Maybe it's just as well. I was going to ask your aunt to walk across the street and keep you company while I followed Melissa home. Now you can come with me. Stay in your pj's, but put some shoes on. Then we'll leave."

"I'll be right back!" Casey took off with Dexter at his heels.

Knowing this wasn't the time for a postmortem with Melissa, Travis escorted her through the house and out the front door to her car. After helping her inside, he leaned down for another taste of her divine mouth.

"Travis...Casey can see us." She tore her lips from his, but not before he'd felt her respond. It gratified him to know her emotions were spilling over, too.

He kissed her nose. "We'll be right behind you."

When Travis unlocked the truck, Casey and Dexter climbed in the back. On the way over to Melissa's the boy was still unusually quiet. Travis eyed him through the rearview mirror. "What's on your mind?"

"I don't think Mclissa likes me."

That was a surprise. "Where did you get an idea like that? I seem to recall she's given you lots of presents, and she made more brownies for you tonight."

"I know."

"So what's the problem?"

A haunting sigh escaped before he murmured, "I told her I wished she lived with us all the time."

Travis rubbed his jaw. "What did she say?"

Silence greeted his question. They were almost to Melissa's town house, so Travis prodded, "Casey?"

"She didn't say anything," he answered in a quiet voice.

Travis's earlier conversation with Melissa had come back to bite him. "That doesn't mean she doesn't like you. You have to remember Melissa isn't your mother. She's never been a mother," he said in a burst of inspiration, wanting to help his son get past this hurt.

"You mean she doesn't know how?" Casey sounded as if he couldn't imagine such a thing. It made Travis smile despite the pang in his heart.

"Yeah, that's what I mean. And guess what? *I* didn't know how to be a father until after I got married and you were born. Your mom and I learned how together."

He could hear the wheels turning in Casey's head.

"Do you think if you married Melissa, you could teach her and she'd learn how?"

Travis didn't reply.

MELISSA WAS PACKING hard-boiled eggs and peanut butter sandwiches in her backpack when her phone rang. Maybe it was Travis calling to tell her he was going to be late picking her up. Instead it was her sister.

"Linda?"

"Hi! I know, it's been at least two weeks since I last talked to you. Dad said you've taken the week off and we shouldn't go up to the cabin until the P.I. figures out what's going on. I want to hear all about what's happening up there, but first I need a favor."

"What?"

"My babysitter can't come at eleven, and I have an appointment with my ob-gyn for my annual pap smear. I was wondering if you might be able to help me out. I know it's late notice."

"You know I would in a second, but the guy heading the investigation is coming by for me in a few minutes. We have to go up the canyon again. I'm so sorry."

"Hey, it's all right. I'll call Mom. I hate to ask her, but sometimes there isn't anything else to do. If that fails, I'll cancel the appointment. So how's it going? Do you trust this P.I. to know what he's doing?"

Heat swept through Melissa. The memory of the way Travis had kissed her in his kitchen last night had kept her awake for hours. "He's brilliant."

"Really. Is he young? Old?"

"Mid-thirties."

"Married?"

"Linda…not you, too! Mom and Dad do enough of that."

"I'm getting warmer, aren't I? You've been so quiet lately, something tells me he's a person of interest."

"He hopes to have the case solved soon. That's the only thing of interest to me."

"Liar. But I'm glad to hear you have such confidence in him. One of these days I want the inside skinny on him. In the meantime I'm sure you can't wait to get the cabin back. I know you'd live up there if you could."

"You know me too well." Except that since Melissa had met Travis, she couldn't imagine being up there without him.

"Well, I'd better try phoning Mom. We'll talk later. Have a good day!"

"You, too."

After they hung up, Melissa put her keys in her pocket and left the condo carrying her backpack. Travis was out in front, right on time. She felt an adrenaline rush, something that happened every time she saw him. As she deposited her backpack in the rear and climbed into the truck, she sensed his mind was somewhere else. Whether it was personal or work-related, she couldn't tell.

Probably he was thinking about those men they'd seen on the video, who had to be close to the cabin. Maybe today would be the day she and Travis would catch sight of them, though they'd be hiking in a rugged area she hadn't been in since she was a kid. Still, two pairs of eyes were better than one.

She put on her best smile and said, "Good morning."

When he turned to her, his gaze traveled over her

and centered on her mouth. "It is now. But I'm having second thoughts about taking you with me."

And here she'd hoped he might kiss her. What was she thinking? "Why?"

"I've decided you'll be safer here."

She frowned. "I thought you had backup for us."

"I do, but even with the best-laid plans, things can go wrong. I'd prefer not to take any chances."

"Why don't you tell me what's really wrong? You think I'll slow you down?"

"You know better than that."

"So how about telling me the truth?"

His jaw tensed. "This has to do with Casey."

She bit her lip. "Is he all right?"

"He won't be if anything happens to you."

Melissa stared at Travis, trying hard to read between the lines. "What you're not saying is that this case has escalated into something highly explosive. Am I right?"

"I'm afraid so. On the way over here, Jose called me from the cabin. The men were there again last night, and he overheard conversation on the listening device that has required us to step up the operation. Now the police are involved."

"So that means the Texas Ranger is once again walking into a situation that could take lives."

"Not if I can help it." His voice was hard.

Melissa felt real fear. "I wish I'd never told my father about the Lufka firm."

"Thank heaven you did," Travis retorted.

"Why?" she cried.

He grimaced. "Never mind."

Now she was terrified. "Travis, if anything happened to you, Casey would never be able to handle the loss, and I'd never be able to forgivc myself." *I'd never get over it.*

"If you're home safe and sound at least I'll be able to concentrate on the job I've got to do. Promise me you'll stay put today. I'll call you before the day is out. I swear it."

Melissa's heart pounded so hard she felt ill. "What about Casey?"

"Deana will pick him up from school. If I can't get home tonight, my sister's going to take care of him."

This was a crisis, but Travis wasn't asking for Melissa's help.

Was that because she'd told him she didn't dare get too close to Casey?

Or had he decided it was best to maintain distance because he'd finally separated her from his wife and she didn't stand up to the comparison?

Whatever the answer, he didn't want her around. Melissa got the message. "Sorry for holding you up." She jumped out of the truck and reached in back for her pack.

"Melissa..." His blue eyes glittered.

"Whatever you do, come home to your son," she said. And without waiting for a response, she raced up the sidewalk to her condo and let herself in. Once safely locked inside, she ran to her room and collapsed on the bed in a paroxysm of tears.

When she finally couldn't sob any longer, she got up and washed her face. After that she left the town house and drove to her sister's home in the Sugar House area of Salt Lake, not far from the university. Melissa wanted the comfort of Linda's toddlers. If her mother came over, so much the better. She'd never needed her family more.

CASEY HAD BEEN IN Travis's heart from the second they'd learned Valerie was pregnant. But recently someone else had joined his son in that secret chamber. Melissa wasn't happy about his decision this morning, but he would no longer subject her to the dangers awaiting her at the cabin.

When it came to his work, he'd learned to separate his personal life from the mission at hand. There was no other way to survive.

On his trip up the canyon he received a call from Roman. "Travis, I just talked to the detective at police headquarters about the fingerprints you lifted at the cabin. The one taken off the pine table was a match for the prints found at the crime scene in Douglas, Arizona, of that elderly couple. It's the man you fingered at Grampy's."

"That had to be a one-in-a-million shot. I can't believe it paid off."

"It's more like a billion. I'd bet on your vibes anytime, comrade. There's more. The left front tire on the camper has the two cuts that showed up on the tire tape at forensics. That puts him at the cabin, to provide the link. One more thing, Travis. He's on the FBI's Most Wanted list. I'm afraid he's right up there with your wife's killer," Roman said in a quieter voice. "At least you have one of them in your sights, and he won't be getting away."

Adrenaline shot through Travis. "What does his rap sheet look like?"

"It's a mile long. His name is Luis Manuel Carvelo."

"He didn't sound or look Hispanic."

"He's probably mixed blood and bilingual. As for his hair, he bleaches it. But his earlier photo shows him with black hair, slicked back. He's wanted for unlawful flight to avoid prosecution, murder, kidnapping, rape and parole violation. In July of 2010 he shot and killed three gang members in Holbrook, Arizona. A year later he kidnapped, raped and murdered a woman in Lake Havasu.

"Carvelo is believed to work for a Colombian drug cartel, and is known to travel between the U.S. and Colombia via Mexico. His rap sheet says he may have a tattoo on the back of his neck—and with you on the case, we know he does. You're a great asset, Travis."

"It works both ways."

"The Feds are ready to move in as soon as you give the signal."

That moment couldn't come too soon for Travis. Jose's latest information via the listening device confirmed what he'd been worried about: the illegals had indicated the coming weekend would be the end of the harvest. By next week they'd have made a haul worth millions on the streets.

It was now or never for Travis. He had to find the marijuana grove while the men were still working it. Otherwise they'd move on and start another plantation somewhere else, and the culprits would slip through his fingers.

"I hope to have news by nightfall."

"Be careful."

"Always."

Travis clicked off and turned onto another firebreak road that gave him access to an area he needed to explore. After climbing out of his truck and locking it, he moved into the shadows of the forest and began hiking quickly. This side of the mountain was definitely steeper. It would be a difficult climb to the mine Melissa had mentioned. Even if gold wasn't what the Colombians were after, it might have been, under other circumstances.

Armed with his heat-seeking goggles, Travis zigzagged up the slope. He'd been walking about ten minutes when his boot tip hit something that pitched him forward, straight into a crop of Early Misty marijuana.

Travis leaned over to find black pipes hidden among the plants, evidence of an elaborate irrigation system. He followed it a few hundred yards to a narrow stream. Careful now, he waded through the twists and turns. At a certain vantage point his goggles picked up human forms. He counted six men working above him. One of them was Carvelo.

After the way the killer had eyed Melissa when she'd walked up to the window at Grampy's, there was no doubt in Travis's mind he was the man who'd had plans for her. *It's not going to happen, you monster.*

Reaching for his camera, Travis took shots of the entire area including the makeshift camp. He saw a couple of rifles propped against a log. Obviously, the illegals were prepared to fight off other traffickers who might want the same rewards.

There were natural springs and hundreds of feet of irrigation piping, with sprinklers to water the plants. Garbage was strewn everywhere, including containers of fertilizer and other chemicals.

It was difficult to guess how many thousands of plants were under cultivation, but Travis had no doubt some of the crap had already been harvested. This close to the firebreak road, it would be easy to haul it off in trucks, with no one the wiser. The Feds would get aerial photographs to identify the perimeter.

Having seen all he needed to see, Travis made a beeline to his truck before it was spotted. On the way down to Kamas, he phoned Roman. "Tell the Feds they can move in. I hit the jackpot. There are six men, Carvelo among them. They're armed. Here are the coordinates."

"I'll relay this to Jose and Lon. They're on their way up. Anything you need, let us know," his boss told him.

"I'm going to park my truck away from the firebreak road, then hike back up and watch for signs of trucks pulling near the camp to pick up the marijuana," he repeated. "I'll get license plate numbers and pictures."

Travis had a personal reason for wanting to see this whole operation go down fast. When it was over, he couldn't wait to see the look on Melissa's face when he told her she had her cabin back to enjoy. And then he couldn't wait to get her alone and make certain things clear to her.

Chapter Nine

Melissa's mother joined her at Linda's house, and they spent the whole day together with the children. After her sister got back from her doctor's appointment, the three of them were able to visit. It gave Melissa a chance to tell them everything she knew about what was happening at the cabin.

Though they were horrified, Melissa assured them that Travis had kept her perfectly safe, and it wouldn't be long before he caught the bad guys. When she told them he was a former Texas Ranger whose wife had been murdered in a revenge killing, the tone of the conversation changed. There couldn't be any question in her loved ones' minds that Travis was of vital importance to her, but for once Linda didn't tease her and her mother didn't pry.

When it got to be seven o'clock, Melissa drove home to her condo, half expecting Travis would have called her by now. Finally the phone rang. She picked up without looking at the caller ID.

"Hello?"

"Is this Melissa Dalton?"

"Yes?" She didn't recognize the voice.

"This is Pat Lawrence, Travis's sister."

"Oh, hello! He's told me wonderful things about you and your family."

"I've heard a lot of good things about you, too, and hope you don't mind my phoning."

"Not at all." Melissa's pulse raced. "Did he call you?"

"No. Travis gave me your phone number this morning before he left for the mountains. He indicated he might not get home before tomorrow, or even the next day. Realizing how Casey worries when he's late, Travis said you would know how to comfort him."

It meant the world to Melissa that Travis trusted her enough to provide backup in case of an emergency. "Is Casey anxious now?"

"He has that solemn look on his face. A few minutes ago he asked if he could talk to you."

"Oh, of course he can."

"All right. Just a minute and I'll get him."

Her heart was racing by the time he came to the phone. "Melissa?"

"Hi, sweetheart. How are you doing?"

"Have you heard from my dad?" He was worried, all right. Otherwise he would have answered her question, if only to tell her what Dexter was up to.

"No, but I do know he's working hard on the case. Just remember he has a whole backup team that works with him, so they keep each other safe."

"I know," the little boy said in a subdued voice. "I want to go home. Could you come to my house and stay with me till he gets there?"

He wants me, rather than his aunt? Melissa's throat

swelled with emotion. "Of course. I'll come now. Do you have a key?"

"Yup."

"Great. When you see my Jeep in the driveway, then run across the street."

"Okay. See ya!" He ended their conversation on a happier note.

Since it was possible Travis wouldn't be home until tomorrow or even the next day, she pulled out an overnight bag and packed the clothes and toiletries she'd need. On top of them she put in some of her art supplies and her portfolio. Casey might like to look through it.

Before long she'd left her condo and driven the short distance to Lone Peak Estates. No sooner had she pulled into the driveway than Travis's sister walked Casey across the street. Dexter came running up to Melissa while the two women shook hands and chatted. They all went inside Travis's house. Casey hurried to his room to put on his pajamas.

"I brought enough clothes to stay through the weekend if I have to," Melissa confided. "Travis has been setting up a sting. I'm presuming it could take several days."

"The idea was that when he moved here and took the P.I. job, he'd be in less danger. But we both know it's *all* dangerous."

Melissa eyed Pat, who resembled her brother and was very attractive. "At the movie, Casey told me his dad went after bad guys. I think it's what Travis was born to do."

"I *know* it was."

"For what it's worth, I have total confidence in him," Melissa said. "There's an authority about him. That picture of him over Casey's bed says it all. Travis has no idea how much I admire him." The throb in her voice had to be a giveaway.

Casey's aunt studied Melissa for a moment. "You're so different than Valerie."

"You're kidding! According to Travis, if you don't look too closely, I'm a dead ringer for her."

"You have similar coloring, but you're nothing alike. She was terrified of the work he did. In fact, she was so scared she begged him to quit after every case. It was a constant source of trouble between them. They almost divorced over it."

This was news to Melissa. Somehow she had this idea everything had been perfect between them. "I didn't realize."

"My brother has gone through hell believing that if he'd gotten out of the Rangers, she'd still be alive. But as I've reminded him, not every man is lucky enough to love what he does and be a natural at it. In Texas he's a hero to many people."

"He's a hero to our family," Melissa confessed emotionally. "Thank heaven he went to work for Lufka's. You should see how fast and thoroughly he set things up at the cabin that first day. I never saw anything like it in my life!"

"He can't stay away from what he knows and does best. Of course it's tragic that Valerie was killed, but none of us has a guarantee in this life. Our own parents were killed by a train."

Melissa nodded. "Casey told me."

"I'd better get home," Pat whispered, as her young nephew came running in the kitchen. "Call me if you need anything."

"Of course. We'll keep in touch."

"Good night, Casey." Pat kissed the top of his head and left the house.

"Will you sleep with me tonight?" the boy asked.

"Sure. Let's go to your room and I'll change into my jammies."

"What kind are they?"

"I don't have Spider-Man. Mine are just navy sweats."

"Oh."

They walked to his bedroom at the rear of the house. She disappeared into the bathroom. When she came out, she'd removed the combs from her hair and was wearing it loose, so she could give it a good brushing.

"Wow! I've never seen your hair like that before! You look different."

She guessed she did. "Don't you like it down?" It touched the top of her shoulders.

"I *love* it. You should wear it that way all the time."

"Well, thank you for the compliment. Why don't you pick out a couple of your favorite books? After you say your prayers, we'll read until we fall asleep."

"Hooray!"

A half hour later they pulled up the covers. Dexter crept into the space between them.

"Night, Melissa. I love you," Casey sighed.

Hot tears trickled from the corners of her eyes. "I love you, too. Sleep tight."

AT SIX IN THE MORNING Travis pulled into the driveway. His heart thudded when he discovered Melissa's Jeep there. He came to a stop and closed his eyes tightly. Casey must have asked Pat to call her or Melissa wouldn't be here. He exhaled a sigh of gratitude that they were both safe inside.

There was so much to tell her. Now he wouldn't have to go over to her house tomorrow to talk to her, or track her down if she wasn't there.

He tried to be quiet as he let himself in the front door, but Dexter was right there to greet him. Travis picked him up and carried him through the house. He passed Casey's bedroom and saw two heads against the pillows, sound asleep. Half a dozen books lay on the floor. What a sight!

"You're going to spend the rest of the night with me," Travis told Dexter, after he'd shut the door to his own bedroom. He set the Scottie down. Taking a few more steps, he fell across his bed, dirty and exhausted.

Nothing else registered until he felt a nudge on his shoulder. Light filled the room.

"Daddy? Wake up. Melissa's fixing us dinner."

Dinner? "What time is it?"

"Five o'clock."

Travis's lids opened. Through bleary eyes he saw his son, and pulled him into his arms. It was so wonderful getting back to normal! He rolled Casey on his back and tickled him until he begged him to stop.

"Hey, what's all that black on you?"

Travis could just imagine what he looked like after the night he'd lived through. "I guess I should take a shower, huh?"

"You need a shave, too. It scratches."

Travis saw movement in the doorway, but almost didn't recognize Melissa with her hair down and flowing around her shoulders. Talk about a vision.

"Welcome back." She smiled. "This room smells like there's been a fire in here. Come on, Casey. While your father does what he has to do to make himself presentable—if that's possible—we'll get dinner on the table."

Travis grinned at her. "That bad, huh?"

She nodded. "Pretty awful. Even Dexter didn't want to stay in here any longer."

Travis barked a laugh. "How come you're not running away?"

"I don't know. There must be something about you, but I'll have to think about it," she teased.

"Give me five minutes."

"Take ten, *please*."

More laughter rolled out of him. After everyone disappeared, he got out of bed and stretched before going into his bathroom to shower. One look at his soiled clothes convinced him they'd need two to three washings to get clean again.

He hurriedly showered and shaved, then pulled on clean jeans and a sport shirt. When he emerged from his room, the smell of Italian food drew him to the breakfast room. Melissa and Casey must have gone to the grocery store during the day. The dinner she had prepared made him salivate. Along with lasagna, there was a fruit salad dotted with fat strawberries and daubs of whipped cream.

Travis sat down at the table, trapping her gaze. "This all looks so good, I don't know where to dig in first."

"Try these bread sticks!" Casey blurted, eating one as fast as he could. "Melissa made them all by herself. She let me twist them."

"I'd say you did a great job." Travis reached for one and ate it in two seconds. "You could make a whole meal of these."

"Hey, Dad," Casey said. "How come you got so dirty?"

"I was just going to ask you the same question," Melissa said.

He checked his watch. "It's almost five-thirty. If we turn on the TV to Channel Five, you'll get your answer."

"TV? I'll do it!" Casey slid out of his chair and ran over to the portable on the counter. When he switched it on, the local announcers were talking about a truck that had overturned near Saint George on I-15, and thousands of bees in their hives had spilled out onto the freeway. Beekeepers had to be sent for to clear up the mess.

"Uh-oh," Travis said. "I hope Abby doesn't see this."

"She'll freak out!" Casey exclaimed.

"Who's Abby?" Melissa said.

"One of our friends, huh, Daddy? She got stung by a bee and now she's afraid of them."

"Oh, dear. That's no fun."

"She's the stepdaughter of my friend Chaz Roylance, another P.I. at the firm," Travis explained. "It might interest you to know she's Lacey Pomeroy's three-year-old daughter."

Melissa's eyes flickered. "My favorite former host of the *Stargazer Paranormal* show?"

"The very one. They got married at the beginning of the summer. That's why she went off the air. He was hired to find the person stalking her. I'll tell you their story sometime. When the guys and I plan the next party, you'll meet her."

"I can't wait!"

"She's awesome," Casey interjected. "She believes in flying saucers."

"I know," Melissa said. "So do I."

"You do?"

Before there was any more talk, the TV announcer moved on to the next story.

"Once again Utah is in the news. Due to a tip-off, federal agents have seized a marijuana plantation in the mountains above Kamas. They estimate the street value of the marijuana, known as Early Misty, is $40 million. Our helicopter news team has been on the scene since early morning as agents and police swept in to confiscate guns and equipment, and burn what these illegals have tended all summer with the hope of harvesting.

"If you recall, there was a seizure of marijuana on Boulder Mountain several years ago. Utah seems to be becoming a prime target of cartels who are having trouble smuggling drugs across the Mexican border. They've chosen to grow their crop here and then ship it to the Midwest. These workers were caught red-handed and arrested on sight.

"It's determined they're from Colombia. They've labored hard all season to produce this huge crop, but sometimes hard work is not rewarded—as they've found out today. In this case, the Feds also captured a Colombian who's been on the FBI's Most Wanted list for close to two years. These mug shots identify him as Luis Manuel Carvelo, a notorious escaped convict now in custody after being wanted in Arizona for the deaths of six people."

Melissa's gasp reverberated through the kitchen. Travis saw her grow pale as she stared at him in disbelief. "That's the vile man at Grampy's!"

Travis walked over to turn off the TV. "He had a rap sheet as long as your arm."

"I can't believe it. How did he get hired?"

"He cut and bleached his hair. Using one of his aliases, he passed himself off as a former waiter from California, bilingual in Spanish, who moved to Kamas. He's been living in a camper parked in the garage of those people you told me about who vacation at Lake Tahoe."

"*That's* why you were asking me about them."

Travis nodded. "That camper was one of the vehicles used to transport the marijuana. He probably drove to your cabin many times. The tires on the vehicle matched the tracks outside your place. The whole thing was an elaborate setup, planned months ahead of its execution. Your cabin was closest to the area and made the perfect hangout."

Melissa shivered before getting to her feet. "All those awful men were living in my family's cabin."

"But they're gone now, huh, Daddy?"

Overjoyed that the danger to her was over, Travis reached for his son and lifted him in the air. "They sure are."

Melissa's eyes had filled with tears. "It's all because of you." Her voice shook. "You single-handedly took down a dangerous drug cartel. That criminal would still be out there, killing other people, if it weren't for you. I don't even know where to begin to thank you and your backup crew. My parents and I will always be indebted to you. I've got to call them right now!"

"Go ahead. We'll keep eating."

She dashed from the kitchen to get her phone. By the time they were finishing their lasagna, she reappeared. He could tell she'd been crying happy tears. "My parents want to talk to you." She handed him the phone.

For the next few minutes Travis explained to them what had transpired. They couldn't have been more grateful.

"When things have settled down," her father said, "we'd like to give a party to honor you and all the people at Lufka's who had any part in this. You've rid Kamas of a terrible menace. I guess you know by now this means more to us, and to our daughter, than words can say."

Travis *did* know. He had evidence of it in numerous ways. "She was a big help, Mr. Roberts. And, I might add, a very courageous woman, to keep going up there with me."

Her dad chuckled. "That cabin is special to her. We'll talk to her later and find a time when it's convenient for you to come to our house for an evening with the family, and of course, bring your son. She says he's a delightful young man. We're glad to hear his broken leg is all healed."

"Me, too."

"See you soon. Good night, Mr. Stillman."

Travis clicked off and handed the phone to Melissa who, along with Casey, was playing tug-of-war with one of the dog's toys. "Okay, everybody. What are we going to do after we clean up the kitchen?" Travis had no intention of letting this evening end.

"Can we go up to the cabin and have a sleepover tonight?"

Trust his son to come up with the perfect answer. "That's up to Melissa." Travis's gaze swerved to hers. "Have you had enough of the Stillman family?"

She hugged her arms to her waist in what he'd come to recognize as a nervous gesture. "I don't know what you're talking about. I was just thinking how exhausted you must be. Too tired to drive to Kamas again after all you've been through."

He put an arm around his son. "We love it up there, don't we, bud?"

"Yup."

"Well, if it's what you'd really like to do, then of course it's what I want more than anything."

Casey ran over and hugged her. "I'll have to drive to the town house first and get some more clothes and fresh bedding," she said, after hugging him back. "All the bedding up there needs to be thrown out. I don't want any reminders of what happened up there."

"I don't blame you. We'll clean up here, then head

for your condo and go up in my truck. On the way we'll buy a couple of bundles of wood, so we can make a fire tonight."

Casey gazed up at him in excitement. "Can we roast marshmallows?"

"In the house?" Travis replied.

"It'll be fine," Melissa assured him. "Our family does it all the time. After we get up there, we'll whittle some long sticks."

"Daddy has a really sharp knife."

"Great!" Her eyes flew to Travis. "Then we're set. When you buy the wood, pick up marshmallows and popcorn, too."

His son's shriek of happiness filled the house.

TWILIGHT WAS TURNING INTO darkness as they reached the cabin. Melissa had to pinch herself to believe they could drive right up to it in the truck without fear that someone was in there or was watching them from the forest.

While she opened the front door and turned on the generator so they could have lights, Casey helped his father bring in the groceries and wood. Dexter ran around sniffing in all the corners, while Travis went outside once more for their overnight bags. Melissa carried in the bedding she'd brought from her condo.

"Will you sleep with me again tonight?" Casey asked her.

Before Melissa could answer, Travis said, "You and I, bud, are going to sleep downstairs in one of the bedrooms. We'll let Melissa decide which one."

She flicked him a glance. "How about the one with

the big family picture on the wall? That bed is more comfortable. While you guys get the fire going, I'll put clean sheets and quilts on the beds we'll use tonight." The thought of those awful men using the bedrooms made her sick. While she was at it, she would give the bathrooms another scrubbing.

Their various jobs kept them busy. "Robin Hood had nothing on you," she said as Travis came in with three long, straight sticks, each with a point.

His wide smile caused her toes to curl. "Anything for you, my lady."

Once she'd microwaved the popcorn and poured it into a bowl, she put it and the bag of marshmallows in Casey's lap. He'd changed into his pajamas and was sitting in the middle of the couch, watching the flames. Dexter had jumped up and was nestled against his other side, inching his way toward the food.

After she'd lit two lanterns and turned off the generator, she brought napkins and planted herself on the couch next to him. "This is what I call cozy."

Travis's eyes when they met hers seemed to smolder, but maybe it was just a reflection of the fire. He asked Casey to hand him the marshmallows. "Don't feed any to Dexter or he'll get sick."

"I know. Can he have popcorn?"

"Maybe a couple."

Melissa watched with silent laughter as Casey fed the dog one piece of popcorn at a time, half hiding it under his leg.

Travis put a marshmallow on the end of a stick. "How do like yours cooked, Melissa?"

"Charred."

"That's funny. So do I."

"Yeah, black on the outside and gooey on the inside."

His deep chuckle seemed to rumble through her body. They'd probably have stomachaches in the morning, but she didn't care as she popped a third one in her mouth. Tonight wasn't like any other.

She was in love. Madly in love with a fabulous man.

As for his son, she loved him so much, she could almost believe she'd given birth to him.

The night wore on and the fire started to die down. Casey grew less talkative and eventually fell asleep against her shoulder. It had been a big day. Travis got to his feet with the stealth of a panther and carefully lifted the boy from the couch.

"Don't go away," he whispered to Melissa before carrying his son to the bedroom. As if she would go anywhere. His words acted like an electrical charge, igniting every part of her. Dexter jumped down and followed him.

Travis, without Dexter, returned in minutes. The look of desire he gave her couldn't be mistaken for anything else. She heard his sharp intake of breath before he got to the couch and followed her down with his body, pressing her against the cushions.

"Melissa," he cried urgently. "I need you tonight. Hold me. Kiss me."

He was actually trembling. In wonder, she wrapped her arms around him and let go of every inhibition, needing his kiss more than she needed air. She felt his fingers work their way into her hair. His touch brought exquisite pleasure.

Tonight she had the feeling he wanted *her.* That he was kissing *her,* not his deceased wife. Melissa didn't know how she knew. Maybe the talk with his sister had helped her turn a corner. All she knew was that this felt right and they were on fire for each other.

"If anything had happened to you..." he whispered against her throat. "The thought of him touching you..."

She cupped his face with her hands. "Him? Who are you talking about?"

He made a self-deprecating sound. "No one." He kissed her lips. "Forget what I said." Once again he crushed her mouth with his, thrilling her. But she couldn't get what he'd said out of her mind.

"Travis, what did you mean? You know I haven't been seeing another man."

A heavy sigh escaped his throat before he lifted his head. "One of the Colombians had been watching you. He talked about you. After Jose translated what was on the listening device, that was it. I couldn't let you come up here again until they were captured."

She wound her arms around his neck. "It was that predator at Grampy's, wasn't it?"

"It doesn't matter. He's been arrested. I can't believe I spoke my fears out loud." Travis buried his face in her hair.

Melissa could believe it. "You've just come off the case. It's only natural. Did you help with the actual arrests?"

"Yes. One of them led me on a wild chase and almost escaped."

She hugged him harder. "I can't comprehend hand-to-hand combat. You're made of sterner stuff than most men. I can't thank you enough for protecting me. To be that brave… As Casey always tells me, you're awesome." Melissa had run out of adjectives, and pressed her mouth to his, needing to show him how she felt.

Travis's hunger matched hers, but she was aware there was something troubling him deep down. As far as she knew, he'd still had no word of his wife's killer. But she didn't want to bring that up now. This had been the most heavenly night she'd ever known.

His mouth roved over her face, her throat, and he moaned. She gave an answering moan—she couldn't seem to get close enough to him, either. Suddenly she felt a shudder rack his powerful body. He levered himself away and got to his feet, putting distance between them. She was reeling. To be so passionately enthralled, and then for it to stop…

"What's wrong, Travis?"

He stared at her so strangely. "*This* is wrong. Several hours ago your parents thanked me for making the cabin safe for you. So what do I do? I bring you up here and ravage you, with my son in the next room."

"It's what I wanted, too. So tell me what really happened just now."

Travis had a habit of rubbing the back of his neck when he was trying to come up with an explanation he thought she could handle. But their relationship had gotten past that stage. "I could feel myself losing control," he said. "When I heard you moan, I remembered what you told me about your ex-husband."

She blinked. "That moan you heard was sheer ecstasy, not terror."

"How can I believe you? The last thing I want to do is make a fatal mistake with you and have you think I've suddenly turned into Mr. Hyde."

The bleak look on his face shattered her. She got to her feet. "Travis, he was a sick man. I've had enough therapy and have been with enough men since my divorce to realize Russ was one of a small few. When I met you, you were so in control there've been times when it's driven me crazy. You're the heroic Texas Ranger around everyone else, but when you're with me, I *want* you to be out of control."

"I want to believe you, but—"

"But what?" she interrupted. "Could this be a smoke screen for what's really going on here?"

His eyes narrowed to dark slits. "What do you mean?"

Sharp, stabbing pain took over. "I think you know. Ironic, isn't it? I can't get far enough away from the memory of my spouse. But you can't get close enough to yours. For a little while tonight you tried to forget, but before we got past the point of no return, you couldn't be tempted, because I wasn't Valerie.

"I'm not blaming you. How could I? She was the love of your life and hasn't been gone that long. It's a fact, and no skirting around the issue is going to change it."

"You're more wrong than you know." His voice sounded as if it came from a deep cavern.

"No. You grew up under a code of honor and couldn't forsake it if you tried. Tonight you proved it by not using me, by not pretending to feel something you couldn't feel. You're a noble soul, Travis. Believe me when I tell you that you're the finest man I've ever known. One day you'll get the reward you deserve simply for being *fantastic you.*" She started for the wooden staircase.

"Melissa…"

She paused at the bottom and turned to him. "When you take me home tomorrow, I want it to be for the last time. I know it will be hard on Casey for a little while, but he'll get over it because he has you for a father. You'll know what to say to comfort him. Let's end it now so Casey won't realize what's happening when you drop me off tomorrow. Goodbye, Travis. Thank you for everything. God bless the two of you."

Chapter Ten

"How come you're not eating?"

Travis looked at Mitch. "I'm not hungry."

"That's what you said when we met here last week," Chaz reminded him.

The Cowboy Grub was their favorite hangout for breakfast, but meeting with his friends this morning had been a mistake. Since the marijuana bust a week ago, Travis had taken on and solved two new cases to keep busy, but his turmoil had reached a level where he could no longer function. The guys didn't deserve to see him like this.

"Is Casey still in as bad a shape as you?"

"Afraid so. He blames me and won't talk to me unless he has to."

"I understand his frustration." Mitch was a straight shooter. "Maybe you need to break down and tell us why you're really staying away from her. If you don't talk to somebody about this soon, you're going to crack."

Chaz nodded. "We'd like to help."

Travis rubbed his eyes, then stared at both of them. "Melissa suffered trauma in her marriage, and then suffered it again when her cabin was invaded. She doesn't need to get any more involved with me when we know Valerie's killer is still out there somewhere, looking for me."

"Chances are the Feds will catch up with him and he'll be locked away soon."

"True, Mitch," Travis replied. "And to Melissa's credit, she never brought it up after the first time I told her, but it isn't something you forget. Valerie hated my job as a Ranger. Melissa probably hates the work I do now."

"I hear you," Mitch said in a solemn tone. "When I asked Heidi to marry me, I have to admit I was relieved that the killer who'd tried to take me out back in Florida was finally in custody. But I wouldn't have let it stop me from being with her. Not unless she'd pulled away from me because of it."

Chaz eyed Travis with compassion. "I made a certain promise after I got out of the SEALs, but as we all know, in our business sometimes things go wrong despite our best efforts. I thought I'd lost Lacey because the stalker turned out to be her sister, but after she was arrested, Lacey found me while I was on vacation, and convinced me she was thankful for the work I did. In the end, she said it helped her sister get therapy, and it brought us together.

"As I see it, you need to go to Melissa. After you've told her the thing you're most worried about, let *her* decide if she wants to continue the relationship."

"If you stay away from her, you could be making the biggest mistake of your life," Mitch warned.

They were right.

Having made up his mind, Travis pushed himself away from the table and got to his feet. "I've got to talk to her. Thanks for being here for me."

"You've been there plenty for us."

Within a few minutes Travis was in his truck and on the way to her clinic. He decided not to phone. He couldn't risk her not calling him back. She'd told him Fridays were her busiest days, but he didn't care. He'd wait there until her lunch hour if he had to, so they could talk.

At nine-thirty he walked through the doors and headed straight for her office. To his frustration it was locked. He went to the exercise room, but she wasn't in there. Without hesitation he approached the secretary at the front desk. They recognized each other and nodded.

"Hi. I'm looking for Ms. Dalton."

"I'm afraid she won't be coming in today. She called in last evening and said she wasn't feeling well. But I'm sure she'll be back on Monday. If you're here to make an appointment for Casey, I'll schedule it in her calendar now."

"No, this is personal. If by any chance she should phone the clinic, will you ask her to call me pronto? She has my number."

"Of course."

Travis hurried outside. When he'd driven to the clinic, he'd been so anxious to see her, he hadn't been looking for her Jeep. Now that he glanced around, he realized it was nowhere in sight. He got back in the truck and took the route she normally drove to her town house. On the way he phoned her, but all he got was her voice mail. He asked her to call him.

When he drove up in front of the condo, one glance revealed her Jeep wasn't there, either. Maybe she'd gone to the pharmacy for some medicine. He knew which one and took off. The parking lot was only semifull. There was no Jeep anywhere.

Maybe she'd gone to her parents' or her brother's house. Travis phoned both numbers on the off chance she'd sought them out because she didn't feel well and wanted their company. Again he was met with voice mails. He left messages for them to contact him if they knew where he could reach Melissa.

His mind turned over other possibilities. She might have gone to the cabin after work last evening, and started feeling sick there. Since it was her favorite place, she'd probably decided to stay up there the whole weekend. Maybe she'd picked up a bug. Children coming in and out of the clinic carried germs and could have infected her.

The worrisome thought that she might be really sick and too weak to drive back down the canyon galvanized him into action. He took off for Kamas, breaking the speed limit all the way up. En route, he phoned Deana and asked her to pick up Casey after school. If he couldn't get back tonight, then she was to take him over to Pat's house for the night. It was time he and Melissa had a heart-to-heart.

AFTER ANOTHER RESTLESS NIGHT, Melissa got up determined to get some artwork done. But the creative juices weren't flowing and hadn't been since she'd said goodbye to Travis. Without bothering to dress, she stayed in her gray sweats and went downstairs in her zip-up slippers with her art supplies.

The generator was still on from last night. She fixed herself some instant coffee in the microwave, then turned off the switch. Silence reigned once more, the way it was supposed to in the forest. She opened the back door to a beautiful fall morning. Utah truly was a land of sunny skies.

Once she'd finished her drink, she put her folding chair outside the back door and set up her easel. She'd brought her big art pad down, along with her acrylics. Being up here, instead of at work at the clinic, should have made her feel guilty. But Melissa had been feeling ill all week and knew she couldn't have made it through today's heavy schedule.

She didn't know how to fix her broken heart.

Travis...

Tears rolled down her cheeks. Without realizing it, she began doing a sketch of his well-shaped head. He was a man in his prime, with lines of experience and character etched into his face. A beyond-gorgeous jaw, a wide mouth that could harden or soften, depending on his mood...

His deep-set blue eyes gleamed with intelligence. His ears and nose were in perfect proportion to his other features. His hair was a dark, rich chestnut. And the way he was put together left every other man she'd known out of the competition.

Her love for him poured out on the paper. She didn't

need to see him in person; he was inscribed on her mind and heart for all time. Anything he wore suited him, but she had to admit she loved the hunter-green shirt he'd worn to the clinic with Casey, a button-down with a collar. She drew it in.

After studying the finished product for a minute, she signed and dated it. Beneath her signature she wrote "My Superhero." This portrait and the one she'd done of Casey were her most prized possessions.

It felt good to spill her emotions onto paper. Once she went back in the cabin and got dressed, she would take a hike with some of her supplies and see if she could find that elk. So noble and majestic. She saw Travis's spirit like that.

She closed her art pad. As she started to gather everything up, someone shoved her to the ground and covered her mouth and nose from behind, cutting off her air. She felt a hard chest as a man slammed down on top of her. In shock, she fought and twisted, managing to bite the grubby hand mashing her face. Blood spurted everywhere.

She heard a string of invectives, but he never let go. There was a ripping sound before he started wrapping her mouth with duct tape. After he got off her and set her on her feet, he turned her around. She made a huge scratch down the side of his acne-pocked cheek before he tied her hands in front of her with a rope.

Melissa's captor was no taller than she was, but he was heavyset and strong as a bull. He put one of his legs between hers so she couldn't move. Blood was now dripping from his face and spattering everywhere.

She'd heard nothing before he'd sneaked up behind her. Her legs shook at the possibility of him having spent the night in the cabin with her, waiting for this opportunity. He had to be one of the illegals who'd escaped the sting operation. She could moan all she wanted for help, but the tape had silenced her, and she was feeling claustrophobic.

"Cooperate with me," he said at last, "and you might live long enough to watch me shoot your boyfriend between the eyes. But I won't do that until he sees you're with me. We'll wait for him to come. After he's dead, I plan to have some fun with you before I finish you off."

This lowlife wasn't a Colombian. In fact, he had a Southern drawl. This monster was a white guy covered in tattoos. About her height, he had stringy brown hair that hung in his face. Each time he tossed his head back, it fell over his brows again.

The second she divined the truth of his origins, he said, "Didn't he tell you about me? I'm sure he did. I'm Danny, the only survivor of the McClusky brothers. We were famous down in Texas. I'm not including Fred, of course. He died a long time ago, when we went swimming and he accidentally drowned. That left Donny and Davey."

Her soul screamed in terror. *This lunatic is Valerie's killer!* Somehow he'd tracked Travis down. Much as Melissa wanted this to be a nightmare, it wasn't.

"We were doing great on our own until some rats squealed on us and we had to kill them. From then on, everything went wrong, and that damn Texas Ranger came after us."

Her captor started leading her into the forest by the rope binding her hands. There was no possibility of getting away from him. He was out of shape and was forced to stop every few steps to take deep breaths, but he continued to pull her through the undergrowth to the top of the ridge behind the cabin.

Where his plaid shirt separated from his pants, she saw another repulsive tattoo. Wanting to take advantage of the early morning light, she hadn't eaten breakfast. That was good, because she would have thrown up.

To her horror, he found two trees growing close together at the edge of a clearing, and spread-eagled her upright between them. Using more rope, he fastened her wrists and ankles so tightly they burned. He groped her on and off. When she tried to elude him, the ropes twisted into her skin. The pain was unbearable. She couldn't sit, bend or lie down.

"I wasn't going to let him put us in prison. But during our escape, Donny and Davey got mowed down by him without them knowing what hit them." While he was stringing her up, the man babbled and bawled like a baby. Then he suddenly turned around with a murderous gleam in his eyes.

"I couldn't let that go, now could I? Not Danny McClusky. So I took my time before I picked off your Ranger's wife so he'd get the message. Then I figured that still wasn't good enough. No siree. The Bible says 'an eye for an eye.' He took two of my family, so I decided to take two of his to make things fair. Don't you see?"

Yes. Melissa saw it only too clearly. But his plan was

faulty. When Travis didn't show up, this madman would eventually get tired of waiting, and come up with another plan. At that point, she would probably be dead. But if by some miracle she was still breathing, she might be able to get away from him.

She had to pray that, with a week having gone by already, Travis had decided not to try to see her again. Surely after this long he'd come to the conclusion that a permanent parting was best for all of them.

What bitter irony! All this week she'd been praying he'd call or come to the clinic, because he couldn't live without her and wanted to convince her of that. She'd lain awake all last night debating whether to call *him*. Life without him was no life at all. While she'd been finishing her portrait of Travis earlier, she'd made up her mind that when she got back to Salt Lake, she'd phone him and ask him to come to her condo so they could really talk.

Incredibly, this killer had kidnapped her at the very moment she'd been planning what she would say to Travis. Now there was no second chance to blurt out her love for him. This monster had the upper hand and would be watching for him if he did come up here looking for her. There'd be no way to warn him except to moan loudly enough that he might hear her. But by then it would be too late.

"I've been looking for over a year. He thought he could escape me, but it just goes to show he isn't as smart as he thinks he is. I have friends who helped me track him down. I found him, all right. And what do you know—he has a kid and a girlfriend."

This was a scene right out of a bad movie.

He was criminally insane and would carry out his plan as surely as the sun went down at night.

"I'm going to keep you tied up right here until he comes for you. I figure if I take you and him out together, that leaves the kid. I'll kill him later."

Oh, my darling Casey!

"Ranger boy sure knows how to pick 'em."

A cold layer of sweat enveloped her body as Danny McCluskey ran his hands over her. She gathered her strength and head-butted him, the impact causing more blood to trickle down his face and chin. She was bleeding, too, but it had been worth it.

With such a short fuse at this point, he was angered by everything. He kept looking around like a crazed animal, obviously expecting someone would come.

She thought again of her last night here at the cabin with Travis. She'd been so afraid he still wanted Valerie that she'd ended it with him. And because she knew her family's plans, Melissa realized no one would be coming up to Kamas this weekend.

For the first time in her life, she had a conviction she was going to die. But not without a fight!

After what seemed like hours of being strung up in this condition, she discovered her eyes staring at the ground cover. Her head drooped, feeling as if it weighed a hundred pounds. If only she could have some water, but there was no way he was going to untape her mouth. Her arms had gone numb and she found it hard to breathe.

It could be days that he left her out here. Or he might

decide to rape and shoot her before he went back to Salt Lake to hunt down Travis and Casey. This maniac would have no qualms about doing something horrible to a boy she loved like her own son. She needed to save them both, but how?

RELIEF SURGED THROUGH Travis when he drove up the road from town and saw her Jeep parked at the cabin. He jumped from the cab and raced to the front door.

"Melissa?" He started knocking. When she didn't answer, he knocked again and waited. He rang her phone once more. No answer. With the sun shining overhead, she might be out in back sketching or painting, even if she didn't feel well.

"Melissa?" he called as he walked toward the rear of the cabin. The last thing he wanted to do was frighten her. "It's Travis! If you can hear me, answer me!" The second he rounded the corner his gut twisted, squeezing the breath out of him.

Not only was the back door open, but there were signs of a struggle. The lawn chair she used had been tipped over and dented. Her acrylic paint tubes were scattered in every direction. He stooped to pick up her art pad, lying on top of an easel that appeared broken.

His heart jumped in terror when he saw blood spatters on the pad.

A few feet away he saw her cell phone, open. He checked her last outgoing call. It had been to her parents at five o'clock yesterday evening. Whoever had surprised her had abducted her too fast for her to call for help.

If she was inside, he had to find out. His training in law enforcement had prepared him for this, but not when the victim was the woman he was crazy in love with.

He hadn't seen Valerie when she was shot. His boss had been the one to tell him. This was different. If he found Melissa lying in there…

Saying a prayer, he went inside. A thorough search turned up nothing. That meant there was a chance she was still alive.

He phoned the firm on his own cell. "Roman?" Travis was in such a rage over the fiend who'd done this, he could hardly manage words. "I'm at Melissa's cabin. Looks like she's been abducted. One of the Colombians must have escaped the net while we were rounding them up a week ago, and has been hiding out. Maybe she caught him using the cabin while she was painting. There's evidence she fought him.

"I'm going after her right now. If this scum thinks he's being followed, there's no telling what he'll do to Melissa. He has plans for her, or he would have killed her on the spot."

"What can I do?" Roman asked.

"Send up Jose and Lon. Tell them to drive to the firebreak road where the marijuana was loaded." There was no doubt in Travis's mind the kidnapper had dragged her to the area where he'd been working most of the summer. "They'll know where to head from there. I'll phone them in a little while."

"I'm on it and will have a helicopter standing by," Roman said. "Go get him."

Travis hurried to his truck. He pulled out his heat-seeking goggles and handgun from his backpack. After putting the weapon in his leg holster, he retrieved his rifle from the locker in the back of the truck. Fully equipped, Travis started through the forest on a run.

He had to find her—find her in time…

Forty-five minutes later he got a call from Jose. The guys were rushing to the harvest site and would stay in touch. He hung up and kept moving until his thermal goggles picked up an image he hadn't expected to see until he reached his destination.

His heart slammed against his ribs when he saw Melissa strung out between two trees, her head down. A man armed with a rifle emerged from the pines behind her. Travis got down on the ground behind a log. Using it as a prop for his rifle, he took aim at the man's shoulder and pulled the trigger.

The wounded man fell not two feet from Melissa. His rifle landed just out of his reach. He howled from where he lay, spewing venom as Travis ran toward Melissa.

In the next instant he was cutting the ropes off her and gently laying her unconscious form on the ground. He removed the tape from across her mouth, careful not to take any skin with it. He felt for her pulse and rejoiced when he found one. It was weak, but it was there.

Then he pulled out his cell to call Roman. "The kidnapper has been incapacitated. I've got Melissa, but she's unconscious and needs medical attention. Send a helicopter to the clearing where the marijuana was burned. Here are the coordinates. Tell Jose and Lon."

Still hunkered down beside Melissa, Travis pulled a

bottle of water from his pocket and talked to her while he sprinkled droplets on her face in an effort to revive her. "Come on, sweetheart, be alive for me and Casey."

He could hear the chopper now. Suddenly Lon and Jose were on the scene, followed by police. In another minute a medical team was running forward with a stretcher.

Once she was safely strapped on, Travis followed and climbed into the helicopter with her. The blades were still rotating. Within seconds, the craft took off and the team began the process of hooking her up to an IV. After taking her vital signs, they put an oxygen mask over her face.

"Do you think she will be okay?" Travis asked.

"Give her time. She's been through a rough ordeal. We heard she'd been spread-eagled. With her arms extended that tight, and above her heart, she's had a hard time breathing. The oxygen will help her. Don't worry. We'll be at University Hospital in a few minutes."

One of the medics told Travis he looked pale, and suggested he sit down, but he couldn't leave her. He looked at her wrists and ankles. The ropes had made angry-looking red rings around them.

It was because of him that Melissa was on the verge of losing her life. He should have made certain they'd caught every illegal operating up there. Maybe since Valerie's death, he'd lost his edge and should get out of law enforcement altogether. He had to be slipping if one of those Colombians had eluded capture. All week the trash had probably stayed at her cabin at night, waiting for her to show up.

By the time they reached the hospital, she still hadn't gained consciousness. Travis's pain was unbearable as he watched them wheel her into Emergency.

Roman met him as he walked through the doors behind the stretcher. "She might not make it," Travis rasped.

"She was alive when you found her. Don't lose hope now."

"I'm no good anymore, Roman. This is my fault. I wasn't thorough enough during the sting. One got away, and now Melissa's life is on the line because of my mistake."

Roman grabbed his shoulders. "What are you talking about? Don't you know it was Danny McClusky who kidnapped her?"

"What?" Travis's mind reeled.

Chaz spoke up behind him. "He tracked you here, but received the surprise of his life when you got him with your rifle."

"It's true," Mitch interjected. "Your wife's death has been avenged in a miraculous way. As I see it, you have smooth sailing from here on out."

Travis grimaced. "Not if Melissa doesn't make it. She must wish she'd never met me."

"You know better than that. Let's go see how she's doing."

The four of them walked toward the cubicle, but were told to wait until the doctors had finished their examination. Travis buried his face in his hands. The waiting felt like an eternity.

"Travis?"

He looked up to see Jose and Lon, who'd just come in on the other helicopter. Lon was carrying her bloodied sketch pad. "We thought you might like to see what's inside." He flipped it open and Travis found himself looking at his own image. He was staggered by Melissa's talent. And the words at the bottom said it all.

Roman's eyes gleamed. "It's a very good likeness of you, comrade. I think we should hang it in the office."

"Notice the date." Chaz was smiling.

It had been this morning.

Tears prickled Travis's eyelids. "If it hadn't been for you guys urging me to talk to her..."

"You'd have gone to find her, anyway. You were a mess without her," Mitch said.

Chaz nodded. "You were."

Suddenly, a doctor stepped from behind the curtain. "Is one of you Travis? The patient's asking for him."

Travis felt half a dozen slaps on his back before he rushed into the cubicle.

She was bruised and banged up. They'd cleaned her forehead and had put a butterfly tape over the cut. She was hooked up to oxygen, as well as an IV, but it didn't matter because her eyes were open. And she was the most beautiful sight he'd ever seen.

Her poor mouth was covered in blisters, and he lowered his head and kissed her cheek. When he met her gaze, his eyes filled with tears.

"I prayed you'd c-come," Melissa said, her voice weak. "Then I prayed you w-wouldn't because he was waiting for you. He threatened to kill C-Casey." Tears gushed from her eyes and down her temples to the sheet. "Is Casey all right? Does he know anything?"

"He's fine," Travis whispered "And no, he knows nothing about this."

"Don't ever let him know. I want him to always love the cabin."

"It will be our secret."

The doctor pulled the curtain aside. "I'm sorry to disturb you, but we're taking her upstairs to a private room. She's been given a sedative. You can come, but she needs to rest now."

"Understood."

"Don't l-leave me, Travis."

"I won't, I swear."

As he left the cubicle, an older couple rushed forward. "I'm Melissa's mother. We're so grateful to you for saving our daughter's life, you'll never know." She hugged him with surprising strength.

Over her head Melissa's father was smiling through tears.

"They're taking her up to a private room," Travis said. "I promised I wouldn't leave her, but I need to call my son. Then I'll join you."

"Go right ahead. We'll see you upstairs."

When he walked outside the emergency room doors to make the call, he announced to his waiting friends, "She's going to be fine."

"That's all we wanted to hear."

Lon handed him the art pad. "I think you'll want to hold on to this. I've got the rest of your stuff and will bring it to the office. A couple of police officers are bringing the truck and Jeep down from the cabin. I told them to drive both to Melissa's house so your son won't be alarmed."

"You think of everything."

Lon smiled. "I'm a father, too."

After everyone left in Roman's big van, Travis phoned Pat.

"Casey's been hoping you'd call," his sister said. "Here he is."

"Dad?"

"Hi, bud. How was school today?"

"It was okay. When are you coming home?"

"Well, I have a date with Melissa tonight."

"You do?" he half squealed in joy.

"Yeah. The problem is, I might get home late."

"Is that 'cuz you're going to kiss and stuff?"

"What makes you think that?" Travis teased.

"I saw you kissing, and Zack told me that's what his parents do all the time."

Travis chuckled. "Will it be okay if you don't see me until tomorrow morning?"

"Yeah. Do you think Melissa will come with you?"

"We'll see."

"You always say that!"

"I know. I love you, Casey." His voice shook. "See you in the morning."

Chapter Eleven

Melissa awakened when the nurse came into her room at 7:00 a.m. on her rounds. That's when she saw Travis seated on a chair next to her bed, studying one of the drawings in her art pad. He looked drained and exhausted. And never more attractive.

The nurse took her vitals and checked the IV. "At this rate you'll be able to go home today." She took the IV out of her arm. "Are you hungry for more than juice?"

"Yes. I'd love some toast."

"I'll bring you some. After breakfast you can get up and shower."

"That sounds heavenly." The nurse's visit reminded Melissa she must look awful.

"The doctor will be in later to check on you."

"Thank you."

Melissa was feeling well enough not to like the way the pretty nurse smiled at Travis before she left the room. Melissa wanted Travis out of the line of fire from all the females working here.

Finally they were alone.

"Hi," she said to this incredible man who'd saved her life.

His warm gaze traveled over her. "How are you feeling?"

"I can't wait to get out of here."

"Ah. If that's true, then it means you're well enough to kiss."

Her pulse raced when he got up and moved close. "You might not like the taste of the salve they put on my lips."

"Don't you know by now that won't stop me?"

"Oh, Travis…" He leaned over and kissed her gently. She didn't want gentle, and flung her arms around his neck to pull him closer. "I love you, I love you. If you don't feel the same way, it doesn't matter."

"But I *do* feel the same way. If you weren't still in the hospital, I'd show you just how much I love you, darlin'. Only you and nobody else."

Though her lips were still tender, she kissed him with all she had. "Yesterday I was afraid I'd never see you again," she said long moments later. "I was a fool to end things with you. It wasn't what I wanted. All week I wanted to call you and tell you I was wrong."

"You don't even *want* to know about the week I had without you." He kissed her neck and throat.

"I'm to blame. You see, I'm a very spoiled girl. But I've repented for wishing to be the first and only love in your life. When I was tied with those ropes, I realized how lucky I was to be the current woman in your life."

Travis raised his head. Even in the dim light, his eyes blazed with fire. "Not only current, but the only one for the rest of our lives."

Her eyes filled. "You mean…"

"I'm asking you to marry me. But before you answer me, I need to ask you something else, and you have to be honest with me."

"Oh, for heaven's sake! I fell in love with a Texas Ranger. That's what you'll always be to me, and I wouldn't want you any other way. As your oh-so-wise sister said to me recently, there are no guarantees in this life. Let's agree to love each other and stop worrying about what might happen. Frankly, I'm sick of it."

A chuckle escaped his throat before he worked an arm beneath her head so he could give her the deep kind of kiss she was aching for. When he finally relinquished her mouth, she whispered, "I'll marry you whenever it can be arranged, but before this conversation goes any further, *I* need an answer to a very important question."

"This wouldn't have anything to do with children, would it? Because if it does, you need to know I want more than one. Valerie was afraid to have more for fear—"

Melissa put a finger to his lips. "Say no more. I've always wanted a family of three or four children, as long as it was with the right man. We've already got our first with Casey. Besides you, he's the light of my life. But there's a cabin up in Kamas with enough bedrooms to house a new generation."

The two of them were laughing when the doctor popped in. "That's a happy sound I hear." He eyed Travis. "If you'll step out for a minute."

"Of course."

When Melissa was alone with the doctor, she said, "If

my heart rate is up, it's because of him. He just asked me to marry him."

The doctor finished checking her over. "I take it you said yes?"

"Oh, yes."

The man smiled. "Under the circumstances, I'll sign you out to go home, but go easy for a few days. Have your regular doctor check the cut on your forehead in a week. If that bandage did its job, there shouldn't be a scar. If there is, you can check with a plastic surgeon. Stay hydrated."

"I will. Thank you."

Melissa couldn't wait to see Casey's reaction to their news.

"IT'S ELEVEN O'CLOCK, Dad. How come it took you so long to pick me up?"

Travis glanced in the rearview mirror at his son and Dexter before he started the truck. "Melissa bumped her forehead getting out of the Jeep. I had to take her to the doctor to get a bandage put on it."

His eyes rounded. "Did she need stitches?"

"Nope. She just has a little headache."

"Oh."

That was the story they felt would go down best with Casey. After going to Melissa's town house in a taxi, he'd picked up his truck and driven back to the hospital to take her home.

"Where are we going?"

"To the grocery store."

"Can Melissa come to our house after?"

"I thought we'd go over to her condo."

"I've never been in it before."

"That's because I've been doing a job for her at the cabin, Casey. When I'm working for a client, I don't generally go to their houses. But now that the case has been solved, she has invited us over, even Dexter."

"I bet she doesn't want me to come."

Travis hadn't been expecting a statement like that. "Of course she does. In fact, she asked me to bring you." He waited for a burst of excitement that didn't happen. "Hey, bud, what's wrong?"

"Nothing."

"I thought you loved her. I know she loves *you*."

"She just says that to be nice."

"She *is* nice, but I don't think she tells that to her other patients. Do you?"

"I don't know." The little boy sighed and looked out the window.

Travis couldn't get any more out of him during their trip to the store. When they pulled up in front of the town house, Casey got out of the backseat with Dexter and headed for her front door. Suddenly it opened.

"Hi, Casey!" That bright voice reminded Travis of those first moments at the clinic. "I'm so glad you're here. Come in!" Melissa stood there in jeans and a creamy, long-sleeved sweater that hid the rope burns on her wrists and ankles.

Amazing what makeup could do. She'd covered up the bruise on the side of her cheek where McClusky had shoved her to the ground. Somehow the lipstick she was wearing disguised the tender spots. Her hair had been freshly washed and left loose to swing against the sides of her neck. On the whole, she didn't look as if she'd been through the ordeal he'd witnessed yesterday.

But one thing was missing. He could tell she was waiting for Casey's hug. When it didn't happen, she darted Travis an anxious glance as he put the groceries on the kitchen counter at the other end of the living room.

An exuberant Dexter danced around her, but Travis couldn't say the same for his son who stared at the bandage. "Does your head hurt?"

"I took a painkiller and now I feel fine. Thanks for asking. You've never been in my house before, have you? It's really little. Would you like to take a tour?"

"Okay."

Melissa worked with children all the time. She was a master at not showing her surprise over his uncharacteristic behavior, and pretended he was delighted to be here.

While they walked around, Travis followed. On the living room walls she'd hung a grouping of large framed prints of Picasso and Matisse. Her contemporary furniture added the rest of the color. The place exuded warmth.

They went down the hall. She'd turned the smaller bedroom into an art studio. He could tell Casey was impressed, but the boy remained sober.

In her bedroom, small framed photographs of her family sat on the dresser. Casey studied everything, and was ready to walk out again when he blurted, "Hey, Dad, look!"

"Where?"

"Over the bed. Melissa painted *me!*"

In a twinkling, his whole demeanor changed.

Travis put his arm around Casey's shoulder and they moved closer to examine the good-size framed painting hanging over her bed. He could have sworn this hadn't been on the wall when he'd helped her into the house after leaving the hospital.

The picture filled him with wonder. It *was* Casey, but an older version, the way he might look around age twelve. Melissa had painted him riding an animal with three horns, a creative figment of her imagination. She'd shown him emerging from a prehistoric forest.

He wore animal skins on his lean body and a thong around his forehead, with his chestnut hair spilling over. One hand clutched a spear. His leg carried a jagged scar from thigh to the ankle. The sight of the young superhero brought tears to Travis's eyes.

"Do you like it?" she asked Casey. Travis heard the tremor in her voice.

"I love it! I didn't know you painted me."

"I did this after I first met you, but I've kept it a secret." The revelation thrilled and humbled Travis.

"How come?" Casey asked.

"Because I take care of children all the time, but I'm not supposed to love one of them so much, that I wished he were my son. I love you, Casey. I think I love you too much. That's why I didn't read a story to you the other night. I wanted to be your mommy, but I knew I wasn't, and I was afraid you'd see me cry."

He walked over and looked up at her with eyes more

brilliantly blue than Travis had ever seen them. "Do you want to be my new mom?"

Tears poured down her cheeks. "Yes. More than anything in the world."

Now came the hug. Casey almost crushed her. They clung for a long time.

"You know how you have that picture of your daddy above your bed because you love him?" she finally asked.

His son nodded.

"That's the same reason I have your picture above mine."

Casey's head whipped around. "Dad?"

"She loves you, Casey. Did you hear that?" His son literally glowed with happiness. "And do you know what's *really* amazing?"

"What?"

"She loves me, too."

"I already know that."

"How do you know?" His eyes met Melissa's while they waited for Casey to come out with something startling.

"'Cuz I've seen you kissing."

Travis laughed for sheer joy. "Well, there's one thing I bet you don't know."

"What?"

"I asked Melissa to marry me last night."

"I *knew* you were going to."

"You knew?" Melissa made a sound between a laugh and a cry.

"Yup. You said you were going on a date with her.

Zack said that after Mitch kissed Heidi on a date, they got married."

"Sheer deduction." Melissa grinned at Travis. "I'm not surprised. It looks like those two are so smart, they'll probably grow up to be P.I.s like their dads."

"Nope." Casey shook his head. "I'm going to be a Texas Ranger!"

Melissa embraced them both. "Your son has mighty big shoes to fill," she whispered against Travis's cheek. "Will you do me one more favor?"

He kissed her temple. "Anything."

"Please don't let me die of too much happiness yet. Our lives are just beginning."

Chapter Twelve

Outside the cabin windows, golden fall colors interspersed with green pines provided the backdrop for the wedding. Inside, the flowers on the stands by the fireplace and placed around the family room mimicked the tones nature had provided: elegant red roses, orange Asiatic lilies, bronze cushion spray and yellow Viking spray chrysanthemums mixed with greenery. Dark red tapered candles had been added to highlight the rustic setting.

Melissa knew how much Casey was looking forward to Halloween, so she and Travis had planned to get married the Saturday before.

They both wanted a small affair. Only family and close friends on either side, with Melissa's pastor officiating. Even so, a lot of cars lined the road into the cabin. Snow was forecast for the late evening, but she wasn't worried, because after the four o'clock ceremony, followed by a celebration, everyone would have time to get home before it started. Then she'd be alone with her husband, able to shower him with the love she felt for him. Just the thought made her pulse race.

Casey would be going back with his aunt Pat and her family. Later on, in the spring, Travis planned to take them on a week's honeymoon. For now, two nights away was probably as much as Casey could handle.

When they came back down from the cabin, they'd drive straight to Travis's home. They'd already moved her things in, and Melissa had arranged to sublet her town house. Everything had been done, except the ceremony to make them husband and wife.

"Melissa?" the pastor said. "If you and Travis will join me and hold hands…"

Travis, stunning in a tux, intertwined his fingers with hers before they moved to stand in front of the pastor. Melissa wore a cap-sleeved, knee-length, raw-silk dress in an eggshell color. She knew Travis liked her hair long, so she'd left it loose, and wore two roses behind one ear.

"Dearly beloved, we're gathered here in the heart of these mountains to join Melissa Jeremy Roberts and Travis Cederlof Stillman in holy matrimony. It was here they found their love, and so it's appropriate they seal their vows on this very spot.

"All of you here know the way the lives of these two have been fraught with difficult and dangerous obstacles. The fact that they've survived so beautifully shows not only the indomitable human spirit, but proves they've literally fulfilled that part of the vows where they take each other 'for worse.'"

He smiled. "What's left is the 'for better,' and then to go on loving each other, whether rich or poor, through sickness and health, to the end of your lives and beyond. Travis, do you take this woman to be your wife?"

"I do," he said in his deep voice.

"Melissa? Do you take this man to be your husband?"

"With all my heart."

Travis squeezed her hand.

"Then by the power vested in me, I pronounce you husband and wife. What God has joined together, let no man put asunder. Casey?" He nodded at their son, who was standing by with a huge smile. "If you'll come forward with the rings..."

Melissa's eyes brimmed with unshed tears as the little boy, dressed in a tux like his father, and carrying the rings on a pillow, stepped forward. At that moment she could see handsome Casey as a grown man, wearing a tux at his own wedding. One day she would paint him like that. But that time was years away yet, thank heaven!

Travis picked up the interlocking rings and slid them on her finger. Two blue-white diamonds sparkled up at her. He'd been extravagant, but he told her that one diamond represented his love. The other represented Casey's, and they came as a package deal.

With a less than steady hand, she took the gold band she'd picked out for him and put it on his ring finger. When she looked up, Travis pulled her into his arms. In front of everyone he kissed her with long-suppressed hunger before the pastor had time to say anything.

"We know how you feel, comrade," Travis's boss called out in his Russian accent, "but it's time to wind this up."

The onlookers laughed. After being congratulated, Melissa was engulfed with hugs and the party began.

Casey and Zack drank a lot of punch and worked their way through the crowd to her. Abby tagged along behind them. Melissa hugged all three of them before she picked up Casey in her arms and kissed him. "You're my boy now," she said, before lowering him to the floor.

"Yup."

"We'll be outside in front of your school on Monday to take you home. Are you going to be all right till then? You can always call us. We told your aunt."

"I know. Are you going to stay right here?"

"What do *you* think?" Travis had come back and engulfed them in his strong arms. "Melissa and I aren't going anywhere. This is our favorite place."

"Mine, too."

"Your aunt Pat and uncle Jerry are waving to us. It's started snowing. They want to get down the canyon before it piles up. I need another hug."

Casey hugged them both hard, but to his credit he didn't break down and cry. With Zack watching, he had too much pride.

"Call us when you get home, okay, bud?"

"Yup."

"We love you, sweetheart," Melissa said emotionally. With that, he ran through the cabin to the front door, where his aunt and uncle were waiting.

Pretty soon everyone was leaving. Her parents were the last to go. "I don't have to worry about you taking care of her." Melissa saw her dad's affection for Travis. Her parents were crazy about him. More hugs ensued before quiet reigned and they were finally alone.

When she heard Travis turn the lock of the front door, adrenaline began to flow through her body. Her breath caught as he turned to her. Those dark blue eyes were burning with desire for her.

Without saying a word, he walked around, blowing out the candles. Without the generator on, all they heard were the sizzles coming from the fire dying down in the fireplace. Only the fading light from the flames lit the room.

He slid his hand to her neck and they walked over to the window looking out on the forest behind the cabin. "Our first snowfall together. It's so beautiful, Travis."

"Not as beautiful as my wife." He unexpectedly picked her up as if she weighed nothing, and started for the staircase. "I wanted to do this the night we came up here so I could plant the cameras. Watching you climb the steps gave me ideas I shouldn't have been having."

She pressed a warm kiss to his mouth. "I had the same ideas, Travis, but no matter how hard it's been to wait, I'm glad we did. It makes this night unique in our lives."

He returned her kiss as he carried her over the threshold of her bedroom. "You're so precious to me, Melissa. I adore you. Love me tonight, darling. You have no idea how much I need you."

Who would ever have thought that helping each other out of their clothes could be such a breathtaking experience? Time and space had no meaning as they became lovers. They became one flesh, giving and taking pleasure throughout the night.

When morning came, and dazzling sunlight streamed in the window, reflecting off the snow, Melissa found herself nestled against his chest with their legs entwined. She lifted her head. With him asleep, she could feast her eyes on him all she wanted.

No woman could possibly feel the euphoria that enveloped her this morning. It was because no woman alive had been loved into oblivion by this particular Texas Ranger.

Unable to resist, she kissed him around his lips to tease him awake. When he responded by searching for her mouth, she kissed his jaw.

His eyes opened. He took a deep breath. "What are you trying to do to me, woman?"

"So you call me 'woman' now."

"That's right." He raised up and proceeded to crush her mouth with refined savagery. At last he raised his head. "And I'm your man."

"Yes," she said breathlessly.

Another hour passed before she was in any state to form a coherent sentence. "Darling? Could I ask you an important question?"

He gazed at her. "Sure, but what else could you want to know?"

"With the threat of that killer gone, would you like to move back to Fort Davis? There must be a part of you that misses the association with your coworkers. After all the phone calls from them and your former boss, plus the citation from the governor of Texas for meritorious service, don't you miss that life? Because if you do, I have no problem with us moving there.

"I can always find a job in my profession, and I can paint anywhere. The important thing is for you and Casey to be happy. I realize the P.I. job saved your sanity when you moved here, but there has to be a huge chunk of your life you still feel is missing."

He leaned over her, plunging his hand in her hair. "After what you just said, I love you more than ever. But you need to know that with Valerie's death, my days as a Ranger ended. I came here to start a new life and I've learned to love it. My new friends at Lufka's are the greatest. The work I do is just as challenging.

"As for Casey, he has family here. Because of that family, he fell off one of their horses, and the accident that followed ultimately brought us into the exciting world of Melissa Dalton. That was the day the whole world changed for the Stillman family." He cupped her face with his hands. "I don't want to change anything. I want my wife right where she is—in my heart and my bed."

She smiled. "That's all I needed to hear. I guess it will have to be up to Casey to continue the Texas Ranger tradition."

"Maybe. If it's what he really wants."

Melissa raised herself on one elbow. "I think we'd better call him and let him know that we're alive and fine. So far he's shown great restraint."

Travis's smile lit up her universe. "He has, hasn't he?"

"I love that boy. I hope we can give him a little brother or sister."

"After we phone him, I think we should do our best to make that happen."

"Oh, yes, please!"

* * * * *

Salty tears trickled from the corners of her eyes.

"Chase—" Annie half sobbed his name. "Is it too late for us?" She could hardly stand it. After everything they'd shared, how was she going to live this close to him? Every time he hugged or kissed their daughter, Annie remembered how his arms felt around her, how his mouth devoured her, sending them both into euphoric oblivion.

What was it Agent Manning had said? *Because your life was in danger, Dr Myers had no choice but to stay away from you.*

That meant Chase had loved her more than his own life. Did it mean that now they were together again and his secret had come out, he would end up fighting for her in this presumably safe haven? Or was it too late? Love had to be fed, and he'd gone hungry too many years. So had she…

Dear Reader,

Not many people have the experience of seeing someone they've loved and lost come back from the dead, so to speak.

In my story, *The Ranger's Secret,* Annie Bower believed the man she'd loved had been killed in an explosion. Imagine her shock ten years later when she suddenly sees him in Yosemite National Park and he pretends not to recognize her. Put yourself in her place. How would *you* feel? Especially when you've been raising the child the two of you had together—the child who had always wanted to know her father, but realized it was an impossible dream.

Of course, there's the hero's side to this emotional story. Chase Jarvis is the assistant head Ranger who's suddenly forced to confide his secret to Vance Rossiter, the hero you met in *The Chief Ranger.* You'll have to read this second book in the series to find out why such a thing happened and how it all ends.

Enjoy!

Rebecca Winters

THE RANGER'S SECRET

BY

REBECCA WINTERS

First published in Great Britain 2013
by Mills & Boon, an imprint of Harlequin (UK) Limited,
Eton House, 18-24 Paradise Road, Richmond, Surrey TW9 1SR

ISBN: 978 0 263 90085 9
ebook ISBN: 978 1 472 00444 4

23-0213

Harlequin (UK) policy is to use papers that are natural, renewable and recyclable products and made from wood grown in sustainable forests. The logging and manufacturing processes conform to the legal environmental regulations of the country of origin.

Printed and bound in Spain
by Blackprint CPI, Barcelona

Rebecca Winters, whose family of four children has now swelled to include five beautiful grandchildren, lives in Salt Lake City, Utah, in the land of the Rocky Mountains. With canyons and high alpine meadows full of wildflowers, she never runs out of places to explore. They, plus her favorite vacation spots in Europe, often end up as backgrounds for her romance novels, because writing is her passion, along with her family and church. Rebecca loves to hear from readers. If you wish to email her, please visit her website, www.cleanromances.com.

Chapter One

The bride had just fed wedding cake to the groom. Now the photographer grouped the wedding party for one more set of pictures. “You’re in this last one, Nicky. Come and join your parents. Everyone smile and keep smiling. I’m going to take several shots in succession. Say cheese.”

Nicholas Darrow, the precocious six-year-old wearing a tux, didn’t need any urging. Happiness radiated from his cute face and eyes. Nicky was now the adoptive son of his aunt Rachel Darrow Rossiter and his new adoptive father, Vance Rossiter, the chief ranger at Yosemite National Park in California.

A half-dozen rangers from Yosemite had gathered for the late September wedding and reception at Rachel’s father’s home in Miami, Florida. Chase Jarvis chuckled over Nicky. The boy was so crazy about his new daddy, all evening he’d been skipping around the flower-filled house and could hardly stop long enough to pause for a picture. Yet no one could be happier for the three of them than Chase, Vance’s best friend and his best man for the church ceremony.

By this time, most of the guests had gone and the festivities were fast coming to an end. Chase, Vance's second in command, had been named acting head ranger while Vance was on his honeymoon for the next three weeks. As such, Chase and the others needed to head for the airport and fly home. First, however, he had to change out of his tux in the guest bedroom.

"Uncle Chase?" The boy came running after him.

"Hey, Nicky—" They high-fived each other. Vance had taught his new son to call him Uncle Chase. Amazing what power the words *I do* could wield. In spite of no blood ties, Chase had become a part of the Rossiter family and loved it.

"Are you leaving now?"

"Afraid so."

"I wish you didn't have to go yet."

This was progress. From the time Nicky and his aunt had first come to Yosemite, the boy hadn't wanted anyone around Rachel except Vance. Chase had been a pariah—but no longer. Now that everything was legally signed and sealed and Vance and Nicky were now truly father and son in every sense of the word, the boy had finally accepted Chase. It was a great relief in more ways than one.

"Believe me, I'd like to stay longer. But somebody's got to run the Park until your daddy gets back."

"Mommy and I will be coming with him."

Chase laughed. "Don't I know it! We're all going to live right by each other. I can't wait!"

Nicky beamed. "Me neither." For the first time since Chase had met Rachel and her nephew in early June, Nicky threw his arms around Chase's legs. It brought a lump to his throat. He picked him up and gave him a long, hard hug. They'd all been through many painful moments together to get to this joyful place in time.

"Maybe you'll see the Queen while you're in London," Chase said. Nicky loved the Harry Potter story and wanted to see the train station where the children took off for Hogwarts wizard school.

"Yup. And castles and tall red buses and white owls."

"If you see a white owl, you have to be sure and tell me about it in a postcard."

"I will! Daddy says they're not as big as our great horned owls in the park. When we get back I want to watch the bears go to sleep."

More laughter rumbled out of Chase as he changed into trousers and a sport shirt. "It's pretty hard to catch them going to bed," he teased.

"Daddy can do it! We'll use our binoculars and sneak up on them!"

Yes, Vance could do anything in Nicky's eyes. In Rachel's, too. Vance was a lucky man to have that kind of love. For a moment, waves of longing for the happiness he'd once known with Annie Bower swept over him, catching him off guard.

Even after ten years, thoughts of her and the life they'd once planned together assailed him, but evil forces had had a way of destroying that dream, snatching away his heart's desire. By now his beautiful Annie was probably married with several children.

"Nicky?" a familiar voice called out. They both turned to see Vance in the doorway.

"Uncle Chase has to go back and run the park now," Nicky announced.

A broad smile broke out on Vance's face. "Yup. It's all on your more than capable shoulders. I leave its headaches to you with my blessing."

Nicky frowned "Headaches?"

Chase rubbed a hand over Nicky's latest marine haircut. "He means the problems that come up."

"You mean like the bear that climbed in that lady's car and wouldn't come out?"

"Yes, and a six-year-old boy named Nicky who hid from everyone because he didn't want to go back to Florida."

A giggle escaped. "Daddy found me!"

Vance laughed before looking to Chase. "Good luck on your first meeting with the new superintendent. Bill Telford's a recent widower with a son and daughter away at college. I understand he's a real go-getter, full of new ideas. Rumor has it he wants to turn the park on its ear. I'm glad you'll be breaking him in instead of me."

"Let's hope he's not as grumpy as the last one."

"Amen to that."

"So *this* is where everyone is!" Rachel swept into the room in her white wedding dress. She was a vision with her gold hair and lace veil. Rachel's charm and personality reminded Chase of Annie. With hindsight he realized those similarities had caused him to be drawn to Rachel when she'd first arrived at the park with Nicky. But she'd only had eyes for Vance. When she looked at her new husband like she was doing now, the love light in her jewel-green eyes was blinding.

Pain twisted his gut. Annie's smoky-blue eyes used to look at Chase like that… He had no doubt that somewhere in the world she was getting ready to go to bed with her husband and love him the way she'd once loved Chase.

Did she ever think about him?

He wondered how long it was going to take him to get over her and fall in love with someone else. Heaven knows he'd tried. The thought that it would never happen frightened him.

On his flight back to California with the other rangers, he'd tell Ranger Baird to go ahead and set him up with his wife's cousin. For over a year the couple had been pushing to get Chase and her together. Why not relent this once? Seeing Vance and Rachel so happy brought on a terrible hunger for that same kind of fulfillment. He needed to try…

Rachel rushed over to hug him. "Thank you for everything. We'll be back at the park before you know it. Take care, dear Chase."

He grasped her hands. "When is your father's operation?"

"The day after we get back from London. We're leaving tomorrow, but we'll only be in London a week. Then we'll spend the next two weeks in Miami to be with my parents. If all goes well with Dad's heart, we'll bring them to California with us."

"Everyone's pulling for him."

"I know. I can't thank you enough." She hugged him one more time.

Vance signaled to him. "Your taxi's here, Chase. I'll walk you out."

He grabbed his suitcase and followed Vance through the house to the driveway where a couple of cabs waited. One of the drivers put his suitcase in the trunk of the first car. Chase turned to Vance. "Enjoy your honeymoon. If you need a couple more weeks than you planned, you've got them."

"Thanks. We'll see how things go, but I appreciate it. Good luck. I'm going to miss you."

Chase grinned. "Sure you are." He climbed in the back with one of the other rangers and told the driver to head for the airport.

THOUGH IT WAS THE SECOND WEEK of October, the days were still hot in Santa Rosa, California. Annie Bower turned on the air-conditioning and waited in her compact car outside Hillcrest elementary school. It was three-thirty. Any second now class would be over for the day. She had mixed emotions about the news she had to tell her ten-year-old daughter, Roberta.

While she pondered the unexpected job offer that had come in the mail, students poured out the doors of the school. Five minutes later she saw her slender daughter walking toward the car with her dark ponytail swinging. Debbie, her outgoing best friend ran to catch up with her.

Debbie's mother, Julie, a single mom like Annie, drove the girls to school in the mornings. Annie picked them up afterward and kept Debbie at their condo until Julie came for her daughter. The system had been working well for the past two years.

To imagine Roberta having to make new friends in a new environment was troubling to say the least, especially since she was a quiet child who didn't have a large group of friends. However, this new job was something Annie had been hoping to get for a long time. In fact while she'd worked for the California Department of Forestry as an archaeologist for the last five years, there'd never been this kind of opening until now.

The pay wasn't that great, but if she didn't grab it, she could lose out on an unprecedented opportunity to do fieldwork on the Sierra Indians, her particular expertise.

Ten years ago Annie's parents, who lived a hectic social life in San Francisco, had welcomed her back from the Middle East with open arms. They'd tried to comfort her over the loss of Robert and his family. No two people could have been more kind and understanding when they'd learned she was pregnant with his child, but they'd expected her to live with them and couldn't countenance the kind of work she wanted to do, certainly not with a baby on the way.

Her goals were so different from those of her parents'. She'd rented a small apartment, taken out a loan to finish her education and had put her daughter in day care after she was born. When Annie received her anthropology degree, she moved to a condo in Santa Rosa where she'd gone to work for the CDF. Slowly she worked her way up the scale while being the best mother she could be to her daughter.

Every month she spent a weekend in San Francisco so Roberta could visit her grandparents, but they continued to complain about Annie's choices and this created more tension, something she knew Roberta could feel.

If Annie took this new position, her parents would throw up their hands in dismay, indicating their disappointment over her doing something so unorthodox while she had a child to take care of. It was either their way, or no way. Since there was no use discussing it with them, she and Roberta were on their own.

So far they'd been doing fine. Other people had to move where their jobs took them if it meant doing the work they wanted to do. Her father's pharmaceutical corporation meant many thousands of people had to relocate to work for him, but that argument didn't fly when discussing his only daughter and granddaughter's future.

What the decision really came down to for Annie had everything to do with Roberta and how she took the news.

"Hi, girls."

"Hi!" Debbie answered, and got in the car first.

Roberta climbed in the back seat with her, both of them lugging their backpacks.

Annie waited until the school crossing guard allowed her to pull out of the drive and onto the street before asking, "How was school today?"

"Good."

"We had a substitute," Debbie offered.

"Did you like her?"

"She was okay, but she made two of the boys stay in for recess."

"What did they do?"

"They laughed at her because she limps."

"Jason and Carlos are mean," Roberta explained.

Annie stared at her daughter through the rearview mirror. "That was mean."

"I'm going to tell Mrs. Darger when she gets back."

"Good for you." The school had a no-bully policy. That went for teachers who were targets, too. Everyone needed to be on the watch for it.

"You might get in trouble if they find out."

"I don't care," Roberta told Debbie.

And her daughter *didn't*. Roberta stood up for injustice no matter the situation. How Annie loved her!

A few minutes later she pulled into the carport of their unit in the eightplex. "I'll make dinner while you two get started on your homework." They always ate an early meal because that was when Roberta was the hungriest.

Annie's daughter was a funny little thing. So far this year the lunches she'd made for her remained in her backpack virtually untouched. Roberta's only explanation was that bullying extended to the lunchroom. If you didn't bring a juice box and packaged snacks of a certain brand, some of the popular kids made fun of you. When she finally admitted what was wrong, Annie was disgusted, but she took her to the store and let her pick out some items that would keep the negative comments down.

If Annie sent a check with her for school lunch, she later found it in Robert's her pack, uncashed. Apparently Roberta was too embarrassed to go through the cashier line. Her shyness might have come from not having grown up with a father. Deprived of a father, as Annie was of a husband. The thought of him came into Annie's mind, and she put it away again because of the pain of that ghastly day in Kabul.

Annie had been walking to the dig site from the hotel when an explosion rocked the whole area. In the aftermath there was chaos. She soon learned that Robert and all those with him, including his parents, had been killed. Even the thought of it was still too excruciating to contemplate.

"The substitute didn't give us any work, Mom. Mrs. Darger will be back tomorrow."

Since Roberta didn't lie, Annie had no reason to disbelieve her. "Then you two can help me make tacos."

"Can I grate the cheese?"

Debbie asked the question first, but Roberta loved to do it and her friend knew it.

"Of course." Again Annie looked through the mirror to see her daughter having a private talk with herself. Her rigid idea of fairness won out and she didn't say anything. A trait that had probably come from Roberta's father. An admirable one.

If Roberta were a boy, she would look exactly like a young Robert. She had his straight nose. It gave both of them character. She also had his wide mouth and dark brown hair. The parts of her features belonging to Annie were a softly rounded chin and blue eyes.

Robert's had been gray with flecks of silver that lit up when he looked at her. During their passionate interludes they turned iridescent, letting her know she brought him as much pleasure as he brought her.

"Be sure you guys wash your hands first," she admonished before opening the front door of the condo.

"Why do you always say that, Mom? We're not babies."

Uh-oh. "You're right. I'm afraid I'm still in the habit of treating you like one." In ways her daughter was growing up too fast, but maybe it was a good thing considering the conversation they would have later when they were alone. A certain amount of maturity was needed for Roberta to consider moving to a unique location.

"My mom says the same thing. Be sure and brush your teeth and say your prayers."

While they ran off to Roberta's room, Annie freshened up before putting some frozen ground beef in the microwave to thaw. Yesterday she'd shopped for groceries and pulled all the necessary ingredients from the fridge.

The girls joined her. While they chopped and grated, she fried the tortillas and browned the meat. Before long she'd whipped up a fruit salad.

No sooner did they sit around the table to eat than Julie arrived. She'd forgotten Debbie had a violin lesson and they needed to leave immediately. Annie jumped up and packed a couple of tacos in foil for her to take with her.

"Thanks, Annie. See ya tomorrow, Roberta."

"Okay. Bye."

Once they'd gone, Roberta came running back to the table to eat. "I'm glad you didn't make me take violin."

"Everyone should learn some kind of instrument. Since I used to play the piano, I thought of renting one so you could start taking lessons this year, but before we talk about it, there's something else we need to discuss first."

Roberta finished fixing herself another taco. "What is it?" she asked before biting into it with enthusiasm. "Did you and Grandma have another argument?"

Annie stopped munching. "Is that how it sounds to you?"

"Sometimes," came her quiet answer.

"I'm sorry. When we talk it may sound as if we're arguing, but sometimes that's just how we communicate. They love you and wish we lived in San Francisco." She studied her daughter. "Do you ever wish we lived there?"

"Maybe. Sometimes." After another swallow she said, "Do you?"

"Sometimes, but I can't do my work there."

"I know. If Daddy hadn't died, we'd live with him and you could do it." Her logic couldn't be disputed.

"That's right, honey." Annie had told Roberta the truth. She and Robert hadn't had a chance to get married before he was killed, but they'd planned to because they'd been painfully in love. He was every bit her father, even if there hadn't been an official engagement or wedding ceremony. "We would have always been together."

Now was the time to broach the subject of her new job offer, but the turn in the conversation had made her reticent. Was she hurting Roberta by living away from her parents? Would her daughter be better off being close to the grandparents who adored her?

"If I were willing to do another kind of work entirely, we could live in San Francisco."

"Like what?"

"I—I don't know yet," she stammered. Roberta sounded interested in the possibility.

"Grandpa said he'd take care of us and you wouldn't have to work."

She let out a heavy sigh. "When I was a girl he took care of me, but now that I'm all grown-up with a daughter of my own, do you think he should still have to take care of me?"

After a period of silence, "If Daddy hadn't died, he would have taken care of us."

"But he did die, and that was a long time ago."

From the beginning Annie had done everything possible to help her daughter know and understand the wonderful, adventurous man who'd fathered her. It had been easy to do because Robert had been a breed apart from other men, academically brilliant yet fun loving and kind. Annie had made certain Roberta understood he was courageous to work in a relatively hostile environment and had made her feel perfectly safe.

She'd assured Annie that he'd looked forward to getting married and having children. The two of them had had dreams of the family they planned to raise. Her photographs revealed a strong, handsome, vital male any girl would love to claim for her father.

As a result, Roberta never forgot for a second that he would have loved her and would have been the most terrific dad in the world to her if he hadn't been killed.

After such praise, to remind Roberta that Annie had been taking care of her since she was born didn't mean the same thing in her daughter's mind.

She straightened in her chair. "How come Julie and Debbie don't live with Julie's parents?"

Roberta shrugged. "I don't know."

"It's probably because Julie likes to take care of her daughter just like I like to take care of mine." Now, no matter the consequences, it was time to ask the definitive question. "Would you feel better if Grandpa took care of us?"

Those clear blue eyes stared at her. "Not if *you* wouldn't."

"Oh honey—" She reached out to grasp Roberta's hand. "Please be honest with me. Do you want to move to San Francisco? We can, you know. I'll find a job there."

"You mean and live with Grandma and Grandpa?"

She bit her lip. "Not exactly. We could find our own place, but that way you could visit them a lot. Maybe ride your bike to their house after school and on weekends."

"Don't you like it here?"

"Yes. What about you?"

"I just want to be with you."

Humbled by the answer, Annie had to believe that sentiment came from her daughter's heart. "Then let me ask you another question. How would you like to live someplace else, just for a year? We'd be together a lot more because I'd do most of my work at home throughout the winter."

"Would it be a long way away from Debbie?"

"No," she said without hesitation. "She could come

and visit you on weekends. So could Grandma and Grandpa. Sometimes we could visit them."

"Where is it?"

"Yosemite National Park."

"That's where they have those big sequoia trees. I think they look like giants."

"Yes. How did you know that?"

"I'm in fourth grade, Mom. We're studying California history. Mrs. Darger showed us a video the other day. We're going to go on a field trip to Yosemite next year near the end of school."

Of course. On back-to-school night the teacher had passed out copies of the fourth-grade curriculum. Annie had only given it a cursory glance. "The park is very famous."

"She said part of our water comes from a dam built in the park. It's in a funny-sounding place. People are fighting about taking it down."

"I know. You're talking about the Hetch Hetchy Valley."

Roberta nodded. "How did you know that?"

"Your grandparents took me to the park a lot when I was young. It's an amazing, beautiful place."

Annie's parents had bought an original black-and-white photograph of Yosemite's Half Dome taken by Ansel Adams from a collector back in the early forties. It was worth a fortune now and hung in her father's den.

"What kind of work would you do?"

"What I always do. Archaeology."

She cocked her head. "In the park?"

"Yes. The Yosemite Valley is designated as an archeological district. It's listed on the National Register of Historic Places in the United States. That's where I developed an interest in archaeology. Do you know it has more than one hundred known Indian sites that give information about prehistoric lifeways?"

"Do Indians live there now?"

"Some. Because of timber falling and rockfalls or slides, the park has archaeological treasures hidden in the ground. My job would be to catalogue data and, when possible, try to unearth some of them."

Annie could hear Roberta's mind ticking. She had her interest now. "Where would we live?"

"Somewhere in the park. I've been waiting years for the opportunity. Finally a letter has come in the mail telling me I could have the job. If I'm interested, the Forestry Department will fly me there for a one-day orientation to see if I want to take it. While I'm there, the director of archaeology will give me all the information we need to know."

Her daughter slid off her chair. "Can I go with you?"

"Not for the fly over. I'd leave early Monday morning and be back that night. If you want, you can go to Grandma and Grandpa's, or we'll make arrangements for you to stay with Debbie or Penny. But I won't do any of it if you don't want me to."

Roberta suddenly darted out of the kitchen, causing Annie's spirits to plummet. "Where are you going?"

"To look up the park on the Internet!"

Her little bookworm was very savvy when it came to grazing Web sites. Annie followed her into the dining room where they'd set up the computer for Roberta's homework and her own work at the CDF in Santa Rosa.

She stood in the doorway, waiting until her daughter figured out the right spelling of Yosemite and pulled up the site on the park. It seemed an eternity before she exclaimed, "You can ride horses there!"

Annie wasn't surprised to hear excitement in her voice. Before the Harry Potter books had arrived to absorb her daughter, Roberta had gone through a reading phase on animals—everything from cats and dogs to wolves and polar bears. However, her favorite animal was a horse.

In another life she would have wanted to be born on a horse farm in Kentucky. Robert had loved horses and would have been thrilled to know their daughter had an affinity for them. Annie had taken them riding at a local stable a couple of times and both of them had loved it.

"That sounds fun."

"This says there are miles and miles of horse trails." After a few minutes she lifted her head again. "I don't see any schools."

"Well, since school is for the children whose parents work there, they wouldn't advertise it on the Internet."

"I forgot about that. They don't want predators finding kids." Her daughter sounded a hundred years old just then.

A shiver ran down Annie's spine. If nothing else, she could be thankful her daughter's school was teaching them awareness of the ugly side of society. To do her part at home, Annie had put a filter on their Internet server to help keep them both safe.

"What do you think?" She held her breath. "Should I go and find out about it or not?"

Roberta was glued to the screen. "Yes. After Debbie's violin lesson, I'm going to call her and tell her to look up Yosemite Park. This says some of the rangers ride horses. Debbie could go horseback riding with me. I'll ask her if I can stay at their house until you get back."

Annie couldn't believe it. Her daughter hadn't said no. Of all Yosemite's wonders, who knew it would be horses that spoke to Roberta. Maybe it was in the genes.

"While you do that, I'll send an e-mail to the director and tell him I'll be ready to go on Monday." That was five days away. Enough time to read up on the latest information he'd sent about a project she would be working on along the Tuolumne River. The Awahnichi had lived there in 500 A.D.

Now that she had a chance to do some fieldwork, she was starting to get excited. Except for Roberta, who was the greatest joy of her life, she hadn't known true excitement since before losing Robert.

AFTER LUNCH, Beth poked her head in the door of Vance's office. "Chase? Ranger Baird is on line two. He says he'll hold until you're off the phone."

Chase nodded to Vance's personal assistant before finishing up his call with Ranger Thompson about the fall cleanup and repair of several of the camping areas. This was Chase's least favorite time at the park. The waterfalls were a mere trickle of their former selves and the trails were well worn from the locustlike traffic of summer crowds. Without rain this season, the controlled forest fires left a smoky smog over everything, especially while the weather was still warm.

Nicky wanted to watch the black bears go into hibernation, but that wouldn't be for a while. Right now they were so active, they broke into cars and camps where they could smell food and stuffed themselves.

His thoughts went to Vance, who would be back at

the park with his family tomorrow afternoon. Chase planned to pick them up at the Merced airport. Where had the three weeks gone? He'd been so busy doing the work of a dozen men, he hadn't noticed the time passing. His respect for Vance just kept growing.

The one dinner he'd had at the Bairds' house last night to meet his wife's single cousin had gone well enough. Susan was a dentist in Bishop, California, and a very attractive woman. Though she'd dropped hints she'd like to see Chase again, he had no desire to encourage her and couldn't pretend otherwise. Frank Baird was a straight talker and so was Chase. He'd understand. Still, Chase didn't like hurting anyone.

Once he'd hung up with Ranger Thompson, he clicked on to the other ranger. "Frank? Sorry to keep you waiting."

"No problem. I figured if there'd been a spark last night, I would've heard from you early this morning. You know—in case you didn't want Susan to leave for another day."

Chase heaved a sigh of relief. "I'm sorry to say you figured right. She's a talented, beautiful woman, but—"

"Don't bother to explain. I've been there and know what it's like. Before I met Kim, I went through women like water. Your problem is, you were married once."

Not quite. "I think it's harder to go through all that rigmarole again."

A sardonic laugh escaped Chase's lips. "I planned to call you tonight and thank you and Kim for going to all that trouble for me. The Sunday dinner was delicious by the way."

"Kim appreciated the bottle of wine you brought, so we're even. Better luck next time."

"You know what, Frank? No more going into things blind. After Vance gets back from Miami, I'm leaving on a long vacation. Who knows? I might actually meet someone." Yet deep in his gut he didn't quite believe it.

The old blackness was starting to seep in, robbing him of even small pleasures. As Vance had expressed after his grandmother, the last member of the Rossiter family, had been buried at the beginning of the summer, he felt empty. Chase could relate. Something had to change.

"I hear you."

"Talk to you later." He rang off and buzzed Beth. "What time is my meeting with Superintendent Telford tomorrow?" The man's ideas for advertising the park's attractions could take them into a lengthy discussion.

"Ten-thirty in the morning."

"Would you call him and ask if we can start at nine-thirty?" Vance's flight was due in at 4:10 p.m. Chase didn't want to be late.

"I'll take care of it. Will you want goodies?"

He chuckled. "Do you have to ask? Bring on the works and plenty of coffee!"

"You're as bad as Vance. I'm going to miss you when you're not sitting in his chair."

"You're full of it, Beth. In case you didn't know, the sacred chair is his with my blessing."

"You mean you don't want to be Chief?"

Chase grunted. "If anyone needs me, I'm leaving for the Lower Pines Campground to inspect the latest damage."

"Good luck."

Laughing because they both knew it was in the worst

shape of all, he hung up and headed out the back door of the visitors' center for his truck. No sooner had he climbed inside the cab than another call came in. It was a typical Monday. The phone had rung off the hook since early morning. He clicked on. "Ranger Jarvis here."

"Chase? It's Mark. Five minutes ago Tom Fuller was at the controls of a forestry helicopter when it went off radar somewhere over Mount Paiute. There's been no contact since. We know that means it's down." Chase groaned. "I've called out air and land rescue units, but it will take a while to get to the crash site. I left word for Tom's wife to phone me immediately."

His hand tightened on the receiver. It was the flight that Superintendent Telford had asked Chase to authorize. He wanted more archaeologists working with the park director of archaeology and had come up with the funding.

"Let's pray they're found soon." Dead or alive, Chase didn't want to think what could happen to them while the bears were actively foraging. "Give me the name of the passenger."

"Margaret Anne Bower from Santa Rosa, California."

Bower?

Just hearing that name after all these years squeezed the air out of Chase's lungs. His mind reeled in shock. It couldn't be Annie. It wasn't possible. Still…

He raked a shaky hand through his hair. His thoughts went back ten years. She would have told him if she'd been named Margaret. He would have remembered. They'd shared everything. And surely by now she would be married with a different name.

"If you've got a phone number on her, better call her family." Chase didn't dare do it or his caller ID would show up and that would involve him personally.

"I already did. An answering machine came on and a man's voice said no one was home. I left a message for her husband to call me."

She *was* married then.

Maybe she went by her maiden name. "That's all you can do for now, Mark. Keep me posted."

"Will do."

After Chase hung up, he started the truck with the intention of talking to the rescue units before they took off, but the hairs stood on the back of his neck when he realized his assumption about Annie being married might be wrong.

Just because a man's voice came on the line, it didn't necessarily mean it belonged to her husband. In order to prove a man lived in the house, she could have asked a male neighbor or friend—or a lover—to program her phone. Even her father. San Francisco wasn't that far away from Santa Rosa.

This woman was an archaeologist. She'd probably been to the park many times. If she were Annie, then he *knew* she had.

Was it possible she'd spotted Chase on one of her recent visits and realized he was alive? Could it be the reason she'd applied for the position Superintendent Telford had opened up, so she could find out the truth without letting anyone else know?

But that didn't make sense. If she'd seen him, she wouldn't have been able to hold back from responding. They'd been too deeply in love. He ruled out that theory.

He shook his head in despair. There were too many questions with no answers. He thought of the downed helicopter. Visions of Annie's lovely body mangled and burned or worse bombarded him until he broke out in a cold sweat and found himself screeching toward the helipad.

Before jumping out of the truck to join the others, he made a call back to Mark. "I'm flying up to the crash site. Tell Beth you're in charge until further notice!"

Chapter Two

Every so often Annie heard a moaning sound. She wished she could see who was making it, but there was something covering her eyes. When she tried to remove it with her hand, red-hot pain shot through her upper arm, causing her to gasp. Her other arm lay trapped beneath her body.

The moaning sounds continued. She could smell smoke. It was as foul as the taste of blood in her mouth. A terrible thirst had come over her. If she could just have a drink of water.

She heard vibrating sounds, which she thought must be coming from inside her head. They'd been growing in intensity and wouldn't stop. Maybe a woodpecker was trying to crack her skull open. It pecked faster and faster, tap, tap, tap, tap, driving her mad.

"There she is." A male voice reached her ears. She heard footsteps coming closer.

"Easy," another voice spoke to her.

"I've got a pulse. She's alive."

"Thank God." Yet another male voice that had a gut-wrenchingly familiar timbre, rousing her more fully.

"She has a possible broken arm. I see a scalp

wound. Could be internal injuries. Let's get her to the hospital pronto."

Whatever had blinded her was taken away. Through veiled eyes she found herself surrounded by men in uniform. Above her a helicopter hovered. There'd been an explosion. It was the rotors she'd heard inside her head. Her adrenaline surged. She had to find Robert. He hadn't died after all. He was here. In the confusion she'd heard his voice.

"I've got her neck and back braced. Ready to lift her into the basket?"

"Take care with that arm," Robert said.

She felt herself being moved, causing her to groan from the pain. Her heavy eyelids fluttered. For an instant she looked into a pair of silvery gray eyes trained on her. They were *his* eyes.

"Robert?"

Suddenly she was hoisted out of sight. They were taking her away from him again. She couldn't bear it.

"Robert!" she screamed, trying to look back, but she couldn't move her head. Searing pain engulfed her. "Don't let me go! Don't let them take me away—" She screamed wildly until she knew nothing more.

CHASE COULDN'T BREATHE.

He heard his name being screamed over and over until it grew faint above him. Each cry staggered him a little more. From the ground he watched the guys ease the basket into the chopper. The other crew was bracing Tom in another basket farther up the slope for the lift into the second helicopter. By some miracle neither person had died in the crash.

Annie was alive. She'd come to the park to work.

Their chances of being together here at this moment in time were astronomical.

He buried his face in his hands. Before long a third helicopter carrying an inspection team would descend to rummage through the smoldering wreck. Chase stayed behind, ostensibly to wait for them and make out the preliminary report.

In truth he was so shaken to discover it had been Annie lying there like a beautiful broken doll tossed out a window, he needed this time alone to recover. The rescue team were professionals trained to hide emotion, yet they too had been noticeably disturbed to see an attractive woman passed out hurt and bleeding in this unforgiving wilderness.

When she'd recognized Chase and cried his name with all the emotion of her soul, he'd come close to losing any composure he had left. More than anything in the world he wanted to go in that helicopter with her and never let her out of his sight again, but he couldn't do that. No one had any idea he was a wanted man. It needed to stay that way. Let her believe she'd been hallucinating. Let the others think the same thing.

There'd been no wedding ring or band on her finger to indicate she had a husband, no suntan mark to prove she'd worn one recently. Did it mean what he thought it meant? That she, too, had never been able to fall in love with anyone else?

Annie, Annie… Those blue eyes with their tinge of wood smoke had deepened in hue the second she'd recognized him. The contrast of shoulder-length hair glistening like dark ranch mink against the pallor of a flawless complexion assailed him with exquisite memories. Though blood had run down the side of her face onto her lips, its stain couldn't disguise the voluptuous curve of the mouth he could never get enough of.

Ten years had added more womanly curves to her body encased in a knit top and jeans that outlined her long, shapely legs. He'd been aware of everything while he and Ranger King had worked to stabilize her.

Forcing himself to do his duty, he walked around the crash site making notes to turn over to the federal authorities, yet all the while he was dying inside because once again—when he least expected it—his heart had been ripped out of his body.

Still drained by shock, he finally drew his cell phone from his pocket and called Mark. "Good news here, under the circumstances," he said. "Both victims are alive and in flight to San Gabriel hospital in Stockton. Until you hear otherwise, they're in critical condition."

A shudder racked his body. If Mark could see the mess the helicopter was in, he wouldn't believe anyone could have survived. Chase tried in vain to quell the tremor in his voice. "God was good to us today."

"Amen," Mark whispered. "With the chief coming back tomorrow, this wouldn't have been the best homecoming, if you know what I mean."

"I know exactly," Chase muttered with his eyes closed. The deaths of Nicky's parents eighteen months earlier on top of El Capitan would always live in the memories of those who worked in the park.

"Thanks for the update. Tom's wife will be overjoyed to know he's alive at least."

Chase cleared his throat. "Any word back from the Bower household?"

"Nothing yet. I checked with the CDF in Santa Rosa.

They have an emergency number for her parents in San Francisco and have already put in a call to them. I expect to hear from them at some point."

Annie's parents were in for a terrible shock. So was the man who was in love with her, whoever he was. Whether married or not, there had to be a man in her life. After seeing her again, the thought of her giving herself to anyone else tore up his insides.

In the distance he could hear the sound of rotors whipping the air. "Mark? I'm going to be here at the crash site for a while. When the inspectors have finished, I'll fly back to headquarters with them. Keep me posted with updates on the patients' conditions." *Annie had to be all right.*

"Will do."

SOMEONE CAME IN THE ROOM. Annie opened her eyes. "Hello."

"Hi. Are you Ms. or Mrs. Bower?"

"I'm not married. Just call me Annie."

"My name's Heidi. I'm your night nurse. How's the pain? On a level of one to ten, ten being the worst, can you give me a number?"

"A two maybe."

"Good. Glad to hear that arm fracture isn't giving you too much grief."

"Not as much as the gash on the side of my head."

"Those stitches always sting for the first little while. Do you want more painkiller? The doctor says you can have what you need."

"I'm all right for now, thank you."

"Are you sure? Your blood pressure's up a little. What are you anxious about? Everything else is fine and you'll be out of here in no time." She proceeded to take the rest of her vital signs.

Annie squeezed her eyelids together. No, everything else was *not* fine.

Unless Robert had an identical twin, and she knew he didn't, Robert was *alive!*

She'd heard and seen him after the helicopter crashed. It wasn't a dream. It was Robert's voice she'd picked out first. She couldn't be mistaken about that. A voice was like a fingerprint, only one individual set of tones per human being.

It was Robert who'd helped place her body in the basket with infinite care, a Robert who'd matured into a gorgeous, bronzed male. If anything he was more attractive now with those lines of experience bracketing his hard mouth. In the past it could soften with such tenderness it made her cry.

Once he'd worn his dark brown hair overly long, but today it had been short cropped. There'd been a lean, hungry look about him. Those characteristics had been absent ten years ago. In one illuminating moment this afternoon she had the strongest impression he rarely smiled anymore. He looked tough. Forbidding. A man who walked alone. With robotlike perfection he'd cold-bloodedly rescued her, never showing the tiniest sign of human emotion.

But all this she kept to herself as she told the nurse, "I'm waiting for my daughter, Roberta."

"How old is she?"

"Ten."

"Ah. Now I understand your agitation."

"My parents are bringing her. I thought they'd be here by now."

"I'll ask the desk if they know anything." She raised the head of the bed a bit for her. "Do you feel up to talking to an official from the CDF? He's right outside and only needs a minute of your time to finish up his report."

"Send him in." Annie had some questions herself.

"Shall I bring you back more apple juice?"

"Could I have a cola instead?"

"Of course. I'll get it right now."

She heard voices in the doorway before the man approached her bed. "Please forgive me for disturbing you. This won't take long."

"It's all right."

"Can you tell me what happened when you knew you were in trouble?"

"Yes. Tom had flown us as low as we could go to give me a look at one of the Indian sites. All of a sudden the helicopter spun around, but it wasn't because we'd hit anything.

"I've been going over it in my mind. It reminded me of the way it is when you're flying a kite and it's riding a current and everything's perfect, and the next second it suddenly does all these crazy spirals for no reason. Tom was amazingly calm. He said we were going to crash and told me to get into fetal position. The next thing I knew I was lying in the brush and smelled smoke."

"You and Tom had a miraculous escape."

"How is he?"

"Other than a broken leg, he's fine."

"Thank heaven!"

"He said the same thing when he heard you were all right."

"What did he say happened to the helicopter?"

"Without a thorough inspection, no one knows

anything official yet, but he's been in other crashes like it in the navy and felt it was an interior malfunction."

"I'm sure he's right. I can tell you right now it had nothing to do with his flying expertise. He kept me from panicking and showed remarkable courage."

"Thanks for your cooperation. As a final note, the CDF will be paying all your medical expenses."

That was a relief. "Thank you for coming."

Alone again, Annie lay there in a frozen state beyond anguish. If Robert had wanted to end their relationship, he could have gone about it like most people and simply told her it was over. Yet for some reason she couldn't comprehend, he'd used the tragic event of his parents' deaths to make the grand exit from her life ten years ago.

It was the perfect plan to bring her permanent closure. No messy explanations had been sought or required. Of course that was when she'd thought he was dead.

If she had the opportunity to confront him right now, would she find herself talking to a true amnesiac? He'd behaved like one during the rescue, but she didn't believe it. In the moment when she'd had a glimpse of him, his eyes had looked fierce, not vacant.

Ruling out that particular mental disorder as the reason for his lack of reaction, she had no explanation for his disappearance from her life. But it was clear he'd wanted no part of her. What a shock to have been found out at the crash site of all places!

She had no doubt he'd already disappeared from the park, but he needn't have bothered. If he thought she would make frantic inquiries and try to track him down after the lie he'd perpetrated, then he'd never known the real Annie.

In the most graphic of ways, the terrifying crash had reminded her of her mortality. One's life could be snuffed out in an instant. By some miracle she and the pilot had survived. She'd learned nothing was more important to her than staying alive to raise her darling daughter. Since Robert had chosen to be dead to Annie for the past ten years, he could continue to remain dead for the rest of her life.

If Roberta were to learn the truth, it would extinguish the flame of love in her heart for the dad she'd never known. Her world would be blighted forever. Annie determined never to tell her or anyone what had transpired on the mountain. That secret would go to the grave with her.

"Mom?"

Her splotchy-faced, tear-ravaged daughter came into the hospital room ahead of Annie's parents and rushed over to the bed. Between the cast on her left arm and the drip on the top of her right hand, there wasn't a lot of space to work with, but Roberta found a way. While she buried her head against Annie's chest and quietly sobbed, Annie's parents looked on through their own tears.

"I'm all right," she assured them before anyone else spoke. "Thanks to the pilot who had the presence of mind to tell me how to protect myself, I only have a fracture in my arm."

"Did he die?" Her father asked the solemn question.

"No. I just found out he has a broken leg. We were both so lucky. It's probably because we were so close to the ground looking at an Indian site when the helicopter malfunctioned and we more or less rolled out before it crashed. The doctor says I'll be able to go home day after tomorrow."

Her parents kissed her cheeks. "You're coming home with us to recuperate. Thank heaven you're alive!" her mother cried. "We couldn't believe it when we got the news from the police."

"I've never known that kind of terror before," her father confided in a low voice.

Moisture bathed Annie's cheeks. "Neither have I." She patted Roberta's head. "I know you were frightened."

"I wish you hadn't gone to Yosemite. Please don't go back." Another burst of tears resounded in the room. Roberta's slender body shook.

Her daughter's heartfelt plea, plus the pain in her parent's eyes, made up her mind for her. "Guess what?"

Roberta lifted her head. "What?"

"I've decided I'm not taking the job. We're going to move to San Francisco."

"Annie—" her mother cried out in a mixture of joy and disbelief.

Roberta's grave eyes studied her. "You mean to live?"

"Yes."

Her dad stared at her as if he'd never seen her before. He knew something earthshaking would have to happen for her to make an announcement like that. Naturally he would attribute her near fatal accident to the reason for this about face.

"If you'd said anything else…" He stood there and wept. So much happiness for the family rode on her decision. No more looking back.

For ten years Robert had been alive! In all these years he hadn't *once* tried to contact her.

It reminded her of a story on the news about a man who'd faked his own death to get away from his wife and family. Twenty years later his wife saw him. He was married to someone else and had another family.

Annie couldn't comprehend anyone doing that, but *Robert had done it.* Her summer in Afghanistan ten years ago had been nothing more than an intermezzo in her life. He'd proposed and she'd accepted. Still, they'd never made it to the altar.

But it had produced her beautiful baby. From here on out she would devote her life to Roberta's happiness and make her parents happy in the process.

"What job are you going to do?"

"I don't know yet. Maybe I'll go back to university and become a schoolteacher." Something unrelated to archaeology and memories. She'd spent too many years honoring a man who'd turned out to be unremarkable after all.

Her dad put his arm around his granddaughter. "The important thing is that we're all going to be together, sweetie."

She looked up at him. "Can I sleep by Mom, tonight?"

"We'll ask the nurse as soon as she comes back in."

"I'm sure it will be okay." Annie's gaze flicked to her mother. "Where are you staying tonight?"

"At a hotel just around the corner from the hospital."

The door opened and the nurse came in with Annie's soft drink. "Looks like everyone got here," she said with a smile.

Annie nodded. "Could a cot be set up so my daughter can stay with me tonight?"

"Of course. I'll see to it right away."

"Thank you. You've been wonderful to me."

"We aim to please. I bet the rest of you could use a soda. How about you?" she asked Roberta, who nodded, causing her ponytail to wiggle. "What's your favorite? Sprite? Cola? Orange soda? Root beer?"

"Root beer."

"Cola for us," Annie's mom spoke up.

"Got it," she said and was gone once again.

Annie's eyes filled with tears. Everyone she loved was assembled around her bed. This morning she'd set out on a new adventure, unaware that before the day was over, her entire life would undergo a dramatic change.

The crash had given her clarity about her priorities. Robert's return had rewritten history, closing the door on the past. From now on she would live for these three precious people and ask for nothing more.

"THERE'S UNCLE CHASE!"

Nicky broke away from his parents and came running toward the car, his cute features alive with excitement. A tortured Chase had been resting against the passenger door waiting for them. He scooped the boy from the ground and hugged him close, so full of conflicted emotions he was dying inside.

"Did you get my postcard? It was the Tower of London!"

"I did and I loved it."

"They used to torture people in it."

"That's what you told me."

Nicky gave him a peck on the cheek. "I brought you a present, but it's in my suitcase."

"I can't wait to see it."

His hazel eyes twinkled. "You'll *love* it."

"You *will*," Vance assured him.

Chase turned to his best friend, who'd never looked better. Happiness radiated from his eyes. In fact, Chase would say marriage had taken five years off him. As for Rachel, she exuded that aura of true fulfillment you felt when you knew you were loved beyond all else.

When Chase left the park tomorrow, this picture of them would be indelibly impressed in his mind and heart. He hugged Rachel extra hard. He was going to miss his friends like crazy. "How's your father?"

"He's fantastic!" she cried. "The surgery was a complete success. They'll be moving out here before we know it."

"That's wonderful," he whispered, but he was functioning on automatic pilot. Since yesterday when Mark had told him the passenger in the helicopter was named Margaret Anne Bower, Chase's life had been turned inside out.

He could feel Vance's eagle eye on him. Already the Chief could sense Chase wasn't being himself. The two men had never been able to hide anything from each other, but this was one time when he'd have to bluff his way through.

"You guys get in and I'll stow your bags." He moved to the rear of the car and opened the trunk. Vance followed him. For the moment they were alone.

"Pardon my English, but you look like hell."

Yup. Chase had been one of hell's occupants since yesterday. It was Mark Sims who'd provided him his only lifeline to the world of the living. Through their communication he'd learned that Annie had come out of the crash with nothing more than a fractured arm and a few stitches in her head. Thank God for that.

"Being chief ranger of Yosemite Park was a lot harder than I thought it would be. Your shoes are too big to fill."

Avoiding eye contact, he shut the trunk lid and got

in the driver's seat. Nicky and Rachel had installed themselves in the back where Chase had put Nicky's car seat. Vance climbed in front. Again Chase felt his friend's laser-blue glance doing a full probe while they fastened their seat belts.

Once they left the airport Chase purposely engaged Nicky in conversation. "Did you see any white owls?"

"I got to see Hedwig!"

"The real Hedwig?"

"Yup."

"The one in the movie?"

"Yup. Except they used seven different owls. The one I saw was really called Oak."

"How did you manage that?"

"Mommy and Daddy drove us to this town. I don't remember what it was called."

"Walsall," Rachel interjected.

"Yeah, and this lady came to the library with some animals. She brought Oak, who was really snowy."

"Well, lucky you."

"Yup. We got pictures of me standing next to her and I also got to touch a pygmy hedgehog."

Chase chuckled in spite of his pain. He'd learned to love Nicky and couldn't imagine not being around him anymore. "I can't wait to look at your pictures."

"Have you ever seen a pygmy hedgehog?"

"I don't think so."

"They're really little."

"I bet. You didn't happen to see the Queen too, did you?"

"Nope, but we saw the guards guarding her with these huge hats. What were they called again, Mommy?"

"Beefeaters."

"Oh yeah, and we rode the red double-decker buses all over London. You can see the river and everything upstairs. Oh, and guess what else?"

"What?" Keep it up, Nicky.

"We rode on a train."

"Did it take you to Hogwarts?"

Nicky giggled. "Hogwarts isn't real. You're funny, Uncle Chase."

Their little blond chatterbox entertained them until they reached the entrance to the park. Chase wouldn't have stopped, but Jeff Thompson, the ranger manning the guard station, had seen them coming. When he spotted Vance, he stepped out to say hello. Chase had no option but to apply the brakes.

"Glad to see you back, Chief."

"It's good to be home."

Jeff tipped his hat to Nicky and Rachel seated in the rear. "Just so you know, Ranger Jarvis did such a great job, no one would know you'd left," he added.

"That's laying it on a little thick don't you think?" Chase scoffed.

"It's the reason I left him in charge," Vance followed up. "What's new with you?"

"Not a thing, but I guess you know all about the forestry helicopter crash over Mount Paiute," he said in a quieter voice.

Vance's head swung toward Chase in consternation.

Chase almost bit his own tongue off. *Thanks a lot, Jeff.* "Let's talk outside," he muttered to Vance, who nodded. They both got out of the car, not wanting Nicky to hear anything.

"When was this?" Vance asked. A grimace had broken out on his face.

"Yesterday."

"Why didn't you tell me?"

"If there'd been fatalities, I would have. Fortunately, the pilot and passenger on board came out of it with only a broken leg and a fractured arm."

"It was miraculous they survived in such great shape, all things considered," Jeff said.

Vance was waiting for a more detailed explanation from Chase. "So far the inspectors think it was a tail rotor malfunction or an in-flight mechanical malfunction. There's no other logical explanation for what happened."

"Who was at the controls?"

"Tom Fuller," Jeff supplied.

Chase elaborated. "The good news is that pilot error has been ruled out. It happened around noon in perfect weather, providing optimum conditions for a happy outcome."

"Who was the passenger?"

The blood pounded at his temples. "A new archaeologist from the CDF on an orientation flight."

"A *new* one—"

"It was Superintendent Telford's idea to hire an additional archaeologist. He found the funding for it."

"The rescue guys said she's a real looker," Jeff said.

"What's her name?"

"Margaret Bower. The guys are lining up to meet her, but I plan to be first to nail a date."

Chase could feel his blood pressure rise.

"She's single then?" Vance muttered.

Jeff nodded. "She has a daughter who'll be living in the park with her."

A daughter? For the first time in Chase's life he nearly passed out from shock.

"How old is she?"

Jeff shrugged. "I don't know. You'll have to ask Mark for those details."

Chase eyed his friend. "I'd hoped to spare you that information until tomorrow, Vance. Welcome home."

"I'm glad I found out tonight. Forewarned is fore-armed. I presume it's been plastered all over the news here."

"Of course, but the positive outcome has caused the clamor to die down."

"The new superintendent must have come close to having a coronary."

Jeff nodded. "It's safe to say we all did until they were taken off the critical list. Superintendent Telford felt so responsible, he wrote out a statement for the park publicist to give to the press so we're covered."

"That's a relief."

Chase couldn't take any more. "It's great talking to you, Jeff, but they've had a transatlantic flight and need to get home." *I have to talk to Mark.*

They both got back in the car. Jeff waved to the two in the back seat. "See you around, Nicky!"

"See ya!"

He backed away so Chase could drive the car on through.

For the rest of the drive to Yosemite Valley they talked shop while Chase brought Vance up to speed. Rachel and Nicky held their own conversation in the back seat. Before long Chase turned into Vance's driveway and shut off the motor.

"I'll help you with the luggage." Chase couldn't talk to Mark fast enough, but that wouldn't happen until he was alone.

Vance helped his family into the house then came back to the car. Together they carried the bags inside the door. As Chase turned to leave, Vance caught his arm. "Hey? Where's the fire? We want you to stay. Rachel's going to fix us a snack. Come on in."

Chase flashed him a wry smile. "This is your first night home with your bride. Four's a crowd, if you know what I mean. Don't forget I'm still in charge until you show up for work tomorrow, so enjoy yourselves."

After clapping a hand on Vance's shoulder, he walked back to the car. Though he felt like running, he controlled the impulse. When he looked through the side-view mirror he noticed Vance still standing in the doorway with a deep frown marring his rugged features.

After rounding the corner, Chase turned into his own driveway and pressed the remote to enter his garage. He hurried inside the house and pulled out his cell phone to call Mark from the kitchen.

"Mission accomplished. Vance and family are back home and safe. All is well."

"Terrific. How does he look?"

"Better than a man who just won the ten-billion-dollar lottery."

"That's very good," was Mark's emotional response. Like all the rangers, the head security officer for the park thought the world of Vance.

"Did Nicky enjoy himself?"

"He's been chattering nonstop. You're going to be hearing all about his trip."

Mark laughed. "I'm crazy about that little guy."

"Everyone is." Until he had the answer to one specific question, Chase's anxiety was so severe he could hardly breathe. "Speaking of children, Jeff told Vance that Ms. Bower has a daughter."

"That's right."

"I didn't realize. By any chance is she Nicky's age? If so, that would be nice for him to have a friend. We'll be in short supply around here this winter."

"According to the information sheet provided by the CDF, she's ten years old, my Carly's age. It says she's in the fourth grade and her name is Roberta."

The phone slipped from Chase's fingers and fell to the floor.

He'd made Annie pregnant. They had a child together—

"Chase? Are you still there?"

A girl—he had a daughter!

"Hello? Chase?"

He had to reach down for the phone, but his hand trembled like a man with palsy, making it difficult. "Yes," he murmured in a daze. "Sorry about that. The phone dropped. Thanks for the info, Mark. Feed all emergencies to me. Vance won't be back on duty until tomorrow. Stay in touch."

"Will do."

The second they hung up, Chase braced himself at the sink. While he stared blindly out the window trying to come to grips with the fact that he was a father, someone knocked on the front door. It was the kind of summons you couldn't ignore. One of the rangers, no doubt, but this was one time when the intrusion seemed more than he could handle.

Still, he strode through the house and flung the door

open wide. Vance took one look at him and said, "I thought so." Sidestepping him, he moved inside.

Chase shut the door. They faced each other like adversaries.

"I'm not leaving until you tell me what's going on."

Chapter Three

A full minute passed while Chase stared at him. It was truth time. "You're not going to like what you hear. When I've told you everything, you're not only going to hate my guts for lying to you, you'll be enraged that my being here has put the park in danger."

All animation left Vance's face. "Why not let me be the judge of that. Let's hear it."

Taking a fortifying breath, he began. "For starters my name is Robert Myers. I was born in New York City, not San Diego. There's no Barbara in my life. I was never married or divorced. Never a navy man.

"Like my parents I too received my Ph.D. from Duke University in archaeology, but I need to backtrack. I didn't grow up in the States. Before I was a year old, my parents left for China. We virtually lived our lives following the Eastern to Western outposts of the Silk Route from the Orient to Afghanistan where we ended up in Kabul to do an excavation.

"As you know from being a marine in Iraq, archaeologists often have entrée into countries where few others can get in. I was a young boy when the CIA approached my parents to do intelligence gathering for them. At the time I didn't understand the significance. All I knew was that I was warned never to talk to anyone about our activities."

Vance shook his head in amazement.

"When Afghanistan was under Russian occupation and subsequent Taliban rule, their national museum in Kabul was looted of its treasure, but it never showed up in the Western auction houses or in Russia. The world was stumped.

"To make a long story short, it was learned that the Afghan government had hidden it in an impenetrable vault beneath the presidential palace complex in Kabul. After the Taliban were expelled, a team of locksmiths were called in to open the seven locks.

"Save for a few pieces, the fabulous Bactrian Gold treasure was all there along with the priceless two thousand coins dating from the fifth century B.C. showing the profiles of successive kings. Other teams of archaeologists including ours were sent in to verify the authenticity of the contents, proving a central Asian identity midway on the Silk Route."

"*You* got to examine it?"

Chase nodded. "A part of it, but victory came at a price. An Al-Qaeda cell still working with the Taliban got their revenge against anyone connected to the find. They set off an explosion at our excavation site, killing my parents and thirteen others. I was given up for dead too, but I survived and was flown to Switzerland by the CIA for rehabilitation.

"I was in the hospital a year to recover. Besides the massive scarring and skin grafts from successive operations, I was told I wouldn't be able to have children. And one more thing…"

Chase could tell Vance was holding his breath.

"There was an inoperable piece of shrapnel lodged in my heart. If it moved, I was a dead man. Knowing it could happen at any time, my life wasn't worth two cents so I agreed to go back to work for the CIA. It was better than waiting around for the end to come. Because of my knowledge of Arabic, Punjabi and Persian Dari, my job was to infiltrate and gather intelligence for them.

"The taste for revenge was strong. To my shock, my heart survived the training. The doctor just scratched his head. I ended up giving them six years of my life. On my last mission where I was embedded with a group of special forces, my cover was blown by a double agent who recognized me from the Kabul disaster. They immediately put me in the witness protection program here at Yosemite where I could fade into the woodwork.

"In case you're wondering how I made it through my physical, the powers that be planted someone else's chest X-ray during my park service physical. For three years nothing has disturbed the tenor of my existence…until yesterday."

Vance folded his arms. "I knew there had to be a reason I felt an affinity to you from day one." He gazed at Chase with a mixture of fascination and admiration. "Go on."

Chase swallowed hard. "I'm in trouble, Vance."

"You mean your identity here has been compromised?"

"Not yet." He rubbed the side of his jaw. "But this is something related and deeply personal. A little while ago I found out I'm a father."

Those blue eyes squinted. "Say that again?"

"I can't believe it either. Apparently I have a daughter. Her mother happens to be the woman who was in the helicopter yesterday, Annie Bower. She's the woman I fell in love with in Afghanistan. She was there as an undergraduate archaeology student from UCLA volunteering for credit."

The news brought Vance to his feet.

"When Annie first appeared at the dig site, no male working there could keep his eyes off her. I took one look and felt an immediate attraction that only grew stronger the instant she smiled."

Her intelligence had fascinated him, drawing him to her. The warmth of her personality captivated him. "We became inseparable…until the day disaster struck and separated us permanently. Thank God she'd stayed at the apartment that morning." His voice trembled.

"Thank God," Vance echoed.

"We'd planned to be married at the end of the summer, but now you know what happened. She went back to California believing I was dead. I'd taken precautions, so I had no idea she was pregnant when she left.

"With Al-Qaeda cells active everywhere in the U.S., I was terrified they'd track her down because she'd been part of the excavation team. I had no choice but to remain dead to her. And let's face it. Who would want a scarred shell of a man who could drop dead at any moment?"

Vance grimaced. "I hear you," he whispered.

"The CIA has kept her under surveillance all these years, but they've never given me any knowledge of her. I guess they knew that if I found out we had a daughter, I wouldn't be able to stay away from her." He sucked in his breath. "Can you imagine how I felt yesterday when I flew to the crash site and there was Annie lying crumpled in the brush?"

"Chase—"

"It's one of those coincidences that has defied all logic. As we lifted her into the basket, she looked at me and cried my name. The guys figured Robert must be her husband's name and didn't find it unusual she'd called out to him."

Vance was quick to put two and two together. "So it was Ranger Thompson who unwittingly broke the news to you tonight that she had a daughter. I swear you turned into a different man just then."

Chase nodded. "I phoned Mark a few minutes ago and found out my little girl is ten years old."

"Did he tell you her name?"

"It's Roberta."

A low whistle escaped Vance's lips. "That's better proof than DNA," he teased. "If Nicky were here he'd say *whoa!*"

His head reared. "What am I going to do?"

"What do you want to do?"

"That's a hell of a question—"

"I was going to tell you the same thing," Vance retorted.

"You don't understand. Even though my heart's still pumping, that piece of shrapnel could suddenly move and that would be it."

"True, but it hasn't happened in ten years. I'd say you've beaten the odds."

"Maybe, but my CIA contact keeps me updated and the fact remains that Al-Qaeda operatives are still searching for me. We know their patience is legendary. Though being in the witness protection program has kept us all safe so far, I'll always be a fugitive looking over my shoulder. Better for Annie and Roberta if I disappear into another world before she leaves the hospital."

Vance shook his head. "Your particular war has been over for a long time. The chances of either of you being traced here is a million times less likely than her being involved in a helicopter crash over the park. What better place for you to protect her where she and Roberta can live in relative seclusion? No way are you leaving here! I won't let you," he vowed with satisfying ferocity.

Chase's eyes smarted. "You have every right to despise me for pretending to be someone else all this time."

"Don't be an idiot. Would you despise *me* if the shoe were on the other foot?'

"You already know the answer to that."

"Then we understand each other. Now that I'm back to being the Chief again, I'm giving you as much time off as you need to take care of unfinished business. I'd say ten years' worth." He headed for the door. "To think Rachel and I were talking the whole trip about how to find you the right woman…"

"Surely not the *whole* trip."

He grinned. "No. I have to be honest about that. Good night, Robert, or should I say Dr. Myers."

"Do you know how weird that sounds to me now?"

"Probably not as weird as the name 'Chase' will sound to Annie. She's going to have to learn to call you that. Of course Roberta won't have any problem. She'll just call you Dad."

"Let's not get ahead of ourselves. Annie knows I'm alive." He sucked in his breath. "I have a gut feeling she'll never forgive my long silence no matter the reason."

"Then make her fall in love with you all over again. Rachel says you're a real heartthrob. By the way, I don't think I had a chance to tell you about my conversation with Chief Sam before I left on my honeymoon."

The old Paiute chief was a visionary man. Whenever he spoke, he gave Chase gooseflesh.

"After he thanked me for fixing the photo of the Paiute lodge in the library, he said he saw a peregrine falcon flying faster than an arrow to her mate nesting in the cliffs overlooking the valley. You realize we haven't seen any falcons nesting there in a decade or more. Kind of gives you chills, doesn't it?"

Before he closed the door behind him he added, "Remind me to give the Superintendent a bear hug for opening up a slot for a new resident archaeologist to the park."

After Vance left, there was no sleep for Chase. For the rest of the night he downed coffee and wrestled with a dozen ideas on how to approach Annie. By morning he'd come to the conclusion that the only thing to do was phone her before she was released from the hospital. It was a place to start. If she refused to take the call or shut him down flat, then he'd find another way to reach her.

At eight in the morning he couldn't wait any longer and rang information for San Gabriel hospital in Stockton. Eventually he reached the hospital operator who told him she was in W423 and rang her room. Between caffeine and adrenaline, he was so jumpy he paced the living room floor while he waited for someone to pick up.

"Hello?" said a young female voice.

If he didn't miss his guess, it was his daughter who'd answered. Unbelievable. "Hello," he said back, breaking out in another cold sweat. "Is this Ms. Bower's room?"

"Yes?"

"May I speak to her please?"

"She can't come to the phone right now. Who's calling?"

"Ranger Jarvis."

After a brief silence she said, "Are you one of the men who rescued my mother?" Her sweet demeanor melted his heart.

"I am." He cleared his throat. "How is she doing?"

"The doctor says she can go home this afternoon."

He swallowed with difficulty. "That's wonderful news. Who are you?"

"Her daughter, Roberta."

His eyes closed tightly. *Roberta...* "That's a beautiful name."

"Thank you. I was named for my father whose name was Robert. He died before I was born."

Chase covered his face with his hand. "I'm glad your mother is all right. Have you been staying with her the whole time?"

"Yes. My grandparents wanted me to stay at the hotel with them, but Mom needs me to do things for her."

"She's very lucky to have a daughter who loves her so much. Do you think she'll be able to talk to me later?"

"If you'll hold on, I'll find out."

"Okay. Thank you."

"You're welcome."

What an amazingly polite, charming girl! He could tell she'd had the right training from her mother. To think she was blood of his blood, flesh of his flesh. Already, he was bursting with pride.

"Ranger Jarvis?" She'd come back to the phone.

"I'm still here."

"Mom's busy with the nurse. She says that if you'll leave your number, she'll call you back in ten minutes."

Annie had guessed who it was.

It appeared she'd decided to face Chase head-on. That put the fear in him. She wasn't twenty years old anymore. She was a thirty-one year old woman who'd been the head of her home for ten years and had carved out an enviable career for herself and Roberta.

"Do you have a pen to write it down?"

"Yes. Go ahead please."

He smiled through the tears and gave it to her. She made the perfect secretary. Such a serious head on those young shoulders. Who could blame her after almost losing her mother? Chase shuddered because Annie had come so close to death. Visions of the twisted wreckage refused to leave his mind.

"I'll read it back." She'd gotten it right. "Don't worry. She won't forget to call you. She said her rescuers were angels."

Except for one… "Thank you, Roberta. I'll be waiting."

"Okay. Goodbye. Thank you for helping my mom." She hung up before he could say anything else.

Chase sank down in the nearest chair, shaken and humbled by the first conversation with his only offspring.

A RANGER JARVIS WANTED Annie to call him back?

Along with flowers sent from friends and staff at the CDF, she'd already received two gorgeous flower arrangements from the park superintendent and the chief ranger wishing her a full and speedy recovery.

So why this phone call from a ranger? Unless it was an official follow-up courtesy call on the part of the park service to anyone who'd been injured within its borders. She had no idea of park protocol and couldn't say with any authority what they did one way or the other.

It led her to the conclusion that if it wasn't their policy to call in these situations, then Robert had initiated it because he knew *she* knew he hadn't died. Out of desperation he'd called on a fishing expedition to find out what she was going to do about it.

How she would have loved to be a fly on the wall when he discovered he was talking to his own daughter! A normal man might have come close to cardiac arrest. But considering Robert was capable of the worst cruelty, nothing short of liquid nitrogen could run through his veins.

Now that the anesthetic had left her body, rage began to take its place, along with aches and pains starting to come out in every part of her. She was infuriated to think it might have been Robert talking to her sweet, innocent girl just now. He didn't deserve to have a conversation with her, let alone be anywhere near her!

Once out of the shower, the nurse had helped Annie dress in a loose-fitting top and skirt, then Roberta took over. She put toothpaste on Annie's brush, then dried her wet hair with a towel.

"Thank you, honey. I don't know what I'd do without you." Annie hugged her with her free arm before more or less shuffling into the other room. She sat down in a chair so her daughter could put her hair in a ponytail. It felt good for someone else to brush it. "Ah, this is sheer luxury."

Roberta laughed gently while she did an expert job on her mom, taking care not to touch the area with the stitches. The two of them had always been close, but this experience had bonded them in a more profound way. Roberta fastened the elastic in place. "I'm all finished."

"You did a perfect job. I love you."

"I love you, too." She walked over to the table by the bed and brought her the cell phone and notepad. "Now you can call that ranger back."

Annie would do it right in front of Roberta. Regardless of whoever answered on the other end, her daughter would never know anything was out of the ordinary. In light of the fact that her parents would be here soon to take her home, she hoped it was Robert so she could get this out of the way once and for all.

She pushed the digits and waited three rings before he picked up.

"This is Chase Jarvis."

No matter how ready she thought she was to handle the call, she hadn't counted on the way Robert's deep voice resonated with her insides, calling up memories she was fighting with all her might to repress.

Her body went rigid. How did he have the gall to do this to her, to them! "I understand you asked me to return your call."

"Annie?" He sounded haunted. No doubt he was. It had taken ten years, but he'd finally been snared in a trap of his own making. "Don't hang up," he begged. "We have to talk."

"I agree," she said. Roberta might be watching TV, but her tender ears picked up on everything. "It would be remiss of me not to express my gratitude to all of you brave men for rescuing me and the pilot. I'll never be able to thank you enough.

"When I'm a little better I'll send an official thank-you to each of you for your extraordinary courage. It took courage to fly up there and perform those rescues knowing what had just happened to the helicopter we were in."

"Annie—" He said her name again, this time in a voice an octave lower and saturated in some indefinable emotion. She hardened herself against its insidious power to break through her defenses.

"If you'd be kind enough to tell the chief ranger I've decided not to take the job after all, I'd appreciate it. He sent a note with his flowers welcoming me to the park. Yesterday I spoke with my boss at the CDF and let him know I've changed my mind. I'm sure the word will be passed along, but since you work under Chief Rossiter he'll probably hear it sooner if you tell him.

"Goodbye, Ranger Jarvis, and thanks again for your uncommon act of valor. It will never be forgotten by me or the pilot." She clicked off, breathing in huge drafts of air to gain some semblance of control.

The moment Roberta could see that she'd hung up, she turned off the TV. "That ranger was nice."

Oh Roberta...

"Yes he was."

"Can we sleep at our house tonight? I want Debbie to come over."

The girls had a lot to discuss. "We'll probably stay there through the rest of the week and leave for San Francisco on Sunday."

"Are Grandma and Grandpa going to stay with us till then?"

"Tonight certainly. Then they'll probably drive back and forth. You know Grandpa. He has a hard time staying put for long."

"Yeah. He always walks around and it drives Grandma crazy."

Annie smiled at her observant daughter. "Now he'll have you to take with him. What you and I should do is get organized and make sure we've packed what we need to stay at Grandma's until our big move."

"When will we do that?"

"We can't move everything out until this cast comes off in six weeks. I don't even want to try. What we'll do when we get to Grandma's is enroll you in school near their house and start looking for a place to live that's close to them. Once that's accomplished we'll go from there. I don't expect we'll leave Santa Rosa for good for at least two months."

The lease on their condo wouldn't be up until the end of December. That gave her enough time to set up a new household in San Francisco without feeling rushed. Right now Annie was jobless, but she'd worry about that later. She had enough savings to take them into the first few months of next year.

"Can I invite Debbie to stay at Grandma's on the weekends?"

"Debbie and maybe Penny."

Penny was a girl who lived in the eightplex, but went to a private school. Annie and Roberta liked her a lot. "We'll ask Julie to come too and sometimes you can stay with them." Julie rented a house only a block away from the condo. In time Roberta would make new friends in San Francisco, but for now this would work.

She heard footsteps and saw her parents come in the room. Roberta ran to hug her grandma. Annie's dad beamed when he saw her. "Looking at you, you'd never know you've been through such a horrendous ordeal. Do you feel as good as you look?"

"Better," Annie lied, giving him a kiss on the cheek.

Every bone in her body ached and the one-sided conversation with Robert had shaken her to the core. Though he'd only said a few words, they'd been enough to disturb her at her deepest level. "The doctor has discharged me. I'm ready to leave."

Roberta gave him a hug. "I've got our suitcases ready."

"Then let's go."

"What are we going to do with the flowers?"

Annie studied her daughter. "We can't take them with us. Shall we ask the hospital to give them to some patients who could use cheering up?"

She nodded. "Here's your purse."

"Thank you."

Her mother peeked out the door. "The nurse is coming with your wheelchair."

"Can I push you, Mom?"

"We'll ask the nurse, but I don't see why not."

FRIDAY MORNING Chase sat in his car in one of the guest parking stalls at Annie's condo. Agent Sid Manning, his contact in the CIA, was parked around the corner waiting for Chase's signal to join him.

The phone conversation with Annie on Wednesday had been a lesson in futility. He'd known it in his bones before he'd picked up the phone. In truth he didn't have much faith in what he was about to do now, but it was necessary if he expected her to listen long enough to hear him out.

Since yesterday he'd been watching the activity at her condo. Last night he saw a man and woman leave her place in their luxury car. They had to be Annie's parents. Both had attractive physical traits she'd inherited.

A few minutes ago he'd had his first glimpse of his daughter. At eight-thirty a woman driving a Toyota pulled into the parking area with a blond girl in the back seat. In another minute a brunette of medium height flew out the front door in a blue and green top and jeans, carrying a backpack. While her ponytail swished back and forth, she waved to her friend waiting in the car.

Chase's hungry gaze took in her slender frame. She moved with nimble grace, like Annie. As she drew closer, he could see her facial features. His heart jolted to realize she bore an almost uncanny resemblance to his family, to him. Tears welled in his eyes. Roberta—his little girl. She was *adorable*.

The moment the Toyota disappeared down the street, Chase phoned Sid. "I'm going to approach her now."

"I'll be right there."

He'd decided to show up without warning. He realized it would be another strike against him. For all he knew Annie was still in bed, recuperating. But this was a life-and-death situation.

His life.

Knowing what he knew now, existence would have no meaning if he couldn't take care of them and love them for as long as he was granted life.

After drawing in a deep breath, he levered himself from the car and walked toward her condo. Sid pulled his car around and met him at the front door. He rang the bell. To his surprise she answered it faster than he would have expected.

"Honey?" she cried. "Did you forget something?"

But the minute she saw Chase, a gasp escaped her throat. She backed away from him. Beneath her mane of dark, glistening hair still in slight disarray from sleep, her features took on a chiseled cast.

"How dare you come here."

She wore a simple pink sundress, no doubt easy to put on over her cast. At second glance he noticed she was barefoot and beautiful. More beautiful than she'd been ten years ago if that were possible.

"Ms. Bower?" Sid spoke up. He took out his ID and held it in front of her. "I'm Agent Manning from the CIA. I need to have a word with you. It's for the safety of you and your daughter as well as Dr. Myers, who worked for us for a time."

"Of course he did," she mocked with a cruel laugh.

"May we step inside please?"

"No," she responded without hesitation or hysteria. "You can say what you have to say right here." She stared directly at them without the flicker of an eyelash to reveal any angst she might be hiding.

Chase wasn't surprised. There were degrees of betrayal. His qualified at the bedrock level. You couldn't go any lower.

Sid remained calm. "This will take some time."

The curve of her normally provocative mouth thinned to an angry white line. "You said you had something to say, so say it, otherwise I'm shutting the door."

"I was only thinking of your physical comfort."

"You people don't give a damn about anyone's comfort."

Sid flashed Chase a covert glance of surprise.

"Agent Manning is my contact here in the States," Chase explained. "I realize I'm dead to you, but as he explained, an Al-Qaeda cell is still hunting for me. For a long time we've feared you and Roberta might be a target. Now that you've learned I'm alive, it's important you know exactly what happened before Roberta was born. The explosion that killed everyone at the site wasn't an accident."

Her eyes darkened to an inky-blue. Finally a connection.

"He's right, Ms. Bower. Both he and his parents were operatives for the CIA helping gather intelligence while they worked undercover as archaeologists. They served faithfully many years until their true agenda was discovered and they were wiped out along with a dozen others.

"Only two bodies in the rubble were found still alive. Both had been given up for dead, but one of the doctors literally brought Dr. Myers back to life. Our people got him out of the country to a hospital in Switzerland where he spent over a year learning to walk again, not to mention undergoing several operations in order to recuperate from serious chest and stomach wounds."

Her face paled. Chase saw her sway and was ready to steady her, but she leaned against the doorjamb. "I don't believe any of it."

Sid reached inside his suit jacket and pulled out an eight-by-ten envelope. "These photos will convince you otherwise. They were taken after the explosion and at the hospital after Dr. Myers was flown there for surgery." When she wouldn't make a move to touch it, Sid tossed it onto the hall floor behind her. It slid across the tile.

"Knowing your relationship with him," Sid continued, "you were flown home immediately and put under protective surveillance in case Al-Qaeda operatives traced you here for retaliation. Because your life was in danger, Dr. Myers had no choice but to stay away from you. He gave up his work as an archaeologist to go to work for us full time."

Chase saw the muscles working in her throat. "I've given you more time than you deserve. You've had your say, now get out!"

His hands formed fists. "I need to talk to you, Annie."

Her face closed up. "I've needed to talk to you for ten years. Now it's too late." She shut the door in his face.

Sid turned his head toward Chase. "I've been in this business a lot of years, but I never met anyone as hard to crack. I'm not sure it's possible."

"It isn't," Chase whispered in shock. When he'd told Vance he feared she wouldn't be able to forgive him after she'd learned the truth, even he hadn't counted on the depth of her trauma. Pain consumed him.

He *was* dead to her.

Chapter Four

Annie stared at the brown envelope lying at the edge of the tile. Wherever she moved, it followed her like a living thing. Her survival instincts told her to burn it without viewing the contents.

If by any chance Agent Manning had told her the truth, more than ever she had no desire to see pictures of the man who'd never once tried to contact her since he'd been released from the hospital, not even through a third party.

Danger be damned! He'd seen a way out of their relationship and he'd taken it. There was only one reason he was making contact with her now. He'd found out he had a daughter. On Wednesday he'd spoken to Roberta on the phone. This morning he'd been stalking them out in front and had seen her leave the condo and get in Julie's car.

Who did he think he was to be absent for over a decade, and then swoop in to demand he and Annie talk?

There was no way she'd let him have access to Roberta. Annie needed to talk to her father's good friend, Clive Radinger. She'd met him several times at her parents' home when they'd entertained. He was supposed to be the best attorney in Northern California.

She would hire him to put a restraining order on Robert, but she'd keep it a secret from her family.

If Robert was so paranoid he'd actually chosen to remain dead to her until now, she reasoned he would shy away from undue publicity that could attract public attention to him or Roberta. Not wanting to waste a second, she snatched the envelope from the floor and went into the bedroom to make that phone call.

In a few minutes a receptionist answered. "Radinger and Byland."

"Hello? This is Annie Bower, Joseph Bower's daughter." She couldn't remember the last time she'd used her father's name for an entrée, but this constituted an emergency. "Is Mr. Radinger in?"

"He is, but he's with a client."

"If you'll put me on hold, I'll wait for him. This is extremely urgent."

"It could be a while."

"I don't care."

"Very well."

While Annie waited, she put her phone on speaker and sank down on the side of the bed. In case he wanted to know what was in the envelope, she thought she'd better open it. With only one arm free, it took some ingenuity to undo the seal. Out fell six glossy black-and-white photographs.

Her gaze fell on them. All she could see was a blood-spattered male body lying on his back with his arms and legs flung wide. The huge, gaping wound in his chest looked like a heap of spaghetti. It brought bile to her throat. There was so much blood on his face, she wouldn't have known who it was if she hadn't recognized the shape of Robert's head.

Her eyes traveled to another photo showing him lying on a stretcher facedown. The base of his spine looked like someone had taken a hacksaw to it. His trousers were totally drenched in blood.

Her cry resounded in the bedroom before she rushed to the bathroom and lost her breakfast. Five minutes later Annie returned to the bedroom, shaking like a leaf. For a moment she didn't realize the sound she could hear was a dial tone. She put a hand to her mouth, having forgotten all about the call to the attorney.

On rubbery legs she moved to the bed to hang up, then redialed the number.

"Radinger and Byland."

"H-hello. It's Annie Bower calling back."

"I'm glad you phoned. He's still on that other call. Do you really want to wait?"

She swayed in place. "N-no. I've changed my mind about talking to him. Please don't say anything. If I need him, I'll call and make an appointment."

"You're sure?"

"Yes. Thank you."

Annie clicked off. She was in shock over the pictures spread out on the bed. One photo showed a close-up of his bloodied face covered in cuts. This picture was exceptionally gory because he was such a striking man. The sight of him riddled with bits of the bomb brought home as nothing else could the evil of those who'd caused the mutilation done to him.

By rights he should have died with the others, yet it was no dead man who'd appeared at her door a little while ago.

She shoved the pictures under her pillow out of sight, not knowing what to do or where to turn. In agony she collapsed on her back and sobbed. This was a new horror on top of the old.

When her cell phone began ringing she was in no shape to answer it, but the person on the other end wouldn't give up. Using her free arm for leverage, she sat up and checked the caller ID in case it was her parents or the school phoning, but she knew full well who it was. Naturally the ID was blank.

Annie feared he was still outside the condo. What if he waited until Roberta got home from school and then approached her, forcing a confrontation of the three of them.

Today Annie's mother planned to pick up the girls and bring dinner home with them. She started to panic because, if either of them saw Robert, they'd recognize him at once.

She'd brought back photographs from Afghanistan. Most of them had been framed and were placed around Roberta's bedroom. Annie kept several framed pictures on her own dresser and by the bed. The rest had been put in an album Roberta went through all the time and showed her friends.

Robert had put her in an untenable position. She was damned no matter what she did, but if she refused to talk to him, he was capable of anything and it could affect Roberta. She would do whatever it took to protect her daughter.

Her hand reached for the phone and she clicked on. After a brief hesitation she said, "What is it you want?"

"To talk."

"There's nothing to discuss. I could have done without the photographs and am deeply sorry for the horror you went through, but have no fear. You're still dead to me and Roberta. That's the way I want it to stay."

"At any moment you might get your wish."

His comment brought her up short. "You mean you're going to be disappearing again? If that's the case, why bother telling me?"

"I'm not going anywhere, but there's something else you need to know about me. Unfortunately when we came to the door earlier you were so upset, I held back."

"Held back what?"

"Let me backtrack for a minute. When I heard you had a daughter and learned that her name was Roberta, I realized she was my daughter, too. Knowing I'd made you pregnant, I wanted to be a part of her life and help care for her. But you need to know about my medical condition. It might influence you not to tell Roberta about me. I would understand that and leave you alone."

His words rocked her. "That sounds very noble. What medical condition?"

"There's a piece of shrapnel lodged in my heart." When the words sank in, Annie felt a tight band constrict her lungs. "It's in an inoperable position. As long as it doesn't move, I'm all right. After ten years I'm still here, but there are no guarantees. Roberta would have to know that."

Annie could hardly swallow, let alone respond.

"Every two months I have it checked at a private clinic. No one knows about my condition except Agent Manning and Chief Rossiter. Because ten years have gone by without incident, it gives me hope for a few more. How many, only God knows. At this point you deserve—no, you have the right to know everything about me before you decide to let Roberta know I'm alive. I'm aware it could influence your decision."

A cry escaped her throat. "Are you telling me you

were afraid you might die of your injury and that's the reason you never tried to contact me?"

"No. I've already given you my reasons for remaining dead to you, but now that I know I have a daughter…everything's changed," he said emotionally. "I know you're going to say that it hardly makes sense for me to show up now and endanger both your lives, but I've talked with my superiors.

"We've come to a consensus that ten years has minimized the threat of danger as long as I remain at the park. The uncanny coincidence that you applied for the archaeology position will make it possible for me to see our daughter on a daily basis."

"That's out of the question. I've already withdrawn my application."

"If you take the job," he said, ignoring her, "there'll be no safer place in the world for all of us where I can protect you. Homeland security is especially tight there. I want to get to know my daughter, Annie. As long as she's told the whole truth about me and you think she can live with it, then this is the one way we can be together."

By now she was shaking. How could she tell Roberta her father was alive in one breath, and then in the next, tell her he could die any time from an injury to his heart? This was insanity! "I've told you I don't want anything to do with you."

"I'm well aware of that fact, but would you punish Roberta who has her own father ready and willing to love her? How do you think she'll feel if later on she finds out you made the decision to keep her away from me after you found out I'm alive?"

Her breath caught. "The only way she'd find out would be if *you* told her!"

"I've already told you I wouldn't do that, but can you be positive there won't be another coincidence down the line that brings an accidental meeting of the two of us?"

Her thoughts flicked back to a recent conversation she'd had with Roberta. *We're studying California history. Mrs. Darger showed us a video the other day. We're going to go on a field trip to Yosemite next year near the end of school.*

Annie shook her head. "This is a nightmare."

"Why? What did you tell her about her father? Does she even know the truth?"

"Yes—" she almost shouted in defense. "Yes," she mumbled, trying to calm down.

"Then why is this a nightmare? Unless you're on the verge of marrying someone else and she already thinks of him as daddy."

Her hand tightened on the phone. "There isn't anyone else," she admitted in a weak moment. She'd dated other men, but she'd only allowed those relationships to go so far before she backed off because she couldn't commit.

Only now did it occur to her Robert was probably involved with some fascinating female. The women she knew in Kabul, foreign or American, had coveted her relationship with him. Since she'd been younger than any of them, she couldn't believe it when he'd singled her out. He was one man who could have had any woman he wanted and was an even more arresting male now. How many had there been since he'd left the hospital in Switzerland?

"When will Roberta be home from school?"

The unexpected question set off alarm bells. "Why?"

"Because I'm walking up to your door as we speak.

In case you feel she can handle all the truth, we need to work out a plan face-to-face before I meet her for the first time. In the event you don't end up taking the job in the park, we have to talk about visitation rights."

"No—"

"Don't you think her input will be crucial when she learns she can visit me at the park any time she wants to? It's your choice how we handle it."

"Robert? Please don't do this—" she begged frantically.

"My name is Chase Jarvis. It's just one of the many things about my fictional background Roberta and her grandparents will have to have explained to them. I saw them leaving the condo last night, by the way. Ages ago I told you I was looking forward to meeting them, but I didn't realize it would take ten years before I had the opportunity. There's no time like right now to talk this through."

He'd run her to ground. "Y-you'll have to give me five minutes."

"No problem. I'm not going anywhere."

Annie knew that. The ramifications terrified her.

WHEN THE DOOR OPENED and a pale Annie with her arm in a sling stood back so Chase could enter, he could breathe again. He saw no change in her except she'd put on sandals and had run a brush through her glossy hair.

Once inside the condo he noted the yellow-and-white color scheme in the front room with its splashes of blue. She'd placed potted plants around with an artistic eye. A basket of fresh violets sat perched on the coffee table in front of the yellow-and-white-striped couch. Two French provincial chairs in a taffeta plaid of blue, yellow and white completed the living room arrangement.

Everything reflected the warm personality of the woman he'd fallen in love with. She'd decorated her condo along traditional lines, creating a cozy, comfortable atmosphere for herself and their daughter. Give her free rein with his house in the park and they'd have a showplace.

It had been needing a woman's touch. Her touch. He'd needed, craved her touch for too long. Being with her like this again made him want to catch up on ten years all at once. He wanted an on-the-spot fix that would obliterate the pain of the past so they could take up where'd they'd left off before the explosion, but he knew it wasn't possible. He had to slow down and let her set the pace.

She shut the door behind him. "Come in the living room."

As he moved out of the foyer, he felt inquisitive eyes wander over him, undoubtedly trying to see through his sport shirt and trousers to the massive scars on his torso and lower back. The shrapnel in his heart wouldn't be visible without an X-ray, of course.

Several plastic surgeries had helped make the damage somewhat more presentable to human eyes, but even the doctors who'd attended him had to admit those photographs weren't a pretty sight. However, their shock value had at least made a fissure in that wall of ice encasing Annie, otherwise he wouldn't have made it inside her home.

Standing in the middle of the room, he said, "I fell in love with our daughter over the phone. When I saw her leave the condo earlier, my entrancement was complete. She has a faint look of me, but all the important parts are you. To say that you've done a superb job raising our child would be a colossal understatement."

She stood opposite him. He noticed her breathing had grown shallow. "The last thing I want is for her to be hurt!" she cried. "You suddenly show up back from the dead with your pretty speech, not having a clue what this could do to her."

"I know what it has done to me," he said calmly, "so I think I have some idea of the impact it will have on her. But if we do this right, then she'll have the benefit of being loved by the two people who love her more than anyone on earth. I'll love her and protect for as long as I'm granted breath."

He could see she was trembling. "How do you do something like this *right*?" She was fighting for Roberta's life. The anguish in her tone cut him to the quick.

"You're still recovering from the crash and look pale. Before we talk about it, I'm going to get you a glass of water."

Despite her protests, he walked through the dining room to the sunny kitchen. He checked a couple of cupboards until he found a glass. As he turned on the cold water tap she joined him. One glimpse of her drawn features and he forced her to sit on one of the white wood-and-wicker chairs placed around the breakfast table.

"Drink this, Annie. You look ready to pass out."

Incredibly, she did as he asked.

"Do you need more painkiller for your arm?" When she didn't immediately answer, he told her he'd get it and headed down the hall to her bedroom. Going on instinct he found the medicine on an end table next to her bed.

Beneath the lamp he saw a framed picture of the two

of them with their arms wrapped around each other. He remembered when and where it had been taken as if it were yesterday. His heart gave him a karate-sized kick, sending him back to the kitchen.

He opened the bottle and shook out the prescribed two pills for her. She swallowed them with the last of her water.

"More?"

She shook her head.

"You need to be in bed. I'll help you."

"No—you've done enough. The weakness has passed."

Her color had improved. It was the only reason he didn't pick her up and carry her to the bedroom.

Chase stood next to her chair. She refused to look at him. "I realize the shock has been too much for you so I'm going back to my motel. It's only a mile from here. Just understand that I want to have a full relationship with our daughter, but I'll honor your wishes if you decide she can't handle learning about my heart condition.

"Please let me know one way or the other. Depending on your decision, we'll come up with a plan to be introduced. I'm on vacation and will wait as long as it takes for your phone call."

"I can't give you a timetable for anything."

"You need to keep in mind there's an endless line of archaeologists waiting for the opportunity you've been offered to work in the park. Roberta's too young to know you were singled out from all the others because of your outstanding credentials and experience in Afghanistan. Superintendent Telford is counting on you to vindicate him in adding an archaeologist with your particular expertise."

She made no response, indicating she was barely

tolerating his presence. He doubted she'd been listening.

He ground his teeth in frustration. "Before I leave, is there anything else I can do for you?"

"Nothing." It was clear Annie wanted him gone.

"Don't forget I'm only five minutes away if you need anything." With those parting words he strode from the kitchen to the front door and let himself out. From now on it was a waiting game.

LATE SATURDAY AFTERNOON, Annie poked her head inside the door of Roberta's bedroom. The girls had been playing with their Polly Pocket figures. "Debbie? Your mom's here."

Roberta looked up from the bed. "Does she have to go?"

"I'm afraid so."

"Mom's boyfriend is taking us for pizza and a movie." She put the figures she brought in a little case and jumped off the bed.

"Do you like him?" Roberta asked as they walked through the house. Annie followed them.

"Not very much. When he comes over he always turns off my show so he can watch sports."

"That's not fair."

Annie could have predicted her daughter would say that. They waved Debbie off and shut the door. "How soon are Grandma and Grandpa coming?"

"They're bringing Chinese for us and should be here by seven." It was four-thirty now, giving Annie a two-and-a-half-hour window to talk about the elephant in the room, the one Roberta didn't know had been living with them since Monday.

She made a detour to the laundry room to pull the clean clothes out of the dryer. "Would you mind carrying the basket to my bedroom so I can fold them?"

Roberta did as she was asked and trudged behind Annie with it. "I'm glad you don't have a mean boyfriend." Roberta set it on the bed. Her daughter had just given Annie the opening she'd been searching for since Robert had made his demand before leaving the condo yesterday. No matter how he'd couched it, he'd let her know he was going to have his way and there was no escape.

"Would you like me to have a nice one?" she teased.

"Would *you*?"

Either Roberta was a crafty soul or unsure of herself. Maybe she was a little of both, because she often answered Annie's questions with another question, thereby excusing herself from incrimination.

"I haven't given it a great deal of thought. We've been happy together, haven't we?"

Roberta nodded. "Nobody would be like Daddy."

Annie struggled to breathe normally. "How do you know that?"

Roberta gave her one of those innocent stares that seemed to go clear through to Annie's soul. "Because you *loved* him."

In an abrupt move, Annie turned the basket upside down on the bed and started separating their clothes. Halfway through the process she sank down on the edge, praying for inspiration.

"Honey? Let's play a game."

"Which one?" She was carefully folding her tops and stacking them. Roberta was a much neater person than Annie.

"It's one we've never tried before."

"Okay. What's it called?"

"What if?"

"We used to play that in kindergarten."

"Can we do it anyway?"

"Okay."

"I'll start." Annie's heart hammered so hard, she wondered if it would pound her right into the floor. "What if you found out a miracle happened and your daddy didn't die in that explosion?"

She'd begun folding her school pants in another pile. "I'd be the happiest girl in the world."

"I know that. What if you learned he had a piece of metal in his heart from the explosion that the doctors couldn't get out?"

Her hands stilled on the clothes. "You mean he could die."

"It's possible."

"But he hasn't died yet so maybe he won't."

Oh, Roberta... "What if it took him ten years before he could let me know he was alive?"

She lifted her head. "Why would he take so long?"

"Because he was in a war and bad people were looking for him. He didn't want to put you and me in danger." For the time being she had to accept Agent Manning's explanation.

Roberta went perfectly quiet. "Are we still playing what if?" Her daughter knew the answer to that question before she'd asked it.

Annie shook her head. "No."

Solemn eyes mixed with fear clung to Annie's. "Is he still in danger?"

"Not in the same way he once was. That was a long

time ago, but he's been using a different name for years just to stay safe."

She twisted her hands together like she often did when she was her most insecure. "Does he know I was born?"

"He does now."

Roberta bit her lip. "Does he want to see me?" she asked in a quiet voice.

"Oh yes, darling. The second he found out he had a daughter, he phoned me in the hospital." She tried to swallow but couldn't. "Do you remember Ranger Jarvis? The one you said was so nice?"

She nodded.

This was it. "He's your father."

Annie could hear her mind trying to take it all in. "The ranger who rescued you?"

"Yes. He's been a park ranger for three years, but I didn't know it. I only saw him for a moment when they were lifting me into the helicopter. H-he wants to meet you as soon as possible." Her voice faltered. "How do you feel about that?"

Her daughter blinked. She was in a daze. "Is he at the park now?"

An adrenaline rush made Annie so jumpy she stood up. "No. He's staying at a motel here in Santa Rosa waiting to meet you."

"Do you think he would come over?" Her daughter was holding in all her feelings of excitement. Annie could tell she didn't quite believe this was happening. Who would? The whole situation was too surreal to comprehend.

"Why don't you call him? I have his phone number, the one you wrote down. It's in my purse." Before she could ask Roberta to hand it to her, her daughter rushed to the dresser to get it. Annie handed her the cell phone lying on the bedside table. "If he doesn't answer, leave him a message. I know he'll return it."

Roberta punched in the number and put the phone to her ear. Annie held her breath.

CHASE HAD JUST PULLED AWAY from a drive-through when his cell phone rang. One glance at the caller ID showed it to be Annie's number. His heart thudded against his ribs. This call had come sooner than he'd anticipated. How would he handle it if she shut him out for good?

He rested the sack of food on the seat and answered. "Annie?"

After a silence, "It's Roberta."

Warmth flooded his system. This could only mean one thing. Annie had told their daughter about him. That meant she'd told her about his heart condition. He didn't know how much other information she'd given her, but under the circumstances it was a miracle she'd unbent enough to let them get acquainted.

"Hi, sweetheart."

"Hi," came the timid greeting.

"I can't wait to meet you."

"Me, too," she admitted quietly.

"Are you afraid?"

"Kind of."

"So am I. What if you don't like me?"

A nervous little laugh escaped. "I have pictures of you."

"I wish I'd had one of you all these years. I'm afraid I look a lot older now."

"Like my grandpa?"

He chuckled. "Maybe not quite that old."

"Mom told me about your heart. Does it hurt?"

Chase had to clear his throat. "No, sweetheart. I feel perfectly normal."

"That's good. Can you come over to our house?"

There was no other place he wanted to be. "I was hoping you'd ask. If you want, I'll drive there right now. What do you think?"

"Mom says you can come for a little while."

Chase took that to mean they were expecting company later, probably the Bowers. "I'm on my way. See you in a minute."

"Okay."

He didn't remember the short drive to the eightplex or the walk from the guest parking stall to the condo. Before he reached it, he saw her standing in the open doorway wearing a pair of jeans and a bright red cotton top.

As he approached, they studied each other for a long time. Now that he had a frontal view of her, he detected a lot more of Annie in the oval shape of her face and the feminine way she stood and moved.

"Do I look like a grandpa to you?"

"No."

That was something anyway. He smiled. "With those sky-blue eyes, you're even more beautiful than I had imagined. Am I the luckiest father in the world or what?"

Her Myers mouth curved into the sweetest smile he'd ever seen.

"I never got to change you or feed you when you were a baby. Would you mind very much if I gave you a hug?"

She shook her head, causing her dark brown ponytail to swish.

He made the first move, but when he swept her into

his arms and lifted her off the ground, she lost her reserve. Her arms crept around his neck and clasped him tightly. The slight weight of her body satisfied a deep ache that had been gnawing at him since he'd been torn from Annie.

"Roberta," he murmured against her temple, giving her kisses. "I love you." He could hardly bear it that he'd missed her first ten years.

"I love you, too."

She broke his heart with her unqualified acceptance. "Will you be my big girl from now on?" He felt her nod. "Some of my ranger friends have children. They won't believe it when they find out I have a daughter. I guess you realize we look alike."

"That's what mom says."

He lowered her to the ground. "Where is she?"

"Inside." She stared up at him. "Do you want to come in?"

"If it's all right with her."

"She said you could."

"Then I'd like to." Before he walked inside with her, a girl Roberta's age came skipping down the sidewalk from another condo and asked if she wanted to play.

"I can't. My dad's here."

The auburn-haired girl gazed at him in shock. "I've seen your pictures. I thought you…died."

He laughed inwardly. She'd said it the way it was. "I was in an accident and Roberta's mother thought I was dead. When I woke up in the hospital I had amnesia and didn't know who I was. Over the years I eventually regained my memory." That was the story he and Sid had come up with to tell everyone. "Roberta, sweetheart? Who's your friend?"

"This is Penny."

He smiled. "How do you do, Penny."

"Hi." She kept looking at him. This was what it felt like to be an alien.

"Have you two been friends a long time?"

Penny nodded.

"Penny's dad is the football coach at St. Xavier high school."

"That's exciting," Chase replied. "Do you attend all his games?"

She nodded. "Sometimes Roberta goes with our family and Dad takes us for hot dogs after."

He glanced at his daughter. "Lucky you."

Roberta nodded. "My dad's a ranger at Yosemite Park," she announced unexpectedly.

To hear her say "my dad" filled him with joy.

"You are?"

Chase chuckled at the expression of amazement on Penny's face. Kids often responded that way. Soon after he'd started working at the park he discovered there was something of a mystique about the rangers in tourists' eyes.

"That's right. You'll have to come horseback riding at the park with me and Roberta sometime. We'll take a picnic with us and I'll show you a fabulous beaver pond. There's an old granddaddy beaver we've named Methuselah because he's been around so many years. When he slaps his big tail, it's so loud it scares all the animals away."

Suddenly it was his daughter who looked awestruck. "How soon can we go?"

"Whenever you want."

Out of the corner of his eye he saw Annie appear in

the entry. He'd been waiting. Every time he saw her, those old feelings of desire took over.

"Hi, Penny. How are you?"

"Good. Does your arm still hurt?"

"Not when I wear the sling."

"Mom!" Roberta cried. "Dad's going to take us horseback riding!"

"So I heard."

Chase had a feeling she'd been listening and had decided to break things up when the conversation started to get out of her control.

Roberta must have heard Annie's guarded answer. On cue she said, "I have to go in now, Penny, but I'll call you later."

"Okay. See ya. Don't forget."

"We won't," Chase assured her. "It was nice to meet you, Penny."

"You, too." She hurried down the sidewalk.

Annie flicked him a glance out of shadowed blue eyes. "Come in. We need to talk."

His words exactly.

He ushered Roberta inside and shut the door. It was déjà vu except that they congregated in the living room. Roberta sat next to him on the couch. Annie stood behind one of the chairs. Negative tension radiated from her.

"Honey?" she began. "Before you start making any plans with friends, we have to be very careful about what we say. Not even your grandparents know your father is alive yet. Whatever we tell people has to be the same story. No one can know he was once Robert Myers."

"Your mother's right," Chase corroborated. "We'll tell everyone I lost my memory and barely got it back. That's all people ever have to know. As for you,

Roberta, you have to be told the truth. You know there's a war in the Middle East, right?"

She nodded.

"After the explosion, I was in a hospital in Switzerland for a long time. After that I fought in the war for our country."

"You did?"

"Yes. But one of the terrorists who'd planned the attack on my parents recognized me and word went out that I was still alive. That's when the CIA flew me to the States and turned me into a park ranger to keep *me* safe. For three years everything has been fine, so I don't want you to worry about being in danger.

"When you visit me, it will be in the park where my colleagues are on the alert for all bad people and terrorists living in our country. In fact you'll probably be safer at my house than here in Santa Rosa because of the tight security. Chief Rossiter was a marine in Iraq. He knows the danger to me and has heightened security to keep us all safe."

Annie finally sat down in the chair. "After we move to San Francisco, we'll work out a schedule so you can go see your father when it's convenient for us and for him."

"But now that Daddy's here, I don't want to move to San Francisco."

Chase kept his head bowed. *Did you hear that, Annie?*

"It's all decided," she declared in a no-nonsense tone. "Grandma and Grandpa have been making plans for us."

Roberta slid off the couch and stood up. "I know I told you I didn't want you to work in the park, but I've changed my mind."

"You can't just change your mind. I've already turned down the job offer."

Her daughter's eyes filled with tears. "Can't you get it back? All you have to do is call them up and tell them you're feeling better now."

Nothing pleased Chase more than to watch Annie squirm over this.

He raised his head, focusing on her. "It's not too late. For the last three weeks I was acting head ranger for the park while the Chief was on his honeymoon. I'm the one the new superintendent asked to arrange for your flight over the park. All I have to do is say the word and the position is still yours."

"You were the head of all the rangers?" Roberta questioned while her mother looked poleaxed.

"I'm the assistant head ranger. When the Chief has to leave the park or go off duty, I'm in charge."

Her face beamed. "I can't wait to tell Debbie."

"Who's Debbie?"

"My best friend."

"I'd like to meet her. In fact I'm anxious to get acquainted with all your friends. They can come to my house anytime and sleep over with you. Of course if you lived in the park too, your house would be right around the corner from mine and you could run back and forth between us."

She gave a little jump of happiness.

As long as he'd gone this far to undermine Annie's plans to stay away from him, he might as well go all out. "You'll be a welcome addition to the school. The kids in the Yosemite Valley are homeschooled."

"You mean they get to study in their own house?"

"Not exactly. Ranger Farrell's wife, Kristy, is a professional teacher from the Mariposa County school district. You attend school at her house just like you go to school here. It's about two blocks away from mine. If you end up living in the park, that will make ten students for this school year."

"Are there kids my age?"

"Yes. Ranger Sims has a daughter named Carly who's your age and Ranger King has an eleven year-old boy named Brody. You'd like both of them."

At this point Annie had vacated her chair. "I'm afraid we're getting way ahead of ourselves."

Roberta ran over to her. "Mom—please say yes! Please! Grandma and Grandpa can come and stay with us all the time. I want to live by Daddy."

Satisfied to have created this much chaos, Chase rose to his feet. "Roberta? Your mother was kind enough to let me come and meet you, but I'm going to leave now. This is a situation you two need to discuss in private. You can call me anytime."

She looked alarmed. "Are you going back to the park?"

"Yes, but I'm only as far away as a phone call." He turned to Annie, who couldn't sustain his glance and had averted her eyes. "Annie? You'll never know what this day has meant to me," he whispered. "I'll let myself out."

He walked to the front hall. Roberta darted after him. "You promise you won't go away from the park?"

"I promise, sweetheart. It's my home." As if he'd been doing it all his life, he hugged her hard and was rewarded with a surprisingly strong squeeze. It came so naturally to him, he marveled. When he raised up he caught a glimpse of Annie, whose tortured expression he carried with him as he strode swiftly to his car.

Chapter Five

After Annie heard the front door close, she hurried into the kitchen to get herself a drink of water. It was an excuse to gather her wits, but Roberta stuck to her like glue.

"Daddy said you could work in the park if you want to. Don't you want to?"

She drained the glass she'd poured before turning to her daughter. "Actually I don't."

"Because of the accident?"

"No."

"Then why?" she persisted.

"Roberta, I realize this is hard for you to understand, but your father and I have led separate lives since before you were born. The park is his home now. I have to respect his privacy."

"Why? He wants us to come."

"No, he doesn't." The bewilderment on Roberta's face prompted her to sit down and draw her daughter to her. She brushed the tears off her cheeks with her free hand. "There's something you need to know. After you left for school this morning, he came to see me."

"You didn't tell me that. Neither did he."

"I know. He was trying to respect my feelings. We

talked for quite a while. A lot has happened in ten years. We're different people now. Everything has changed except for one thing. He loves you more than anything in the world and wants you in his life."

Roberta looked heartbroken. "Don't you love each other anymore?"

Annie had to be honest with her. "We have our memories, of course. No one can take those away from us, but we've both moved on. He said he never contacted me in all that time in order to keep me safe. I think that's a wonderful, noble excuse, the best excuse there could be, but I don't think it's the real reason he let me believe he had died."

Her daughter's blue eyes implored Annie. "What's the real reason?"

"If he'd truly been in love with me, I don't think he would have been able to stay away from me. When two people love each other more than anything in the world, nothing can separate them."

"Oh." Roberta's lips trembled.

It killed Annie to have to be this brutally honest with her, but it was the only way. "While he was rescuing me, he pretended he didn't know me. Honey, he was ready to leave the park and go someplace else without ever talking to me again, but by then one of the rangers told him I had a daughter. That changed everything for him. You see, I didn't know I was pregnant with you when I left Afghanistan, so of course he didn't either."

"I know. You told me that before."

This was developing into a new nightmare. "It's his love for *you*, not me, that brought him to the condo this morning, otherwise he'd be somewhere else far away from here by now. No one but his own little girl could have made him decide to call me at the hospital. That's because he wants you in his life and the only way he can make that happen is to talk to me and work things out."

Tears poured down Roberta's cheeks. "But he wanted to marry you."

"We said a lot of things to each other once. That was a long time ago. The fact that he hasn't ever married proves to me he's happy with his life the way it is and doesn't want a wife.

"You have to understand that before he fought in the war, he was an archaeologist who traveled from China to Afghanistan. In many ways, it's a lonely occupation. He lived in far-off places where the dig sites were hard to get to and he kept strange hours. Robert isn't a man like Penny's father, who has a normal kind of job with normal hours and time for his family."

"He's not an archaeologist anymore," Roberta said. She wasn't willing to let this go.

"That's true, but as you can see, he still lives alone because it's difficult to change old habits. In ways a ranger's life isn't that conducive to having a family either." She needed to squelch Roberta's hope that the two of them would get together.

"He said some of the rangers are married."

Annie sucked in her breath. "I know, but the last thing he wants is to see me working in the park, wishing I weren't around. He used the explosion that ended our relationship to make certain the situation remained permanent, but that was before he was told he had a daughter. We'll work out visitation for you to see him."

"Don't you even like him anymore?"

"Roberta, this doesn't have anything to do with liking him. He was a part of my life. Of course I like him, but to find out he's alive has been a great shock to me. I know you've always wanted your Daddy and by some miracle he's here for you, but our lives are more complicated than that."

"Daddy said he would protect us. Are you scared those terrorists are going to hurt you now?"

"Oh no, honey—"

She frowned. "Then I think you're being mean."

In Roberta's vocabulary the word *mean* had many definitions depending on the situation, but she'd never used it against Annie before. It was like a dagger plunged in her heart. "In what way?"

"If we lived in the park, I could see him every day. I don't want to live in San Francisco and have to wait all the time to be with him. He said he loves me more than anything." Her body shook with emotion. "When I talk to him again, I'm going to ask if I can live with him." On that note she ran out of the kitchen, leaving Annie absolutely devastated.

To her dismay the doorbell rang. Her parents' timing couldn't be worse. Thank goodness, Robert had already left. Attempting to pull herself together, she walked through the house to the entry, but a tear-ravaged Roberta had beaten her to it.

"Daddy?" she cried as she flung the door open. Obviously she thought he'd come back for some reason.

Caught off guard, Annie's parents' shocked gazes traveled from their granddaughter to Annie, who groaned in reaction. With that one telling word, the water had spilled over the dam, never to be recovered.

While her father stood there holding a sack of

Chinese takeout food, her mother bent over Roberta. "What's going on, dear?"

"Daddy didn't die in that explosion!"

She cupped Roberta's face in her hands. "I don't understand."

"Grandma—Daddy's alive! He's the assistant head ranger at Yosemite who helped rescue mom. He wants us to live in the park!"

Her father shut the door. He shot Annie an inquisitive glance mixed with hurt surprise that she hadn't confided any of this to them earlier. "Is this true?"

More groans.

"Yes. I—it's a long story," she stammered.

AFTER THE DRIVE from Santa Rosa, Chase let himself in the rear door at headquarters and entered Mark's office. Since he knew he wouldn't be able to sleep, he'd phoned Mark to tell him he would cover the Saturday night shift so the chief security ranger could have some much needed time off.

Vance had told Chase to go on vacation, but being alone in a motel waiting for the phone to ring was the kind of torture he couldn't tolerate.

The other man tried in vain to hide his excitement. "You're sure you want to do this?"

"Get out of here, Mark."

He grinned. "I'm going. I'll be back on duty at noon."

"Show up at two instead." While Chase waited for Annie to make the next move, the only panacea was to stay too busy to do a lot of thinking.

"You're on!"

Ten minutes after he left, the rangers stationed

around the park phoned in their status reports. The last one to come in was Ranger Farrell on duty at the base camp of the Tuolumne Meadows.

"We've got a situation, but I don't know how serious yet. There's been an outbreak of gastrointestinal illness."

"Who's been affected?"

"Some of the lodge employees and hikers."

"How many?"

"At least thirty so far. Three people were sick enough to be taken to the hospital in Bishop."

"I'll get right on it. Give me an hour-by-hour report."

"Will do."

After hanging up, Chase phoned the hospital to talk with the lab. In a few minutes he learned they suspected it was a norovirus infection illness. So far no fatalities. They didn't expect any.

Chase asked them to phone him when they had more information, then he left word for the county health inspector to get busy on it. He made a third call to the lodge to offer any assistance they needed, then he phoned Vance.

"At last! I've been waiting to hear from you. Have you met your daughter yet?"

"I'll tell you everything in a minute. Business first."

"What are you talking about?"

"I gave Mark the night off."

"You're here?"

"Drove in about a half hour ago."

"I'll be right there."

Within five minutes Vance walked into Mark's office. Chase was on the phone with one of the rangers reporting on a deserted car found on the road near Wawona.

While he told the ranger to impound the vehicle and send out a search crew for the missing driver, he handed Vance the faxed report from the lodge about the outbreak. Once he hung up, Chase brought him up to speed.

"Okay—" Vance sat back in the chair facing him. "Now that we've got business out of the way, I want to hear it all."

It was a relief for Chase to unload. "My Roberta is adorable. Perfect."

"Yeah?" Vance was grinning. "Has she called you Daddy yet?"

Chase nodded, still incredulous he was a father.

"So how soon can we expect her and her mother? Rachel and I are dying to meet them."

His smile morphed into a grimace. "That part isn't resolved. Annie's fighting it all the way."

"Is there another man?"

"No. I'm dealing with something much more formidable. She won't consider taking the job. We're down to visitation rights."

Vance sat forward. "Your daughter holds all the power right now. Do I have to remind you that Nicky was the one who brought Rachel back to the park a second time when she had no intention? Give it time."

Chase needed to hear that about now.

"You'll hate me for saying this, Chase, but patience is the key. I know because I've been there."

Chase shook his head. "After ten years, I don't have any." Just then the phone rang. "Let me get this."

"I'll go find us a couple of sodas."

Chase nodded and picked up. "Ranger Jarvis here."

"This is the hospital lab in Bishop calling." Chase

was crushed it wasn't Annie or Roberta on the other end. "What's the verdict?"

"Our assumption about the virus was correct. It comes on fast but everyone should recover without problem."

"I'll get the word out."

Good news for the park, but he needed even a modicum of good news from another quarter or he wasn't going to make it. He hoped to heaven Vance was right about Roberta working on her mother. Like Nicky, who'd been Vance's cheering section and had brought Rachel around, Chase's daughter was the key to his happiness.

ROBERTA ALWAYS GOT in bed with Annie in the mornings, but not this Sunday morning. All the way around, last night had been a total disaster. After she'd sat down with her parents to explain the incredible news that Robert was alive, Roberta had been so upset with Annie for insisting they were moving to San Francisco anyway, she'd gone to bed utterly inconsolable. Not even her grandparents could get her to come out.

Every time Annie peeked in the bedroom, she heard Roberta crying into her pillow. With each quiet sob it tore her apart a little more and she tiptoed back to the living room to talk to her parents. Mostly they listened while she unburdened herself.

"Do you have any idea how hard it would be for me to live at the park in such close proximity to him after what's happened?" Her voice throbbed in pain. "All these years I've kept a myth alive for Roberta. I've been such a fool."

"No, Annie," her father said. "He intended to marry you before terrorists destroyed his world. They could have destroyed you too if he hadn't protected you the way he did. The way he still has to!"

Annie hid her face in her hands. Somewhere deep down her father was making sense, but the shock of seeing Robert alive had prevented her from taking it all in.

"Don't blame him for deciding not to recognize you in front of the other rangers at the accident scene," her dad continued. "He was trying to protect you until he got you to the hospital, but the moment he felt it was safe, he phoned you. I'd say he's been perfectly clear about his intentions. He wants to be a father to Roberta now that he knows of her existence."

"Your father's right," her mom agreed. "When he first saw you, he could have asked the witness protection program to hide him away at another undisclosed location. Instead he called his superiors and now he has told you he wants you and Roberta near him, but he can't leave the park. My advice is to take the job. You have to admit it would make the problem of visitation a lot easier."

She stared at her mother. "I thought you were on my side. Don't you want us to live by you?"

"Margaret Anne Bower, that question doesn't deserve an answer." Her mother hadn't called her that since she was Roberta's age. "Do you honestly believe you'd be happy in San Francisco when you know how unhappy it would make your daughter? From day one you put her father on a pedestal and now he's here to claim her. You're changing the rules and she doesn't understand."

Annie didn't want to think about her parents' logic. She was in a kind of hell where there was no way out.

"All we're suggesting is that you don't let your pride get in the way of making such a vital decision where Roberta is considered," her father reasoned.

"Pride?" Annie questioned in surprise.

"Isn't that what this is all about?" He studied her for a moment. "If he'd come right out on the phone and declared that he was still in love with you, would you have given him the time of day…considering your frame of mind?"

The question went to the heart of the matter.

Her mother's eyebrows arched. "Where you're concerned, no one can presume to know what's in his mind and heart right now, but if I were you I'd show Robert you've matured into a woman who moved on a long time ago. He can see you've been leading a fulfilled life without him. Prove to him you'll continue to do what's right for your daughter. The future will take care of itself."

"Let him spend time with Roberta," her father said. "That will relieve you to enjoy yourself in the process. Have fun for the first time since you came home from Afghanistan. He'll soon realize you haven't lost that sense of adventure he was drawn to in the beginning. If you and Robert aren't meant to be, don't shut yourself off to other possibilities. You might meet someone exceptional while you're working in the park."

Annie wasn't a complete fool. She knew that deep down they worried she would never get married. Thirty-one wasn't an old age, but if she didn't put herself in a position to meet men, opportunities would be missed.

Her dad got up from the couch and came around to kiss her cheek. "We're going to the hotel, but we'll be back in the morning. The offer still holds to drive you to the park tomorrow. Roberta's never been there. It wouldn't hurt for her to see if she even likes it."

"Oh, Dad—with Robert there you *know* Roberta will love it."

That salient fact had kept Annie tossing and turning all night. Needing to talk to her daughter before any more time went by, she moved carefully off the bed and headed straight for Roberta's room.

She was still burrowed under her covers, but Annie knew she was awake. Her daughter was an early riser, always had been. When she was a baby, Annie would discover her in her crib in the wee small hours wide awake and playing with her toes. When she moved into the toddler years, she would be standing at the bars talking unintelligibly to herself before the sun was up.

Finally came the morning when Annie heard a loud thump and went running to Roberta's room. Her little girl had climbed over the railing and landed on the floor. Instead of a cry, Annie had been met with a smile and it was only six o'clock. It wasn't much past that time now.

"Roberta? Time to get up."

"I don't want to," came the smothered response.

Annie moved over to her and sank down on the bed. With her free hand she pulled the covers back so she could see her. "Do you know last night was the first time we ever went to bed without kissing each other good night?"

When she encountered only silence, Annie leaned over and kissed her brow. "In a little while your grandparents will be coming to take us to Yosemite for the day. We both need to get up and eat breakfast so we'll be ready."

Movement at last. Roberta shot up in the bed, her eyes shining from a puffy face. "Does Daddy know?"

"Not yet. I have no idea if he's on duty or not. We'll call him after we get there. If I'm going to take the job, I thought we'd better look at the house we'd be living in."

Roberta threw herself into Annie's arms. Tears of joy spilled everywhere, wetting them both.

Courage, Annie. You're about to go onstage in a new role. It will have to be so convincing, even you will be blessed in time with the gift of forgetfulness.

BETH SLIPPED inside Mark's office. She put coffee and a paper plate filled with breakfast fare on the desk for Chase. He'd just answered the phone and mouthed her a thank-you before she left.

"What were you saying about the abandoned car?"

"A tourist ran out of gas and hitched a ride back to Wawona. Problem solved."

"Good. How's the smog from the burn in that section?"

"Average."

"We can be thankful for light wind today. Keep in touch."

Chase clicked off and reached for a slice of toast. His gaze flicked to the clock. Ten to ten. Four more hours before he went off duty. After working all night he ought to be exhausted, but his inner turmoil over Annie had sent out hot, wirelike tentacles to every atom of his body, preventing him from relaxing.

A call from the hospital indicated no more new patients had been admitted because of the virus outbreak in the park. Chase sent a fax to the superintendent with the latest update, then settled down to eat his breakfast.

While he was swallowing the last of it, Jeff Thompson phoned in. Curious to know what was up when he'd just talked to him a half hour ago, he clicked on.

"Ranger Jarvis here."

"I thought you should know the park's most famous female just passed through the entrance."

He frowned. "Whom are you talking about?"

"Margaret Bower."

The disposable cup slipped from Chase's fingers. Fortunately he'd drunk the contents.

"Her daughter and parents were with her. Because of her cast, her father's driving. She said they were visiting for the day. For somebody who was in a crash just a week ago she looks fantastic, you know what I mean?"

Chase shot the cup in the direction of the wastebasket and missed. He couldn't answer. Too many emotions had seized him at once.

"Thought you should be informed in case they show up at the Visitor's Center. The Chief will want to meet her."

"He's off today. Got another call coming in," he lied, and ended the conversation before he had to listen to anything more that idiot had to say about Annie.

Last night Chase had been so negatively charged, he'd told Mark not to report for duty until two today. He groaned to realize Annie and Roberta would in all probability be arriving shortly and he couldn't leave his post.

He didn't know what was behind Annie's agenda. Chase would be a fool to assume she'd done a 360-degree turnaround. In all likelihood she wanted Roberta to get a feel for the park before she allowed visitation. To ask for more than that would only result in dashing his dreams. For the moment he had to squelch the desire to phone her. Until she made contact with him, he had no choice but to wait.

Everything seemed to be working against him. For once things were slow around the office despite the fact that this was one of the biggest traffic weekends for the park would have until spring.

At eleven-thirty he sent out the latest weather report to each ranger station. In the process, Cindy rang him from the information desk in the visitor's center.

"What's happening, Cindy?"

"There's a cute young lady out here named Roberta Bower who's asking for Ranger Jarvis." Elation brought him to his feet. "She says you're one of the rangers who helped rescue her mom from the helicopter crash and she wants to thank you." Clever girl. "What should I tell her?"

"Bring her back to Mark's office."

"Will do."

He walked around the counter to the door and opened it. A few seconds later he saw them coming down the hall. His first reaction was to run out and sweep her into his arms, but he restrained himself.

Cindy smiled at Chase. "Ranger Jarvis? Meet Roberta Bower."

He tried to dislodge the lump in his throat, but it was no use. "We met once before didn't we, Roberta."

"Yes."

They were both playing a game in front of Cindy. Behind Roberta's reserve, her blue eyes glowed like hot stars. As she surveyed him in his ranger outfit, he saw her heels go up and down, as if she were barely holding on to her excitement. Join the club.

"Where's your mother?"

"Outside in the car with my grandparents. She said I could visit you for a minute if you were free."

"You picked the perfect time. Come in." He flicked his gaze to Cindy. "Thanks for bringing her back."

"You bet. See you later, Roberta."

"Thank you for helping me."

His daughter's excellent manners delighted him all over again. He shut the door so they could be alone. Smiling down at her, he said, "Aren't *you* a sight for sore eyes!"

She looked so cute in her long-sleeved pullover and jeans, he couldn't resist picking her up to hug her. Roberta was right there hugging him back with all her might. She smelled fragrant, just the way her mother always did.

Naturally the phone rang while they clung to each other. "I've got to answer it." He carried her around the counter with him and set her on one of the stools before he picked up. "Ranger Jarvis here."

"It's Ranger Hawkins reporting from Tamarack Flat. I found five dead skunks in the latrines. This is a new one on me."

It surprised Chase, too. The park's chief biologist would need to investigate. "I'll get right on it. In the meantime, seal them off to the public."

He hung up, then called Paul Thomas's office and explained the situation. "Give me your best theory after you've investigated. Mark will need to know if they wound up in there because of a malicious prank."

"That was my first thought. I'm leaving now."

"Thanks, Paul."

Finally he could give Roberta his attention. "Is your mom still out in front?" She nodded. "Maybe I'd better talk to her."

"She wants to know if you have to work all day."

"I'll be off at two, then I'll show you where I live."

Roberta slid off the stool. "I'll run out and tell her, then I'll come right back.'

"Okay."

She darted around the counter and out the door. A couple of staff came and went from the room. He answered another call. The next time the door opened he thought it would be Roberta. Instead, Nicky popped in carrying a long, thin, gift-wrapped package.

"Hi, Uncle Chase!"

"Hi, yourself! Did you come over with your dad?"

"Nope. He's home with Mom. We wanted you to come for dinner so I could give you my present, but Daddy found out you had to work. He said I could come over and give it to you, but first I have to call him and tell him I'm here."

Chase handed him his cell phone. "Press two."

While Nicky was making the call, Roberta came running inside. She swept right past their visitor and hurried around the counter. "Grandma and Grandpa have to get back to San Francisco so Mom says we have to leave the park by three."

Stifling his disappointment, he said, "Then we'll have an hour to talk. What does she plan to do in the meantime?"

"We're going to look at the falls and walk around, but I'd rather stay here with you."

"Then run back out and tell her I'll keep you with me."

"Can I?" she cried with excitement.

"I want you to. At three we'll meet in my office with your mom and talk."

By now Nicky was off the phone. He stared from her to Chase. "Who's that?"

This was going to be fun. "Nicky Rossiter? I want you to meet my daughter, Roberta Bower. Roberta? Nicky's father is Vance Rossiter, the chief ranger and my best friend."

Nicky giggled. "You don't have a daughter, Uncle Chase."

Chase put an arm around her shoulders. "Are you sure? Take a close look." He lowered his face next to hers. "What do you think?"

At least a half minute passed while Nicky scrutinized them. "You kind of look like each other. Is he really your daddy?"

Roberta nodded. "He had amnesia for ten years and didn't know I was born until a few days ago."

"What's amnesia?"

Chase straightened. "Tell you what, Nicky—I'll explain all about it in a minute. First though, why don't you go with Roberta while she runs outside to talk to her mother. On your way back, show her where my office is and then stop in at your dad's office and get both of you a soda from his mini fridge."

"Okay." Nicky put the unopened present on the counter. "What kind of soda do you like?" he asked as they started to leave the office together.

"Root beer."

"So do I! It's my favorite! Have you ever been to the park?"

"No."

"What grade are you in?"

"Fourth."

"You're old. I'm only in first. Are you scared of bears?"

"I'm scared of grizzlies."

"Don't worry. We only have black bears. Yosemite doesn't have any wolves."

As their voices faded, Chase broke into a broad grin because Nicky would be pure entertainment for his daughter from now on. That is, if Annie allowed him liberal visitation rights.

His hands tightened into fists. To think she was right outside the building behaving as if they'd never known each other. How ironic when in reality their precious go-between was no one less than the child they'd created together.

Annie couldn't have forgotten those early mornings of passion years ago before they left for work. They took turns fixing each other breakfast, then went back to bed, unable to leave each other's arms. Once at the site they had to be careful not to give in to their desires around the others. Knowing this, they made the most of every moment alone.

Annie's open, loving nature had been a revelation to him on a spiritual as well as a physical level. No woman since had the depth of character to tug so powerfully at his emotions. Having seen her again, her magic was stronger than ever. She'd given birth to their beautiful daughter. This new dimension of motherhood left him in awe that she'd had sole responsibility of their daughter from the moment she'd conceived.

Chase knew it was late in the day, but everything in him yearned to be a part of their lives. He ached for what he'd been missing. No matter how hard Annie fought him, he intended to live the life with them that had been denied him.

As he was making that vow to himself, the young lady who was going to help him achieve that joy came into the office with Nicky, both of them drinking root beer. From the way he was still chattering, it sounded like he'd been giving Roberta the guided tour.

"Hi, sweetheart. Did your mom say it was all right to stay with me?"

Roberta darted him a glance. "Yes. She says she'll be in your office at two."

Good. He wondered if her parents would come in with her. It was long past time they all met.

"Here." Nicky picked up the present. "This is for you. I hope you like it."

"I'm sure I will." Chase removed the wrapping paper and opened the long box. Inside the lining lay a silver, batonlike object, smooth and slim. "What is it?"

"It's your wizard wand. The man put your name on the handle. See?"

Chase lifted it from the box and examined it. Sure enough the words *Uncle Chase* had been engraved. "I love it! How did you know this is exactly what I wanted?"

Roberta looked fascinated. "Where did you get it?"

"In London at the Harry Potter shop. We all bought one."

"You went to England?"

Nicky nodded.

Pretending he was a wizard, Chase wove it around in the air. Making his voice scary he said, "Double, double toil and trouble, fire burn and caldron bubble—cool it with a baboon's blood, then the charm is firm and good."

While the children laughed, someone started clapping. Chase looked up to see Vance in the doorway. "Well, well, well. Shakespeare at Hogwarts. I believe you've missed your calling."

Chase chuckled. "Something my English tutor in Pakistan had me memorize, but I only remember the last four lines." He rubbed the top of Nicky's head. "Thank you for the terrific gift. I'm going to keep it on the desk in my office. When the rangers get out of line, I'll put a spell on them."

"You can't really do that." But he looked at Vance before he said, "Can he, Daddy?"

"I guess we'll have to wait and see," he teased. His gaze fell on Roberta. He studied her before sending Chase his nod of approval. "I'm already crazy about your little acorn," he murmured quietly. Then he turned to Nicky. "Aren't you going to introduce me to your new friend?"

He took another sip of his soda. "This is Roberta. Uncle Chase is her daddy."

Vance hunkered down in front of her. "I can see the resemblance, but you're the pretty one." Roberta blushed. "It's a pleasure to meet you."

"Thanks. It's nice to meet you, too."

"You've made your dad very happy by coming to visit him."

Nicky put his arm across Vance's shoulder. "Daddy? What does amnesia mean?"

The two men exchanged meaningful glances. "In Uncle Chase's case it means he had an accident ten years ago and it took away his memory. When he woke up in a hospital, he didn't know where he was or who he was."

By now Nicky was mesmerized. He eyed Chase with a worried glance. "Were you scared?"

"Very." *In fact you'll never know, Nicky. For years I had petrifying dreams that Annie had been found and tortured.* "Roberta's mother thought he died and she moved back to California," Vance continued. "Then just the other day she was in that helicopter crash and Uncle

Chase found her. Suddenly he remembered who he was, and to his joy he found out Roberta was his daughter."

After the explanation sank in, Nicky stared at Roberta. "Are you glad your daddy found you?"

She nodded.

"Next to Daddy and my grandparents, I love Uncle Chase best."

Chase's eyes smarted. "Ditto, sport." Just then Roberta slid her hand into Chase's.

She looked up at him. "I love you, too."

He squeezed her fingers. Those words had just melted his heart.

"Are you going to live with him?" Nicky asked.

Vance got to his feet. "Nobody knows what's going to happen yet. That's why Roberta's mother has come to the park today." He picked him up. "Now that you've delivered your present, we're going back to your mom and let Roberta and her father spend some time together alone."

"Okay. See ya, Roberta."

"See ya."

When the door closed Chase looked down at his daughter, who was drinking the rest of her root beer. "Now where were we?"

Chapter Six

"Hi. My name's Cindy. What can I do for you?" The cute, blond female ranger taking in the sling holding Annie's broken arm, had a charming Southern accent.

"I have an appointment with Ranger Jarvis at two."

"You have to be Roberta's mother. She's a darling girl."

Annie warmed to her. Anyone who liked Roberta was an automatic friend. "Thank you. I think she is, too."

"We're all so sorry you had to be in that crash. I'm sure it was horrible for you, but everyone's thankful you survived. I must say you look wonderful."

"Thank you, but the credit goes to the pilot. He told me what to do and it saved both of us."

"Tom was a crack naval pilot."

"So I've heard. I'm just glad he was at the controls."

"You were doubly lucky that day. Ranger Jarvis is a natural-born hunter. He's the one everyone wants on a rescue like yours. Chief Rossiter says he has superhuman instincts. Coming from the Chief, that's real praise."

A shiver ran down Annie's spine. Now that she knew Robert had trained with the Special Forces in Afghanistan, nothing surprised her. The look in the female ranger's eyes as she spoke about Robert told Annie a lot. So did the fact that there was no engagement ring or wedding band on her finger.

Annie probably had that same look in her eyes when she'd first met him. It seemed a century ago. "I realize I was very lucky. Do you think he's free now?"

The other woman checked her watch. "He's just going off duty. Why don't you walk back to his office? Go down that hall on your left and you'll come to another hall. His is two doors down on your right."

"Thank you. I'll find it."

She looked around the visitor's center filled with tourists checking out the exhibits and getting information. Slowly she threaded her way through the crowd to the hallway in question. It was almost impossible to believe this had been Robert's world for the past three years. His life here was far removed from the work he'd done as the brilliant archaeologist with whom she'd fallen in love.

Only now was she starting to recognize the sacrifices he'd made to prevent disaster from striking again. For him to live and work in this environment when it was so foreign to him helped her to see what she couldn't see or accept before now.

He'd wanted to get in touch with her and would have. She was beginning to understand. Deep in thought, she almost ran into him in the hall outside his office.

With or without his ranger outfit, his striking physique and features caused her to stare at him the way she'd once done. He was such an attractive male, she'd been caught off guard and didn't realize Roberta was already waiting inside.

"Hi," he said in his deep, husky voice. His questing gaze wandered over her figure clothed in pleated tan pants and cotton sweater in a tan-and-white print. Roberta had been the one to tie her hair at the nape with a white scarf.

She took a steadying breath. "I'm sorry if we disturbed you while you were on duty."

He put his hands on his hips in a purely male stance. "Let's get something straight. Roberta's our daughter and is a permanent part of my life any time of the day or night."

Averting her eyes, she walked into his office ahead of him and found her daughter sitting on a chair playing with a silver baton. Annie sat down on another chair next to her. "What's that, darling?"

"It's a wizard's wand Daddy's friends brought him from England."

Annie examined it and saw the engraving *Uncle Chase.* "This is beautiful."

"I wish we could go to the Harry Potter shop, too. Nicky was so lucky."

Robert closed the door and sat on the corner of his desk, bringing him much too close to Annie. "Do you love those books?"

Roberta nodded. "I've read all of them."

"Nicky loves them as well. I think his mother has read every one of them to him. Did you know he met the real Hedwig while they were on their trip?"

Her eyes rounded. "How did he do that?"

"The next time you see him, you'll have to ask him about it."

"Speaking of next time," Annie broke in. Her heart was racing. "I phoned my boss at the CDF and told him that after consideration I've decided to take the park job after all."

There was a palpable silence before he said, "That's great news for the park. I'll inform Superintendent Telford." His silvery eyes swerved to Roberta. Their luminescent color revealed his satisfaction. "For me personally, I'm thrilled to know you'll be living so close."

"Me too, Daddy. Now we can be together all the time."

Annie cleared her throat. "Would it be possible to see the house Roberta and I will be living in before we drive back to Santa Rosa?"

"We'll do it in a minute, but first we have to decide how to proceed. From here on out my name is Chase Jarvis. For reasons of safety, the name Robert Myers no longer exists."

"We know, don't we, honey?"

Roberta nodded.

"Good. When we walk out of this room," he continued, "I'll be introducing Roberta as my daughter and you, her mother. Among the park personnel Vance will spread the news that following an accident, I had amnesia and was confused about my past until the helicopter crash."

Annie had so much energy to expend she recrossed her legs. "In case someone asks, we need to agree on where your accident took place."

"At Newport Beach in Southern California," he said without missing a heartbeat. "We met there on vacation from college. When I got run over by a speedboat way offshore, my body was never found and authorities theorized sharks might have been responsible."

"Dad!" Roberta cried in reaction.

Annie shuddered. The scenario he'd just painted was ghastly, but nothing could compare to the unspeakable horror of what had literally happened that day in Kabul.

"Any other questions?"

When Annie realized he'd been staring at her and had seen more in her eyes than she wanted him, she said no and looked at Roberta. "What about you? Is there anything else you want to ask your father?"

"No. I just want to go see our house."

"We'll do it right now." He stood up. "Come down the hall with me while I get the key, then we'll leave through the rear door and walk over there."

"I didn't know the houses were so close to your work."

"Years ago the planners built everything that way on purpose. The rangers have to be ready at a moment's notice."

Roberta followed him out the door. "You're like a fireman."

"That's right."

Their conversation floated back as Annie put the wand in the box and hurried after them. Robert appeared to be in high spirits. So far everything was going according to his wishes. Annie had to pretend she didn't mind the way things were turning out because she had her own life to lead. However, that was easier said and done in theory.

She had to admit it hurt to see how quickly Roberta had bonded with him. He held her hand as they stepped outside, as if they'd been doing it for years. Of course Annie wanted them to bond, but that insidious emotion called jealousy had squeezed in there to add to her turmoil.

Someone else in her daughter's world now had a claim on her heart. A legitimate claim. Annie had to learn to share her daughter. Correction. *Their* daughter. Somehow she hadn't expected to be pierced by this new form of pain.

It took only a few minutes walking through the pines to reach the cluster of houses used by the rangers. The forties ranch style was typical of the many tracts of housing built throughout California seventy years earlier.

Robert—Chase, she corrected herself mentally—led them to the end of a street where three houses stood. He walked up the steps of the middle one-story house and unlocked the front door.

Once inside, Roberta darted through the rooms making excited noises while Annie surveyed the living and dining room. She wandered through the rest of the house. Most of the rooms were carpeted. The maple furnishings were fine…homey, but the orange and brown decor was something she would change in a hurry.

Chase followed her around. They ended up in the postage-stamp-size kitchen. It meant their meals would have to be eaten in the dining room, but she couldn't concentrate on much of anything because of his close proximity.

"What do you think?"

She pinned on a smile and turned to him. "I think Jack Frost lives here."

His dark brown head reared back and he laughed that deep laugh she hadn't heard in years. Just then he sounded younger. It brought back too many memories, wounding her all over again.

Roberta came running to find them. "What's so funny?"

He threw an arm around her shoulder. "Have you ever heard of Jack Frost?"

She shook her head.

"Jack's a little elf who paints all the leaves in fall colors. Your mom thinks this is his house."

Annie could hear her mind digesting everything. "When we bring our things, it won't look so bad, Mom."

Chase burst into more laughter. Annie had to fight not to break down, too.

"Can I have the room next to the bathroom? There's a cute little squirrel running up and down the tree outside the window. Come and look!"

Relieved to put distance between herself and Chase, Annie followed Roberta down the hall past the bathroom to the bedroom she'd chosen. They moved beyond the queen-size bed to the screened window. Roberta's pink and white quilt would do wonders for the room.

"See!"

"There's a family living up there," Chase informed her. "You'll have to invite Nicky over. He has a pair of powerful binoculars. The two of you can watch them for hours."

"He's funny. How come he doesn't look like his daddy?" Annie had wondered the same thing.

A shadow darkened Chase's eyes, drawing her attention. "His real parents flew out here from Florida a year ago last spring. I was on duty when a freak winter-type storm was forecast. We warned everyone off the mountains and formations, but the Darrows didn't obey it. They were caught in a blizzard on top of El Capitan and died of hypothermia."

"That's awful," Roberta whispered, echoing Annie's thoughts.

"It was terrible for a lot of reasons. Vance went up in a helicopter to rescue them, but it was too late. We all knew they had a five year-old boy at home. Last June Nicky's aunt Rachel brought him to the park so he could see where the tragedy had happened. It was hard for him to understand that his parents had died. He'd been having nightmares and never wanted to go to school or play."

Roberta's lower lip trembled. "I don't blame him."

"But then a miracle happened. Vance became Nicky's hero and the three of them fell in love with each other. In time they decided to become a family and get married. Now they've adopted Nicky as their son. To make it fun for him, they took him to England on their honeymoon and just barely got back."

Annie lost the battle of tears. "What a touching story," she whispered, wiping her eyes with the back of her free hand.

Chase's solemn gaze switched from her to Roberta. "Nicky needs good friends. I know you're older, but you were very accepting of him today. I can tell he likes you already. Thank you for being my wonderful girl."

She hugged him before looking at Annie. "How soon are we going to move in?"

"Sometime next week. Your grandfather is arranging for a moving truck to bring the things we want here. The rest we'll put in storage."

"I wish it were tomorrow."

"Do you know what?" Chase intervened. "You'll probably need a few days to decide what you want to keep with you. If there are some things you want moved out of here to make room for your furnishings, I'll take care of it. This is going to be your new home. You need to feel comfortable."

Chase was behaving exactly like the accommodating, sensible man she'd once loved. In fact he was being so reasonable and understanding without trying to take over, Annie wanted to scream.

She checked her watch. To her shock, the time had flown. "You know what? It's ten after three right now. Your grandparents will be waiting for us."

"But I want to see Daddy's house first."

"We don't have time today."

"Your mother's right, sweetheart. After you move in, we'll have the rest of our lives to do everything."

Roberta wiped her eyes with the end of her sleeve. "Okay. I'll call you when we're coming. I've memorized your number."

"I was hoping you would. I'll be waiting to hear from you."

Annie started for the front door ahead of them. When he'd locked it behind them and they'd walked down the front porch steps, he turned to her and handed her the key. "The place is yours."

As their hands brushed, she felt the contact like a hot current of electricity. The same thing had happened when she'd first met him. "Thank you for making this so easy for us. I appreciate it."

His eyes gleamed silver. "You're welcome."

Roberta hung on to his arm. "What are you going to do now?"

"Run home, have a shower and go to bed. I've been up close to twenty-four hours and need sleep."

"Where's your house?"

He pointed to his left. "Right around the corner."

That brought a smile to her face.

"Come on," Annie urged.

"Okay. See ya, Dad."

While they hugged, Annie began walking in the direction of the visitor's center. His charm was lethal. In that regard nothing had changed in ten years.

ON THURSDAY MORNING Chase was in his office dealing with the latest faxed reports when Vance came through the door. They eyed each other for a brief moment. "Isn't this the big day or did I get it wrong?"

"You know it is."

"It's after ten now. What are you still doing here?"

"I've got to be careful, Vance. Roberta phoned to let me know the day and time, but Annie was coaching her because there was no invitation for me to be a part of things. Let's face it. I had nightmares at the thought of working out visitation, never dreaming Annie would take the job.

"We might be living around the corner from each other now, but if she thinks I'm trying to manage her in any way she'll shut me out so completely I'll never get to first base."

Vance smiled out of one corner of his mouth. "I'd say you've already done that."

"Not because of me," Chase muttered in a morose tone. "She wants this job no matter what. To be frank, I'm terrified of doing something wrong."

"I hear you, so this is what we're going to do. My wife's making food for them."

He sat back in the chair. "She's incredible."

"I agree. Rachel can't wait to meet her. We've arranged for Nicky to come home from school at noon.

He wants to help. We thought we'd go over there around twelve-thirty. I'll give her an official greeting. If you're with us, Annie can't object."

"You mean even if she wants to." Chase let out a sigh of relief. "You've just solved my immediate dilemma. While we're there, I'll take care of anything that needs doing."

"Good. See you later. For the moment I've got a camper accident to investigate.

He got up from the desk. "I'm headed into a meeting in the conference room."

"The new housing project controversy?"

"I'm afraid so. As you know, the arguments never end. I'll put the report in your basket." Chase followed him out of the office, grateful to Vance for helping him make it through the last few endless days of waiting. It was a miracle he and Rachel put up with him.

Chase still had a hard time believing this day had come. Once the news got out that his daughter and ex-lover were living in the park, the three of them would be an item of speculation and gossip.

He'd give anything to spare them, but nothing short of marriage could stem the tide of curiosity. That was the bad side of living in a closed community. But there was an upside. One way or another he'd be seeing both of them on a daily basis. For now he'd take whatever he could get.

Two hours later he left headquarters and sprinted through the trees to the housing complex. When he rounded the corner, he saw a small moving truck in her driveway. The front door of the house was open. He noticed her blue Nissan parked in front. He'd seen it in her parking stall at the condo. There was no sign of Vance yet.

As Chase approached the entry he slowed his pace, unwilling for Annie to detect the degree of his need for her. Nothing would turn her off faster.

A couple of men came out the door with a dolly. They nodded when they saw him.

"How's it going?"

"We just finished." They slid the plank into the truck and shut the back. As Annie came down the steps wearing a pair of jeans and a yellow top, one of them reached inside the cab and pulled out a clipboard. "Someone needs to sign. Are you Mr. Bower?"

"No, I'm not. You need to get Ms. Bower's signature." Chase remained in place while she walked toward the man and signed the release form with her free hand. "Thank you." Her crisp remark of irritation was wasted on them.

To his chagrin Chase was afraid he'd be silently blamed for showing up at the wrong moment. He was damned either way.

"Daddy!" Roberta came flying out of the house into his arms. She saved the day.

"How are you, sweetheart?" He swung her around and kissed her. In the excitement, Vance showed up. He waited for the truck to back out and drive away before he pulled into the driveway. After shutting off the engine, everyone got out of the car carrying sacks.

Nicky made a beeline for Roberta. "Hi! We brought your lunch. Where do you want me to put the bread sticks?"

Rachel must have just taken them out of the oven. Chase could smell the aroma and started salivating.

"Mom? Where should they put the food?"

It was clear the arrival of company had caught Annie

off guard. "Well, how about the dining room? There's no room in the kitchen until we get things put away."

"I'll show you," Roberta told Nicky. The two of them walked up the porch steps into the house.

Chase stepped forward. "Annie Bower, I'd like you to meet my closest friends, Rachel and Vance Rossiter."

"Hello," she said, shaking both their hands. Her hair swished like a glossy dark pelt against her cheek. "You've already done enough with the gorgeous flowers you sent. I can't believe you've come over with food, too."

"It's our pleasure," Rachel assured her. "Another neighbor is really welcome around here."

"Thank you. I feel the same way. Roberta's already charmed by Nicky. For one thing, they have Harry Potter in common."

"Don't forget root beer," Vance interjected with a warm smile. "I wanted to see our newest resident archaeologist in person. Let's hope that fractured arm and the attendant memories will be the only unpleasant moment you experience here."

"I'm hoping for that as well."

"Vance and I knew you'd get hungry at some point. If you don't feel like eating right now, that's fine. I'm aware how busy you are today and thought you'd like something to munch on."

"To be honest, I'm starving. We had breakfast with my parents before leaving Santa Rosa at six. They're taking charge of putting the rest of my things in storage and won't be visiting until tomorrow. Please, come in and eat with us."

Even with the invitation extended, Annie hadn't looked at Chase yet. He needed to get used to being invisible if he was going to survive.

Vance turned toward the car. "I'll get the casserole out of the back."

"Let me do it," Chase insisted.

Their eyes met in quiet understanding. In the next instant Vance escorted the women into the house while Chase walked across the street and opened the rear door of the car. The large covered casserole had handles, making it easy for him to carry the delicious smelling lasagna. Rachel had gone all out.

No sooner had he entered the house than Nicky came darting toward the front door with Roberta behind him. "Where are you two going? We'll be eating in a minute," Chase said.

"Roberta's running home with me so I can get my binoculars! We'll be right back!"

Watching them together, Chase's thoughts flew to a week ago last Monday when he'd been in such a severe depression he didn't know how he was going to make it through the rest of his life. Then came the phone call about Annie, followed by the news that they had a daughter.

Instant fatherhood. As if by magic a whole family came into being, illuminating his world. The only thing missing was his wedding ring on Annie's finger and all that went with it.

"Put the casserole here," Rachel called to him. She'd placed a hot pad down on the round maple table. While he did her bidding, he noticed there were only four matching chairs. He'd seen two of Annie's white chairs in the living room and brought them into the dining room.

As he fit them around the table, his arm brushed against Annie's, sending a rush of fresh longing through his body. She jerked away from him. Whether anyone else noticed her reaction or not, it left him pondering two possibilities. Either she didn't welcome his touch, or it had electrified her because she still felt an attraction.

It was a subject he intended to explore at a later date. Again he had to remind himself this was only her first day here. She might tolerate one accident, but he didn't dare start to experiment with another one yet.

When the kids came back to the house, he arranged for Nicky and Roberta to sit on either side of him. That way Annie couldn't accuse him of purposely manipulating the situation to his advantage.

Once the salad was passed around and everyone was served, Nicky lifted the binoculars to his eyes and surveyed each person.

"That's not polite. Put the binoculars in the living room for now," Rachel admonished. Darting Annie a covert glance, Chase saw a smile break out on her flushed face. She found Nicky as funny and irresistible as the rest of them did.

"Okay," he said in a pretend grumpy voice and got out of the chair. In a second he was back to make inroads on his breadstick. "This is fun." He munched a little more. "I wish we could eat together all the time, don't you, Roberta?"

While the others chuckled, Chase exchanged a private smile with his daughter. For the next half hour Nicky kept them laughing in his inimitable way. As Chase was thinking that he hadn't known this kind of happiness since sharing all his meals and the aftermath with Annie, there was a knock on the front door.

His first instinct was to answer it, but this wasn't his

home. He watched Annie get up from the table. Maybe her parents had decided to come after all.

It had been so different back in Kabul. Though they'd had their own accommodations, they'd been like a married couple. To go from that kind of intimacy to this situation was killing him.

Bill Telford's voice preceded his eventual entry into the dining room. The mid-forties superintendent had a golfer's build and most of his blond hair. He couldn't seem to take his eyes off Annie. "I only came to welcome our new resident archaeologist to the park. I don't want to intrude," he insisted.

The hell he didn't. The man hadn't wasted any time. The widow and the widower.

"You know everyone here except my daughter. Roberta? This is Bill Telford, the superintendent of the park. He made it possible for your mother to have this job."

"Hi! It's nice to meet you."

"It's a pleasure to meet you too, Roberta." He moved around the table to shake her hand. He hid his surprise well as his gaze traveled over Vance and Chase who got to their feet. "You're in celebrated company."

"What's celebrated?" Nicky piped up.

"Very famous," Bill explained.

"Oh." He wiped the milk off his mouth with a napkin. "Did you know Uncle Chase is Roberta's daddy?"

Nicky had just given Chase another reason to love him so much.

Bill's head jerked toward her. "Were we misinformed? I didn't realize you were married." The man looked as if he'd just been hit in the jaw by Tiger Woods's line drive.

Chase shot Vance a glance. This was a job he

intended to leave for the Chief. Annie would appreciate Chase's absence.

"Bill? Why don't you take my place and enjoy some of Rachel's fabulous lasagna. I'm going to help the kids sneak around the tree outside and look for squirrels."

Nicky clapped his hands. "Hooray! Come on, Roberta. I'll get my binoculars."

Chapter Seven

"Rachel, after bringing over the delicious meal, I won't have you helping me with the dishes, too," Annie declared.

"I want to. The guys are busy putting all your electronic equipment together in the spare bedroom and loving it. I'm afraid Nicky is driving Roberta crazy while she's arranging her room. That leaves *moi* with nothing to do. If you'll give me directions, I'll empty a few boxes and start putting dishes and pans in the kitchen cupboards."

"If you're sure."

"Of course. That cast on your arm is there for a reason. If you'll let us help, we'll have you settled in no time. It isn't as if you've just moved into the Palais Royal with a hundred rooms to fill."

Annie laughed. "No, but it's cozy and it's our new home for now."

"You don't plan to stay here for long?"

"I've signed a year's contract. At the end of that time the superintendent will decide if the progress made warrants more funding."

Rachel eyed her speculatively. "I'm pretty sure that won't be a problem. I've only met Bill Telford one other time, but if I don't miss my guess, he showed an inordinate interest in you today. I heard him ask you to go to dinner with him next week. It might have been a purely professional invitation, but in case you didn't know, his wife died of cancer last year."

"Thanks for telling me." That missing piece of information hadn't passed Chase's lips, but in all fairness she hadn't encouraged conversation with him. Her boss at CDF hadn't mentioned it either.

"Earlier today Vance came home from headquarters and let me know you were gorgeous." Annie shook her head. "I've discovered he was right, so I'm pretty sure you'll be seeing a lot more of Bill. That is, if you want to. His house is only three blocks away."

"My boss at the CDF says he has impressive credentials."

"He's attractive, too, if you're partial to blond men."

Annie took a steadying breath. "If I could speak frankly with you for a minute, I'm sure you're wondering about Chase and me."

"Listen," she said in a quiet voice, "you don't owe anyone an explanation, least of all me. Vance told me the whole story. To be honest, I would feel so betrayed if Vance had been alive ten years without telling me, especially if we had a child between us, I'm not sure what I would do."

Annie's eyes smarted. "At first I was in shock and so hurt, I was convinced Chase couldn't have been that in love with me."

"And now?"

She lifted her chin. "Now I understand why he didn't ever get in touch with me, but the fact still remains that after ten years we're strangers to each other."

"Of course you would be," Rachel agreed.

This woman understood and could be a real friend to Annie. "Thank you, Rachel," she whispered.

"Just know I'm around if you ever need a shoulder to cry on."

"Careful." Annie sniffed. "You may live to regret that offer. You don't know how grateful I am over your being so candid. I'm aware you've been through a horribly painful experience yourself. Chase told me about your brother and his wife. Poor little Nicky. I understand he went through a terrible struggle."

"He did. My parents and I almost lost our minds wondering how to help him. Then I flew him out here and he met Vance."

Annie smiled. "I can tell they're joined at the hip."

"One day I'll fill you in on the details."

"I think I can guess. Your husband has the most beautiful blue eyes I've ever seen. When he looks at you, they glow."

"I love him so much, it hurts."

Annie bowed her head. She and Chase had once felt that way about each other. Now that he was back in her life she hurt all the time, but that was because… because she wanted him to love her that way again, but she didn't dare think it might happen. The difference in Annie's and Rachel's personal lives was off the charts.

"Annie?" At the sound of Chase's low voice, her pulse raced. It seemed her body recognized it whether she tried to shut him out or not. She turned around to meet a pair of shadowed gray eyes. No silver in them right now. "We've finished setting up your computer. Where do you want the television?"

"I think against the wall opposite the couch. Thank you."

He glanced around. "It looks like all the boxes have been emptied. I'll get my truck and we'll cart them away. The kids want to go with us. Is that all right with you two?"

They nodded.

He made quick work of removing the cartons. After he left, she could breathe more easily. A few minutes later the kitchen had been put in order and the dishes were done.

Annie turned to Rachel. "I can't believe how fast everything's been set in place. Without your help, Roberta and I would have been putting things away for days. Thank you for all you've done, including that delicious meal."

"You're welcome."

"I owe you. If you're free on Sunday afternoon and your husband isn't on duty, I'd like you to come over for dinner."

"That sounds wonderful. When I know his schedule, I'll call you. It changes all the time depending on emergencies."

"So I understand. Let's go to the other room and take a break. You've worked long and hard enough for one day."

They moved through the dining room to the living room. Already it looked better, with her occasional pieces of furniture placed around and her framed prints hanging on the walls.

Rachel went over to the Renoir. "I love this one of the mother and daughter."

So did Annie. "My mother gave it to me after Roberta was born."

"Roberta is so sweet to Nicky. I'm really glad you've

moved here. He needs friends. I'm hoping to provide him with a brother or sister."

"Maybe that will happen one day."

"We're trying," Rachel confessed. "Vance's first wife served in the military when he did, but she was killed during the war in the Middle East. They'd wanted children, but there wasn't enough time."

A hand went to Annie's throat. "I didn't know he'd been married before." Vance had lost his wife the same way Annie had thought she'd lost Chase.

"That was a little over five years ago. He loves Nicky like his own, but he's such a wonderful father I want him to experience the whole business of childbirth. Needless to say, I can't wait to have a baby."

Annie took a deep breath. "There's nothing like it." Chase had missed out on it. He'd missed Roberta's first ten years. It was time to change the subject before she broke down. "I understand you're barely back from your honeymoon. Are you still moving in?"

"Not in the way you mean. My father just had a heart operation which was successful. They're moving out here from Florida right before Halloween and will be bringing my things in the van with them. Then Vance's house is going to undergo a big renovation. It needs it."

They both laughed as they looked around Annie's living room, observing its lack of a uniform theme or decor.

"Will your parents live here in the park, too?"

"No. Vance owns a house right outside the park entrance in Oakhurst. It was his grandparents'. They raised him. In June his grandmother passed away and willed it to him."

"That's wonderful you'll be so close to them," Annie

cried softly. “My parents live in San Francisco so it’ll be a bit more of a drive for all of us, but not impossible.”

“Family’s everything. That’s why Chase—” She suddenly stopped talking. “I’m sorry. I didn’t mean to bring him up.”

“Please, Rachel, it’s all right to talk about Chase. He and Vance are best friends so it’s inevitable.”

“I was only going to say that for him to discover *you* again has caused as dramatic a change in him as turning on a blowtorch in a pitch-dark room. He’s overjoyed to realize he has a daughter.”

“It’s been a shock for all of us.” Annie’s voice trembled.

“My husband told me Chase was in a depression when he came to work at the park three years ago. Over time it had gotten worse. When I met him in June, I liked him very much, but I sensed a deep sadness in him and thought it was due to his divorce.”

Annie blinked. “What divorce?”

“The one he manufactured as part of his fake persona once he was put in the witness protection program.”

“I had no idea. Naturally he would have to create a background for himself.”

Rachel nodded. “You know what’s odd? Even though it was fiction, I bought the emptiness I heard in his voice. Something was definitely missing. Now that I know the whole truth, I understand it. In order to keep everyone safe, he’s been forced to deny his whole former existence for years. I can’t imagine anything worse.”

Their conversation was throwing Annie into more turmoil. It had only started to dawn on her he’d put his life in jeopardy every day while he’d worked undercover. He'd seen so much of war. It had to have changed him in so many ways and she hadn't been able to share any of it with him.

"What does Vance think now that he knows everything?"

"The only argument Vance and I have come close to having is the one over whether it was wrong of Chase not to contact you from the hospital in Switzerland. If you're asking me if Vance would have chosen to remain dead to his wife, Katy, under Chase's circumstances, the answer is yes. He's seen the evil of the enemy in the Middle East firsthand. It's the warrior in them that vows to protect their women at all costs, I guess."

"Women can be warriors, too."

"You and I know that, but Chase and Vance are honorable to a fault. It puts them in a class by themselves. You should have seen how angry I was when I first met Vance. I blamed him for my brother and sister-in-law's deaths. He was the chief ranger and they died on his watch. I was ready to prosecute him for criminal negligence."

"You're kidding!"

"Afraid not. We got off to the worst start imaginable. I stormed out of his office in a fury."

"I can't imagine it."

"You don't know the half of it. Later that night he found me and Nicky eating dinner at the Yosemite Lodge with Chase."

Annie fought to hide her dismay. "You mean you and Chase went out together?"

"Yes. It was all very innocent. He offered to watch Nicky while I was in with Vance. When I left, I was in turmoil and Chase knew it. He asked me if he could meet us for dinner at the lodge. I said yes, but Nicky didn't like it at all.

"Then Vance came walking into the dining room. Ignoring me, he got down in front of Nicky's chair and started talking to him about what happened. I learned it was my brother who decided not to heed the blizzard advisory.

"While I sat there feeling like the world's greatest fool, Vance was able to explain things in such a way that Nicky broke down and they ended up hugging each other. From that moment on, my nephew started to heal and they bonded.

"After Vance left, Chase asked if we'd like to go horseback riding the next morning. Nicky didn't want to, but I accepted. A huge mistake. Nicky was positively atrocious to Chase. The reason I wanted to go was because he was easy to talk to. You see, I'd broken my engagement to my fiancé and he was begging me to get back with him.

"Chase said he had the same problem with his ex-wife. We talked about our emotional problems. At the time I didn't know he'd fabricated the story about his divorce. We commiserated. I told him I was going back to Miami and, on the advice of my psychiatrist, I was going to make an effort to talk to my ex-fiancé and see if anything could be salvaged.

"I knew in my heart it wouldn't work because I was already attracted to Vance. What an irony when you consider we started off striking sparks against each other. He didn't show me anything but professional courtesy, but the way he treated Nicky was another story.

"The reason I'm going into all this detail is because

I want you to know the truth of everything. I liked Chase a lot because I could tell he's an exceptional man, but when I came back to the park a second time, it wasn't just for Nicky's sake. I couldn't wait to see Vance again. I knew when he picked us up at the airport in Merced, that I'd fallen hard for him.

"It took forever for him to reciprocate because he thought I hadn't let go of my ex-fiancé. I, in turn, was afraid he would never get over Katy. Of course we were both wrong. During a hike in the mountains, Vance kissed me for the first time and suddenly we were pouring out all our feelings. That was a glorious day."

"I can imagine," Annie murmured, but she was strangely conflicted. She already liked Rachel so much, but apparently Chase had been drawn to her, too. Even if it was one-sided, was it possible he still had feelings for Rachel? They were all exceptionally close.

Swallowing hard, she said, "I'm so glad everything turned out for the three of you, Rachel. I—" She stopped talking. "Uh-oh, I can hear them in the driveway." They both got up from the couch and walked out onto the front porch.

With the boxes disposed of, the men helped the children down from the empty truck bed. Chase gave Roberta a long hug before lowering her to the ground. The part that had been missing in her daughter's life was now complete. She had her very own father and a built-in set of new friends.

Vance hoisted Nicky onto his shoulders. "Rachel? I have to get back to headquarters. What would you like to do?"

"I'm coming."

Nicky frowned. "Do we have to go?"

"Afraid so," Rachel answered. "You still have a little homework to do for school in the morning."

"Is Roberta coming to school?"

Annie nodded. "She'll be there."

Rachel turned to her. "If you want, Nicky and I will come by for you at eight-thirty and we'll all walk over."

"Terrific. We'll be ready. Thanks again for all the help and the fabulous lunch."

"It was really good," Roberta called to her. "See ya tomorrow, Nicky."

"Okay. Bye."

After they drove away in their car, Chase turned to Annie. "Roberta wants to come to my house. Why don't you come in the truck with us so you can see where she'll be spending some of her time."

Annie wanted to see where he lived, *how* he lived. "I'll be right with you. Let me get my purse and lock the door."

A minute later she joined them. Always the gentleman, he helped her into the cab. When his arm accidentally brushed against her thigh before shutting the door, she hoped he hadn't felt her quiver in response. Roberta sat between them with a smile of contentment on her face.

Chase backed the truck out of the driveway and they headed for his house around the corner. On the way they passed a ranger who stared at them and waved. He waved back.

"Who's that, Daddy?"

"Mark Sims, the head of security. He's Carly's father. You'll be meeting her at school tomorrow. She only lives a half a block from you. Kind of like you and your friend Penny."

They headed for the house on the next corner. He pulled into the driveway and pressed the remote above the visor to open the garage door. From the outside at least, all of the houses looked pretty much the same.

Annie jumped down before Chase could come around. She didn't want any more contact with him. Twice today was enough. She could still feel his touch. It would stay with her and conjured up intimate memories. Within five minutes she'd walk back to the house and Roberta could come home later.

She waited till he'd opened the door to the kitchen, then followed Roberta inside. Right away she noticed differences. His kitchen could accommodate a breakfast table and the attractive sage and wood décor throughout the main rooms came as a surprise. She assumed the contemporary dark brown leather furniture facing the fireplace was his own.

"Look at all the books!" Roberta cried. Annie *was* looking. Walls of them from floor to ceiling in the living room. It took her back to his apartment in Kabul, which had been more library than living quarters. They spent most of their alone time in hers. "Have you read every one?"

Chase laughed. "That's the idea, sweetheart. Most of them are historical journals of the explorers and early frontiersmen who came to Yosemite. The rest are reference materials for a series of books I'm writing on the park for people who enjoy hiking in the wilderness."

"Mom said you're the smartest man she ever knew."

Yes. Annie had told her daughter that and couldn't take it back. He scoffed. In that regard he hadn't changed. Chase had always been a modest man.

"It's true, Chase. To be honest, I'm not surprised you've immersed yourself in another field besides archaeology. Are you published yet?"

He stood in the middle of the room with his hard-muscled legs slightly apart. "I haven't even picked an agent yet."

"With your credentials you don't nee—" She suddenly broke off talking. Heat crept into her face. "I forgot you've had to give up that whole life."

A grimace marred his rugged features. "I wish I could."

In that moment Annie heard a bleakness in his tone that haunted her. Once again it hit her that the explosion had not only robbed him of his parents, he could no longer continue to pursue archaeology, his life's work and passion.

A lesser man might have given up, but not Chase. The dining room was the proof. He'd turned it into an office with file cabinets and state-of-the-art electronic equipment. On two walls hung several giant U.S. geological survey maps of Yosemite with all kinds of colored pins he'd placed to set off various coordinates. Fascinated, Annie walked over to study one of them.

"I love your house, Daddy!"

"That's good, because it's your house too when you want to come over. Would you like to see your bedroom?"

"You made a bedroom for me?" She squealed for joy. That didn't sound like the more sober minded daughter Annie had raised. Chase's advent in her life was transforming her.

"Who else? I used it for a storeroom, but as soon as I found out you'd be coming for visits, I cleaned it out and got it ready for you. Come on and take a look."

Roberta walked off with him, leaving Annie drowning in a flood of new feelings and sensations. Since Rachel had confided in her, jealousy had reared its ugly head again. She needed to get out of there before her natural curiosity took over and she gave herself away.

"Hey, you two—" she called after them. "I've got a lot to do back at the house so I'll see you later. Okay?"

"Okay!" Roberta shouted back.

She heard nothing from Chase, but then why would she? Upset with herself for even questioning it, Annie left his house via the front door and hurried home. Except that once she was safe inside, her house didn't feel like home. Though she'd brought their most important possessions from Santa Rosa, she realized inanimate objects didn't mean anything without her daughter here.

From now on Roberta would want to spend equal time with Chase. Annie couldn't blame her. He'd embraced her so completely, you would never have known they'd been apart since her birth. Moreover, he was a striking man any child would be thrilled to claim as her father.

Realizing she was spending too much time focusing on Chase rather than her new job, she got busy arranging her bedroom the way she wanted. By the time she was ready for bed, darkness had fallen over the park. She was about to phone Chase when she heard the front door open and close.

"Mom?"

"In the bedroom!"

She ran down the hall to Annie's room. "Daddy's outside. He wants me to call him and tell him you're here before he leaves."

Annie handed her the phone. She appreciated Chase being so careful, but again it didn't surprise her. He'd always been protective of Annie. Naturally he'd be even more so with their daughter

"I will," she heard Roberta say. "I love you, too. Good night, Daddy. See you tomorrow." After she hung up, she grabbed Annie. Her eyes were dancing.

"Daddy's going to take me and Nicky horseback riding on Saturday! Is that okay?"

If it weren't, Annie wouldn't have the heart to tell her. "Of course!"

"He loves horses just like me! I can't wait!"

While Annie locked up and turned out lights, her daughter bubbled over with excitement. "I wish I could call Debbie tonight."

"It's too late. You can phone her after school tomorrow."

"Okay."

Later, after they'd both gone to bed, Annie turned on her good side, wishing she weren't tormented by memories of one glorious horseback ride with Chase in the Khyber Pass. They'd camped out several nights in a row, eating food they'd packed and making love while their handpicked guides kept guard over them. She'd never known rapture like that. On one of those two nights she'd gotten pregnant.

Had his horseback ride with Rachel this past summer become a standout memory for him? In the dark hours of the night did he envy Vance?

Salty tears trickled from the corners of her eyes. "Chase—" she half sobbed, "Is it too late for us?" She could hardly stand it. After everything they'd shared, how was she going to live this close to him? Every time he hugged or kissed Roberta, she remembered how his arms had felt around her, how his mouth had devoured her, sending them both into euphoric oblivion.

To think he now lived around the corner from her and

Roberta! For the past three years he'd been hibernating here in relative contentment, obviously dating other women. He'd wanted a relationship with Rachel. She could hardly bear it, but she had to.

What was it Sid Manning had said? *Because your life was in danger, Dr. Myers had no choice but to stay away from you.*

Since that was true, it meant Chase had loved her more than his own life. Did it mean now that they were together again and his secret had come out, he would end up fighting for her in this presumably safe haven? Or was it too late. Love had to be fed and he'd gone hungry too many years. So had she…

Pain ripped through her body. Annie flung around in bed, forgetting the cast on her arm. It cost her as she cried out in discomfort. Another night like this and she'd have to have it reset.

Tomorrow couldn't come soon enough. Her parents were going to stay with them through the weekend. However, before she'd left Santa Rosa this morning her dad had said, "Don't you think it's time we met Roberta's father?" She'd put it off as long as possible while she'd sorted out her feelings, but there was an inevitability about anything having to do with Chase.

THE CHILDREN RODE on either side of Chase as they left the beaver pond and headed back to the stable. They'd been discussing their Halloween costumes. Halloween was only three days away. Nicky had decided to be Harry Potter and Annie was going as Hermione. Chase couldn't wait to take them trick-or-treating with Vance and Rachel. This was the kind of fatherhood experience that had passed him by, but no longer.

Today he was especially proud of how well Roberta handled her horse. She was a little camera buff, too. She'd taken pictures of everything.

"Can we come again next Saturday, Uncle Chase? That Methuselah's funny. He got me wet when he slapped his tail."

Chase smiled. The beaver wasn't half as funny as Nicky. "I'll check my schedule."

"Maybe my friend Debbie could come with us?"

"Since that's the only day your friend's mom can bring her, I'll trade with one of the guys for some time off." He glanced at his daughter, who'd started school yesterday. "What did you think of Carly?"

"She's okay."

That didn't sound very enthusiastic. When they were alone Chase would find out what was wrong.

"Do you guys like Mrs. Farrell?" They both nodded. That was a plus. "Is it strange only having a few kids at school?"

"Kind of."

"I like it," Nicky exclaimed.

"What did you think of Brody?"

"He's *mean*." Again this from Nicky.

"What does he do?"

"He's eleven. And when we have recess out in back he always gets to choose what we're going to do, huh Roberta."

"He tells everybody what to do, Dad."

"Yup. He said his dad was more important than *my* dad. I said he wasn't and he almost hit me."

That didn't sound good. "Brody has two older brothers, sport. They probably boss him around. Did you tell Mrs. Farrell?"

"If he's mean again, I'll tell her," Roberta said.

Good for her. "Looks like you two will have to stick up for each other."

"Yeah. Can I play at your house when we get back, Roberta?"

"I'm staying at my dad's today." She looked over at Chase. "Do you think Nicky could come over for a while?" She obviously liked him a lot. Nicky won everyone over.

"Sure."

"Hooray! Where's your mom?"

"In Wawona." Chase didn't know that. "What's she doing there?" Nicky asked.

"To have lunch with the other archaeologist. He just got back from a trip to Mexico."

Nicky sidled closer to Chase. "In class I heard Brody tell Carly he got a divorce. What does that mean?"

Gossip always abounded among the park employees, but that was news to Chase. He'd assumed Ron Saddler and his wife had a solid marriage. Annie would be working with him all the time. He took a shuddering breath. "It means his wife and children aren't going to live with him anymore."

"Oh."

On the trip back Roberta remained unusually quiet, causing him concern. When they reached the stable, he helped Nicky down. Roberta got off the horse on her own. She was already independent, just like her mother. Chase needed to find a way to get to Annie.

They piled into the truck and headed back to the house. When they walked in the kitchen, Chase told Nicky to go in the bedroom and call his parents to let them know where he was.

While Roberta washed her hands in the kitchen sink, Chase took advantage of being alone with his daughter for a moment. "I know something's wrong," he murmured. "Did Carly ignore you yesterday?"

She shook her head.

"Well, she did something."

Without looking at him, Roberta said, "She asked how come my parents didn't live together."

His heart thudded. "What did you tell her?"

"That they didn't want to." She finally lifted her head. Those pure blue eyes were swimming in tears. "She asked me if you two got a divorce."

"How did you answer her?"

"I told her no."

Chase had known there'd be talk, but he hadn't counted on it reaching Roberta's ears through Carly. He'd hoped the two girls would become friends. In time they probably would, but it didn't make Roberta's first days happy ones.

He hugged her before letting her go. "I'm sorry she made you uncomfortable."

She wiped her eyes. "Dad? Do you like Mom?"

Roberta, Roberta. "I never stopped, but I hurt her without intending to. I don't think she'll ever be able to forgive me." He waited for the protest from her telling him he was wrong in his assessment, but one never came, because Roberta knew exactly how her mother felt.

"I wish we all lived together."

"So do I," he whispered.

She looked stunned. "You do?"

"What do you think?" He tugged on her ponytail. "You're my daughter. All these years I'd given up hope of ever having a child. There's nothing I'd love more, than to be surrounded by my family in my house."

"Mom, too?"

"I loved her before I loved you, sweetheart. To have my own beautiful women living with me would be my heart's desire."

They heard feet running through the house. "Mommy said I can stay until she picks me up in an hour. We're going shopping."

"Terrific. What do you guys want for lunch?"

"Can I have a peanut butter and jelly sandwich?"

"Sure." He got busy fixing it. "What about you, sweetheart?"

"I just want a glass of milk. I'll get it."

Chase didn't press Roberta to eat. After telling her how he felt, he'd lost his appetite, too. Once the news reached Annie's ears—and it would—he feared she'd keep putting emotional distance between them because she couldn't love him the same way anymore.

His admission might spell the coup de grâce for Chase, because he knew he shouldn't have revealed his deepest feelings this soon. He'd promised himself to go slowly and give it time, but he hadn't been able to hold back any longer, not in front of Roberta.

While Nicky finished off half a sandwich, Roberta poured them each a glass of milk. Chase eyed the two of them. "When you're finished, do you guys want to go out in back and play a game of horseshoes with me?"

His daughter nodded. "I've never done that before."

"It's fun!" Nicky cried, "but it's kind of hard."

"There's a knack to it, but anyone can learn. I'll teach you." Chase needed to keep busy so he wouldn't think about Annie spending time with every damn man in the park except him.

Chapter Eight

After the drive from Wawona, Annie drove straight to Chase's and honked the horn for Roberta. It was after five o'clock. There'd been so much to talk about with Ron, time had gotten away from her.

What a difference it made to live here. If she happened to be late for Roberta, which she didn't intend to happen again unless it was unavoidable, she knew Chase would always be available to their daughter.

A few minutes later Roberta came running out to the car. "Honey," she called to her from the open window. "Your grandparents are waiting for us at the Yosemite Lodge for dinner. Do you want to ask your father if he'd like to join us? I don't know if he's free or not."

"He doesn't go on duty until tomorrow."

"In that case, your grandparents would like to meet him."

"Okay. I'll be right back."

Annie only had to wait a minute before her daughter got into the front seat. "Dad said he'll shower and be right over."

"Good." She backed out of the driveway. "Did you have fun horseback riding?"

"I loved it!" In the next breath she gave Annie a rundown of everything she'd done all day. She was still talking when they reached the village and parked near the lodge. Chase was responsible for the light in her eyes. Only the father who loved her could have put it there.

No matter what, Annie had to concede that the move to the park was already good for her daughter in the most fundamental of ways. There was no substitute for one's own daddy, especially not Chase, who was an exceptional man. Nicky adored him, too. You couldn't fool a child. As for Annie's parents, they'd see through to Chase's core right away and be impressed.

Roberta got out of the car ahead of her. Together they entered the hotel and made their way to the dining court. Through the crowd Annie saw her parents waving them over to their table. After hugs, they sat down and a waiter brought menus.

"I thought your father would be with you."

"He'll be here in a minute, Nana."

Annie's father studied her. "How's everything going?"

"Good. Ron Saddler and I outlined a work schedule. Until my cast comes off in another month, I'll be recording data while he's out in the field. Most of the time I'll be home for—"

"There's Dad!" Roberta slid from her chair, all conversation forgotten. She hurried toward the tall, fit man who'd drawn every eye in the room. He walked toward them wearing a stunning pearl-gray suit paired with a white shirt and striped gray-and-silver tie. Annie's breath caught because it had been so many years since she'd seen him formally dressed.

His dark hair and tanned complexion provided the perfect foil for his pewter eyes. Ten years ago she'd thought him incredibly handsome in the guise of archaeologist and, how, more recently as a park ranger. But tonight he gave off an air of urbane sophistication that did away with labels and distinguished him from the other men in the room.

Though her parents had seen pictures, she could see in their eyes that they hadn't been prepared for the attractive, compelling reality of him. Roberta gazed up at her daddy in hero worship. To Annie's dismay she was caught staring, too.

"Annie," he said in a deep, husky voice before walking around the table to shake her parents' hands.

"Mom and dad? This is Chase Jarvis."

"Mr. and Mrs. Bower? Meeting the two of you is a great honor and pleasure. Once upon a time I'd hoped to marry your daughter and become your son-in-law."

The use of the words *I'd hoped* put in the past tense caused Annie's heart to fall into the pit of her stomach.

"After the explosion, I never could have anticipated this moment. Though I'd go undercover again to protect her, my sorrow for all the pain I've caused will never leave me."

Despite her renewed pain, his soul-felt delivery shook her to her foundation. Judging by her parents' silence, the words had made an indelible impression on them as well.

Her father recovered first. "I'd say the smile you've put on our granddaughter's face has gone a long way to dry up the tears. Tonight should be a celebration of life."

Annie's misty-eyed mother nodded. "My husband

just took the words out of my mouth. Please sit down. Roberta has been living for tonight."

"She's not the only one." The smile he flashed their daughter lightened Annie's mood.

"I can't get over how much you two look alike," her mother commented.

Chase winked at Roberta. "I don't know about you, but I'll never complain."

Roberta's gentle laugh coincided with the waiter's arrival to take orders. From that point the dinner conversation centered on Roberta's new world with her daddy. Aching with the pain of Chase's first remarks to her parents, Annie mostly listened, only here and there offering a comment as they ate.

While she battled with her emotions, she heard Chase's cell phone go off. After he answered, lines darkened his face. Before he'd hung up, he'd already gotten to his feet.

"What's wrong, Daddy?"

"I have to go, but I'll tell you about it later, sweetheart. Sorry everyone. I hope to see all of you again soon." His sober gaze met Annie's for a brief moment before he strode swiftly from the room.

"I wish he didn't have to go."

Contrary to her daughter's desire, Annie was relieved he'd been called away. To be all together at last like they were a real family hurt too much.

Her mother patted Roberta's hand. "It's nice that you live here now and can see him whenever you want."

"No I can't," she corrected her grandmother.

"What do you mean?"

A tear trickled down her cheek. "We don't live with Daddy. Can we go home now?"

Annie's parents didn't try to respond to Roberta or ask her if she wanted dessert. "I'll take care of the check," her father murmured.

"We'll see you back at the house. Come on, Roberta." Annie reached for her daughter's hand and they hurried out of the lodge to the car. The old adage that hope sprang eternal was still alive in her broken heart.

"Do you think Daddy's going to be okay?"

"Of course. He's just doing the job he's been doing for the last three years."

"I wish I knew where he went."

Roberta wasn't the only one. Chase's reaction revealed more concern than usual. It would take time for her and their daughter to acclimatize to his world of emergencies. A ranger never knew what situation he was going to face.

Annie pulled into the garage and shut off the engine. "Have you forgotten your daddy was in the military?" She asked the question to reassure both of them. "He can take care of himself better than anyone."

"Except he couldn't save my other grandma and grandpa."

"Honey—" Devastated by Roberta's fears, she reached across the seat and pulled her against her chest. "I thought you weren't worried about that anymore." She pressed kisses on her head. "The rangers protect each other and everyone in the park, remember?"

Roberta's slight body trembled as she sobbed. Annie had no idea all this had been going on inside of her daughter. It was too late to wish they hadn't moved here. Whatever they did now, they were caught in an emotional trap.

Roberta eventually eased away from her. "Why can't we live together? Daddy wants to."

"No he doesn't."

"Yes he does!" she argued in a louder voice than Annie had ever heard before. "He told me today!"

Her daughter was overwrought. *How to get through to her?* "Okay." Annie wiped the moisture off Roberta's cheeks. She didn't want to get into a battle with her. "Tell me what he said. Take your time."

"After we came back from riding, Daddy and I were in the kitchen and I told him I wished we all lived together and he said 'I do too.'"

A frustrated cry escaped Annie's throat. "Don't you think he was just saying that because he loves you?"

"He loves you too, Mom!"

How many more nightmares were in store before any normalcy dominated their lives? "Why do you think that?"

"Because he called us his two beautiful women. He said he loved you before he loved me and he wants us to be a family."

Annie started to tremble. Did he really mean it? It was evident that Roberta believed he did. Before any more time passed Annie needed to have a private talk with him. Tonight, if it was possible.

"Your grandparents have driven up. Will you let them in the house? We'll talk about this later, all right?"

Roberta's glum expression was her only answer before she got out and hurried into the kitchen. Annie remained in the car and phoned Rachel. *Please be home.*

After four rings the other woman picked up. "Hello, Annie?"

"Hi. I'm so glad you're there," she said in a shaky voice.

"You sound upset. What's wrong?"

"I—it's a long story," she stammered. "First I need to ask you if Vance is there."

"No. He's on duty tonight."

"Could you do me a favor and find out what emergency caused Chase to leave dinner tonight? Roberta has some deep-seated fears and it upset her terribly. If he isn't gone too long, I need to talk to him when she's not around. Since my parents are staying overnight, this would be a good time to have a much needed conversation with him."

"I'll call Vance right now and phone you back."

"Thank you so much."

She clicked off and waited, not wanting to go inside the house until she was armed with some information that would reassure Roberta. One minute passed, then two. She was about to get out of the car when Rachel rang her back.

"Hi! Did you find out anything?"

"Yes. Vance said there was a very small rockslide at Curry Village a little while ago. Nothing serious. No one hurt, but he wanted Chase with him while they took a look around and made recommendations. He said it wouldn't take more than an hour or two at the most."

Annie let out a sigh. Under the circumstances she'd probably be able to talk to him before he went to bed. "I'm relieved everything's all right."

"So am I. Vance said you should explain to Roberta that slides happen quite often because the granite walls are so sheer. In fact it's amazing there aren't a lot more of them."

"Thanks, Rachel. I'll tell her. I'm indebted to both of you."

"Nonsense. Call me anytime."

"You know I will. The same goes for you. Good night."

She rang off and hurried in the house. Though her parents liked to stay at a hotel, Roberta had talked them into sleeping at their house tonight. Annie had given up her bed for them and would sleep with Roberta.

When she walked in the dining room, they were already seated around the table. Roberta had the Monopoly game set up ready to play. Annie took an empty chair next to her.

"I just talked to Rachel. Everything's fine with your dad. There was a small rock slide they needed to investigate." After she told her what she knew, Roberta seemed to relax, but she still wouldn't look at her. Annie exchanged silent glances with her parents, who were aware Roberta wasn't acting like herself.

The game took a long time. Annie's mother turned out to be the winner. When her father declared he was ready for bed, Annie suggested Roberta get into her pajamas. "You've had a big day considering you started out with a long horseback ride."

That brought her head up. She stared at Annie. "Daddy says I'm a natural rider."

"I'm not surprised. He did a great deal of riding years ago and is an expert horseman himself. You're a lot like him."

Her eyes filled. "I'm glad he didn't die." She put the top on the Monopoly box and hugged it to her chest. "Good night."

"Don't I get a kiss?"

She gave her a peck.

"Good night, honey. Sweet dreams."

Annie's father followed Roberta out of the room. That left her mother who gazed at her with troubled eyes. "What can I do to help?"

"Keep being there for me."

"Always that."

"I know. I don't deserve you."

"What in heaven's name are you talking about?"

A noise sounded in her throat. "I adore my daughter, but I made a serious mistake when I slept with Chase. You raised me differently than that. I was so in love that in my weakness, I let my emotions rule my good sense. Who would have thought that ten years later there'd be a price to pay…"

"Because?" her mother prodded.

"You already know the answer to that question."

"You mean that you're still in love with him?"

She smarted. "Is it that obvious?"

"Yes, but that's because I'm your mother. If it makes you feel any better, I almost had a heart attack myself when he walked into the dining room tonight. You wouldn't have been human if you hadn't been attracted to him. He's everything you claimed him to be, and maybe more."

Annie sat up straighter. "More?"

"He's been through hell, darling. You can see it in his eyes. There's a desperation in the way he clings to Roberta. When he looked at you before he left the table tonight, I saw a flash of fear."

She lowered her head because she'd seen it too, but she didn't know what it meant. Was he afraid she would change her mind and leave the park, taking Roberta with her? She sensed he walked on eggshells around her. In that regard he was so unlike the decisive, take-charge male she'd once known and loved. That man laughed in the face of danger. His highly adventurous nature had drawn her to him.

Maybe he was afraid that he really wouldn't be able to protect Roberta if his cover at the park were ever compromised. What if he was living with a new nightmare that the unspeakable would happen and she'd disappear?

Annie needed answers to so many questions she didn't know where to start.

"Mom? Roberta confided some things to me earlier. For her sake I've got to talk to him tonight if I can. Do you mind if I slip over to his house? It's just around the corner. He may not be there, but if he is you'll understand why I might not be back for a while."

"Go ahead. If Roberta asks where you are, I'll tell her the truth. That will comfort her more than anything." Annie's mother understood a lot.

After getting up to hug her, she went to the hall closet for her parka. The temperature outside had to be in the upper thirties and was still falling. She put one arm in the sleeve and pulled the other over her shoulder. Once she left the house, she jogged around the corner to Chase's.

When she reached it, there was no light on. Maybe he'd already come home and was in bed. After a slight hesitation she knocked on the door several times. No answer. She tried the bell. Nothing. Disappointment washed over her.

She could wait on the porch, but the cold would get to her before long. On a whim she tried opening the front door. It was locked. Annie would give it ten minutes before she went back to her house.

THE CLEANUP PHASE HAD STARTED. Vance walked over to Chase. "All things considered, what do you think?"

"As long as even one tent cabin was damaged, I think

we were wise to evacuate everyone in the perimeter. I say we keep these dozen or so cabins in the vicinity closed until next summer."

"Agreed." Vance looked at the sky. "Our first snowfall in the valley is forecast for tomorrow night. From then on, the cliffs will be at their most vulnerable."

"Yup. If there's going to be another slide, it'll happen now that the weather's starting to turn cold. It's good the people in that cabin were out to dinner when it occurred."

"You can say that again. As it is, it'll be all over the news. I'll phone Bill Telford when I get home."

Chase nodded. Right now he wasn't in the mood to talk to the superintendent. He didn't want Bill anywhere near Annie and Vance knew it. "Are we all set for Halloween?"

"I've arranged the watch in two shifts so the rangers with children can do the trick-or-treating with the kids. That means you and me." Vance flashed him a grin. "Last year you and I volunteered to cover for everybody because we didn't have any little Rossiter or Jarvis goblins of our own. Remember? My how things have changed."

"It's so incredible I still don't believe it," Chase whispered.

His friend studied his taut features. "How did it go with Annie's parents?"

"Now I know why she's so remarkable. Unfortunately, the slide happened before I had much of a chance for an in-depth conversation."

"Sorry about that. Can't run this place without you."

"That's good to hear. I like my job."

"But—"

He sucked in his breath. "But my life's not going to turn out like yours. I feel it in my bones. Don't get me wrong. Roberta's the blessing I never expected. Annie…is a different matter. She'd just as soon I faded from existence."

Vance cocked his head. "If that's true, then how come Rachel got a frantic call from her a few hours ago wanting to know where you went in such an all-fired hurry?"

Chase blinked. "Say that again?"

"You heard me."

He shook his head. "If she did that, it was because she was calling for Roberta's sake."

"I don't think so, otherwise Roberta would have called Nicky herself. As you well know, my wife's pretty intuitive. She asked me not to tell you this, but I'm going to anyway. The other day she had a talk with Annie and got the impression you're the one keeping a distance."

"That's because I am! Hell, Vance. One misstep with her could spell disaster."

Those brilliant blue eyes stared him down. "Maybe in the beginning you had to be careful, but the shock has worn off. Rachel could be wrong of course, but I say it wouldn't hurt to turn the tables on Annie and see what happens. It couldn't be any worse than the way things are going now. In any case she'll never take Roberta away from you. She needs to be reminded that once upon a time you two were lovers."

"That's right, until I stayed away from her for ten years!"

"And she knows why. Maybe you should show her some pictures of families of other CIA operatives who were butchered because they *didn't* enter the witness protection program."

"I've thought about it," Chase said.

"Good. Now go on home and think about it some more."

"I'm going."

Vance eyed him narrowly. "You're brooding again. What else is bothering you? If you think Annie will be turned off by your scars, then she's not the woman you thought she was."

Chase couldn't hide much from his friend. "As the doctors told me, I'm not a pretty sight."

"Let her be the judge."

Terror filled him whenever he thought what her reaction would be.

"See you tomorrow, Vance." He wheeled around and headed for his truck. If there was any truth to what Rachel had told Vance—if Annie did worry about him a little—he needed to explore it. Having his darling daughter restored to him wasn't enough. Not nearly. He wanted the woman who bore his child.

Chase rounded the corner of the housing complex in time to see a feminine figure leaving his property. As he drew closer and noticed the cast, he slowed down and lowered the window.

"Annie?" She looked up. "Turn around. I'll meet you at the house."

"It's late and you're probably tired."

"I've never been more wide awake." He drove past her and pulled in his driveway. Shutting off the motor, he jumped out of the cab. "Come on. I'll let us in the front door."

She followed him inside. He turned on the light and

shut the door. "Excuse me for a minute while I shower. If you're hungry or thirsty, help yourself to anything in the fridge."

"Thank you."

"I'll hurry."

AFTER HE DISAPPEARED, Annie eased off her parka and put it over one of the leather chairs. She'd been wearing the same tan pleated pants and white cotton sweater since morning and could use a shower herself.

Another time and she'd pore over the titles on his bookshelves, but tonight she was too restless to concentrate. Maybe she'd take him up on his offer and get herself a soda if he had one. Anything to keep busy while she waited.

One lone can of cola among several root beers beckoned to her. She didn't recall that he drank root beer. They had to be for Roberta. He wasn't a big soda drinker. The only kind she liked was cola.

Her thoughts drifted back to Kabul. When they'd come home to either of their apartments at the end of the day, he'd crush her in his arms and say, "My kingdom for a drop of cold water, but first I have to have this." They'd kiss until there was no beginning or end. Inevitably they gravitated to the bedroom. The water and room-temperature cola came much later.

So deep was her reverie, she didn't realize Chase had come into the kitchen until he turned on the cold water tap and drank for a good half minute. When he lifted his head, his glance fell on the can in her hand. "Some habits never change."

Annie realized he remembered too. "No," she whispered.

"Thank you for that much honesty."

Her pulse picked up speed. He smelled and looked wonderful. The black T-shirt and well-worn jeans molding his powerful thighs took her back in time. He needed a shave. He always did at the end of the day. It added to his sensuality, making her ache to the palms of her hands. She had to take an extra breath to regain her equilibrium.

He lounged against the edge of the counter. "What brought you over here tonight?"

"I need to talk to you about Roberta."

"Go ahead."

He stayed where he was, which was too close to her. Right now he reminded her of the old Robert. The only way to describe him was that he seemed more aggressive, yet he'd done nothing overt. She drank nervously from the can.

"She has this fantasy about you and me."

"So do I," came the quiet assertion. He put his hands on either side of her neck, rubbing his thumbs in circles over her tender skin. His touch hypnotized her. "You and I haven't had a chance until this minute to give each other a proper hello," he whispered against her lips. The warmth of his breath seemed to ignite her whole body.

"Robert—" she gasped softly.

"The name's Chase. An hour before the explosion that changed our world, we had just made passionate love. It was the morning we set the date to leave for the States and get married."

"I remember."

"So do I. Every detail," he insisted. "Afterward I very reluctantly left your arms for work and let you sleep in.

My mind was so full of the future and how gorgeous you were, I didn't notice until the second before oblivion hit that a couple of unfamiliar trucks had pulled up to the site."

The moan she heard was her own, resonating in the kitchen.

"It's taken longer than I expected to get back to you, Annie, so don't refuse me now. I couldn't take it."

There was no escape route as his lips closed over hers and she was pulled into his embrace. Ten years might have gone by, but her mouth and body recognized him and responded as if it had only been an hour since he'd left their bed. The frustration of not being able to use both her hands and arms was driving her insane. She realized the only difference between then and now was that her cast prevented their bodies from achieving a total melding.

He kissed her with a hunger that kept growing more voracious even while it was being appeased. How she'd lived this long without knowing his possession again was anathema to her. She could no more stop what was happening than she could stop breathing. There was a reason she shouldn't be doing this, but so help her, coherent thought had fled and she couldn't remember why.

Somehow her back ended up against the counter until there was no air between them. Without conscious thought her free hand slid up his chest and started to wind around his neck, but the pads of her fingers had run over ridges and bumps beneath his T-shirt that hadn't been a part of his torso before.

Visions of the photos Sid Manning had tossed on the floor illuminated her mind. Horrified once more, she gave an involuntary gasp and slid away from him, forcing him to relinquish his hold. She started to lift his shirt so she could see, but he took her wrist in a firm grip, preventing movement.

"No, Annie. Not yet."

She stared into his eyes and saw the same fear she'd seen in them earlier. "What do you mean not yet?"

"You don't want to look. Trust me." He averted his eyes.

"But I've seen the pictures."

"Those are nothing compared to what's left."

"That's ridiculous. The blood-spattered man I saw riddled in bomb fragments had been given up for dead. You're alive!"

He rubbed the back of his neck in a gesture she interpreted as a sign of insecurity. She couldn't comprehend him falling victim to that weakness. Not Chase.

"You mean what's left of me."

Her hand knotted into a fist. "I didn't think you had a vain bone in your body."

"I don't remember thinking much about it either until I looked into a full-length mirror and found myself staring at one of Dr. Frankenstein's experiments."

"Don't say that, Chase! Don't ever speak like that again." Her body shook so hard she had to hold on to the sink for support. "No one would ever guess in a million years."

He smirked. "With clothes on, you mean?"

She had trouble swallowing. "What do you do when you swim?"

"I don't."

Annie bit her lip. "Are you telling me you've never been with a woman since?"

"No, I'm not telling you that," he came back with brutal honesty.

"Does that include Rachel?" she asked before she could stop herself.

Chase had enviable control. "Rachel was never interested in me. It was Vance from the moment tempers flared in his office. If she told you anything different, she was lying."

"No," Annie answered honestly. "She said as much to me, but evidently you were interested in her."

His eyes narrowed. "You want your pound of flesh, don't you. Well here it is. Rachel had a sweetness about her including an inner strength that made her attractive to me. The truth is, she reminded me of *you*, but Vance had already gotten under her skin. There was no contest. Does that answer your question?"

She looked away, ashamed she'd brought Rachel up to him.

"Why don't we talk about the number of men who found you attractive over the intervening years. Roberta has told me about one of them. Greg somebody? The whiz kid from Pennington Mutual your parents introduced to you? She said he flew the two of you to his yacht moored in the San Francisco Bay area several times.

"I also remember her talking about a professional golfer named Lucky Sorenson who invited you to see the PGA Open at Pebble Beach. I understand you stayed overnight at his home in Carmel."

She should never have opened this up. "You've made your point, Chase."

"Did you sleep with *them*?"

Annie would love to lie to him, but she couldn't. "No," she answered in a quiet voice, "but you've been with other women who've seen your scars."

"They could handle it," he fired back.

"But not me."

"Especially not you."

Flame stained her cheeks. "Why?"

"I'd rather you remembered me the way I was."

"If you mean dead, it's too late for that now!"

His eyes grew bleak. "I know."

Full of pain she cried, "Evidently you always thought of me as a high-maintenance princess who needed to be pampered all the time and couldn't take anything the real world handed out."

She watched his features harden. "I asked you to marry me a long time ago and you said yes. Shall we see if your answer is the still the same now?"

In front of her eyes he pulled his T-shirt over his head. Next came his jeans, leaving him stripped down to his boxers. "Behold the man you once said was the embodiment of your every fantasy."

Looking at Chase was like looking at a picture taken at a carnival. The kind where you stood behind a cardboard stand-up that distorted a portion of your body. She'd always considered him the personification of male beauty. In her eyes he always would be.

"This is only the frontal view."

He turned around so she could see his back all the way to where the scarring was covered up by the waistband. "More plastic surgery might make me a little prettier, but with all my dreams obliterated, I never had the incentive to do anything about it."

When he faced her again, his hands were on his hips in that warriorlike stance she and Rachel had talked about. One brow dipped. "What do you think? Shall I have it done for your wedding present, or don't I stand a chance in hell?"

Annie couldn't talk. It wasn't the scarring that stopped her, although it was massive and no doubt represented years of pain and anguish while he healed. What wounded her was the darkness that had crept into his psyche over the intervening years. A menacing grimace distorted his smile.

"I'm waiting for an answer, my love. Even if our dreams were shattered, do you have the guts to make our daughter's come true?"

Suddenly she was reminded of Roberta the first year she took swimming lessons. All the other kids in her class had finally learned to dive off the side. When it came to her turn, she backed away from the edge. The teacher urged her to try it.

Roberta had denied that she was scared and insisted she didn't feel like diving right then. That look in her eyes was identical to the one in Chase's. Pure, unadulterated, defiant fear.

Chase had said he still wanted her, that he wanted to marry her. He'd kissed her tonight as if he'd never stopped wanting her. If marriage could take away his inner demons, maybe it could heal her demons, too. Nothing mattered except that he was back in her life, a man who'd faced terror and was still standing.

Her chin went up. "I do if you do. Your scars change nothing. I love you, Chase. How soon do you want to plan the ceremony?"

"Annie—" he cried, but as he reached for her, his cell phone rang.

She felt as well as heard his frustration at being interrupted. It frustrated her too because she knew he had to answer it. With one arm still around her, he reached for the phone lying on the counter, and clicked on, but whatever he heard on the other end changed his entire countenance. His arm slowly fell away.

Even in the light she could see he'd paled. All the joy in his expression of moments ago was gone. Extinguished. Annie felt sick to the pit of her stomach.

He covered the phone. "I'm afraid this is going to take some time," he said in a gravelly voice she didn't recognize.

"You want me to leave?"

She'd never seen Chase look more tormented. "It's the last thing I want and you know it. But under the circumstances it would be better. I'll come to your house later."

He gave her a swift, hard kiss on the lips before she grabbed her parka from the chair and left the kitchen. All the way to her house she hugged her cast against her chest to subdue the fierce pounding of her heart. She had the awful premonition something was about to threaten her happiness all over again.

Chapter Nine

Annie slipped in the house, relieved to discover everyone had gone to bed. She wasn't in any condition to face her parents or Roberta. Tonight she'd known such intense joy in Chase's arms, and the shock of having to leave him the second she'd told him she'd marry him had filled her with paralyzing fear.

Once before he'd left her to go to work, and he'd never come back. It couldn't have been normal ranger business making demands on his time tonight; for that, he wouldn't have lost color or sent her away.

He'd said he would come to the house later.

She glanced at her watch. Now it *was* later. What was going on?

If he didn't knock on her door in five minutes, she would run back to his house to find out why. While she was pacing the living room floor, her cell rang. Annie lunged for her purse lying on a chair. She pulled out the phone and clicked on.

"Chase?" She hadn't even looked at the caller ID.

"It's Vance."

"Oh, Vance. Forgive me. I—I've been waiting for Chase."

"That's why I'm calling. He's dealing with an emergency in another part of the park and doesn't know how long he'll be. Since he knew you'd be worried, I told him I'd call you."

She gripped the phone tighter. It was much more serious than Vance was making it out to be or Chase would have called her. Maybe there'd been a bear attack on a camper, or a shooting he had to investigate. As much as she wanted to ask Vance for details, she held back. He'd been kind enough to phone and assure her everything was all right.

What kind of a ranger's wife would she make if she fell apart every time Chase had to respond to a crisis? "You don't know how much I appreciate your call. Thank you for being so thoughtful, Vance."

"You're welcome. We'll be seeing each other soon. Nicky's living for Halloween."

"So is Roberta."

"Tonight he reminded us it's only three days away."

She laughed in spite of her anxiety. "We've been going through a similar countdown here."

"It'll be a fun night for everyone. Don't tell Nicky, but I'm just as excited as he is." Vance was a wonderful man. "Good night, Annie."

"Good night."

Once she'd hung up, she got ready for bed and slid in next to Roberta. But after an hour of tossing and turning she grabbed a blanket from the hall closet and spent what remained of the restless night on the couch instead.

When morning came, Roberta was up and ready for school, none the wiser that Annie had gone over to Chase's last night. By the time Annie had prepared breakfast, her parents had joined them.

Her mother gave her a searching glance. Naturally she wanted to know the outcome of last night's visit, but she didn't say anything in front of their sober granddaughter.

"Aren't you going to finish your toast?"

"I'm not that hungry, Mom." She looked at her grandparents. "I wish you didn't have to go back to San Francisco today."

"Don't you worry. We'll drive up here next week," Annie's father assured her.

"Okay." She slid out of the chair and kissed them, then grabbed her backpack from the chair in the front room.

Annie followed and gave her a hug. "See you after school."

"Daddy said Nicky and I could drop by headquarters for a root beer on our way home."

"That sounds fun." What else could she say? Hopefully Chase was back at his house in bed by now.

"Bye!"

All three of them watched her from the porch until she disappeared around the corner, then they went inside. "I guess we'd better get going too," her dad muttered without his usual enthusiasm.

"Before you do, I have something important to tell you." That got her parents' attention in a hurry. "Last night Chase asked me to marry him and I said yes."

Their eyes lit up. "That's the best news we've ever heard." The next thing she knew they were hugging her, cast and all. While she wiped her eyes, her mother said, "Why didn't you tell Roberta this morning?"

"Chase and I want to do it together." Their conversation hadn't gotten that far last night, but she knew *him*. He'd missed out on everything else to do with their daughter. Annie wasn't about to take that moment away from him.

Her father kissed her cheek. "How soon do you plan to be married?"

"Soon—" she blurted, feeling her face go hot. They hadn't talked about that either, but their hunger for each other demanded nothing less. She couldn't wait to go over to his house later.

"Well, don't keep us in suspense long."

"I promise to phone you the moment we've set a date. Last night he had to go out on an emergency before we could make plans."

"Oh, Annie!" Her mother embraced her again. They'd all been through so much since her return from Afghanistan. She knew what her mom was saying without any more words having to be said.

A few minutes later she walked them out to their car. "Drive safely."

"I will." Her dad gave her another long hug. "Tell Chase we said welcome to the family."

Annie nodded. She couldn't wait!

Once they'd gone, she rushed inside to do the dishes and take a shower. Though she couldn't do anything about being ten years older than she'd been when they'd met, she intended to make herself look as beautiful as possible for him.

By the time she was ready, she phoned headquarters first, just to make sure he wasn't in his office. The dispatcher, Ranger Davis, said he hadn't been in and she didn't know when to expect him. Annie had thought as much.

Five minutes later she discovered his truck wasn't in the driveway, nor did he answer the door. If he was in a deep sleep, she didn't want to rouse him from it. It looked like she had no choice but to go back home and start doing the job she was getting paid for.

The minutes crept into hours while she waited for him to phone at least. When the call never came, she phoned headquarters again. Still no sign of Chase being in his office. By quarter to four she was ready to call Vance when Roberta ran into the house. "Mom?"

Annie hurried down the hall from the room she'd turned into an office. "Hi, honey! How was school today?"

"It was okay, but Dad wasn't at headquarters. Can I go over to his house?"

"Of course," she said, not having to think about it, "but he might not be there."

"I know. If he's not, I'll come right back." She dropped her pack on a chair and took off out the front door.

Please be home, Chase.

Fifteen minutes passed, long enough for Annie to assume all was well. Giddy with relief, she had decided to walk over there and join them when Roberta came through the front door with a long face. "You were right. He wasn't home. Has he called?"

"Not yet, but I know he will the minute he can. Vance said he was called out on an emergency last night, so we don't know how long he'll be gone. Do you want some fruit or a sandwich?"

"Maybe some string cheese."

Good, Roberta wasn't too upset to eat. Annie was determined to keep things normal no matter what. "Why don't you ask Carly to come over. I'd like to meet her."

"I don't know her phone number."

"I'll get it from Ranger Sims. He's probably on duty."

She walked back to her office for pen and paper. While she was at it, she'd find out if he knew Chase's whereabouts.

Carly's father was clearly pleased that Roberta wanted to play with his daughter. He gave her their home phone number but, to her disappointment, his explanation didn't help her.

"He's been working on a big case with the feds to arrest the men responsible for growing marijuana in the wilderness areas. I happen to know they have a manhunt on to ferret them out and need Chase's help. That's probably what's keeping him."

"I'm sure you're right. Thanks, Mark. Talk to you soon."

Annie clicked off, but she wasn't reassured. Mark had been too ready with an easy answer. She knew what she'd seen last night. Chase's sudden pallor had given him away.

"Here's the number." She'd crossed over to Roberta's room to hand her the paper and phone. "I'm still working if you need me."

"Okay. If she can come, can we make popcorn?"

"Sure," she said, convinced his emergency didn't have to do with park business. The pit in her stomach had enlarged to a cavern.

"AREN'T YOU READY YET, honey?"

"I don't want to go trick-or-treating without Daddy," Roberta called out from her bedroom. "Do you think something bad has happened to him?"

"No, I don't."

"But he's been gone three days," she said in a mournful tone.

"He's a federal park ranger with important responsibilities. Sometimes he has to be gone on business he can't discuss with us. I'm afraid it's something we're going to have to get used to." This speech was for Annie's benefit, too. "If you stay in your room all night, you're going to disappoint Nicky, not to mention that you'll be miserable. Do you think that would make your father happy?"

After a silence, she finally said, "No."

"So what do you say?"

"Okay. I'll come."

"Have you taken out your curlers?"

"Yes. I used your hair spray to fluff it."

"I bet it looks perfect. I can't wait to see you and Nicky in your wizard robes. Luckily you can wear your coats under them."

"Rachel bought him a wig and glasses. He looks just like Harry and practices walking around like in the movie."

Annie chuckled. "You two will be the hit of the night."

"Daddy was going to bring my wand from his office."

Don't think about Chase right now. "Maybe it's better you don't have it. All the children will want to hold it."

"I know. Nicky's bringing his." Roberta opened the door, but it was Hermione who marched toward Annie with her Myers nose slightly in the air. The white blouse with the pointed collar was perfect beneath her black robe.

"Oh honey, you look just like her!"

Still staying in Hermione's character, her daughter eyed Annie up and down. "You must be some kind of Indian princess. Who are you precisely?"

"It was supposed to be a secret. I wanted to see if your father could figure it out."

"My father is brilliant," she stated in a superior tone. "Of course he would figure it out, *if* he were here."

They both broke into laughter. Bless her daughter for deciding to be a good soldier. It helped release some of the tension they were both feeling with Chase gone. This was the most animated her daughter had been in several days. Annie hoped this new mood would last, at least for tonight. They hugged, but not too hard. She didn't want her makeup to get on Roberta.

Heavy eyeliner and darker pancake makeup helped create the rest of the illusion that she was Princess Tee-Hee-Neh. Ron Saddler had managed to borrow the dress for her from a friend. Much as she would have loved to wear the moccasins she'd bought in the gift shop, she would have to save those for the party at Mark Sims's house after trick-or-treating because it had started snowing.

The only authentic part of her costume was a woven headband worn by the Ahwahnee women once living in Yosemite. After a couple of tries with her free hand she lowered it around her head so it gripped her forehead without dipping in the wrong place. As the legend went, Tee-Hee-Neh had long, dark hair. Annie wore hers the same way. She hadn't had this much fun in years, hoping to impress Chase, even if she was in a cast.

As if her thoughts had conjured him up, the doorbell rang. "I'll get it!"

Roberta zipped out of the room. With her heart in her throat Annie hurried after her. When she opened the front door, a freezing blast of air blew in. There stood Harry Potter carrying a plastic pumpkin to hold his candy. He was accompanied by a witch and a grim reaper in black, at least seven feet tall.

"Oh my gosh!" Roberta took the words right out of Annie's mouth. Vance was frightening!

"Come in, everyone, and shut the door," Annie urged. They all had a slight dusting of snow. "Well, Mr. Potter, I can't believe I'm not at Hogwarts."

Nicky giggled. "Thanks. You look pretty."

"Thank *you*. Roberta? Give Nicky some candy, then I think we should start our trick-or-treating."

"Goody!" Nicky took two Tootsie Pops before darting out the door first.

"Let's leave the rest of them on the porch for the other children when they come."

"Okay."

Soon everyone had gone outside. Annie followed with her parka around her shoulders and locked the door. They stepped into a winter fairyland. Magic filled the air. With everyone in costume, the scene could have been taken right out of a fantasy where anything was possible and wonders were expected to happen.

Where was Chase? How would she stand another night without him?

After stops at the various houses, they ended up at the Sims's house with plastic pumpkins full of goodies. There had to be a good thirty people assembled. Between all the food and the prizes to be given out, everyone would be on a sugar high for days.

Among the many awards, the most hideous costume went to Vance, of course. Rachel was dubbed the best "bewitched" witch. Nicky and Roberta garnered the "most lifelike impersonations of the cinema" award. Carly won the prettiest award for her Tinkerbell outfit. Three of the kids came as vampires. Brody won the bloodiest award, the other two walked away with the creepiest and the scariest. Everyone won something. Annie was given the best award for an historical figure.

After she'd been given a prize of a free coupon to rent a movie, she wandered over to the punch bowl. While she was helping herself, the grim reaper appeared at her side.

"You're terrifying me again, Vance."

"I was just going to say that if Princess Tee-Hee-Neh looked as beautiful as you, then I can understand how the legend got started."

"Chase!" she cried, so overjoyed he was here she almost spilled her punch on the floor.

He put it back on the table. "Come with me," was all he said. To her shock he led her to the laundry room between the kitchen and the garage. Once he locked the door, they were alone.

"Before we do anything else, I have to have *this*." Off came the fake head of his costume. She caught the gleam of his silvery eyes, then he was kissing her the way he used to do after they got home from the dig site. Their hunger for each other had been insatiable then and was worse now.

For a few minutes they fed from each other's mouths, needing this rapture after three days' deprivation. Transported by desire, neither of them was aware of the passage of time.

Finally he allowed her to come up for air. "I've been worried sick, darling."

"I know," he whispered against her lips. "Forgive me again."

"There's nothing to forgive—" she cried. "I'm just happy to be holding you again."

"I never wanted to let you go. That phone call the

other night came from Sid Manning. Since Vance knows about my being in the witness protection program, Sid worked out an emergency code among the three of us. It was a necessary precaution in case of other people present or electronic surveillance on our phone lines. I'd hoped none of us would ever have to use it, but it happened."

Annie hugged him tighter.

"Right after you left, Vance came for me and drove me to the pad. He said Sid would meet my helicopter in Bishop. The pilot was told it was emergency ranger business."

"Did Vance say anything else?"

Chase grimaced. "I'm afraid so." She shuddered. "Sid told him to be prepared in case Vance had to make someone else his assistant head ranger."

She drew in a sharp breath.

"At that point I told him to turn around because I was taking you and Roberta with me. I'd already been to hell and back. No way would I ever leave you again, but Vance was way ahead of me. He said it was *me* Sid wanted to see, that every safeguard had been put in place to keep you safe while I was gone. Not to worry."

His hands gripped her shoulders tighter. "Can you imagine Sid saying that when you'd just told me you'd marry me?"

"You went so pale," she whispered. "It was an awful moment."

Their eyes met in pained understanding. "For the last few days I've been sequestered with men from counterintelligence reviewing tapes that picked up chatter relevant to the planting of the bomb in Kabul ten years ago."

"Why now, when we've just been reunited? Is that the reason?"

"No, darling." He hushed her with his lips. "This had to do with Lon Wiseman."

"I remember him. The Israeli from Jerusalem University working at the site."

He nodded. "Lon's the other man who escaped death like me. Lately his name has come up in the chatter. It seems they finally have proof he's hiding back in Israel. Clearly the terrorists have never given up hunting for him or me, but the arguments have been loud and long as to where I'm hiding."

"So they're still actively looking for you."

He drew her head against his chest. "They never stop. One of the most outspoken operatives insisted that the double agent who recognized me before I left the military believes I'm being protected by friends in China. Another one is convinced Pakistan. Still another is clinging to the theory that I'm back in the States, yet none of them can be sure I'm not still embedded with American troops."

"Thank heaven they don't know anything yet."

"It's clear they don't, but those killers are some of the best trackers in the world. Though I've been at the park three years without incident, the day could come when a lead might bring them to Yosemite. Knowing Al-Qaeda hasn't relented in their pursuit makes it imperative we be proactive."

Annie looked into his eyes. "What are you saying exactly?"

"That this menace isn't going to go away. When we tell Roberta we're getting married, we have to let her know that the situation we're in means we might have to relocate at a moment's notice. In the meantime you and I have to decide if we're going to continue to stay here at Yosemite or not."

"Because of the danger to everyone else."

"Yes. Our friends, your parents."

"Oh Chase!" She wept quietly against him.

He rocked her in place. "How to protect all of us…that's my torment."

She sniffed and finally lifted her head. "We're together again, aren't we?"

"Yes."

"That's the most important thing, isn't it? We have time to decide what we're going to do?"

"Yes, yes, yes!" His eyes burned with love for her. "You're so strong, Annie. With you I know we're going to make it."

As his mouth descended once more, they became aware someone was trying to open the door. With reluctance Chase eased her out of his arms. "When we're back at your house, we'll pick up where we left off. Right now, let's enjoy the party."

He put the top of his costume back on before unlocking the door. Mark's wife stood at the kitchen sink. Annie flashed her a guilty look. "Sorry about that."

The other woman in the vampire outfit grinned. "No problem. Here—" She handed Annie a napkin. "Your makeup's all smeared."

By now Chase was chuckling. He took the napkin and fixed her face before declaring she was presentable. When they joined the others he whispered, "Do you know every man in the room is envious of me?"

It appeared Chase and Vance had planned ahead of time to wear the same costume. Now there were twin terrifying figures in the house.

"Thank you for the compliment. I wish I could return it, but I have to agree with the MC. Vance won the award for the most hideous costume. You two should be banned to extinction."

His husky laugh played havoc with her insides, turning her legs to mush. While she was trying to recover, Roberta ran up to them. Nicky was right behind her, casting spells on everyone. He was hilarious as usual. Evidently they didn't know what to think with two grim reapers in the room.

"Hi, sweetheart." He picked her up and hugged her.

"Dad!" she squealed in delight and hugged him back. "When did you get here?"

"A little while ago. I came in through Mark's garage."

So that was where he'd come from. Nicky looked shocked. "I've got to tell Daddy you're here!" Everyone was relieved Chase was back, but no one more than Annie.

While he ran off to find his parents, Roberta showed him the coupons for ice cream she and Nicky had won for their costumes. Chase was like a magnet. The rangers congregated around the witch's brew punch bowl to talk to him. Annie didn't mind.

Nothing mattered now that he was back. Before long they'd be alone.... Her body filled with heat. What if she'd stayed home wallowing in pain like she'd wanted to, like Roberta had wanted to do? His arrival had turned the place into a real party that went on for another half hour before some of the rangers had to leave to go back on duty.

Vance gathered up their party of six. After saying goodbye to their hosts, they started walking home. En route their group agreed it had been a perfect Halloween. The kids groaned when Annie and Rachel reminded them they had school in the morning and needed to get to bed. The two families parted at the corner.

"See ya tomorrow, Roberta. Be sure and bring your candy. I'll bring mine."

"I don't think so," Vance interjected.

"How come?"

"Because Chase and I plan to eat all of it at work."

Chase burst into laughter. It sounded so funny, especially while he was still in costume, but Nicky didn't find it at all amusing.

"Mom? Can he do that?"

"I'm afraid so. He's the chief ranger."

"But that doesn't give him the right to eat our candy," Roberta whispered to Annie. It was always the fairness issue with her.

"He's only teasing."

"Oh." Roberta was still a little in awe of Vance. "See ya, Nicky," she called over her shoulder.

As they went their separate ways they heard Nicky giggling again. "You see? Vance adores Nicky."

Roberta nodded.

"What are you two whispering about?" Chase wanted to know.

Annie winked at him. "We were hoping you'd come home with us. We're going to make a fire and watch *The Great Pumpkin*."

At the unexpected invitation, Roberta looked like she was going to explode with joy. This was only the beginning. Annie couldn't see Chase's face to register his expression, but she knew how he felt.

"I haven't seen a Charlie Brown cartoon in years. Let's

do it." He reached the front porch first and scooped up the bowl she'd left out for the kids. It had one Tootsie Pop left.

Once inside the house she said, "I'll change my clothes and be right out."

He took off his costume, revealing the man she loved beyond comprehension. His eyes swept over her in intimate appraisal. "I like you the way you are," he murmured.

Roberta smiled up at him. "Have you guessed who she is?"

"Could she be the Princess Tee-Hee-Neh?"

"How did you know that?"

"I know many things," he teased. Yes he did, Annie mused excitedly to herself. "She was a beautiful princess, the fairest of the daughters of the great chief Ahwahnee. She captured the heart of every young chief in the Yosemite Valley. Legend has it she was erect as the silver fir and supple as the tamarack. Her raven hair was silky as milkweed's floss, her movements graceful as a fawn's."

Annie trembled. When had he taken the time to learn that particular legend by heart?

"Each morning she stepped from her wigwam and would go to her secret place to meet her beloved. But one morning she found him dead from a fallen piece of granite where he'd been shooting arrows. She knelt down beside him. When he wouldn't wake up, she died, too. From then on the place with the giant slab above them was known as Lost Arrow."

While Annie realized it could almost be their story, Roberta looked mesmerized. "Nicky told me Lost Arrow is up by the falls. Are we going to climb up there someday?"

"We'll do it all, sweetheart."

"Roberta? Why don't you change into your pajamas before we start the movie."

"Okay. We'll be right back, Daddy. Don't leave."

"I'm not going anywhere."

Chapter Ten

A few minutes later the sight of Annie in the blue velour robe he'd once given her took him back ten years, causing his pulse to race. The dim light from one of the lamps threw her features into exquisite relief. She'd removed the pancake makeup that had turned her into an Indian princess. He desired her either way. It hurt to breathe.

"Annie?" His voice sounded hoarse even to him. Out of need he grasped her free hand, drawing her over to the couch where he sat down and pulled her onto his lap. Unable to resist, he brushed his lips against the soft warmth of her throat and mouth.

"There's something else I have to tell you before Roberta comes in."

Annie's body quivered. Her solemn eyes, almost a lavender-blue in the semidark, stared into his. "How could there be any more?" A haunted look had entered her eyes.

"This has to do with my physical condition."

Her eyes glistened with unshed tears. "Do you have a disease or some such thing you picked up in the Middle East?"

Close. "I still have the ability to make love to you but, according to the doctor, I'll never be able to give you more children. In case you were hoping for more, I need to know how you feel about that before we talk to our daughter."

She stunned him by wrapping her arms around his neck. After pressing her mouth to his, she said, "You already gave me the most wonderful child in the world. If we decide we want more, we can always adopt. How do you feel about that?"

He buried his face in her neck. "I think I can't believe this is happening at last."

Unable to hold back any longer, he kissed her with a hunger that was growing out of control. "You're beautiful beyond words, Annie. I need to love you so badly."

"I need you so much I'm in pain," she whispered and proceeded to show him. With his passion ignited he forgot where he was. In the next breath she was covering his face with feverish kisses the way she'd done years ago.

"Don't you want to watch the movie?"

Exulting in her love, he didn't realize Roberta had returned to the living room. Chase lifted his head in time to see his daughter standing by the TV in pink pajamas. Her Hermione hairdo still bounced.

"Put the DVD in, sweetheart, then come and sit down by me."

A slow smile broke the corners of Annie's mouth, captivating him. Easing out of his arms, she got to her feet. "I'll microwave the popcorn."

"Sounds like a plan."

He had a surprise plan of his own and would implement it during intermission. Annie knew it was coming, but she was letting him pick the moment. Chase checked his watch. It was ten-fifteen. He would announce the break in ten minutes. That was all the time he could stand to wait. Just thinking about it changed the rhythm of his heart, that violated, vulnerable organ he'd thought would have let him down by now.

Roberta took over. All he had to do was sit back on the couch and get comfortable. He played with her ponytail while they began chuckling over the charming characters. Chase saw a little of Nicky's and Roberta's most endearing qualities in them.

Annie came into the room with the popcorn and sat on the other side of their daughter. It was a good thing their offspring was around, considering his desire for her.

This was heaven, the kind of scenario he'd dreamed of so many times in the past ten years.

"I wish Snoopy were my dog, Mom."

"Every child who sees this film wishes the same thing."

Chase pressed the pause button. "Why don't we get one?"

Roberta leaped to her feet. "You mean and keep it here?"

"If this is where we decide to live."

"But you live around the corner."

"True." He could see he was confusing her. "I've decided I don't like going from your house to mine. What if we decide which house we like the best and all live in the same one together? Would you like that?"

Shock rendered her speechless for a moment. He saw fear creep into her eyes as her focus settled on Annie. "Would *you*, Mom?"

The blood pounded in his ears while he waited for Annie's answer.

"It's what I want more than anything in the world."

"You mean it?" she cried in joyous disbelief, throwing herself at Annie.

"Your mom and I are going to get married as soon as possible." He reached in his trouser pocket and pulled out a ring. "I've been wanting to give this to her since I first came to your condo in Santa Rosa."

He looked straight at Annie. "Before the explosion I asked the question and you said yes. Now I'm making it official in front of our daughter. Be very sure what you answer because this is forever."

"Say *yes*, Mom!"

"Yes," Annie answered in a tremulous voice.

"I'm planning to get two weeks cleared from the duty roster for our wedding and a honeymoon. It'll start Thanksgiving weekend."

"That's in about three weeks!" Roberta squealed. Now he was the one being hugged to death.

"By then your mother's cast will come off."

"Where will you get married?"

"Here in the park in a very small, quiet ceremony with only a few rangers to witness it. I wish it could be in a church and we could all go to some exotic place for our honeymoon, but that wouldn't be wise."

"So what will you do?"

He kissed her forehead. "We'll get married here at the house and honeymoon here. I'm thinking your grandparents could come and stay in your house while your mom and I get to know each other again in mine. After I'm back on duty we'll decide where we're going to live permanently."

Annie caught his hidden message before she put her arms around Roberta. "I think we're going to have to take a little shopping trip to San Francisco to find us something beautiful to wear for the wedding. Your grandmother will know the exact place."

Roberta cried with happiness against her. Annie's eyes, almost a violet-blue in the light from the television, stared into his without fear or striving.

This was the supreme moment of his life. He moved to Annie's other side and slid the solitaire diamond home on her ring finger. Once Roberta went to bed, he would show this amazing woman what she meant to him. The sooner the movie was over, the sooner he could get her in his arms.

"Darling," she said, pressing an avid kiss to his mouth.

"We'll celebrate after she's asleep," he whispered.

They all settled back on the couch. He had reached for the remote to release the pause button when a sound like the crack of thunder overhead went out like shock wave. It shook the ground. Roberta jumped and cried out at the same time.

Annie stared at him. "Was that an earthquake?"

Chase was already on his feet, putting on his parka. "No. A rockslide. It has a distinct sound. That one came from Curry Village."

"Wasn't that where the other one happened?"

He nodded. "I had a gut feeling it might happen again, but this was a much bigger one." Hopefully the tent cabins still available to the tourists had escaped catastrophic damage. He knew Vance was praying for the same thing.

"Don't either of you go out. When moisture gets in the cracks and a slab falls and breaks up, it sends pulverized debris called granite flour into the air for several hours. I don't want you breathing it."

"What about you?" Annie cried.

"I keep a mask in the truck. We'll do the rest of the movie tomorrow evening and invite the Rossiters. Be my good girls and mind me."

"Be careful, Daddy."

"That's my middle name." He gave her a hug, then caught Annie's face between his hands and kissed her thoroughly before taking off out the door.

The drive to Curry Village didn't take long. Already some of the guys were on the scene. It looked like a war zone. As he drew closer he saw Vance helping a dazed tourist out of her damaged tent. He reached for the mask in his toolbox and raced toward the others, grateful Annie and Roberta weren't anywhere near.

By morning he and the others had helped evacuate the 400-plus tourists to other lodgings. Only two had needed medical assistance, and they weren't seriously injured. As he was climbing back into the truck, Vance approached. "I guess you saw the damage to the tent cabins we closed off the other day."

He nodded. "If that first slide hadn't happened, we would have been digging for bodies. We dodged another bullet tonight."

"Yup." The chief wiped some of the powdery substance off his lips. "It's time to go home, but I'm afraid Nicky will think I'm the abominable snowman."

Chase let out a low laugh.

His friend's eyes flashed an electric blue. "I had the time of my life earlier tonight. How about you?"

"You don't know the half of it. Bring your family over to Annie's tomorrow night. I guess that means tonight. I've lost track. We'll watch *The Great Pumpkin*."

"That'll be a hit with Nicky. I'll tell Rachel."

Drained physically yet emotionally hyper where Annie was concerned, Chase drove home at a fast clip. She would be getting their daughter ready for school before she put in a day's work. He couldn't wait to be with her, but first he needed food followed by a shower and sleep. Their honeymoon couldn't come fast enough.

"MOM?" ROBERTA CALLED from the living room. "Nana wants to talk to you."

That was the second call today from her. Though her parents remained calm, she knew they were concerned about the rock slide. Annie on the other hand was coming to learn that something was always going on in the park, but she was so in love with Chase, nothing seemed to faze her.

"Bring the phone to the kitchen, will you?" She had decided to make a big dinner for them. The potatoes and carrots had been cooking around the lamb roast. After school Roberta had peeled the vegetables while Annie had made rolls. They'd be able to eat soon.

"Here."

"Thanks." She grabbed hold with her free hand. "Hi, Mom."

"The news on TV is full of the story about the rock slide."

"I know. I drove over to see the damage on my way to the store. It's pretty terrifying to think huge parts of boulders just fall away."

"What does Chase say about it?"

The mention of his name set her pulse off and running.

She stared at her diamond. "I don't know. I haven't seen or talked to him since last night, but the rangers worked till this morning so I'm sure he's still asleep."

Bill Telford had called her earlier in the day, reminding her they were having dinner tomorrow night. If he tried to turn it into something more than business, she would tell him she was getting married, but it was still a secret. For Roberta's sake she asked him if they could eat earlier than later. He was agreeable and they settled on six o'clock.

She had no way of knowing if Chase would be available for Roberta tomorrow evening. In case he had to be on duty, Rachel said Roberta could go over to their house and play with Nicky.

"You sound happy, darling."

"I am, Mom. He and Roberta are my life."

"That's the way it should be. Well, keep us posted."

"I promise to call you after I've heard from Chase."

"Good."

"Mom?" Roberta said after she'd hung up. "Can I call Daddy and see how soon he's coming over?"

"Go ahead. Dinner's ready." After pulling out the roast, she put the raised rolls in the oven to bake.

"I don't think he's there. It just keeps ringing."

"Then phone headquarters. They'll know where to find him."

"Okay." A minute later she said, "Daddy's off duty until tomorrow."

"I'm sure he's sleeping, so I have an idea. Let's pack up the food and take it over to his house. We'll drive over as soon as the rolls are done."

Roberta didn't need any urging. "I'll bring the key he gave me to get in."

"While we're loading the car, bring *The Great Pumpkin* movie with you."

"Okay."

In a few minutes they backed out of the garage and drove over to his house. If both his vehicles were in the garage she couldn't tell because the snow had melted on his driveway.

They phoned again and rang the doorbell, but there was no answer. Roberta looked up at her. "I'll let us in."

"Go ahead. If we have dinner waiting for him, he'll be thrilled." Together they carried the food to the kitchen. "Why don't you set the table? I'm going to tiptoe down the hall and see if he's asleep."

"Do you think he still is?"

"Or maybe he's in the shower. I'll be right back." The last thing she wanted was for Roberta to find him. If he were uncovered, the shock of his scars would be too much. When he decided to let her see them, he would have to talk to her about them first and prepare her.

With her heart in her throat, she peeked inside his room. To her relief she found him sprawled on top of the bed on his stomach, the sheet twisted around his long, hard-muscled legs. Realizing his back was exposed to his hips, she closed the door and collapsed against it.

"Chase?" she called out softly. At the sound of her voice, he flung out an arm of whipcord strength. "Darling?" she said a little louder.

He stirred before sitting up in the bed, taking the sheet with him. "Annie?"

"I'm sorry, but it's six o'clock. We brought you dinner. If you're not ready to eat, we'll leave you alone so you can go on sleeping."

He raked two bronzed hands through his hair. It was dark and rich, like the color of coffee beans. "I actually slept eleven hours?" he muttered. "I don't believe it." That aura of vulnerability he rarely showed to anyone tugged hard on her emotions.

"You needed it."

"Roberta's here?"

"Yes. She's going to hold you to that movie. Right now she's busy setting the table. I made sure she didn't find you first."

Their eyes met in silent understanding. His gave off a clear silver-gray. It appeared his sleep had done him a world of good. He rubbed his jaw. "I'll shave and join you in a few minutes."

Annie would have preferred to stay and feast her eyes on him. That summer in Kabul they'd gone without a lot of sleep in their desire to bring each other pleasure. Too many times she'd seen him in bed just like this, waiting for her to come back so they could love each other all over again. Stifling a moan, she slipped out the door to find Roberta.

"Your dad *was* asleep."

The tension lines in her face relaxed. "He must have been really tired."

"He was up all night. Do you think you can find some butter for our rolls?"

"I already have. Some jam too."

"Perfect."

A FEAST FIT FOR A KING.

That was Chase's first thought when he entered the kitchen wearing khakis and a sport shirt. His long sleep had made him feel like a new man.

The aroma of lamb roast flavored with fresh mint filled the room. Annie remembered. How many times had they camped out and eaten lamb kabobs roasted over the fire? It was his favorite meat, though he'd rarely eaten it since he'd come to the park. That was because he liked sweet onions and carrots with it and those items took additional preparation.

A few minutes later he caught hold of Roberta's hand and squeezed it. "This is the best meal I've ever eaten."

Her guileless smile got to him every time. "I peeled the vegetables."

"Well, they're perfect. So's everything." His gaze swerved to Annie. *"So are you."*

Their eyes held. "The feeling's mutual."

"I brought the movie over, Dad."

"Perfect," he said, still looking at Annie. "Roberta?"

"Yes?"

"Will you do me a favor and call Nicky? My phone's in the bedroom. Press two. I invited them to come over to your house tonight to watch Snoopy. Tell them to come here instead."

She let out another sound of happiness and ran to the other room to find the phone.

"Annie, come here to me. We never have a second alone."

They reached for each other at the same time. Chase didn't try to talk. All he could do was tell her with his lips and his body as he drew her into him, forgetting there was a cast between them.

Eventually they ended up in his living room on the leather couch. She looked beautiful and sophisticated in a navy blouse and tailored gray wool pants. He couldn't get enough of her.

Too soon for Chase his euphoria was broken by the sound of voices at the front door. He fought against relinquishing her mouth for any reason.

"Hey—" Nicky's bright voice filled the room. "How come they're kissing?"

Chase's body started to shake with laughter. So did Annie's. Slowly he raised his head. In that moment before he looked at the others, he saw the love light in her gorgeous eyes. If he could always have this effect on her, he wouldn't ask for anything else.

He turned to their friends, smiling at Nicky. "How come your dad kisses your mom?"

"'Cause he loves her!"

"And how come she kisses him back?"

"'Cause she loves him."

Annie decided to help him out. "I love your uncle Chase very, very much, so we're going to get married. He just gave me this diamond. Do you want to see it?"

He ran over to look at it.

"Would you like to be in our wedding?" Annie asked him.

Nicky gave a little shriek of excitement and turned to his parents. "Can I?"

Pandemonium broke out as Vance grabbed Chase and they gave each other a bear hug. She couldn't hear all they were saying, but she'd never seen two men so happy.

Annie shared a private glance with Rachel. In a short time they'd become good friends. Nicky's mother moved closer. Her eyes glistened with unshed tears as she inspected the one-carat solitaire.

"Thank heaven you've found each other again. Tonight Chase is such a different person from the man

I met last June, I hardly recognize him. I can see that you're changed, too."

She nodded. "We've had a lot to work out." They still did. Annie wasn't unaware Chase would always have certain demons to deal with from his past. But there was great satisfaction in knowing she would be there to love him through all of it.

"I want to help with your wedding any way I can."

"We both do," Vance declared, giving Annie a big hug. "Congratulations," he whispered. "You're about to be married to the greatest man I know." She nodded. Coming from the chief, there was no greater praise.

After putting his arm around his wife, Vance said, "Since your wedding has to be low-key, why don't you get married at our house? The minister in Oakhurst would be happy to officiate."

Annie checked with Chase. His wide smile said it all. "That sounds wonderful to us, Vance. Thank you so much."

"It'll be our pleasure, believe me. We'll keep everything quiet until the big day. Did you hear that, sport?"

When Annie looked, Nicky and Roberta were both eating rolls. He looked back at his dad. "Hear what?"

"We have to keep their wedding a secret for now."

"Okay. I won't tell anybody. Can I wear a tux like I did at our wedding?"

Chase rubbed the top of his head. "I insist on it. We're going to take lots of pictures of you and Roberta."

"Guess what, Nicky?" she piped up. "Daddy says we're going to get a dog."

"What kind?"

"Snoopy."

His eyes widened. "Hey, Dad—"

Vance laughed. "I heard. Maybe we'll all go together and you can pick out yours at the same time."

"What kind do you want?" Roberta asked.

"A mutt like Daddy used to have."

"That's not a breed."

"Actually it's a combination of several kinds of breeds," Annie corrected her daughter so it wouldn't hurt Nicky's feelings.

"Yeah."

"Do you want to watch *The Great Pumpkin*?" Roberta was a quick study.

"I think that's a terrific idea, sweetheart. Come on. Everyone sit down and we'll all watch it." Chase turned off the lights. The next thing Annie knew he'd pulled her onto his lap, her favorite place. He moved her hair to the side. "Almost heaven," he whispered against her neck, sending rivulets of desire through her body.

It took the greatest control to sit through to the end of the film without devouring each other, but somehow Chase managed. Annie had the more difficult time. Rachel's announcement that it was time for Nicky to be in bed didn't come too soon.

Annie got to her feet on rubbery legs and saw everyone to the door. Chase joined her. When she shut it, she found herself trapped by a powerful body. He found her mouth. The kiss they'd been craving went on and on and was quickly turning into something else. "I could eat you alive."

"We can't—even though Roberta's half-asleep on the couch, we're not alone."

He groaned. "I know. We can't be alone until you're my wife. That's three and a half weeks away. I want a real wedding night. We'll pretend it's our first time together."

She bit her lip, knowing it was going to kill her to wait. "I want that, too."

Chase gave her a thorough kiss. "Come on. I'll see you two home."

"The dishes—"

"I'll do them. After I get back from your house I'm going to have so much excess energy, I'll be glad for something, anything to do until I can do what I really want for as long as I want."

Annie knew exactly what he meant.

THREE WEEKS LATER while Roberta looked on, the doctor removed the cast and carefully washed Annie's arm. "There. How does it feel?"

She smiled. "Like my body's a lot lighter on one side."

"The feeling will pass in a day. Your X-ray indicates you've healed beautifully."

"That's a great relief."

"I bet you're glad it's off, Mom."

"You can't imagine." It had been like a wall separating her from Chase, but in retrospect she knew it had been a good thing. Forty-eight hours from now she'd be his bride. She was running a temperature just thinking about it. "How much can I do with it?"

He winked. "Enough to enjoy your honeymoon." Annie blushed. "I'm teasing."

She chuckled. "I know." This doctor was a stranger, but since her parents had driven them to San Francisco to pick up their dresses, Annie had decided to see the orthopedic surgeon her father had said came highly recommended.

"Just ease back into the normal activity of your life and you'll be fine."

The doctor smiled at Roberta. "When's the big event?"

"It's the day after tomorrow."

"I bet you have a beautiful new dress."

She nodded. "It's long and white with a blue sash."

"Are you excited to be getting a new daddy?"

Roberta sent Annie a secret glance. "Yes. I love him."

"Well, I'd say he's the most fortunate man on the planet." His gaze included Annie as he said it.

"Thank you, Doctor. I appreciate you fitting me in so fast."

"It was a pleasure. Congratulations again."

"Thanks." She got up from the chair feeling free as a bird without that deadweight. "Shall we go? Your grandparents are waiting outside the clinic."

"Bye." Roberta waved before they left his examining room.

Her parents beamed when they saw her approach the car unencumbered. Everything had been accomplished so they could head straight back to the park. She'd told Chase they wouldn't arrive until late so she wouldn't see him until the eleven o'clock ceremony the day after tomorrow. It was better that way. She didn't trust herself within a mile of him now.

On her shopping spree she'd bought his wedding ring and a special wedding present. She'd also purchased a gift for Rachel and Vance for being such wonderful friends. Roberta had picked out a unique surprise for Nicky. The car was also loaded with everything her parents would need while they took care of their granddaughter for a week.

Seven days entirely alone with Chase. How would she live till then?

VANCE SPREAD the double-bed air mattress on the floor in front of Chase's fireplace and started to fill it using his old bicycle pump.

"Does that old relic still work?"

"Let's find out."

Who would have guessed? Chase had to admit it still did the job perfectly.

Vance looked up. "You're going to have to tell me how this setup goes over with Annie. After you guys come out of hibernation, I'm thinking Rachel and I will take up where you left off and have a honeymoon at home, too."

Chase had chopped wood all afternoon and was still stacking it on the hearth. "At least your first one was in a hotel with food and maid service."

His friend paused in his task for a minute. "Do you want to know the truth?"

"Always."

"I'd have much rather stayed right here and done what you're doing. The trip to England was for Nicky."

"I know, but think what great memories you made." He set the last load of wood on top of the stack. "One of these days I'll take my family somewhere."

Vance eyed him intently. "Annie was forced to live ten years without you. I'd say she and Roberta are ready to stay put with you. I think it's time for a beer. Our last together while you're still a single man."

"Whatever you say, Chief."

"BY THE AUTHORITY invested in me, I now pronounce Margaret Anne Bower and Chase Jarvis, husband and wife in the bonds of holy matrimony. What God has joined together, let no man put asunder. You may kiss your bride."

Chase's bride stood in two-inch white high heels. No cast in sight. She was a vision in a stunning white lace suit with pearl buttons. A matching strand of pearls encircled her throat. She reminded Chase of a confection too exquisite to touch.

"I don't know if I dare," he whispered in earnest. "I've needed to be your husband for too long."

Her surprised expression was underlined by Nicky's loud whisper. "Isn't Uncle Chase going to kiss her?" His question produced a ripple of stifled laughter that traveled around the room. Their minister laughed out loud.

The comic relief helped Chase give his new wife an appropriate kiss that lasted just the right amount of time, surprising her even more. But he'd done it this way for self-preservation. Otherwise the half-dozen rangers he'd invited would know he was out of control and they'd never let him live it down.

Roberta was the first to break out of line and hug them. Nicky came next in a black tux that matched his father's and Chase's. He kept tugging on her to run into the dining room with him so they'd be the first to get food and wedding cake.

Then came the onslaught of family and well-wishers packed into Vance's living room. Stands of flowers had transformed it. Chase loved the smell of the gardenias pinned to Annie's shoulder.

The small, intimate crowd they'd first envisioned had grown to a considerable size. Besides Annie's parents, Tom Fuller had come with his family. His leg was still in a cast. Ron, Annie's colleague, was also invited and milled around chatting with the guests.

Beth had come with her family. Of course Rachel's parents were here along with the families of the rangers invited. The brotherhood that Chase felt was something to treasure. Only one thing was missing.

His parents would have loved to be here. From the beginning they'd treated Annie like a daughter. They would have adored their granddaughter.

He felt Annie squeeze his hand. "I miss your parents, too. Wherever they are, I'd like to think they're watching."

She was so in tune with his feelings, he drew her into his arms and rocked her for a moment. "How soon do you think we can leave?"

"Right now if you want."

"It wouldn't be rude?"

"Yes, it would be very rude."

He tightened his embrace, relishing the fact that the cast was gone. "We'll stay twenty more minutes."

"In that case we'd better find our daughter and say goodbye."

"Do you think she'll be able to handle it?" he whispered against her neck.

"As long as we're just around the corner, I'm sure of it. The big question is, can you?"

"You know me too well, Annie."

"There's no rule that says you can't phone her."

"How many men do you know phone their children on their honeymoon?"

"Well, I know *one*. The chief ranger of the *whole* park, as Nicky loves to say, took him on their honeymoon. He's grinning at us right now, by the way."

"So are the other guys. We need to get out of here. Let's find our daughter."

Chapter Eleven

Chase lay in front of the crackling fire, his heart pounding unmercifully as he waited for Annie to come. During the hours they'd made love in the bedroom, the afternoon had melted into evening. Now it was night.

After showering together, he'd left her alone long enough to warm up food from their wedding reception. He had everything ready so they wouldn't have to move again for hours.

Outside a wind had sprung up. Snow had been forecast. In the past, a night like this with the advent of winter always made him feel lonely in a way too desolate to describe. Though there weren't any wolves in the park, he'd felt like one who'd been trekking in the forest on a search for his lost mate, an endless lesson in futility. On such a night, he'd wished himself thousands of miles away from Yosemite.

Not tonight. Not ever again.

While the wind moaned around the corners of the house and beat against the windowpanes, he simply crushed Annie against him and let her heat consume him. She filled the empty spaces in his soul. All he had to do was open his eyes and drink in her beauty. He never again wanted to be anyplace other than right here, safe in the arms of the woman who'd cried out her love for him over and over again.

Her body had grown more voluptuous since giving birth. Between her satiny skin and dark, glistening hair, he couldn't stop telling her she was a living miracle.

"Darling? Did you think I was never coming?"

His gaze took in the mold of her body wrapped in the blue robe. "I can't believe you still have it."

She knelt next to him and kissed his mouth before eating several small rolls filled with crab salad. "For one thing, a lovely robe like this never goes out of style. For another, it's the one item saved from our past I can put on and pretend I can feel your arms around me. I remember you bringing it home from the bazaar."

He ran a hand under her sleeve to feel her warmth. "It looked like you, all filmy and silky."

Annie smiled down at him. "I remember thinking it reminded me of you. The material is shot through with silver threads very much like the color of your eyes right now. I'd never received such an intimate gift before. You thrilled me with it. I loved Robert Myers with everything in me. He was exciting and dashing to an impressionable young woman who'd never been in love before. I thought I'd lost him forever." Her voice caught.

"But tonight I see him in the guise of Chase Jarvis, a man whose suffering and heroism have added stature to that other man. I love this new man, now a devoted father, with all the intensity of my soul. Somehow—I don't know how—I'm the blessed woman privileged to be loved by both men. For however long we have together, you're my heart's desire, Chase."

"And you're mine, my love."

They'd already said their vows, but her words just now wrapped right around his soul. He traced the line of her chin with his index finger. "I wish I had something from my past to give you in remembrance, but I'm afraid every possession was confiscated."

Her eyes darkened with emotion. "Since you've come back into my life I've suffered in new ways for you." Tears clogged her voice. "To think your whole identity was just wiped out—everything gone." She took a deep breath. "Wait here for a minute."

She got to her feet and disappeared. The swishing sound he found provocative because the fabric lay next to the lovely mold of her body. While he half lay there in anticipation, he finished off more rolls and a skewer of fruit.

"Close your eyes, darling." He did her bidding and felt her come closer. "Now open them."

He had no idea what to expect, but when he saw the large framed oil painting of his parents as he remembered them weeks before they died, he made a sound in his throat and wept.

"Mom and Dad know an artist who took one of my photos and reproduced it on canvas. Roberta and I made a special scrapbook for you of every picture I brought back from Kabul. She'll give it to you later, but I wanted you to have this now."

Chase pulled on a pair of sweats, then carried the painting to the couch. On the lower part of the frame was a plaque with their first names engraved. He studied their faces. Annie's gift had brought them back to him in living color. Their resurrection was almost painful in its intensity.

Robbed of words, he did the next best thing and reached

for her. They began kissing all over again. Short kisses, long kisses and everything in between until they clung in a wine-dark rapture and found their way to the mattress.

Later, after being temporarily sated, Chase got up to put more wood on the fire. It had burned down to embers. She stared up at him from beneath the quilt. "I'm so happy, I can't believe I've lived as long as I did without you."

He was beyond happy. "I don't want to think about it. All that matters is the here and now."

She reached for him. "Come and get under the covers, darling. I need you within touching distance."

"And I don't?" He growled the question playfully against her tender throat. "How come you never told me your name was Margaret? When Mark said the passenger in the downed helicopter was Margaret Anne Bower, I thought the 'Anne Bower part' had to be an uncanny coincidence, but I didn't believe it was you."

She buried her face in his bronzed neck. "My mom's mother was named Margaret. When I was young I didn't like being called that. It sounded old-fashioned to me, so I only went by Annie."

He pressed a swift kiss to her lips. "I prided myself in knowing everything about you. Until I saw you lying unconscious in the foliage, I couldn't be positive of anything."

She returned his kiss several times. "I heard your voice before I saw you and thought I was back in Kabul. The explosion had just happened and I was trying to find you."

"I know." His voice throbbed. "You called me Robert. I'm still having difficulty realizing it was you lying there too still for my heart to handle."

"Chase?" She cupped his cheeks. "Did you ask to be placed at Yosemite?"

"No. The witness protection program made all the arrangements. I had no say in the matter. I've been thinking about what we should do."

"So have I."

He studied her beautiful features, the singing curve of her red mouth. "What decision have you come to?"

"That we stay here no matter what and brave whatever comes."

"Oh Annie, if you'd said anything else—"

"How could I?" Her eyes filled. "Our life is here. We'll just have to have faith and take every precaution to stay safe. It was all meant to be."

He agreed. In the grand design he believed they'd been reunited for a reason, but to what end? How could anything be more cruel now than to be aware his life was hanging in the balance because of that piece of metal?

Annie smoothed the frown lines between his brows. "What dark thought passed through your mind just then?"

Chase caught her hand and began a nibbling foray up the arm that had been fractured. She was doubly precious to him now. "Do you have any idea how much I love you?"

"Yes," she said emotionally, "but you didn't answer my question."

He rolled her on top of him, tangling her long silken legs with his. "It was nothing, my love. Let's not talk anymore. There are other ways I want to communicate with you and I don't plan to waste a second of them."

Chase needed her with a desperation that put new fear in him. Throughout the rest of the night he found himself loving her with refined savagery, trying to make time stand still while he worshipped this woman with his whole body and soul.

EIGHT DAYS LATER Chase opened the front door to Annie's house. She rushed inside. "Roberta?"

"No," said a voice from the hallway. "It's only me." Her mom chuckled. "She's going to jump for joy to know you're back."

Annie ran toward her mother and hugged her for a long time. "How are we ever going to thank you for what you've done?"

Her mom teared up. "Seeing the two of you looking like a pair of lovesick teenagers is all the thanks I'll ever want."

"We couldn't have had the kind of honeymoon we needed if we hadn't known she was with the two people she adores." So saying, Chase engulfed Annie's mother in his arms.

"Where is she?" Annie could hardly wait to see her.

"She and your dad walked are over to the Rossiters to visit with Rachel's parents. The drove up from Oakhurst this morning to spend the weekend. I just took a pie out of the oven and was about to go over there myself."

"It smelled like heaven when we walked in."

She smiled at Chase. "Roberta told me apple was your favorite. I wanted you to have something to munch on when you got back."

Annie's husband gave her mother another squeeze. "If your daughter didn't make me so happy, we would have come home yesterday as planned. I think I'll grab myself a slice of it right now while it's hot."

He headed for the kitchen ostensibly because he was hungry, but he'd left them alone on purpose for a moment to let them catch up in private. The two women shared a knowing glance.

"You've turned him into a different man."

"I'm married to the most wonderful man alive."

"So am I. Aren't we lucky?"

"Oh, yes—we are!" Annie couldn't resist hugging her mom again. "How did Roberta handle it? Really, I mean."

"Much better than I would have supposed. Chase's decision to stay in his house made all the difference. She and Nicky have drawn close over the last week. I heard her tell your father she wouldn't mind a little brother."

Annie needed to squelch that dream right now. "Chase's injuries have made it impossible for us to conceive, Mom. I'm glad Annie likes Nicky so much because he'll be the closest thing she ever gets to a little brother."

"Oh, honey. I'm sorry."

"I am too. Chase is such a loving father, he deserves to go through the whole experience with me, but we have to be grateful he came back to us at all. And we could adopt."

"Of course." She cocked her head. "You've matured beyond belief, you know that?"

Knowing your husband could die at any time had a way of waking you up to reality, but Annie kept that painful knowledge to herself. "I recognize a miracle has happened. I'll never take it for granted."

Chase walked in on them. He flashed her mom a guilty look. "I think there's a half a pie left. It was ambrosia. I hope you don't mind."

"I'd mind if you didn't eat it."

"Let's all go over to Vance's and pick up our daughter. Where's your parka?"

"In the closet."

"I'll get it for you."

As soon as Chase helped her mom on with it, they left the house. The snowfall of a few days ago still glistened pure white. When they rounded the corner, Annie spotted the kids out in the front yard with Vance and Rachel. They'd made a snowman with a ranger's hat on top.

Wouldn't you know it was Nicky who spotted them first. "Uncle Chase! Hooray!" He jumped up and down like a crazy man and started running toward them.

Roberta just came running and passed him. Chase ran to meet her and scooped her up in his arms. He carried her to Annie and all three of them hugged. Then Nicky joined them and there were four.

Chase kissed her. "I believe you've gotten heavier while we've been gone."

"It's only been eight days, Dad."

Annie smiled to herself. Nothing got past her Roberta. The girl had been marking time.

"Was it that long?" he teased.

"Yes." She hugged him hard around the neck.

Nicky demanded to be heard. "Did you guys have fun?"

"That's what I want to know." Vance had just walked over to them, his blue eyes dancing.

Annie picked up their son and hugged him. "We had so much fun we couldn't believe it." Rachel burst into laughter.

"What did you do?"

Chase lowered Roberta to the ground and took Nicky from Annie's arms. "We played Fish and Monopoly and read books to each other."

"You did? What kind?"

"I'll tell you about them as soon as I look at your snowman." In the distance Annie could see her father with Minnie and Ted, Rachel's parents, coming down the front steps. She gripped her daughter's hand and they all headed toward it.

"Roberta and I made his stomach."

"Good job! Hey—" Chase blurted. "How did he get hold of my hat?'

Nicky burst into laughter. "It's Daddy's old one! You're funny, Uncle Chase."

Roberta smiled up at Annie. What a perfect day.

Don't think anything but perfect thoughts, Annie. Not today.

WHILE ROBERTA WAS in the tub, Annie walked Chase out to the garage. After he climbed in the cab of his truck he leaned out the window to kiss her. He didn't dare engulf her the way he wanted to or he'd never find the strength to leave.

"I'm worse than Roberta. I don't want you to go to work."

"We knew this day had to come."

"I didn't know it was going to be this hard."

"You think I did?" he said in a husky voice before opening the door so he could feel her in his arms once more.

"We're pathetic."

"We're worse than that. I'm an hour late."

"The guys will understand."

"That's the problem. I'm going to be the butt of every newlywed joke for weeks!"

Her eyes glowed. "If I can stand it, you can."

As long as she was here when he got home, he could stand anything. "If there are no emergencies, I'll be back at seven."

"Stay safe, darling." She plied a hot kiss to his mouth before backing down so he could start the engine.

He pressed the remote to the garage door and backed out. She was still standing in place when he closed it.

Through a special arrangement with Mark on the phone last night, Chase was able to wangle another day off. After a certain private discussion with his daughter, he'd decided to consult with his heart doctor in Merced.

Roberta had talked with Ted about his heart condition. She'd learned that his doctor told him his heart would never get better because the technology wasn't there to repair it. Then everything changed and a revolutionary operation had made him a new man.

After hearing that, Roberta urged Chase to have his doctor get in touch with Ted's doctor in Miami. Maybe something could be done. With so many soldiers returning from war carrying injuries like Chase's, Ted said it might be possible new surgical techniques were developing that could help.

Chase had just spent a week in paradise. He wanted it to go on. If something could be done for his heart, he was prepared to go through with it, especially with Roberta urging him. Indebted to his wonderful daughter, he drove as fast as conditions allowed to reach the clinic.

Dr. Winder's staff said they'd find a way to fit him in. He didn't mind waiting. An hour later he was shown into an examining room. When the doctor came in, Chase didn't waste any time explaining why he'd come without an appointment.

The doctor took another X-ray. With his own eyes Chase saw that the shrapnel was still in the same place.

"It's a good sign that nothing has changed, but I understand if you want to consult with another surgeon. Of course, anything's possible. Leave the information with my secretary and she'll fax your records to him today. When he's looked at the film, we'll consult and I'll get back to you."

Chase couldn't ask for more than that. He thanked the doctor and headed back to the park, still able to put in a half-day's work. Around quarter to four Roberta showed up at his office. They had a root beer and talked about his appointment with the doctor.

For the next week he led the life he'd always envied the married rangers. The three of them had decided to live in Chase's house. With everyone's help they'd started moving Annie's things in after work each evening. Before long her home would be freed up to house another ranger.

At this point Chase's house looked like a furniture store, but he'd never been happier. Once everything was accomplished, they'd drive to Oakhurst with Vance and his family. He knew a place where they could pick out dogs for the children. Life didn't get better than this.

He tried to keep his negative thoughts from surfacing. On Tuesday morning while he was in a conference with Vance and a group of rangers, his doctor's office called him. He flashed the chief a message that he had to take it and stepped out of the room to his own office.

"Chase? Dr. Winder here. This is what I've learned."

After he'd explained everything he said, "Think about it and then get back to me."

"Of course. Thank you."

While he sat there shaken by the information, Vance slipped in and shut the door. "What's going on? The look on your face wasn't normal. Is Annie all right? Roberta?"

He expelled a heavy sigh. "They're fine. This has to do with me."

"Go on—"

"Last week Roberta urged me to get another opinion about my heart, so I went for a checkup in Merced."

"*That's* why you weren't around."

Chase nodded. "A new X-ray didn't show any change, but he agreed to consult with Ted's heart surgeon in Miami."

A stillness surrounded Vance. "What was the outcome?"

"He's done half-a-dozen successful surgeries with my particular kind of injury."

Vance let out a low whistle. "What's the ratio of failure?"

"It's still experimental. If mine were to fail, they'd install a pacemaker. Of course there's always the risk of death with any surgery."

"So you have to decide whether you want to live with what you've got and wonder every day if it's going to be your last—"

"Or I can go for the surgery and take my chances. At least with a pacemaker I wouldn't have the same kind of worry unless it malfunctioned."

His friend muttered something unintelligible under his breath. "Does Annie know any of this?"

"No. I'll tell her tonight."

He threw his head back. "Just when I thought things were going to get fun around here..."

Tell me about it.

Later that evening, after they'd kissed Roberta good-night, Chase led his wife to the living room. "Do you mind if we talk for a little while?"

She grinned. "What's the matter? Do you have a wife who's too eager and wearing you out already?"

"Yes, thank heaven!" He drew her into his arms and they sank down on the couch together.

"All right," she said, moving off his lap. "I know when there's something on your mind besides me."

They smiled at each other, but his slowly faded. "I need to tell you about something I've done." Without wasting time, he related everything. She was so quiet afterward, he picked up her hand and kissed her finger-tips. "What do you think?"

An eternity passed before she said, "I think you have to do it for all our sakes. We're a family that has to take every day on faith."

THE WAITING ROOM for heart surgery patients was on the sixth floor of the hospital in Merced. Annie had been sitting there over ten hours, trying to be brave for Roberta, who was watching cartoons with Nicky. Vance and Rachel had come with them yesterday when they'd checked Vance in to get him prepped. They'd been here for her every second and had taken turns entertaining the children.

Though he was heroic himself, Vance was looking more grim with every second that passed. Due to the secrecy involved, Ted's doctor had flown out to do the surgery with Dr. Winder. Early this morning, before they'd begun giving him the anesthetic, she'd kissed her husband one more time.

"Children have God's ear," she whispered. "He's not going to fail us or our daughter now."

His eyes were the color of storm clouds outlined in silver. "You're my life. I believe it if you say it."

She fought the emotions threatening to overwhelm her. "I say it because I believe it, too."

"Annie?" he cried.

"Yes."

"I love you."

"I love you too, darling. See you this afternoon."

Except that it was early evening now. The memory of their conversation kept playing over in her mind until she wanted to scream. Rachel had brought her a sandwich and a drink, but she'd only been able to eat a portion of it.

Convinced something was wrong, she sprang to her feet and hurried out of the room toward the nursing station. She saw Dr. Winder come out of the no admission doors.

He lowered his mask. "Mrs. Jarvis? I was just coming to tell you the shrapnel was removed and Chase is going to live a long life." She almost fainted for joy. "We had a tense moment when he started hemorrhaging, but we were watching for that to happen and stanched it in time."

The tears gushed down her cheeks. "How soon can I see him?"

"He's been closely monitored all day. If everything proceeds on schedule, he'll be transferred to a private room soon. Call the nursing station at nine o'clock. They'll know where he is so you can visit him for a minute."

She nodded. "I don't know how to thank you."

He waved her off before she flew down the hall to the waiting room. Everyone got up when she appeared. "The operation was a success!" Rachel let out a cry of joy. "Chase is going to be fine!"

"Oh Mom!" Roberta launched herself at Annie, sobbing her heart out for happiness.

"Thank God," Vance whispered.

Annie repeated the same prayer in her heart.

"MR. JARVIS?"

He turned his head toward the nurse who'd just entered his room.

"Do you feel strong enough to have a couple of visitors?"

Chase felt like cursing—he'd been waiting for his family to come for what seemed like hours—but he said simply, "Yes."

"We don't want you getting tired. They can only see you for a minute."

The suspense was killing him until he saw his precious daughter approach the side of the bed. Annie was right behind her.

"You're a sight for sore eyes, sweetheart."

"Hi, Daddy. How do you feel?"

"Wonderful."

"Mommy said your heart is all better now."

"It is, and that's because of you."

"How come?"

"For showing me what I needed to do."

"I can't wait till you come home."

"I'll be there soon."

"The nurse says I have to leave now. I love you."

"I love you more. See you tomorrow."

After the nurse walked her out, Annie drew closer. Their eyes clung, saying all the things they couldn't say aloud.

"I was told not to touch you, darling. Do you have any idea how hard that is for me after learning that you're never going to have to worry about your heart again?"

"They told me I couldn't touch you either or I might get too excited. The problem is, I can't shut off the memories of our honeymoon."

"Chase? You sound tired. I'm going to leave. The nursing station knows where to reach me. We're at a hotel around the corner. I'm only a minute away. Is there anything you need before I go?"

"Besides you?"

She made a sound that could have been a laugh or a cry. "Besides me."

"Tell the chief we're going to start having fun around here. He'll know what I mean."

"I adore you, Chase. Sweet dreams, darling."

Sweet dreams after all these years…

Who would have thought.

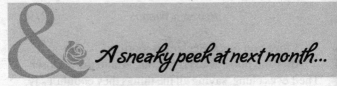